J.D. GRUBB

Three Shades

This novel is entirely a work of fiction. The names, characters and incidents portrayed in it are the work of the author's imagination. Any resemblance to actual persons, living or dead, events or localities is entirely coincidental.

First published by LOD Press 2023

The Library of Congress Cataloging in Publication Data:
Grubb, J.D.
Three Shades/J.D. Grubb--1st ed

ISBN: 978-1-953028-03-7

1. Multiple Perspectives Story—Fiction. 2. Mystical Encounters—Fiction. 3. Navigating Language Barriers—Fiction. 4. Journey of Identity—Fiction. 5. Finding Life Purpose—Fiction. 6. Relationship with Time—Fiction.

To those who dare to look beyond.

Contents

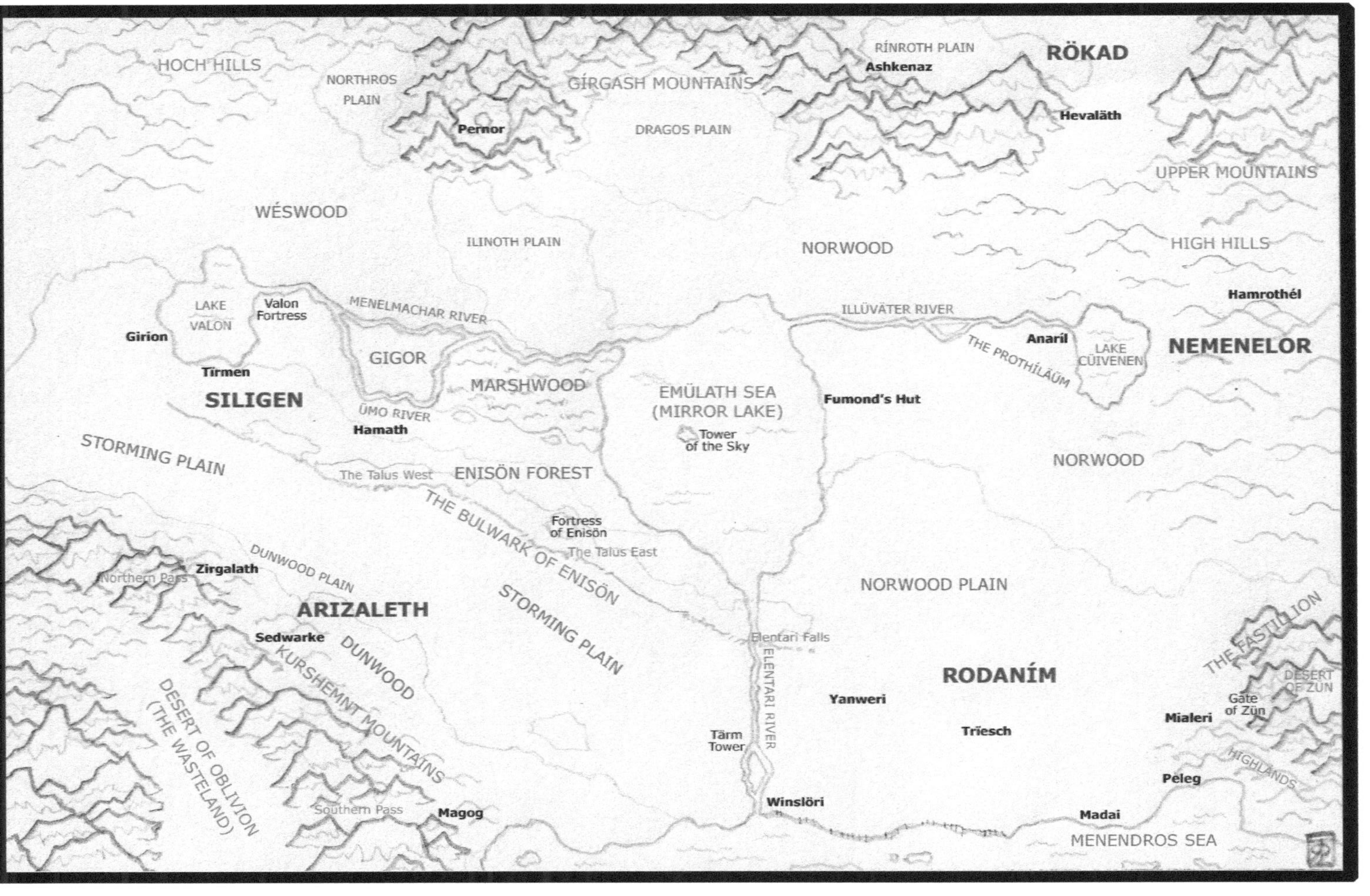

HOCH HILLS
RÍNROTH PLAIN
RÖKAD
NORTHROS PLAIN
GÍRGASH MOUNTAINS
Ashkenaz
Pernor
Heväläth
DRAGOS PLAIN
UPPER MOUNTAINS
WÉSWOOD
ILINOTH PLAIN
NORWOOD
HIGH HILLS
Hamrothél
LAKE VALON
Valon Fortress
MENELMACHAR RIVER
ILLÜVÄTER RIVER
Anaril
THE PROTHÍLÄÜM
NEMENELOR
Girion
GIGOR
LAKE CÜIVENEN
Tirmen
MARSHWOOD
EMÜLATH SEA (MIRROR LAKE)
Fumond's Hut
SILIGEN
ÜMO RIVER
Hamath
Tower of the Sky
NORWOOD
STORMING PLAIN
The Talus West
ENISÖN FOREST
Fortress of Enisön
The Talus East
Zirgalath
DUNWOOD PLAIN
NORWOOD PLAIN
Northern Pass
THE BULWARK OF ENISÖN
STORMING PLAIN
THE FASTILLION
ARIZALETH
Elentari Falls
RODANÍM
DESERT OF ZÜN
Sedwarke
DUNWOOD
KURSHEMNT MOUNTAINS
Yanweri
Gate of Zün
Mialeri
DESERT OF OBLIVION (THE WASTELAND)
Tärm Tower
ELENTARI RIVER
Trïesch
HIGHLANDS
Southern Pass
Magog
Winslöri
Peleg
Madai
MENENDROS SEA
iii

I

ASHE

1

Fumond's Hut

Warmth caresses my skin. I welcome it ever deeper. With a fluttering heart, breath faltering, there is a surge of pleasure in dropping from a high, bright vastness toward an expanse of brown, grey, and green below. Closing my eyes, leaning back, arching my spine, I release my hands to feel my face, hair, and the wind, all the while my thighs squeeze a power pulling me downward—diving into liberation.

Almost.

The stirring in my stomach recedes. Opening my eyes, I recognize the mass of abstraction widening before me to be a mountain range. A desert borders its left side. A forest clings to its right. Shadows lengthen.

No, not there. Not now.

The winged mount beneath me shifts upward, whipping my torso forward. I cling to its neck, and must not let go.

Sensations diminish to a gentle rise and fall across the air—warmth once again lifting us in slow spirals. Darkness is beneath, grey above, and ahead a line of crimson light: the horizon.

Do not let go.

Do not let me go.

Ashe opened her eyes to a room illuminated with amber light. Rolling onto her back, she stretched her arms above her head while reaching in the opposite direction with her feet, inhaling slowly to remove a lingering shroud of sleep. Tossing the warm blanket aside and sitting up, she felt the coolness of the room seize her bare skin.

Someone knocked at the door.

Retrieving her cerulean undershirt from the floor, she promptly put it on and walked with a mild limp to the door. Opening it, she met Heben, one of two bodyguards stationed outside, who offered her a sealed envelope.

"This just arrived for you," Heben said with a deep, quiet voice. "The Sky Rider asked that it be delivered immediately."

Ashe received the envelope. "Thank you."

The guard nodded then closed the door behind her as she turned away and sauntered to the nearest window. She could not clearly see through its paneled glass, but used the light to better read the brief message contained inside the envelope.

"What is it?" Fumond asked.

Ashe glanced at the man now sitting up in bed with a glass of red wine in his hand. His trimmed beard and hair, once black, were graying, yet his features still emitted a youthful energy. "Well?"

"It is from Däne," Ashe replied.

"Oh? And what does the Lord of Hamrothél want?"

"For me to come back."

"Really?" Fumond took a sip from his drink. "Why?"

"He does not say." She put the letter aside, came to the bed, and crawled a few steps on her hands and knees until her nose brushed against Fumond's. Kissing him lightly on the lips, she added, "But wants me to come right away."

Fumond stroked her exposed leg, sliding his hand up to her hip. "I thought you were done serving Nemenelor."

"The empire may be gone," she commented, "but the Alöweans are still my people." The words felt hollow. For eleven years, she had done all she could to stay away from her people's fading empire. She did not really want to go back, but Däne's letter stirred her curiosity.

"Can't you stay a few more days?" Fumond asked.

Ashe stared into his green eyes, searching their intent. She considered

Fumond a good man, intelligent and capable. Being with him was never dull, yet she felt no lasting attachment to him. Gently, she kissed him again. "No."

Grinning playfully, she withdrew from the bed and retrieved her trousers from where they lay next to other assorted clothing on the floor. The request from Däne served as a timely excuse for her to depart. She had lingered too long with Fumond this time, probably because she did not know where else to go or what to do. If she stayed, the short-term contracts with local tradesmen could continue—serving as a messenger, transporter, or bodyguard was lucrative enough—but money mattered little to her. The work had become too predictable.

Having put on her tan trousers, which were padded at the knees, she noticed her wooden pipe waiting on the bedside table. The thought of another smoke of mip weed tempted her, but she resisted and looked away knowing that she needed to keep her mind alert. Besides, the effects of the previous night's blissful escapades still clouded her attention—not ideal for flying, yet she did not regret her choices.

"I am a Sky Rider, after all," she commented, putting on her insulated, knee-high riding boots. "With so few of us left in Illirium, our expertise is a rare commodity."

"Indeed," Fumond said with a glint of mischief in his eyes. "One that I've long admired. You're special, Ashe Pethus, and it's not only because you're a Sky Rider, though I dare say that gives you a distinct kind of . . . drive . . . even fearlessness. There's something else about you, something different from the other Alöweans I've met. I'd like to understand what it is. I want to know you better."

This kind of talk made Ashe uncomfortable. "What are you getting at?"

"For one, you look different than most of your Alöwean peers," he said. "Your silver hair is thicker, skin a darker crimson, and features fuller." Having put his emptied glass aside, he leaned forward and patted the space next to him. "Come back to bed."

She could use some more sleep, but the thought of fresh air held greater appeal. "You did not answer my question." She knew that Fumond had other intimate companions, and that she was not the first Alöwean to share his bed. Neither bothered her in the least. "I am nothing special."

"I disagree." Once more, Fumond motioned for her to join him.

She relented, but merely rested on top of the bedcovers. "It is out of character for you to be obsessing about me like this."

"'Obsessing' is such a strong word." Fumond shifted to lie on his side. He studied Ashe and traced the profile of her face with his forefinger. "I'm transfixed by you, from your fairly crooked nose to your feet."

Ashe chuckled. "Well, my nose was broken when I was young, and did not heal straight. As to my 'fuller' features, as you call them, they are common to the people of Chaléth."

Fumond shrugged. "I've not heard of Chaléth."

"Most of you Illiri have not," Ashe replied. "Few Chaléthians settled here in Illirium—even before the war." The sea was far to the south, and countless miles farther in its midst waited the island of Alöwe, of which Chaléth was part. Her homeland seemed unreachable to her now, like a memory.

"There's so much you can teach me," Fumond said, smiling anew. "What can I do to entice you to stay?" He ran his finger across Ashe's lips and down the front of her neck. "A new, high-paying contract perhaps—something more permanent?"

Unlikely. "What is the job?" she asked.

"You could be my personal emissary. A Sky Rider would expedite communication with my contacts in the west, for example."

"You know how I feel about Dwairian and his empire."

"I did not say my contacts are associated with the new king."

"Everything about the west is associated with Dwairian," Ashe countered. Dwairian's claim to kingship is what had provoked the war, he and his allies driving most of her people out of Illirium. Nearly twenty years had passed since, but that felt like only a few years to an Alöwean. Many scars remained, and some were not yet healed.

"Come now, you aren't so narrow-minded," Fumond pressed. "You've wanted to explore more of the world. What better opportunity do you have?"

Ashe felt a pang of grief in her heart. "I have already seen enough of the west."

"Do it for us then."

"Us?" This surprised Ashe most of all. She sat up and left the bed. "You and I both know that what we share here is casual, even transactional. You are a businessman, and I am a practical woman." Fumond gazed at her with a solemn demeanor. Softening her tone, she added, "That is not to say that I do not savor your company. You make me feel good, and help me focus on the present."

"Is that me or the mip weed?"

Fair question. She considered this for a moment then smiled wryly. "Both."

Fumond nodded with a trace of equal amusement shaping his eyes. Grabbing the robe draped over the end of the bed, he stood, put it on, and went over to a small wooden desk at one corner of the room. After opening and closing a drawer, all the while keeping his back to her, he turned and tossed her a pouch, which she caught.

"Your next batch," Fumond commented, pouring himself a fresh glass of wine. "You've earned it."

Ashe brought the pouch up to her nose to smell the rich earthy fragrance of the dried mip weed. She looked at Fumond and grinned. "If there is a bond between us, this is its foundation."

"As you wish." Fumond sounded mildly disappointed.

Sunlight now shone directly through the windows.

"Anyway," Ashe said, "you are simultaneously too old and too young for me."

"What does that have to do with anything?" Fumond looked intrigued.

"For an Illiri, you are already middle aged—what is that, about fifty years old?"

Fumond's eyes narrowed, but he retained the trace of a grin. "Something like that."

"Well, for an Alöwean, I am still in the youthful prime of my life. Furthermore, as that is measured by having already lived about three centuries, your short lifespan suggests a disparity of experience between us."

"Experience, like appearances, is an illusive concept," Fumond commented.

"Either way, I am not ready to settle down."

"Who said anything about settling down?"

"I mean that people like you and me are not meant for anything long term."

"On the contrary, most of my work is defined by a long-term vision. This place"—Fumond motioned at the space around him—"was not built quickly. It took many years of patient work."

"You know what I mean," Ashe said. "I will not be bound to you."

"You're already bound to me." Fumond nodded at the pouch of mip weed Ashe still held in her hand. "But that's not my point. While your help this last year has been valuable, it's only a taste of what's in store. You could be part of something greater, Ashe. You could experience lasting purpose again."

Who said I care about lasting purpose anymore? She turned away and placed the pouch of mip weed into her riding satchel. Acquiring the mip weed was a simple enough exchange, but only possible through Fumond's facilitation—some secret provider from the south. She retrieved her pipe and packed it away, anxious to get out in the open sky again. After putting on her sleeveless brigandine tunic and then a thick wool outer coat, which she kept unfastened for the time being, she strapped her unstrung bow and satchel across her back, secured her quiver full of arrows at her waist belt, and gripped the head of her lightweight war hammer like a cane, placing some of her weight on it with each step.

Fumond watched her, drinking occasionally from his wineglass while sitting leisurely on a high-backed leather chair. "When will I see you again?"

"Who knows?"

"That supply of mip weed could last a few months," he said, looking at her satchel. "That is, if you control your appetite." He smiled shrewdly.

She smiled back. "No promises."

Accompanied by the steady thud of her makeshift cane on the floor, she walked to the door and left Fumond's room. She nodded at the two bodyguards stationed outside then advanced through a dimly lit corridor.

Outside Fumond's small mansion, a chill lingered in the early spring air. Glistening frost covered the surfaces of walls and windows still in shadow. Above, the azure sky shone clear. The cold weather did not deter Ashe; she had navigated far harsher conditions. It would be a good day for flying.

Once she left the mansion's guarded main gate, she walked along a sun-warmed cobblestone street toward the western end of town. Trying to maintain a relaxed pace, which was difficult considering how her feet ached with any sustained effort, she enjoyed the freshness of the morning air. The prospect of a new day, especially one defined by flying, invigorated her spirit.

Various two or three storey structures lined the narrow street. Though now comprised of thousands of residents from every region of Illirium, the town retained the name "Fumond's Hut" in honor of its founder-overseer and as an affectionate understatement. No one agreed about when Fumond had established the trading post, for he had done so alone, but anyone who inhabited it or visited agreed that Fumond's Hut was the most welcoming and diverse municipality in Illirium.

The town's western end bordered a stretch of high steep banks that dropped into a large lake the Alöweans called the Emülath Sea. At the edge of the slope, Ashe gazed across the glimmering water to a distant island with a tall rectangular structure at its center: the Tower of the Sky. Abandoned after the war, it had once housed Nemenelor's main host of Sky Riders. The sight stirred memories both good and grievous. She knew the tower and surrounding waters well.

Turning away, she focused instead on a lesser stone and wood tower to her right. The tower was the tallest structure in Fumond's Hut, set apart from the main township cluster with its own palisade. Years earlier, with some feedback from Ashe, Fumond had commissioned the tower to be designed by an Alöwean master mason from Hamrothél. Most people called it Mirror Tower, for the Illiri referred to the Emülath Sea as Mirror Lake. Overseeing the staffing and maintenance of the tower was one of Fumond's personal priorities.

As Ashe reached the open gate, the two sentries moved aside in recognition, letting her pass without a word. As a Sky Rider, she frequented the tower more than anyone else. She suspected that Fumond had built it for her, which did make it easier for her to come and go. She also appreciated having an official place to house her mount while staying in Fumond's Hut. Talking briefly with the tower warden, she learned that no other Sky Riders were currently in residence. The messenger from Hamrothél had simply landed on the topmost platform of the tower, the fourth level, which was reserved for brief visits, and then left after delivering the envelope from Däne.

Methodically, one hand gripping the railing while the other clutched her war hammer for stability, Ashe ascended the tower's internal, square-angled spiraling stairway. Accompanying her, the warden had learned not to offer assistance, for Ashe would receive none. Three levels up, they left the stairs and approached one of two adjacent archways. There, inside a tall chamber waited Ashe's brown-feathered mount, Lüfet.

Lüfet was an Erïeth, a rare breed of bird akin to an eagle with a body the size of a horse. Captured as an eaglet thirty years earlier, Lüfet had been trained by Ashe, serving as her third mount. Ashe had lost none of her mounts in battle, but tamed Erïeths tended to only live up to seventy years.

"How are you, my friend?" Ashe greeted softly, reaching up to stroke Lüfet's smooth neck, which was at her eye level. Lüfet chattered softly in reply, glancing sidelong at Ashe with her large black pupils and yellow eyes. "Ready to get out of here?"

The Erïeth adjusted her weight from one leg to another, scraping the floor with strong, sharp talons.

"Good." Ashe smiled. "Me too."

The Sky Rider walked carefully around her mount while the warden unbolted the outside door, which served as one of the compartment's main walls. Using the windlass affixed to the adjacent framing, the warden lowered the door like a drawbridge.

Guiding Lüfet to bow, Ashe placed a small riding saddle on the base of the eagle's neck. The saddle's straps and harnesses were lightweight, but strong, carefully designed to allow the Sky Rider to sit at the Erïeth's center of gravity, overall constricting its flight as minimally as possible. Having closed up her outer coat, retrieved and put on her masked helm with its two small round holes for visibility, Ashe at last strapped her war hammer across her back and climbed up a three-step rope ladder hanging from the base of the saddle along Lüfet's back. Once on top, Ashe tucked her knees under her, placing her feet into hardened leather slots at the side near the back of the saddle. She then further secured herself by clipping a leather harness to her riding belt. A well-trained Erïeth would not let its rider fall, but safety precautions were wise, especially when a Sky Rider needed to free his or her hands to wield a weapon.

Ready, Ashe unclasped the leash that kept Lüfet loosely tethered to the chamber, gripped a short stirrup with her right hand and, using her hips and legs, directed Lüfet out onto the lowered door. Lüfet was relatively light for a creature of her size, but the chains holding the door still tightened and the wood underneath creaked as the bird walked out on it. The twin supporting chains of the platform were fastened to the middle of its length to allow greater space at the end for the Erïeth to expand its wings. A cool breeze brushed against Ashe's outerwear, which had felt too warm inside the tower. The insulation would soon serve her well.

Gazing out at the open expanse above the glistening water of the Emülath Sea, Ashe inhaled through her nose, leaned forward and said, "Fly."

Lüfet lowered her head, partially opened her massive wings, and flapped with a few tight strokes as she launched straight out from the edge of the platform. Ashe cherished the exhilaration of takeoff. The eastbound breeze blowing across the lake and up the slope provided lift while the interaction of lake and land temperatures provided a thermal on which to more easily gain elevation. Keeping her wide wings extended, Lüfet spiraled gracefully upward.

Watching the details of the tower, town, and surrounding lands slowly shrink, Ashe felt focused and at ease. The sky was her true homeland, a place of belonging and perspective. Riding Lüfet thousands of feet high,

Ashe felt no pain in her feet, but rather entered a happy realm of choice. She could go anywhere.

Looking south, she once again imagined the wide coastline of the sea. Far across that sea waited Chaléth and her mother. Could she reach her homeland atop an Erïeth? As the feat had never been attempted, the notion enticed her. Yet, Däne's message contained a curious urgency. At the pinnacle of the thermal, Lüfet glided southward for a moment until Ashe leaned left, directing the winged mount east toward Hamrothél and what remained of Nemenelor.

2

The Old Empire

One of the three largest rivers in Illirium, the Illüvatár flowed into the Emülath Sea from the High Hills in the east. At dusk, having followed the course of the river all day, Ashe landed Lüfet on an isle to make camp. Though the night was cold, sleeping out under the stars reminded her how much she had missed the sensory spread of nature.

The next morning, they continued east above the river, reaching the border of Nemenelor by midday, and not long after the ruins of its old capital, Anaríl, which bordered the northwestern shore of Lake Cüivenen. The city once provided a direct passageway to Alöwe through the Door of Anaríl at its center, but the Door was now closed. Even before the city's fall, most Alöwean noncombatants had been evacuated through the Door, leaving those in Illirium who had survived the war separated from their families and homeland.

Passing over the desolate city, Ashe looked away. Onward she focused, beyond the dark waters of the lake to the rising forested expanse of the High Hills. The temperature dropped. Patches of snow lingered in the shadows of the leafless gray forest below. Ashe listened to the empty sighs of the wind against her helm, and suddenly felt alone in an immeasurable world. As melancholy weighed on her heart, she stroked Lüfet's neck, grateful for the bird's company.

Enough, she chided herself.

Leaning forward, she directed Lüfet to dive. A torrent of wind rushed past as they swooped down and glided just above the bare fingers of trees—some swaying in the wake of the Erïeth's passing. A flock of birds erupted from one cluster of trees, a pair of black ravens separating from them, croaking as they veered to the north. The thrill of the swift descent lifted Ashe's stomach and caused her heart to pulse euphorically.

Do not let go, she reminded herself, cherishing the liberation of the moment as Lüfet ascended in slow spirals up a thermal. Once again, the world seemed full of possibilities; there was too much to explore and enjoy. She had no time for despondency.

During the afternoon of the third day, they reached the Wall of Nemenelor. Though the wall provided a large defensive perimeter around Hamrothél, the last city of Alöweans in Illirium, Ashe considered it more a symbol than provider of strength. She doubted that Lord Däne had the numbers to truly secure it, at least against a prolonged siege. Däne had ordered the wall constructed soon after the war's end, in part as a way to better defend the refugee camp that had formed outside Hamrothél's original city walls. In the years since, the camp had developed into a quiet outer town. Though larger than ever before, Hamrothél had become little more than a last bastion of a faded civilization. The bordering forestland of the High Hills could be deemed both a barrier against aggression from the outside world as well as a marker of deepening isolation.

I will not stay long.

Two Sky Riders swooped down to either side of Lüfet. Their appearance did not surprise Ashe, for she had spotted them flying above her an hour earlier, tracking her progress from the concealment of the clouds. The two Sky Riders wore green tunics lined with black, the colors of Hamrothél, over their protective layers. Their helms were the same design as Ashe's; two pairs of shadowed circular holes studied her. They rode sea Erïeth, which were smaller in size and lighter in plumage than a mountain Erïeth like Lüfet, but they were also faster and better suited for short distances. The rider to Ashe's left held a nocked bow pointed calmly in her direction, while the one to the right bore a long spear. With her free hand, the second pointed down, indicating that Ashe land ahead.

Ashe nodded and raised a hand in consent, directing Lüfet toward a wooden platform that crowned a nearby hill. The structure employed rooted tree trunks for support, their tips trimmed to allow Sky Riders unobstructed landing and takeoff. A bowman patrolled the circular perimeter, while another guard watched from under a shelter built within the center of the platform—little more than a roof jutting up, the narrow gap in between it and the platform floor providing a vantage point. Noticing Ashe's approach, the second guard stepped out using a steep, narrow stairway, and walked to the edge of the gazebo with a spear at hand, awaiting her landing. Meanwhile, the two airborne Sky Riders drifted back, the archer circling above Ashe's position while the other landed on the opposite side of the platform.

"Please dismount," the spearman said to Ashe once she had landed. Holding his weapon loosely, he kept the tip oriented toward Lüfet.

"Of course," Ashe replied, having removed her helmet. She unrolled the rope ladder from the back of her saddle, and climbed down off Lüfet's back.

"I wondered if you would ever return," a woman's voice said behind her.

Ashe turned to see the Sky Rider with the spear take off her helmet to reveal a pale crimson face and graying auburn hair. "Hello Räshan," Ashe said.

"'Captain' to you," the older Alöwean woman replied.

Ashe nodded with an acquiescent grin. "Captain."

"What is your business in Nemenelor? Bored of self-indulgence, are you?"

"I do not get bored," Ashe replied, ignoring the other's antagonistic tone. "Lord Däne sent for me."

"Do you have proof?"

Ashe handed the Sky Rider captain the letter.

After a cursory glance at the letter's content, Räshan returned it to Ashe. "I am surprised you came."

"I like to keep people guessing."

"You do what suits you, and you alone," Räshan commented, turning away. She gazed out at the rolling forest landscape. "What does the Lord of Hamrothél want with you?"

"You saw the letter."

"You had a chance to be a leader, but rejected it." Räshan looked back at Ashe. "That opportunity has passed."

"You need not worry," Ashe said calmly. "I am not here to disrupt your equilibrium."

"Even if you wanted to, you would find it difficult." The Sky Rider captain studied Ashe for a while longer. "Well, you had best be on your way."

By nightfall, Ashe reached the Sky Rider tower in the citadel of Hamrothél. Nethelen stërne, stones of the stars, lined the branchlike posts jutting out from the tower, illuminating it with soft blue light. Once Lüfet had landed on one of the posts and stepped onto the flat walkway surrounding the tower, an attendant walked out to take the reins from Ashe.

"Make sure she is well fed," Ashe said, dismounting. She stroked Lüfet's neck. "We have been traveling for three days."

The attendant nodded then guided Lüfet inside to one of the tower's stalls.

After following them inside, Ashe proceeded through the stall to the tower's central stairway. There, she met the tower warden and inquired about where she could find the lord of the city.

"I will send word to the steward," the warden replied. "In the meantime, may I offer you a place to clean up and rest from your journey?"

"Some hot water and a bed would be wonderful," Ashe replied.

"Excellent." The warden motioned to a young aide. "We will arrange a place for you in the tower barracks and bring fresh linens. Are you hungry?"

"Definitely."

"Well then, some food will also be provided."

Ashe knew the tower well, and could fend for herself, but appreciated the hospitality. She felt tired, and her knees were stiff from riding. Using her war hammer once more as a walking cane, she followed the young aide a few levels down to the tower's main hall, the dimensions of which were larger than the tower, being adjoined to Hamrothél's central keep. There was no activity inside. As it was later in the evening, Ashe presumed supper had concluded hours earlier. She also surmised that there were few Sky Riders stationed in Hamrothél, for she had spotted only three other Erïeth occupying tower stalls. Most of the Sky Riders in Illirium had been killed during the war. Capturing and training new Erïeth was difficult enough, let alone instructing new riders.

The aide indicated that Ashe sit at one of the main hall's long dining tables. An oil lamp lit the table, and a fire flickered behind her in the hearth, which cast a soft glow over the room and warmed her as she waited. Soon, the aide brought out a plate with bread, butter, and cheese, and then a cup of wine. The food was not warm, but Ashe enjoyed its simple heartiness. The drink complimented the flavors well, and eased the ache rising from her stomach to her head.

Not long after she had finished eating, the warden returned. "A bed is ready for you, as is a hot bath. You will not be disturbed."

"Thank you."

"I have also received word from the steward of the citadel," the warden added. "The Lord of Hamrothél welcomes you, and will speak with you tomorrow morning."

Ashe nodded. She felt too tired to speak with Däne that night anyway.

The warden had arranged for Ashe to stay in a room designated for a Sky Rider lieutenant. To access it, she passed through an adjacent room with ten vacant bunks—housing for one squadron of Sky Riders: twenty riders subdivided into five flights, four riders each. Hamrothél's garrison had once held two squadrons. A somber quiet filled the room, reminding Ashe of the cost of war. The barrack had once been a bright, lively environment, brimming with interesting Alöwean men and women. She cherished the memories.

The officer's room contained a simple, freshly made bed, desk with oil lamp, and a round window looking northward across moonlit hills. A small tub had been brought in and filled with hot water, steam rising invitingly from its surface.

Once again thanking the warden, and assuring him that she had all she needed, Ashe watched him withdraw and close the door. She locked it behind him, tossed her riding satchel onto the bed, and promptly undressed. Stepping into the bath, the water felt soothing. Bending her knees, she could lean back and rest her head against the rim of the tub. With her pipe, she smoked some mip weed, closed her eyes, felt her body numb and her mind meander.

Gentle hands hold me close, warming. We were so alive together, so comfortable in uncomplicated pleasures. There was no obstacle too high, no path too long. We embraced every moment, invigorated by our togetherness.

Nothing has compared since.

I miss you.

* * *

"How long has it been, Ashe Pethus?" The Lord of Hamrothél rose from behind his ornate wooden desk. Behind him, through the wide glass window, snow fell in a flurry.

"Eleven years," Ashe replied, meeting the other's gaze.

Däne's posture was tall, strong, and rigid, his eyes brooding. "Thank you for coming so quickly."

At his beckoning, Ashe settled on a cushioned sofa beside the hearth to her right while he sat across from her on a high-backed chair. She appreciated the warmth of his study—much cozier than her chamber in the empty barrack. Elegant carpet covered most of the floor. A set of shelves full of parchment and even a few books covered the wall to her left.

For a while, studying the map of Alöwe above the fireplace mantle, she contemplated the topography of its southeastern shoreline: Chaléth, her homeland. "Any news from across the sea?"

Däne brushed a loose strand of silver hair from his face. "None." His deep voice sounded gruff. "We remain alone."

"You appear to be doing well enough."

Däne glanced at the map of Illirium mounted next to that of Alöwe. "It is still a wonder that Dwairian did not finish us after the Battle of the Prothílaüm."

Ashe recalled being in Hamrothél during the final months of the war, preparing her unit of Sky Riders for the city's last defense. "The Illiri need Nemenelor," she commented. "You provide a buffer between Dwairian's empire and Rodaním, maybe even Rökad."

"Dwairian is not concerned with Rökad," Däne stated grimly. "The Dwarves are not interested in his ambitions; not while the Illiri clans of Rodaním pose a more immediate threat. There is indeed a buffer, as you suggest, and we can thank our Illiri neighbors to the south." He frowned. "For now."

"Traders passing through Fumond's Hut say that Rodaním has its own troubles," Ashe commented, rising to examine a book on one of Däne's shelves titled *The Rise and Fall of Emülath,* which was presumably about the first Alöwean settlement in Illirium. "Everyone is tired of conflict."

"There will always be conflict," Däne retorted with an edge of weariness in his voice, "especially concerning the Illiri. They are opportunists, and Dwairian's appetite for expansion is insatiable." He met her eyes. "We are fortunate that you found the rebels in Wéswood those years ago."

Ashe smiled to herself at the memory. "And how is Captain Hectiliath?"

"I have not heard from him in weeks, but the last report affirmed that his forces are holding our old territory well enough. Hectiliath will not abandon his post." Däne gave her a wry look.

Ashe did not understand why the Alöwean rebels continued fighting in the northwest, against the expansion of Dwairian's new empire. What was there to preserve but ruins? "Why not command Hectiliath and his forces to return to Hamrothél? Surely, you could use his strength here."

Däne leaned back, resting one leg on the other while he stared at the fire. "You have been gone a long time, Ashe, and are now a mercenary—or whatever you wish to call yourself. Granted, if we had more Sky Riders . . ." He took a long, slow breath. "The years you gave as a trainer after the war were valuable, but not enough."

"My answer has not changed." Still, she was curious about how Hectiliath was doing. A judicious leader, he had slowed the enemy's advance in the early months of the Illirium War. Yet there had to be something more to their protracted fighting than preserving land.

Däne leaned forward. "We need you, Ashe."

"I am done with war," she replied. "It accomplishes little." Military stratagems intrigued her, but she had resolved to separate herself from Alöwean political affairs.

"War is not done with us," Däne said, once more gazing at the fire, "not while there are kingdoms and borders."

"Then why not abandon such notions?"

"You are not so naïve," he replied. "Not after all you have been through." He sat pensively for a time, his arms crossed. One hand rose to stroke his short beard.

"No," she said, "yet I have explored that way before. It only leads to frustration." The old world had vanished, lost in a bog of pride and grief. Why did men like Däne or Hectiliath fight so hard to reclaim the ghosts? "Why did you ask me to come?"

Däne looked up at her, seemingly coming out of wandering thoughts. "When were you last in Rökad?"

She recalled the postwar years spent traveling around Illirium, especially the kingdom of the Dwarves to the north, trying to understand its people and customs. "It has been at least five years."

"I received word from King Nodshek about seven days ago," Däne began. "He asks for as many Sky Rider scouts as I can provide."

Ashe straightened. "That is a bold request."

"Indeed," Däne said. "He needs help hunting some kind of pestilence antagonizing their northern border. He recently lost his son, Prince Halirothos, to it."

"What kind of pestilence?"

"Some foreign race referred to as 'the Erog,'" Däne replied. "A new Rök contingent has been mustered and specially trained to hunt them, and they would like our Sky Riders to act as scouts."

"For how long?" Ashe asked, "and to what end?"

Däne stood and walked over to the window. Outside, the snowfall had ceased, yet grey clouds lingered. "King Nodshek did not say."

"What will you do?"

The Lord of Hamrothél continued to stare out the window, his hands clasped behind him. "I want to accommodate them, for our alliance with Rökad is essential to our survival. Yet, I cannot spare the few Sky Riders I have."

"You have no reserves?" She immediately realized that it was a foolish question. She had seen the answer for herself.

"Not at the present." Däne turned to face Ashe. "That is why I sent for you. You are one of the best Sky Riders I know; and what is more, you are familiar with Rökad and its people. Therefore, I see you as the best choice I have." He returned to his seat across from her. "Whether you admit it or not, you are still a part of Nemenelor. Think of this as a small way to honor all that it has done for you."

Ashe was not sure about what she had gained in service to Nemenelor, but could not deny that the so-called northern pestilence appealed to her curiosity. She wanted to learn more about this new race, the Erog, but more so considered whether she could seize the opportunity to establish something more permanent back in Rökad. It had felt like home once. Not knowing where else to go or what else to do, except that it did not include staying in Hamrothél or returning to Fumond's Hut, Rökad seemed to offer a chance for new meaning—or at least some distraction.

"By giving our aid," Däne continued, "the Rök will lower trade tariffs on ore and crafted stone, which would provide relief to our already strained resources. Both Rodaním and Rökad have long taken advantage of our isolated state, raising trade expenses. We cannot afford to lose this opportunity."

Ashe hesitated, not liking the idea of fulfilling some part of a political negotiation. "There are other mercenary Sky Riders in Illirium. Why not ask them?"

"None are in good standing with me," Däne replied flatly.

Ashe smiled mischievously. "Is that to say that you and I are in good standing?"

"Perhaps more to the point of your interest," Däne said, ignoring her comment, "King Nodshek will compensate any Sky Rider involved with hunting the Erog."

"What kind of compensation?"

Däne met her eyes and offered his own sly smile. "Enough." He stood and began to stoke the embers in the hearth. "So what will it be, Ashe Pethus? Will you represent Nemenelor for the benefit of your people?"

Ultimately, she had nothing better to do. Slapping her thighs, she stood and smiled. "Why not?"

"Good," the Lord of Hamrothél said, focusing on the renewed flames. "You are to be in Ashkenaz in a month, once the summer begins." He returned to his desk and retrieved a folded piece of paper. "This provides further instructions, such as the name of your contact in the city."

Ashe received the letter, glanced at it, and then tucked it away in the small pouch hanging from her belt.

"Until then, you are welcome to stay here," Däne said. "I only ask that you make yourself useful."

Offering a grin, Ashe nodded. "Of course."

"Good day."

Turning away to the study door, Ashe determined to depart Hamrothél as soon as possible.

3

The Upper Mountains

Ashe felt happiest when flying, rising above what felt like the material bounds of existence. Soaring above the world, she could go any direction she desired: down, up, south, east, west, and north. To be on land recalled the limitations of weight, friction, and the pain of every footstep. There, life became too serious. Though at times she was at the mercy of the wind, thrust wherever it blew, she preferred that to the so-called normalcy of grounded people.

Hamrothél had become an empty tomb of fading memories. What was once familiar now offered only sadness, and she had resolved not to dwell on the past. Rather, future possibilities and their seduction of present-mindedness were what held her interest. Therefore, not being expected in Rökad for a month, Ashe decided to venture north of Nemenelor into the Upper Mountains. No one dwelled in those mountains, for they were said to be reserved for the dead—a passageway to the invisible world beyond life. She had investigated the feet of the mountains years ago, but now wanted to explore deeper to comprehend why others, Alöwean and Rök alike, referred to the tall peaks with quiet reverence.

She reached the mountain border two days after leaving Hamrothél. There, she directed Lüfet to land on the rocky shoulder of a low mountain, and then gazed south across the rolling High Hills. The air spoke in whispers. Landscapes untarnished by civilization were to be relished. Looking right, westward, Ashe's eyes wandered across a flat stretch of forest, fifty miles long, to the far end where the eastern fist of the Girgash Mountains began.

"We will visit your homeland soon, my friend." Ashe stroked Lüfet's large feathered neck. The Erïeth's yellow eyes glinted amber against the lowering sun.

Somewhere at the base of the distant Girgash range, nestled in the folds of rock, was Hevaläth, the capital of Rökad. The forested gap between the two mountain ranges marked the border of the Rök kingdom. Weeks from now, if she loitered in the Upper Mountains that long, she would fly west across that flat forestland, turn north to cross the Rínroth Plain, and then west once more to Ashkenaz.

But not yet.

Turning away to face the Upper Mountains, she felt a thrill fill her heart. A gust of cold wind rushed down the mountainside. Though daylight would last a few hours more, Ashe decided to set up camp for the night. Considering winter's lingering unpredictability, it would be safer to proceed with a new day. "No need for us to hurry," she commented to Lüfet, guiding her by the reins toward the shelter of a nearby lee.

As she walked, Ashe spotted movement to her right. The mountain sloped down to a narrow ravine formed by a small stream. Across the way, within a mile, an escarpment rose to a similar height as the mountain shoulder upon which Ashe stood. There, a lone ram with thick grey fur and a pair of mighty curved horns ambled uphill along the edge. It halted to look at the Alöwean and her Erïeth mount, staring so directly that Ashe wondered if it meant to tell her something. Lüfet also studied the ram, but did so only briefly, averting her eyes as if in deference.

"Is there something I should know?" Ashe asked Lüfet, but the Erïeth acted preoccupied with preening her feathers.

When Ashe glanced back at the escarpment, the ram had vanished.

The next day, the sky shone clear and bright. Ashe welcomed the cheery atmosphere, especially the calm airflow through the mountains. It allowed for more leisurely flying.

Gliding up along a narrow arête, and then out across a wide glacier, Ashe perceived nothing unusual about the Upper Mountains. Except the silence. Nothing stirred. While it was not uncommon for creatures to hide from the presence of an Erïeth, this was unprecedented. Was there something else to fear?

As the sun reached its apex, Ashe directed Lüfet to land beside a small milky blue lake formed beneath two sharp peaks. There, having undressed, she jumped into the water, intending to swim across, but as her body immediately went numb from the near-freezing temperature that made her head scream, she quickly climbed out. She sat for a while, trying to calm her pounding heart, and then laughed at how alive she suddenly felt. Nearby, Lüfet watched Ashe with what she assumed was amused befuddlement.

After resting on a flat sun-warmed rock for an hour, Ashe opened her eyes to discover the same grey ram from the evening before. It stood amidst the col between the two peaks, the shadows of which now covered half the lake. Upon being seen, the ram turned and disappeared beyond the ridge.

Hastily, Ashe dressed and mounted Lüfet. A strange compulsion drove her to follow the ram, as if doing so would somehow reveal the mystery of the mountain silence. Gaining altitude from the bowl of the lake took some effort for the bird, but she soon found an updraft, which helped them rise above the height of the twin peaks. There, gusts of wind increased. Ashe realized with some concern that a host of clouds was approaching from the north.

We have time.

Gliding across the nearby col, Ashe glimpsed the ram moving steadily along a high crag. She directed Lüfet to track the ram's path over and along the sides of the mountain, keeping at a mild distance, yet the ram always managed to keep one stretch of land ahead of them.

Strange, Ashe thought.

The strength of the wind grew to where Lüfet struggled to maintain a straight course. The clouds had come quicker than Ashe anticipated, darkening the sky with menace, now looming only a few miles away. Contrasted with the last rays of sunlight, which illuminated a green mountainside, Ashe found the scene both beautiful and disquieting. She embraced the adrenaline coursing through her body, and inhaled deeply. *Come and get me*, she thought to the approaching storm. She had outflown many before.

A rumble of thunder echoed across the range. Ashe noticed dabs of rain landing on her sleeves. Her hands were growing cold, which made it difficult to grip the reins. Looking once more at the ram as it traversed a saddle ahead, Ashe turned Lüfet to the right, southward away from the storm, and descended swiftly into a rocky canyon. As they glided through the canyon, a rushing stream at its center flanked by scree, Ashe's eyes searched for shelter. She began to feel a clattering vibration upon her helmet. Lüfet cried out. Soon, the sting of hail pellets barraged them furiously. Lightning struck the top of the canyon wall above them, sending a subtle surge of energy tingling down Ashe's body. The situation had escalated so quickly.

Fine, she thought. They had to land or risk being struck.

The stream dropped away into a waterfall at the low end of the canyon. From there, the mountains opened to a misty breadth of rounded summits and lower valleys. The hail intensified. Desperate, Ashe landed Lüfet on a ledge of solid stone. The top of the ledge provided enough space for her to dismount and walk Lüfet closer to the overhanging mountainside, which provided some shelter from the wind and hail. The Erïeth also tried to shield Ashe from the weather with her larger body, but it was too late. Dampness soaked through the Sky Rider's layers to her skin. She shivered as snow began to fall. Visibility diminished to a whiteout. Ashe hoped the storm would pass quickly, but knew it was unlikely. This was early spring, and no summer deluge. There was nowhere to go. They would have to wait.

From her riding bag attached to Lüfet's saddle, Ashe retrieved a blanket. Wrapping it around her, she sat against the wall with her knees pressed to her chest, which helped only a little. The Upper Mountains now felt fiercely alienating, yet Ashe imagined how the experience added to her anthology of adventure stories, how she would enjoy sharing it with others in the warm, dry comfort of some dining hall. She pulled out her pipe and smoked some mip weed, both for a sense of warmth as well as to help the moments pass.

As night settled over the mountains, the storm did not recede. A dark, howling blackness surrounded Ashe's position. She could not grasp time, but merely experienced it in an endless, repeating cycle of shivering, nodding off, imagining herself falling from the ledge, and waking with a disorienting jerk. A vague silhouette in the night, Lüfet kept her head down beside Ashe, looking as though she too was struggling to cope.

"I am sorry," Ashe whispered gruffly to the Erïeth. Trembling, she realized now how grossly unprepared she was to spend the night in such a place. *Fool.* "I know better than this." Leaning her head against Lüfet's neck, she added, "We will make it through, though. . ." She felt so tired of resisting the cold. "We will make it through . . ."

Silence.

I crouch before a small pool shrouded in fog, admiring the water's glassy silver surface—for a moment, questioning whether it is actually water. I could touch it with my fingertips, but hesitate, perceiving an immeasurable depth beneath the surface—a vastness that could consume me. Glancing down, I cannot see the ground of the shore, yet it feels firm like smooth stone. All around, clouds swirl along the perimeter of the pool, yet they do not or cannot glide out upon the water. High above the pool, beyond the ring of fog, the sky is clear and radiant. Crimson gradates to bronze and then azure. Brighter it becomes, illuminating the surrounding cloud cover to the extent that I must avert my eyes, using my hand for added protection.

Glimpsing through my fingers, a white swan approaches across the pool with a gentle ripple in its wake. It whispers to me, "Be wary."

Ashe perceived a dazzling light through her closed eyelids. Uncertainly, groggily, she opened them, hoping that the morning had finally come. Instead, she saw a figure materialize through the haze. The figure resembled a man; his form shimmered as if robed and hooded in translucent white light, beneath which his body was faintly visible: skin with undulating gold and red shapes, like the surface of water reflecting a sunset. His presence began to warm and ease the tension in Ashe's body.

Do I still dream?

Lüfet also stared at the figure. Ashe was surprised that the Erïeth did not stir in fear. Rather, as with the ram, the giant eagle lowered her head and eyes as if in reverence.

The figure halted before Lüfet at the edge of the ledge, and reached out to touch her hooked beak.

"Who are you?" Ashe asked. Her throat felt raspy.

The figure looked at her in surprise. "You see me?" His voice rumbled gently, carried with a breathy timbre like a breeze through trees.

"Yes," she replied, somewhat uncertain. *Of course I do.*

"I am glad," the figure replied, smiling. "Do not be afraid."

Ashe heard a crackling noise behind her. Glancing back, she saw a sheet of ice forming over the rock wall. It crept down the cliff and across the entire ledge, yet she did not feel its touch.

"What do you want?" she asked the figure. Her cold cheeks made it difficult to articulate words.

"You should not be here," he said. "The storm is a warning."

The warmth of his proximity was unmistakable, starkly contrasting the ice thickening below her feet. Lüfet appeared unconcerned. The figure knelt on one knee before Ashe. Looking closer at his eyes, she thought they resembled a night sky full of stars.

"You should accompany me to the safety of my home," he continued.

"Where is it?"

"Measured by the flight of a bird, it is not far," the figure answered. "You cannot linger here in the mountains. Nïmwé will not allow it. Worse than winds and snow could beset you should you dare venture any farther."

Ashe did not understand what the figure was talking about, but also felt too cold to care at the moment. "If your home is warm, I will go with you."

The figure smiled. "I am glad."

"But who are you?"

"I am Thian Darhe."

"I mean . . . what are you? Not some blend of exhaustion, hunger, and mip weed, I warrant." She meant this partially as a joke.

Thian looked confused, both by her statement and as though the answer should be obvious. "I am a Séoran."

Ashe stared at him with renewed wonder. Questions multiplied. "I did not know that Séorans still dwell in Illirium."

Thian nodded. "Come." He looked up as the clouds began to break.

Ashe followed his gaze and saw an indigo sky brightening in the east. Though the Séoran's presence provided warmth, the grip of cold had reached deep within Ashe's body. Her senses felt so numbed, she doubted she would be able to ride.

Thian offered her his hand, which continued to emit a triad of white light over fluctuating crimson and gold.

Receiving it, Ashe felt a surge of soothing energy flow into her hand down to her feet. The Séoran helped her stand, holding her in place until her equilibrium was restored.

"There will be time for talk soon enough," Thian added with an edge of urgency. He looked around. "First we must leave this place."

Keeping Ashe's hand secure in his own, and placing his other hand on her shoulder, Thian ensured that she did not slip as she approached and climbed onto Lüfet. Throughout the process, Ashe's throbbing head made it difficult to keep her eyes fully open.

After helping strap her feet and legs to Lüfet's saddle, the Séoran said, "Follow me."

The transformation happened instantaneously: air surged past Ashe, first warm then cold, tufts of mist swirling toward Thian as he seemed to absorb the air surrounding him; meanwhile, he extended his arms, brought his knees up to his chest, and tilted forward, floating; with the top of his head facing Ashe, the Séoran's body rotated smoothly, the glow of his white outer layer expanding to the point that Ashe could no longer see his inner form; despite the steady flow of air, she heard nothing—as if all sound had been also absorbed—until, at last, the blinding white light contracted, air and sound returned to normal, and what remained of Thian was a small brown sparrow. It glided past Ashe's face and then out from the ledge toward the south.

Remarkable. Watching, Ashe struggled to track the sparrow's progress. How he navigated the mountain wind and mist so effortlessly, she could not say. She clenched her teeth against the pain in her head, closed her eyes, and rested her forehead upon Lüfet's neck. "I am going to need your help, my friend."

The Erïeth evidently required no further instruction. Ashe felt the eagle leap from the ledge and drift smoothly through the air. A bitter wind rushed over them, yet Ashe hardly noticed. Instead, she imagined herself sinking into a bottomless pool: cold, calm, and quiet.

Be wary, a voice echoed in her thoughts.

✳ ✳ ✳

The buzz of insects and the chirp of birds welcomed Ashe to consciousness. Tree trunks creaked while boughs clattered softly in the breeze. Nearby, water dripped steadily.

She felt cocooned in flowing warmth. Opening her eyes, a blue sky greeted her through the budding fingers of trees. A pair of brown sparrows sat perched on one of its lower branches, watching her. As she sat up, she realized that her head had been resting upon a bank of soft grass while her body soaked in a steaming thermal spring. Heat emanated from an unseen passage in the water near her feet, its temperature sometimes almost scalding. The pool was half sheltered by an overhanging outcrop, rivulets of water trickling down its rocky surface.

"How do you feel?" a quiet, sonorous voice asked.

Looking right, Ashe saw Thian sitting cross-legged beside the pool. His figure still shone marvelously, white with traces of crimson and gold underneath.

"Warm," she replied. Investigating her hands, she added, "and pruning." She could not remember arriving. "Did you place me in the water?"

The Séoran smiled. "I did what I could, for the cold had nearly reached your heart. I did not act alone, however. The spring was kind enough to offer its help."

A curious way of phrasing it. "How long have I been here?"

"The first full day already wanes," Thian answered.

"Where am I?"

"Come." Shifting to his feet, Thian indicated a crude wool robe, predominantly silver in color, draped over the back of a doe. "I made this for you."

She rose from the water, retrieved the robe from the doe and slipped her arms into its sleeves, securing its folds around her body with a woven rope. The robe felt soft and insulating. Thian offered his arm for support.

"Thank you," she said, still feeling a little disoriented. The Séoran's touch felt more like water than another's arm, but nonetheless provided some warmth and clarity of thought.

Pleased, the Séoran led her arm-in-arm from the thermal spring onto a meadow of long grass and mossy stones. Ashe's bare toes enjoyed the soft soil underneath as she walked, though her sense of balance and alertness remained hazy. A gray hare stood on its hind legs as she passed, its long ears perked. It seemed more curious than fearful of her presence. On the opposite side of the meadow, a wooded landscape rose steeply toward the snowcapped sentinel peaks of what she assumed were the Upper Mountains.

A larger pool sat at the center of the meadow. Though various streams, including what came from the hot spring, fed into it, the primary source of the pool could be traced left to where the land rose into a cirque partitioned by a cascading waterfall. Beavers had partially dammed the lower end of the pool; she spotted a pair scurrying across. A cluster of white-barked birches lined the far end of the meadow, budding in anticipation of spring.

"This is my home," Thian commented, standing beside her.

"It is beautiful." Ashe breathed in the crisp air, reveling in the scent of damp earth and vegetation. *So alive and content.* Looking around further, she gathered that they were at the center of a dell. "Do you live here alone?"

Thian looked bewildered by the question. "I have many companions. Life here is abundant."

Ashe noticed a stag with great antlers approach the pool across the way.

"Can you speak with all of them?"

"Of course. I am charged with stewarding the beauty of life, especially its smaller features. There are others who do the same, some with their own specialties."

"Smaller features?"

"I adore the myrtle and roses, sparrows and doves."

"Interesting choices," Ashe said.

Thian tilted his head slightly, as if considering her statement. "Why?"

"No reason, really." How could she explain it? "Out of nature's immense selection, they are just unassuming." She thought of the symbolism of the eagle, tree, or mountain as contrary examples. "I suppose that is your point, though."

"Every element has a place of prominence," Thian said. "All are cherished and cared for by my kind. Or so it was in the beginning, before the Corruption when the natural order was altered."

If you say so. Ashe's stomach began to rumble. "Do you have anything to eat?"

With a widening smile, the Séoran nodded. "Come."

Now clearer headed, she slipped her arm from Thian's arm to walk on her own, and followed him around the pool, across a shallow stretch of creek, toward the birch grove.

She suddenly remembered Lüfet. "Wait."

Thian faced her attentively. "What is wrong?"

"Where is my Erïeth?"

"Lüfet is well," Thian replied affably, though his expression once more suggested he did not understand the urgency of such a question. "She rested this morning, but is now out hunting for her supper. You need not worry. She is strong and sagacious."

"How do you know her name?"

"She told me." Thian resumed his previous course across the meadow. "She trusts me to look after you, though I admit that required some convincing at first. Erïeth can be protective."

"Will she come back?"

"Lüfet is fond of you," Thian answered. "She will return."

Ashe began to question how well she really knew her mount, and envied Thian's ability to communicate with her directly. "Could you teach me?"

"To speak to Lüfet?"

"Yes."

"I can show you certain signs, but, alas, nothing more."

"I learn quickly," Ashe pressed.

"It is not that," Thian commented. "There is a kind of intuition unique to my race, an unspoken connection between us and all creation." He showed her to a flat stone upon which was set an assortment of seeds, roots, mushrooms, a few berries, lichen, and even sap gathered on a plate of smooth bark. "Please," he said, indicating the spread. "Eat all you like. More can be brought."

"Will you join me?"

Thian grinned. "I will sit and talk with you, if you wish."

She sat beside the stone. "Do you not eat?"

"Not in the manner of your kind."

Together, they watched the light fade over the dell. To Ashe, the food tasted wholesome and satisfying. Thian brought her some cool water from the stream, served from his hands. As she ate and drank, Ashe felt her vigor slowly returning. Her skin still felt tender from the abuse of the mountain storm, especially her hands and face, but she was thankful for Thian's hospitality, as strange as it seemed, and for such a place of rest.

She studied the Séoran. Though the light of his being no longer blinded her, it still glowed brightly. *Should I be wary of him?* Thian's eyes focused on the violet sky above. *What does he really want?* "Tell me about yourself, Thian."

He looked at her with tender eyes. "What do you wish to know?"

"Have you always lived here in this dell?"

"No."

"In Illirium?"

Thian shook his head.

"What brought you here then?"

"That is a long story," the Séoran answered, "which holds much that you could not imagine."

Probably true. Thinking about it, she was amazed at their interacting at all. "Could you at least tell me where the story starts?"

"I rose from the foaming surf of Oceanus," Thian began, "early in the creation of the world, in the Middle Kingdom on the island of Paphélos."

Ashe straightened attentively. "I lived in Paphélos for many years, and was born on the neighboring island of Lemnas."

"Really?" Thian mirrored her eager expression. "I am glad." After staring at her pensively for a while, he returned his gaze to the dell. "Eventually, my sister and I journeyed across the sea to the shore of the Lower Kingdom you call Illirium."

"Where is your sister now?"

Thian's voice quieted. "Lost."

Why Thian referred to Alöwe as the Middle Kingdom, Ashe did not know. She wanted to ask more, but from the Séoran's downcast demeanor decided against it. This was not a place or time for heavy conversation. Instead, she said, "We Alöweans are taught so little about your kind these days. To me, you are like the spirits of another world."

"There is truth to that," Thian commented.

"But—I mean . . . what is the nature of your power here?"

"My power?"

"Your stewardship," she tried to clarify, though felt unequipped with adequate language, "as a Séoran?"

After a period of silence, Thian said, "In the creation, Elíbom Prímom imbued all living things with the power to exist autonomously, while only thriving through relationship—not only with similar kind, but a diverse host of fellow beings. Since the Early Years, we Séorans have been charged to cultivate that design. There are many tasks, some small and others great, but all are essential for the health of the world. For my part, I have been allocated certain smaller tasks. Think of me as a gardener. The lives of the sparrows, for example, do not depend solely on me, but I am available to them to offer nourishment, healing, and even wisdom should they wish it.

Does that answer your question?"

Ashe shrugged. "I suppose I am beginning to understand, at least in a general way."

"To perceive the universal is to grasp the framework of the truth." Thian eyed her once more. "Though much remains unseen. . . . Now tell me about you. What brought you to Illirium?"

"Opportunity," Ashe replied. At first, she thought to mimic the Séoran's elusiveness, but then resolved to assume a more open, casual tone to lift the mood. "I was young. My uncle served as one of the lead trainers in the Tower of the Sky, on Paphélos. I lived and worked with him there, learning how to train and ride Erïeth. In fact, I became a Sky Rider because of him. Once Nemenelor's dominion was established in Illirium, my uncle introduced me to one who oversaw the new Tower of the Sky, which had been established at the center of the Emülath Sea."

"Is that the name of the island's stone stronghold?" Thian asked.

"Exactly," Ashe affirmed. "They wanted to build their ranks with young, seasoned Sky Riders from Alöwe. I seized the opportunity to leave Chaléth and discover a new world."

"A perplexing world at times," the Séoran commented, "but full of good."

To Ashe, goodness was a misleading concept. "More or less," she commented, considering recent events. A question lingered. "Have you seen a grey mountain ram in this region?"

"There are many rams in the Upper Mountains."

"Not like this one," Ashe pressed. "It was alone and larger than any I have ever seen, with mighty curved horns. I spotted it only days ago."

Thian remained quiet.

"You mentioned someone who would not allow me to venture further into the range."

"Nïmwé," he answered quietly.

"Is Nïmwé the mountain ram?"

Meeting her eyes, Thian shook his head. "No . . . but the creature you saw was another who helps protect these lands."

"Another Séoran?"

"Yes. We are the wakeful ones, the stewards, always attentive and seldom seen in our primordial forms."

"I see you," Ashe offered.

Thian smiled. "I am glad."

As shadows settled over the land, a thin crescent moon ascended. Ashe's eyes became heavy; she was surprised by how tired she felt.

"Come," Thian said. "I will bring you to a place where you can sleep in comfort and peace."

Going further into the woods away from the meadow, Thian brought Ashe to a dense cluster of birches. At their center, grass grew long and voluminous. Some dry strands had been woven into a sheet placed over a layer of gathered moss. Though darkness deepened under the trees, the light of the Séoran's form helped Ashe see clearly.

"Nothing will trouble you here," he said, "not even in your sleep."

Recalling the swan, she wondered what a Séoran could know about her dreams. "Where do you rest?"

"Séorans do not sleep," Thian replied, "not in the way you mortals require." He grinned slightly. "I am glad that you and I have found each other in this land between waking and sleeping. I would like us to be friends."

"I would like that too," Ashe replied, intrigued by her new companion. Wrapping the wool robe tighter around her, she sat down on the makeshift bed. "Until tomorrow then."

"Yes." Thian smiled. "I will not be far if you need anything." He turned away.

"Wait." Ashe suddenly remembered something. The Séoran paused, glancing back at her. "I have not told you my name."

"I know who you are, Ashe Pethus."

"How do you know?"

Thian's smile widened. "Lüfet has told me much. Goodnight."

For days, Ashe resided with Thian in the dell. It could have been weeks; she could not entirely tell. She did not really care to know. She had experienced nothing like it—so carefree and present-oriented. Each day, she woke from uninterrupted sleep feeling sharper of mind and stronger of limb. As their walks throughout the dell lengthened, even her feet ached less than normal, allowing her freedom from relying on her war hammer or even the mip weed.

The Séoran was always accommodating. He talked to her about the manner of living things they saw: the habits of animals, the moods of the rock, the aspirations of the foliage. If only she could remember it all. Nonetheless, she absorbed the memories as a sustained state of tranquility and bliss. She wanted to know the world through Thian's eyes. He seemed unconcerned with the past or future, but rather focused on fostering contentment with the immediate. She liked such simplicity. For a while, she imagined that she would never grow tired of it.

Yet, as they ventured beyond the shelter of the dell to its neighboring lands, as vantage points offered views of the High Hills, her thoughts returned to Nemenelor and her mission in Rökad. She also missed flying. Lüfet had kept mostly to herself during their stay, but Ashe often spotted her soaring around the feet of the mountains, sometimes calling out with single, high-pitched notes. Perhaps the Erïeth was also getting restless.

"Soon, I must go," Ashe said to Thian late one morning. They had climbed to the top of the cirque, and sat beside the waterfall as it gushed down a series of stone steps hundreds of feet below into the dell.

Thian looked at her with concern, his light fading somewhat. "Why must you go?"

"I have an errand—in Rökad, the kingdom of the Dwarves." She told him what little she knew.

"That sounds like a violent prospect," Thian said. "You said you were done with that kind of life."

"I have not severed all strands," Ashe replied, wondering if she had been speaking too openly with the Séoran. "The Alöweans are still my people, and I care about their survival. Anyway, my role in Rökad need not be violent. That is the advantage of a Sky Rider. Above all, we provide perspective."

Thian's posture slouched. His voice quieted. "I do not want you to go."

Ashe did not know what to say to that. Her connection with Thian was unique, his company enjoyable, but she had other places to be. "This is not the end of our friendship," she offered. "We will see each other again."

The Séoran did not appear convinced. "When?"

"I do not know," she replied. Her departure felt increasingly necessary. Not knowing exactly how long she had lingered added to the sense of urgency.

As Thian stared at the ground, Ashe took his hand and squeezed it between both of hers—an unsubstantial sensation, still like touching water. It did not convey the warmth of their first meeting.

"I could come with you," he suggested, staring at her hands.

Wary about the Séoran's growing attachment as well as the distraction he would likely create, she removed her hands from his. "No." It would be simpler for her to continue on alone as she had always done.

"Why not?"

"It would not be good for you," she tried to reason. In their conversations, Thian had seemed ignorant about the occasional necessity of armed conflict. More than a distraction, he would be a liability. *What are you doing here, Ashe? You have let your guard down for too long.*

"Must I let you go?" Thian pressed, looking her in the eyes.

Must? What did he mean? "A friend would understand," she replied, selecting her words carefully. Could he keep her there against her will?

"Yes." With his free hand, Thian reached out to caress her cheek. "Friends. I am glad that we met. You have opened my eyes to a broader world of possibilities. You give me hope that barriers can be overcome, and broken pathways mended."

All that from me? What could she say to that? "You saved my life. I will not forget that."

"Good," Thian said. "Come." He stood and gazed down at the dell. "Lüfet is waiting for you."

4

Ashkenaz

Ashe left Thian's dell with only a few parting words. A drawn-out farewell would only make the situation worse, she decided. Ascending into the sky, she felt the Séoran watching. Only once the dell was out of sight did she feel herself relax again.

It took longer to cross Rökad than Ashe anticipated, for the wind subsided soon after she reached the southern border of the Rínroth Plain. Lacking the wind, Lüfet could not soar without effort. Not wanting the Erïeth to expend more energy than required, and thinking that she was not expected in Ashkenaz for a week, Ashe rested for a day on a north-facing slope overlooking the plain.

The days spent in the Upper Mountains faded in her memory like old dreams. What had felt so immediate, so tangible in the present, upon further consideration became vague and transient. Even flying Lüfet left Ashe with a sense of detachment, her mind elsewhere while her body fulfilled a routine.

As the sun hid its face behind the jagged line of mountains on the fifth day, Ashe mustered herself to concentrate on the sight of Ashkenaz. In the darkening shadow of the Girgash Range, the Rök city was distinguishable by the lights twinkling from its ramparts, towers, and dwellings. It had long been known as a prison city, a third of its space dedicated to containing Illirium's criminals. Before the war, all kingdoms empowered Ashkenaz to hide away individuals deemed most dangerous to society; however,

Dwairian's uprising, including the fall of Tïrmen, Nemenelor's western capital, which now served as his empire's own prison city, had diminished such a need. Behind the citadel's high walls, and accessible only by passageways carved deep into the mountain, was Ashkenaz Prison. Ashe had never seen its corridors or cells, and had no desire to.

The city proper was formidable, its base the solid rock of the mountain. Three great towers oversaw its outer defenses, and a fourth, the tallest, rose from the central keep. Waterfalls, surging with spring runoff, poured into pools and streams that bordered the outer foundation of the city, engineered to serve as a moat. The Rök were excellent craftsmen.

In her final approach to the city, Ashe pulled out a length of white cloth with a small clip at one end. She attached the clip to her saddle then let the cloth unravel in the wind. Slowing Lüfet, bringing her down to a few hundred feet, Ashe trusted that the cloth still served as a sign to the city sentinels that she was not an enemy. She was watched closely until landing—archers glaring at her as she glided over the outer wall atop Lüfet. Only rarely did the Rök accommodate Sky Riders. The city maintained a basic landing platform atop a square building near its outskirts. Once landed, Ashe greeted the armed warden, Rëg, amiably, recognizing him from when she had dwelt in Ashkenaz five years earlier. Two other guards stood on the platform behind him. Bearing longbows, they eyed the Alöwean suspiciously while keeping a wary distance from the Erïeth.

"Welcome back, Sky Rider," the warden said huskily in the common tongue. Broad-shouldered with muscular limbs, he stood as tall as Ashe's collar bone. A thick, braided beard covered half his face. "What brings you back to our corner of the world?"

"Business." Ashe winked then showed him the letter from King Nodshek.

"Hm." Rëg skimmed the message. "I didn't know the king to approve of using Sky Riders. It's just as well, though." He returned the letter. "Ever since the prince steward was killed, tensions've been increasing and communication lacking. They tell us little to none here. And with the pestilence getting worse, or so I'm told, I'm glad you've come."

"Who oversees the city now?" Ashe asked.

"General Hélgorsh." Rëg stepped back nonchalantly, as if to subtly distance himself from Lüfet. "For now, anyway."

"Do you know where I can find Captain Makhai?"

"Makhai?"

"He is mentioned in the letter." Ashe indicated the document. "I understand that he leads a new unit formed to hunt the Erog pestilence."

"Ah yes, the Alödïm," Rëg commented. "That's what they're calling themselves. I'm not sure if any're still here; most've been deployed north to the Rínroth Outpost, I gather. You'd best report to the general. He'll be one to better inform you."

"Well, it is good seeing you again, Rëg." Ashe offered a faint smile. Indicating Lüfet, she added, "She will not cause you any trouble if you keep her well fed."

The three Rök looked at the Erïeth nervously as Ashe walked past to descend the building.

The cobblestone streets were quiet for the night; that is, except for the faint chorus of hammers clanging throughout the city. So it would be for hours, a common refrain in Ashkenaz. Ashe slowly made her way up toward the citadel, inhaling deeply against the pain swelling in her feet and ankles. The added weight of her side satchel and riding pack with extra gear did not help. She noted a couple of Illiri traders pass by, but felt conspicuous being the only visible Alöwean—and one of the few noticeable women for that matter. It also did not help that she stood taller than everyone else. Ignoring the onlookers, she gripped her war hammer tighter, leaning on it for support, and pressed ahead, the metal end of the cane tapping as she went.

Spotting a pair of sparrows resting on the edge of a shingled rooftop, she was reminded of the two she had seen in Thian's dell. As they promptly fluttered away, she wondered whether they were the same pair; and if so, why they were there. *Nothing to gain by dwelling on it now*, she mused.

With the gate of the citadel's high wall finally in view, she turned right to follow along its base. Despite her weariness and the discomfort of walking, she decided to take a detour. A pair of Rök soldiers carrying poleaxes passed her going the opposite direction. She glanced at them, nodded, but then focused ahead. They spoke softly to one another after she had passed, but she could not hear them well enough to understand what they said.

A few blocks away, a familiar sign came into view, hanging from the side of a three-storey building. The sign contained a red, upright forging hammer inside a brown mountain. The two large doors of the shop were still open, soft light flickering from within. A sturdy Rök reclined below the sign smoking a large pipe, his legs fully extended and crossed. A few scars marked his bald head, and his white beard was cut short so as to not interfere with his work. He wore a sleeveless shirt, which exposed bare arms with thick muscles. Hazel eyes calmly tracked Ashe's approach, and a smile formed at the corner of his lip. Gripping the stummel of his pipe with his right hand, the Rök withdrew the bit from between his teeth.

"Ashe Pethus," he said affectionately. "Is that really you?"

Ashe smiled in return. "Hello, Khïrem."

"Come now." The old blacksmith stood and placed the stool before her. "Please, have a seat." He retrieved another stool and sat in front of her, back erect with his hands placed on his thighs.

"Thank you," she said, relieved to take the weight off her feet. "I am glad to see your shop still open. How is business? How are you?"

"Good, good," Khïrem replied. "I have no complaints."

"You seldom do," Ashe said sincerely. She glanced inside the shop, reminding herself of its features: the glowing forge, the shape of the anvils, containers of water and oil for quenching, and the organized collection of hammers and tongs hanging from wood pillars and crossbeams. Nothing appeared to have changed. Even Khïrem seemed the same, except that his face looked leaner than she remembered.

"I need nothing more than I already have," the Rök said, gesturing back toward his shop. "Work is steady—returning clients for the most part—and my name still brings some impact among the guild." He took a puff from his pipe, securing the bit at the corner of his mouth. "I am content." He nodded at her war hammer. "How is it holding up for you?"

"I have not seen its equal," she replied, "though it has been used more as a walking support than a weapon. I do your work some disservice, I am afraid."

"Nonsense." Khïrem waved the comment aside and removed his pipe. "The absence of violence is never a tragedy."

"I suppose you are right."

"Of course I am." The Rök blacksmith smiled and winked at her. "Shall I have a look?"

"Oh, you need not trouble yourself. It is getting late."

"Nonsense." Khïrem stood, received the war hammer from Ashe, and took it into his shop.

She followed him inside. The smell of coal dust and molten iron brought her back to the years she spent assisting Khïrem, learning from him. Though her father was also a blacksmith whom she had worked with, she had gained more from her friendship with the Rök. The two men were incomparable. Her father's work was undeniably elegant, but it proved an ironic counterpoint to his aggressive character. Khïrem's craft, by contrast, was more robust; all the while he maintained a gentle demeanor. Ashe had long viewed him like another uncle.

"Where is Thella?" she asked, casually crossing her arms and leaning back against a wall while the Rök tended to her war hammer.

Khïrem put the weapon down. His voice lowered. "She died last year."

Ashe's heart dropped. "Oh no . . ."

"She got sick." He resumed his work.

"Khïrem, I am so sorry."

The Rök shrugged. "We have both been getting on in years. Eventually, inevitably, the body no longer has the strength to keep fighting. With it being just the two of us . . ." He looked at Ashe. "Anyway, I am heartened to see you again. It has been too long. Remember that you are welcome here anytime."

"I will come visit you more often," she replied.

Part of her regretted not being there in Thella's final days, more to offer her support to Khïrem. She had not felt as close with the blacksmith's wife. Death seemed to follow Ashe wherever she went, leaving its stain on every chapter.

As Khïrem worked, Ashe tried to repel darker thoughts by helping where needed, which included tending to some final tasks for the night. They talked throughout, shared some food and drink, and caught up on stories of recent years. The rhythm of their partnership returned easily. Being back in the shop with Khïrem appealed to Ashe's desire to focus on what was right before her, and the manipulation of metal felt empowering. Yet, the shop also seemed too small and contained, even suffocating. Despite admiring the Rök, she remembered never having felt like she belonged in Ashkenaz. Such reasons had contributed to her departure.

When they were ready to close the shop doors for the night, Ashe heard the approach of heavy boots and the clatter of arms. She retrieved her war hammer while Khïrem stepped onto the street to investigate.

The boots stopped.

"Good evening, gentlemen," she heard Khïrem say. "What can I do for you?"

"We're here for the Sky Rider," a deep voice replied.

Using her war hammer as a cane, Ashe slowly walked out to stand behind Khïrem.

Five grim-looking Rök soldiers dressed in grey brigandine, dark helms, and armed with poleaxes stood before the blacksmith. Seeing Ashe, the leader of the group said, "You're to come with us."

"Is something wrong?" Khïrem asked, still facing the soldiers. His posture tensed, while his voice remained calm.

"None of your concern, blacksmith," the leader replied, still looking at Ashe. He stepped toward her. "Let's go." As he said this, the other four soldiers spread out to hinder a chance of escape.

Khïrem turned to Ashe, keeping his back to the soldiers. Softly, with a calculating gaze, he told her, "I will accompany you."

Glancing past him at the soldiers' stern expressions, Ashe chuckled to herself. She shook her head and placed a tender hand on her friend's shoulder. "Thank you for your hospitality. I will be fine."

Khïrem came closer, almost whispering. His eyes conveyed caution. "Are you sure?"

She assessed the unmoving soldiers once more, each gripping his poleaxe. *Why the spectacle?* "Yes," she replied, feeling relaxed. The soldiers did not intimidate her in the least. "I will see you again soon." Stepping away from her friend, she faced the leader of the group. "Lead on."

The soldiers steered Ashe away from the citadel wall, which surprised her somewhat. They descended a main street toward the outer reaches of the city. Seeing the Sky Rider platform nearby, she wondered if they meant to expel her, but the soldiers directed her to a barracks instead. Inside, she was brought to a room with a round table at its center. A young, blonde-bearded Rök stood at the opposite side of the table, leaning over to inspect a map of Rökad's Northland. Like most Rök, his burly stature was at least a head shorter than the average Alöwean. Five parallel scars, apparently claw marks, ran at an angle down his face. He wore a plain brown tunic and dark green trousers.

As Ashe and the soldiers entered, the Rök looked up. "At last," he said, sounding annoyed. "That'll be all, lieutenant." He waved the soldiers away and indicated that Ashe approach the table. "You're late, Sky Rider."

The abrasiveness of his tone seemed unmerited. "Excuse me?"

"I expected you here three days ago."

Three days? She thought she had arrived early. "Are you Captain Makhai?"

"Who else would I be?" He rubbed his eyes. "This is the headquarters of the Alödïm. I heard that you arrived this afternoon. Why didn't you come to me directly?"

With such vague instructions from the king, what did this captain expect? "I did not know where to look. The tower warden—"

"Yes, clearly, word didn't reach him in time." Makhai exhaled slowly, staring at the map on the table. "It's late, but I need to brief you now so that you know what's going on. The Alödïm currently have two companies. The larger is stationed at Rínroth Outpost, establishing stability in the Northland. The second will leave in the morning, ultimately reuniting with the first. Are you the only Sky Rider that Lord Däne could send?"

She did not feel the need to explain Nemenelor's position. "I will be enough."

The Rök captain did not look convinced. "What is your name and rank?"

"I am Ashe Pethus. I concluded my career in Nemenelor as a captain."

"Concluded?" His expression conveyed suspicion.

"I have worked as a mercenary for the last ten years."

"I suppose you're only here to get paid," Makhai commented curtly, looking back at the map.

More or less true.

Under his breath, the Rök mumbled, "I didn't like the idea of partnering with the Alöweans to begin with." He returned his attention to Ashe. "You know about the Erog, right?"

"Only that King Nodshek has declared them a pestilence," she replied.

Makhai nodded slowly, pensively. "They're violent creatures. We hardly recognized Prince Halirothos when the Erog were done with him. We've yet to discover their dens, but do begin to grasp their hunting habits. They're particularly fond of our tzëg herds." His forefinger fell upon the line of mountains comprising the western border of the Rínroth Plain. "That's where we'll set our next trap. We'll need your eyes from above."

Ashe noted an armor stand behind the captain. The material of the armor was unlike any she had ever seen.

Noticing her gaze, Makhai said, "Made from Erog hide—nearly as strong as steel, but lighter. Come, have a look and meet our quarry."

Using her war hammer for support, she limped around the table to examine the armor. The breastplate was covered in thick, yellow-tan scales, rough to the touch, and the shoulder plates were decorated with what appeared to be scaly, clawed hands with five fingers. The helm was made from the head of a dragon-like creature, nearly twice as large as a man's skull. Two round eye sockets stared vacantly from the sides, each brow defined by a short boney spike. A pair of horns as long as Ashe's arm jutted out from the top-back of the head, and two lesser horns framed what could be considered the cheek line. The wide lower jaw, with a series of small, sharp teeth, had been fashioned into an adjustable visor.

"Impressive," she commented, also finding the display barbaric.

"The Erog adorn themselves in a similar fashion—with the skins of their enemies, we presume." Makhai indicated the belt, which held various horns. "That is my own touch—one for each adversary slain."

Ashe counted. "Only six?"

The Rök captain straightened. "We've had but five skirmishes with the pestilence, and an Erog is incredibly difficult to kill. When standing on their hind legs like us, they are at least twice as tall as a Rök, and can double their girth to intimidate. As quadrupeds, they move in quick powerful bursts, with exceptional climbing skills. They can even change their skin color to better blend into the environment." He stared at Ashe's feet and makeshift cane. "Will that limp be a problem?"

"I have lived with it most of my life," she replied, "since I was a girl."

"Were you born with it?"

"No," she replied. She had nothing to hide. "Early in my training as a Sky Rider, I fell from an Erïeth and broke the bones in my feet and ankles. They now have limited mobility, but the right side is worse. I cannot run or walk long distances without pain, and even riding a horse can be difficult." She came within a step of the Rök captain, looking down at him. "But to assume I am a helpless cripple would be a mistake. It was I who commanded the Sky Riders that defended your capital against the Ülak during the war."

Makhai raised a brow. "You were at the siege of Hevaläth?"

"We drove them from the foothills," she said. "So, understand that when I ride an Erïeth, it will be you who slows me down. . . . Will that be a problem?"

He stared back at her.

Ashe suddenly grinned and slapped the Rök on the side of the shoulder. "Come on, captain. No need to be so serious. I am one of the best Sky Riders in Illirium, here at your service." She bowed playfully. "You need not worry about me."

"Your payment will depend on it," the captain commented without humor, turning away.

Sleepiness began to threaten Ashe's attention. She yawned. "Is there anything else I should know before tomorrow?"

Makhai leaned over the map once more. "For too long, too many months, we've underestimated the Erog invaders. That time is over. Like wild boars, they must be respected." He met Ashe's eyes, and raised a finger. "But not feared."

"I understand," she replied, wondering if the Rök was being a bit melodramatic. She wanted to conclude the matter, wash, and find a comfortable bed.

"You'll scout our perimeter and provide air support when needed, directly under my command."

Ashe nodded.

"That's all for now, captain." Makhai straightened. "A room's available for you upstairs, if you'd like. We'll leave at first light."

In her room, Ashe splashed her face and neck with cold water from a small wooden wash basin. She felt coated in dust and dried sweat—days of travel and the evening working in Khïrem's shop—so undressed and did what she could to clean the rest of her body, concentrating on the areas around her joints, which felt the grimiest. *If only I had soap.* Though not as effective as bathing, the process still revived her spirit. She put on her spare undershirt, pulled out her blanket from her riding pack, and settled herself on the room's lone cot.

Sleep claimed her at once, but she woke disoriented, wondering if hours had passed. It had only been an hour, she realized, judging by the short distance covered by the waxing crescent moon visible through her window. The air in the room felt cold. Closing the window would help, but Ashe did not want to get out of bed. Instead, she closed her eyes and pulled the blanket tighter.

Never cold with you. Never lonely or uncertain.

Cradled by your tenderness, long hours not long enough.

So tired, but awake, desiring to know all—affectionately, tirelessly, giving all I have.

Where are you now?
You changed everything.

Monotonous chirping called her back to consciousness. Opening her eyes, she saw the silhouette of two sparrows perched on the room's windowsill. The sky beyond glowed a faint blue. Dawn approached.

She scrutinized the sparrows. Surely, they were the same pair as before. "What do you want?" she murmured, not expecting a response.

"I asked them to watch over you," said a familiar voice.

Startled, Ashe turned to see Thian sitting crossed-legged in the air next to the head of her cot. The light of his outer form was soft like the moon behind a thin cloud, while a hint of red and gold still radiated beneath.

She sat up. "What are you doing here?"

The Séoran looked confused, and shifted his attention for a moment on the two sparrows. "Osré and Oshrémi followed you from my home, and have kept me informed. They are my servants."

"You should not spy on me," she replied. "A friend does not do such a thing."

"I need to keep you safe."

Need?

He pointed to her body wrapped in the blanket. "You were cold again. I came to warm you."

There had to be more to it than that. "I appreciate your intent," she began, not knowing how to feel about his intrusion, "but this kind of secrecy cannot become a habit. It damages trust."

The Séoran looked grieved. "I want you to trust me."

"Then respect what I am asking," she urged. It had been so long since she trusted anyone deeply. She found Thian's persistence unsettling. "It begins with honesty about your purpose and, as it pertains to me, asking permission to proceed. What do you really want from me?"

"I want us to be friends."

She shook her head. "It is more than that. Why are you here . . . now . . . in this place?"

"Your mission in the Northland is dangerous," Thian answered.

"I have been in riskier situations," she countered. "I cannot have you getting in the way of my work here. Others depend on me."

"You do not understand all that may be at stake," Thian said. "I can ensure your safety."

All that may be at stake? She could protect herself. "How will you ensure my safety?"

Thian extended his legs so that he touched the floor. He then walked over to the window and stared out. One of the sparrows chirped. "Yes," Thian commented, "it is difficult for mortals to comprehend that which is invisible." He faced Ashe. "There is an Unseen War, Ashe, from which the battles you fought were merely ripples."

Aware of the unprecedented speed and destruction of the Illirium War, along with its unresolved mysteries, Ashe found this prospect plausible enough. Yet, why bring it up now—why not before when they were together in the dell? She wondered about the nature of the Séoran's influence beyond what she had so far experienced. What was he not telling her?

"The Rök will not know I am here," Thian continued. "I will be your guardian, providing clarity when your eyes fail to see past the limits of mortal perception. With my help, you will be stronger."

There had to be some kind of ulterior motive. No one did anything selflessly. "Is there a cost to accepting such aid?"

"No cost," Thian answered. "Simply the presence of a friend."

After her rough introduction to Captain Makhai, and not entirely knowing what awaited them in the north, having an ally at hand could be useful. So far, the Séoran had offered her only kindness. That could not be too hastily discarded. He also fascinated her, but more importantly she realized that she preferred the idea of keeping him close as opposed to the likelihood of him continuing to sneak about nearby. She would have to keep a watchful eye on him, while trying to discover more about his purpose along the way. "Very well," she said, offering her hand with a smile. "It will be nice to have the company of a friend."

Thian mirrored her expression, and took her hand. "I am glad."

5

The Northland

The Alödïm's slow pace surprised Ashe, not pushing their ponies farther than twenty miles each day. It made her realize how accustomed she was to an Alöwean standard of speed, the vanguard of which was usually defined by Sky Riders. She did not really mind the delay, however, for the Northland was unfamiliar and she enjoyed gradually taking it in.

Sharp ridges and brittle rock comprised much of the northern Girgash Mountains, which the company kept to their left, paralleling the range as they went. Eventually, the mountains shifted northeast. Riding atop Lüfet, Ashe saw the tips of distant peaks forming a wall from left to right. Having studied Captain Makhai's map of the region, she knew the Girgash framed the Rínroth Plain's southern, western, and northern ends, while the Upper Mountains formed its eastern border. The northwestern corner of the plain marked their destination, where Makhai's contingent would rendezvous with the main company of Alödïm.

Ashe wished the Alödïm were more sociable with her. Each night, after setting up camp, the Rök would gather around fires to eat and converse. Few acknowledged the Sky Rider, however, or included her in their conversation, despite her efforts. She felt alienated, reduced to an onlooker, which gradually confirmed in her mind that Rökad had no future to offer her. The realization stirred pangs of grief in her heart, not for the apparent rejection, but for failing to foster a meaningful choice against returning to Fumond's

Hut or Nemenelor.

After a few days of this, she stopped trying to initiate connection with the Alödïm, and instead made her own fire at the periphery of camp. No one protested. At least Lüfet's presence offered some friendly familiarity. A large predator like the Erïeth could not reside so near the ponies, anyway—not without trouble.

Thian remained mostly unseen during the day. Ashe sometimes spotted three sparrows flying close to the treetops below, paralleling Lüfet's course. At night, the Séoran usually appeared in his primordial form. Far from friendly places and landscapes, she felt more inclined to welcome his presence.

One evening, she watched the glow of firelight dance upon the faces of the nearby Rök. Most leaned toward the warmth of the flames, huddled close, hushed in their conversation. They had made camp in a stretch of forest next to the plain. Patches of hardened snow remained in places. Tufts of cloud, touched by a high steady wind and illuminated by moonlight, filled an otherwise empty indigo sky. The grass of the plain sang a whispered chorus with each swooping gust from above. The trees offered some protection from the wind, but the falling temperature sought to chill Ashe to her core.

That is, until Thian appeared, radiant with warmth. The shadows of the trees darkened and shifted at his approach. His presence mesmerized Ashe. Sitting on her sleeping mat beside her fire, she glanced over at the Rök, sure that they would notice the passing light, yet no one looked her way.

"Why am I the only one who sees you?" she asked the Séoran as he stopped beside her and sat cross-legged in the air.

He smiled. "You have eyes that see."

"What does that mean?"

"You choose to search beyond the tangible, beyond the veils," Thian answered. "Few are born with that kind of sight anymore. For some, however, it can come gradually, even imperceptibly."

"Which am I?" Ashe asked.

"I am not yet sure."

"Well, why are there differences?"

"It began with the Corruption," the Séoran explained, "which occurred not long after the creation of the world. Only Elíbom Prímom truly comprehends the answers. We need not know all. I am not interested in what separates, but rather what can unite us." His dark eyes shifted to study the moon. He assumed a reverent tone. "Though only some can now see what remains unseen, there will come a time when the gates of Rühílis are reopened, when peace will be restored and the spiritual and physical reunited. Then, all will see clearly once again. Already, the Divide has fallen and a new age begun." He looked at Ashe. "The Restoration is coming. More happened in the Illirium War than you mortals realize."

"I do not know about Rühílis or the Divide."

Thian signed. "So much has been forgotten. Rühílis is the dwelling place of the spirit of Elíbom Prímom, the stronghold of my kind." Thian gazed at the fire. "For too long, instability has been allowed to govern this world—an increasingly uncontainable chaos. Some of my brethren tried to restrain it, but . . ."

"But . . ." Ashe waited expectantly. "What?"

"Chaos often precedes restoration," he continued, "like a forest fire cleanses dead soil."

"What are you really talking about?" she asked.

"Confusion can press one toward understanding. In time you will fully see."

"How much time?"

"That is not for me to say," Thian answered. "I look less toward the past and future, but instead serve the present."

"And yet you seem so future-oriented," Ashe countered.

"What I have shared pertains to the present, to what is happening as we speak. That is why I am here."

"The Unseen War?"

"Yes."

Wind stirred the treetops.

Stretching out her arms while yawning, Ashe decided that she no longer cared to continue their conversation. It felt too abstract and detached from her concerns. She preferred to invest more in what was immediately tangible. Nodding toward the Rök, she asked, "What about them? What do you discern of their present? Any advice on what I could do to make them like me more?" She meant the last question more as a joke.

Thian pondered for a while. "They wish too much for an old world, a breadth of history that cannot be reclaimed. Trying to bring it back perpetuates divisions, preventing the current world from growing toward peace."

"Do we not now live in peace?" she asked.

"That which you call 'peace' is merely a bandage over festering wounds. There has been little healing. These Rök cherish their isolation, yet that is exactly what is bringing about their ruin."

"If you are once again trying to discourage me from participating in this mission, my mind is set."

"The Erog are not the real problem," the Séoran said. "The infection reaches deeper. Too many focus outwardly when they should be examining what is inside."

"And the Alöweans?"

Thian looked at her. "You know the answer."

Ashe had a sudden craving for mip weed. She pulled out her pipe and carefully filled it from the pouch Fumond had given her.

The Séoran watched her with interest. "Why do you rely on that substance?"

"I do not rely on it," Ashe retorted. "It just helps me relax." She considered it further. "Maybe it is what allows me to see you."

"Perhaps," Thian commented, pensively. "You do not feel relaxed enough already?"

Ashe shrugged.

"Well, if it gives you peace," Thian said, "then I am glad."

"Do you want to try some?" Ashe offered him the freshly lit pipe.

The Séoran gently held up his hand and shook his head. "It would do nothing for me. We are made from different matter."

Puffing out a ring of smoke, Ashe watched it slowly rise, expand, and dissipate above her. Adjusting her blanket over her legs, she sat up and stoked the shimmering embers of her fire. Having added another two logs, she returned to a reclined position, leaning back against her pack, holding her pipe in one hand. The heat of the fire kept her from trembling, but the cold of the ground had already soaked through her mat, numbing the bottom of her legs. She longed for a soft, dry bed.

"I could help you," Thian said, still hovering slightly above the ground.

She glanced at him in consideration. "With what?"

"Warmth."

The prospect was tempting, but she liked the space between them at the moment. "I will be fine."

He brought his feet to the ground, knelt, and touched her feet with his fingertips.

"What are you doing?" she asked, tensing.

"This fire is inadequate," he said.

The fire fluttered as the heat of the Séoran's proximity intensified. The warmth moved rapidly from her feet up her leg, a pleasant sensation, but also one she had not invited. With her back still propped against her pack, she pointed across the fire. "Get back."

The Séoran looked confused.

"Touch me without permission again, and our friendship will be over."

Thian lifted his hands in acquiescence and moved back. "I meant you no harm."

"I know," Ashe replied, mostly believing it. The Séoran's true intent remained too enigmatic. She kept her voice calm, but even. He had to learn. "This is not like what happened in the Upper Mountains. If I need help, I will ask for it."

Thian stood. "As you wish."

Even after he had withdrawn into the shadows, it took some time for her heart to calm. The intensity of response surprised her, but she also embraced it as a necessary instinct for survival. Finally, staring at the fire, with the mip weed caressing her into a drowsy bliss, she embraced sleep without further delay. Gazing up at the branches of the pine trees, watching them sway, green color brightening, she imagined herself swimming through a glimmering sea—from the shallows near the beach out toward a darker expanse.

* * *

In the northwest corner of the Rínroth Plain, the mountains were less dense, offering more ways to cross the Girgash Range.

"It's here," Captain Makhai told Ashe, "that the pestilence has been seeping into Rökad. I suspect the Erog can't abide the colder temperatures of the high mountain passes to the south, leaving this area as their only option for crossing our border."

"What lies beyond the range?" Ashe asked. Even flying Lüfet, she had been unable to see beyond the dense barrier of snowcapped pinnacles.

"We don't yet know," Makhai replied. "I've sent scouting parties into the passes, but bad weather or Erog ambushes have aggravated our efforts."

"The Erog sound cleverer and more coordinated than you originally conveyed," Ashe commented.

"I'm not sure that 'clever' is the right word," Makhai replied, "but they're certainly tough and aggressive beasts."

Around them, Alödïm finished putting on customized plate armor, the more grizzled soldiers adorned with pieces of Erog hide like their captain. Some sharpened their weapons, such as halberds and poleaxes, while others notched sturdy longbows, but most carried two-handed war hammers with fierce metal heads. From what Ashe had seen of the Erog hide, and considering the height disadvantage of the Rök, she had learned that the strategy was to maintain as much distance from the enemy as possible while ultimately relying on bludgeoning force to slay them. Makhai confirmed that swords and axes had proven almost useless, and that only the best archers managed to cripple their targets with shots to the Erog's eyes or less protected joints.

"I trust you're a good shot with that," Makhai commented, eying Ashe's short bow.

"I hit my mark." Though the regularity of her archery practice had diminished in recent years, not finding a need for it, she remained confident of skills honed by many decades.

"Good," Makhai replied. "It's your eyes that may prove most valuable, however. The Erog have no projectiles that we've encountered, so you shouldn't have to worry about flying out of range. I'll need you to report on their movements. They never hunt alone. Sometimes only a few will nip at our flanks or try to drive us into corners where a larger force awaits."

Like wolves, Ashe thought.

The Alödïm began to form ranks with their allocated unit commanders. Nearby, a herd of tzëg waited in a makeshift corral. The tzëg were as large as ponies, only furrier with features that resembled large mountain goats with curved horns. Seeing them reminded Ashe of the ram she had followed in the Upper Mountains.

The plan was to lure the Erog into the open with the bait of an isolated tzëg herd tended by three Rök shepherds. Such had been the most common prey of the pestilence. All the while, the Alödïm would wait out of sight to encircle and contain the assailants once they struck. Makhai wanted to capture at least one Erog alive. A large iron cage had been specially made in Ashkenaz and brought for that purpose.

"Will the Erog fall for such a simple ruse?" Ashe asked.

"They're driven by hunger," Makhai replied. "This way, we at least choose the battlefield for a change."

"Might they smell your soldiers nearby?"

"The Erog aren't known to have a keen sense of smell, but instead rely on their sight." Makhai straightened and put on his horned Erog helm. "Nonetheless, I've instructed my troops to rub their armor and clothing with local flora. Some Rök activity is not uncommon in this area, particularly with herdsmen; therefore, even if the Erog can smell us, they will hopefully find nothing unusual. We're also establishing our position now to allow our scent to blend into the environment overnight. Furthermore, my main force will wait upwind from where the herd will be grazing."

"As long as the wind does not change direction," Ashe said.

"I understand the risks," Makhai replied, "having studied these creatures longer than anyone else in Rökad. This is my responsibility. Do your job, Sky Rider, and I'll do mine." Striding away, he added over his shoulder, "Signal to me at the first sign of the enemy."

"And the shepherds?"

"The shepherds are prepared," the captain called back.

Ashe appreciated Makhai's resolved preparations, but wondered if anyone had yet tried to communicate with the Erog instead. She did not like entering a conflict this blind, but for the moment would trust that Makhai knew what he was doing. This was a Rök matter. She found some consolation knowing that her position would be detached from the inevitable violence. *I am a scout*, she reminded herself. *Nothing more.*

The following morning, Ashe scanned the surrounding terrain from atop Lüfet. Over two-thousand feet below, the tzëg herd loitered at the center of a field of brown grass. The mountains rose steeply along the south and west sides of the field, while forest partitioned by rock formations marked the descending northern end. Adjacent to that, northwest of the field, a narrow gully ran down from a mountain pass. Makhai anticipated that the Erog would come from there. To the east, the field ascended to an escarpment that dropped a hundred feet to forestland below.

Most of the Alödïm waited amidst the trees and rock formations to the north, ready to bar any attempt at escape by the Erog via the gully. A few archers hid atop the natural rock towers closest to the field. Rel riders were stationed at the brink of the western cliffs, and another unit of foot soldiers watched from the edge of the escarpment.

Another day passed.

Motionless grey clouds covered the sky the following morning. Mist like steam clung to portions of the mountainside, lingering precipitation from the previous night's rainfall. Current visibility was not ideal. Unable to fly higher without losing sight of the field, the Sky Rider wondered if Lüfet's gliding form was too noticeable, and might scare the Erog away as Makhai had warned. She landed Lüfet on a nearby ledge.

An hour passed.

The ding of small bells echoed from below, fastened to the collars of a few tzëg, in part intended to draw the attention of the Erog.

Something stirred in the gully. Strapped to the saddle, leaning forward upon Lüfet's neck, Ashe looked closer. Unmoving, the creature was nearly impossible to identify, its skin mimicking the colors of its environment. But then it carefully crawled further toward the field, moving on four legs like a lizard, its wide oval-shaped back lined with small spikes.

6

Skirmish

Straightening, Ashe slowly waved her arm at the forest where she hoped she was still being watched, and then pointed down at the intruder. After repeating this motion two more times, she returned her attention to the gully, and noticed two other Erog behind the first. A fourth climbed along the bank above them, and then a fifth appeared, even closer to the herd than the first, climbing across the rise west of the field.

The fifth creature moved swiftly and effortlessly, suddenly rushing on all fours down the mountainside to attack the nearest shepherd. As the Rök disappeared underneath the Erog's large mass, the tzëg began to bleat in alarm and press against each other away from the predator. The other two shepherds turned toward the Erog, one drawing a bow, but they were quickly beset by the other four Erog coming from the pass.

Now. Ashe glanced back at the forest. *What are you waiting for?*

She waved in Makhai's general direction and then, not wanting to delay any longer, directed Lüfet to take off from the ledge. A rush of wind blew over Ashe's helm and body as the Erïeth swooped down over the field. She could not spot the Rök shepherds anymore, but glimpsed one Erog seize a tzëg's horns with its clawed hand, slam it down, and bite its neck. Another Erog was already ripping the flesh from its victim's flanks.

Surely, the Alödïm could see what was happening. Turning Lüfet over the top of the trees, Ashe pulled out her already strung bow, accepting that despite her reservations she could not stay idly by. Nocking an arrow, she directed Lüfet with her legs toward an Erog near the perimeter of the herd and loosed the arrow. It struck the creature in the eye, which made it recoil with a guttural cry. It clawed at the arrow desperately, but did not seem lethally hurt.

One Rök shepherd remained standing, and appeared to be trying to drive the tzëg away from the mountainside toward the escarpment. Four Erog formed a line in pursuit, apparently directing the course of the herd more than the shepherd.

Finally, the unit of rel riders appeared from the brink of the western cliff. Slightly larger than the tzëg, the rel had short white or brown fur and long bushy tails. They ran down the cliff on all four legs, and then launched out into the air, using the sail-like membrane that stretched from their wrists to ankles to glide down swiftly. Those that managed to land on top of the rough, spiked backs of their Erog targets, however, tensed in pain and struggled for footing. They were thrust aside, sending their riders violently to the ground, some being crushed underneath their mounts. The rel were not carnivorous, and had no real means to defend themselves. They were meant for speed, but little more. The spears of the rel riders broke as they attempted to penetrate the joints of the Erog's natural armor, leaving the lightly protected Rök and their steeds vulnerable to being clawed and torn apart. The use of the rel riders seemed like a waste to Ashe, though she knew they were meant to stir more confusion than damage, allowing time for the main host of Alödïm to close its trap.

Ashe released more arrows, but most stuck in the Erogs' thick hides, doing nothing to slow their aggression. Trained instincts governed her actions, but she also felt clouded by memories of the war and a desire to withdraw from the battle. Grim focus and revulsion fought for her attention. Some relief washed over her as Alödïm finally moved across the gully entrance, barring the Erog escape, while the main force of Rök advanced with halberds from the woods. A similar line had formed at the escarpment, and began to close in.

Having devastated the rel rider unit, four Erog faced the main Alödïm force; clustering together, keeping on all four legs, each Erog increased its girth like a pouch filling with air. They charged into the front line of Alödïm, driving them back. One Erog faltered with multiple halberds successfully piercing its joints. The next line of Rök came forward to reinforce the crumbling front line of Alödïm, and began battering the heads of the three Erog with their poleaxes. Another Erog went down.

Gliding above in steady circles, Ashe tried to determine how the Alödïm were doing. Only two lines stood in reserve at the gully. As the escarpment unit finally reached the skirmish, completing a circle around the remaining Erog, the advantage in Rök numbers—around three-hundred strong—indicated that the fight would soon be over.

An unfamiliar horn call resonated from the northern forest.

Scattered Alödïm archers and another reserve unit fled from the shelter of the trees. Ashe saw one archer atop a rock formation sent sprawling into the treetops. He was replaced by a large Erog. With a face painted red, the Erog wore pieces of what appeared to be bone armor on its shoulders and covering its joints. In its hand, it bore a black broadsword, which it held high as its voice rumbled.

In response, a line of Erog marched from the trees, staying low while walking upright on their hind legs. Each warrior held a large rectangular wooden shield. The rearmost ranks of Alödïm in the field turned to face their new assailants. Only one of the original Erog attackers remained. The Alödïm charged with ready war hammers, but broke upon the Erog shield wall like dust. The Erog battered the Rök back with their shields, stabbing at them with stone-tipped spears or black swords.

Diving Lüfet toward the line, Ashe loosed an arrow directly into an Erog's eye from the side, penetrating through its skull through the opposite eye. The creature collapsed as Lüfet flew over and then used an updraft against the mountainside to regain altitude.

The clang of weapons, growls of angry exertion, and shouts of pain reverberated across the field. Ashe saw that the force of Alödïm stationed in the gully was beset by additional Erog coming from the pass. The enemy dragged bodies of dead or dying Rök away from the fray. Some even managed to capture stray tzëgs. Ashe recognized Captain Makhai in the thick of the main conflict, rallying his soldiers against the Erog line. The bloodied bodies of the fallen covered much of the field.

Unsure what else she could do to help, the Sky Rider caught sight of a lone Erog watching the scene from a high southern crest. Dressed in what appeared to be a black fur cloak, the Erog bore no weapon. If this was their leader, and if she could take it down, perhaps the battle would be turned. As Ashe steered Lüfet in its direction, the Erog fled, churning a barely contained anger in Ashe's heart. *Coward.*

She clenched her teeth and drove Lüfet toward the retreating enemy. A sparrow fluttered across her visor as she did so, but she ignored it. It persisted, flying back and forth across her view. "No," Thian's voice urged.

"Get out of my way," Ashe shouted.

"Not this one," the Séoran pressed.

Ashe knocked the sparrow aside with the back of her hand. Ahead of her, the lone Erog moved quickly across the wide rocky ridge of the mountainside. Using her legs, Ashe shifted her weight back slightly, bringing Lüfet up over the fleeing target. She released an arrow as she passed that struck the back of the Erog's right knee joint. The creature staggered for a few steps, awkwardly removed the arrow with its left hand, and then continued without hindrance.

The Sky Rider realized what she could do, though it was riskier. She brought Lüfet around to face the Erog, leaned forward, gripped the reins with one hand, and yelled, "Attack."

The Erïeth piped in response, kept her wings straight and steady, and gained speed.

Atop the wide barren terrain, the Erog had nowhere to hide. It faced its doom, lowering itself as close to the ground as possible. It was then that Ashe noticed that the creature was missing its right forearm.

She braced herself. Just before impact, Lüfet lifted her wings, slowing enough to seize the Erog with her mighty talons. The grip was cumbersome, however, for the Erog enlarged its form as she did so. Ashe struggled to see what was happening below her, but felt a jolt in Lüfet's attempt at ascent. She heard the Erog growl beneath her, and then a hiss as they soared unsteadily back toward the battlefield.

Reaching the area where the cliff dropped into the field, Ashe was surprised to see that the Erog forces had dispersed or been killed. Only Alödïm remained standing.

Almost there. She would bring the Erog back as a prisoner.

Lüfet suddenly cried out, and one wing went limp. A smattering of blood and feathers rushed past Ashe's face with the updraft. Flapping one wing, the Erïeth plummeted. The surrounding landscape began to blur in an erratic spinning motion while, a thousand feet below, the crimson-stained field grew larger and larger with terrifying speed.

Ashe gripped the reins tightly with both hands, trying to keep herself close to Lüfet's neck, but felt the momentum pulling her torso backward. Losing her hold, she grasped the air, hoping to stay upright. Though her legs remained fixed to the saddle, she had to keep her back limber, ready for impact.

The earth came.

Shield your head!

7

Away

I fall through a white mist, the damp air chilling my skin.

Under the layer of cloud, as though passing through the surface of water, there is a flash of red light before I slow into a viscous gold emptiness. The deeper I sink, the warmer I feel.

Movement.

Two winged forms land before me, settling on some unseen plane. They are swans—one white, the other black.

"Be careful," says the white.

"I am here," adds the black.

A third form rises behind them, her wings flapping desperately as if to be free of the thick golden void—Lüfet, young or old, I cannot tell, nor whether she is near or far.

"Stay," I call, my voice sounding muted, "or take me too."

Does she not hear? Does she not care? After all, I am the one who took her away. Perhaps I deserve to be left.

"Be careful," the white swan says.

"I am here," repeats the black.

Ashe awoke to a grey-haired Rök kneeling over her, examining her blinking eyes. His mouth moved, but she did not hear him speak. Above him, a faded white canopy rippled with the breeze. A bright orb shone upon its fabric—the midday sun?

"What happened?" Ashe's voice sounded gruff and distant, as if her ears were plugged. She opened her mouth wide, trying to yawn.

"Lie still, please," she heard the Rök say, though his voice remained muffled. Gently, he placed his hand on her shoulder to keep her from rising. "You've been unconscious for a day."

"Who are you?"

"I'm an Alödïm healer. You're safe in camp."

Captain Makhai appeared behind him, looking on with interest. His right eye was purple and swollen shut. He said something to the healer, but Ashe did not understand. She lifted her hand from beneath the blanket that covered her body, and felt her throbbing head. Her brow had been wrapped in cloth, the portion over her left eye rigid with dried blood. Touching her bare forearms, she found that they too had been bandaged. Grazing her shins with her feet revealed the same for them.

"Mostly scrapes and bruises from your landing," the healer explained, "but one of your ribs is also broken." Supporting the back of Ashe's head, he helped her rise to drink a hot liquid that smelled of herbs. It hurt to sit up, but the warmth of the drink felt good flowing down her throat. The healer carefully lowered her head back upon the pillow. It took a moment for Ashe to catch her breath, her side hurt so much.

"Rest now," the healer said. His voice remained stifled in Ashe's ears. "I'll check back on you soon." He straightened, turned to Makhai, and followed him out from under the canopy.

"You fell from a great height," Thian said. His voice sounded clear, but lacked its usual vigor. She was not sure how she felt seeing him. "I slowed your fall," he continued, "to save you." He sat on the ground next to her, his back bent, arms resting limply on his lap. Emitting little light, the Séoran's skin appeared almost as opaque as any mortal. He sighed. "I am sorry, Ashe."

"For what?" she managed to say.

Thian's eyes wandered up, past Ashe to the left.

Turning her head, she saw a sizeable form nearby, shadowed by another pale white canopy. A glint of light fell upon the tip of a large beak.

No. Ashe's heart shuddered. She rolled off her mat, clenching her teeth against the pain, and crawled until her blanket untangled from her legs and fell back. Her forearms and shins stung with each step, but she did not care. Wearing only her cerulean undershirt, the sleeves rolled up to allow space for her bandaged forearms, she managed to rise to her feet and walk barefoot, unsteadily, to the unmoving Erïeth.

Someone called, but she did not listen.

A moment later, the Rök healer came next to her, trying to take her arm for support, but she pushed him back. "No," she said.

At the canopy, she collapsed to her knees and hastily observed Lüfet's condition. The bird lay on her side, her chest wrapped in a large blood-stained cloth. Ashe stroked the feathers of her neck, but there was no response.

Her throat tightened. She could not speak. Resting her head against Lüfet's brow, the Sky Rider placed her arms around her neck.

No.

After some time, a cool hand tenderly touched her shoulder. Ashe placed her palm on the hand, and was surprised to find that it was Thian's.

Lüfet twitched.

With a pang of hope, Ashe sat up and, stroking the Erïeth's neck once again, watched her eyes blink slightly open. "Please." She turned to Thian. "Save her."

The Séoran's expression remained downcast. He shook his head slowly. "I wish I could."

"You said you saved me," Ashe protested. "What is stopping you from doing the same for her?"

"I only slowed your fall," Thian answered. He looked at the Erïeth's chest. "Alas, Lüfet's injuries are too deep, her loss of blood too great."

"We did what we could," the healer said.

Ashe noticed the Rök standing just behind Thian, addressing her.

"I am sorry," Thian and the healer said simultaneously, the Séoran's voice like an airy resonance.

"Please," Ashe began, not focusing on anyone in particular, "do something." She could not accept the thought of losing Lüfet prematurely and after thirty years of shared memories.

The healer drew a long knife from his belt. He knelt down beside Ashe then looked at the Erïeth. She seized the healer's wrist.

"I've been told it's the only mercy," the Rök said. "We would do the same for one of our own mounts. It is a way to honor it."

Carefully, Ashe took the knife from the healer's hand. He nodded somberly and stepped away. Staring at the Erïeth, the Sky Rider could not move. Lüfet's yellow eyes watched her calmly and compliantly. Still on her knees, Ashe lost all sensations and swayed. Thian steadied her by placing his hands on the outside of her shoulders. Leaning back against his chest helped her remain upright. "Do something," she whispered, resting her head back against his.

After some silence, Thian said, "She will feel no pain." He placed his hand down around Ashe's hand, which still held the knife.

"I will do it," she said, retreating from his touch. With her free hand, she stroked the top of Lüfet's head and once again rested her forehead against the bird's brow. *It's the only mercy.* "May you fly free and in peace forevermore, my friend . . . and forgive me." She slid the blade across Lüfet's neck. Tears flowed, followed by a sob.

8

The Prisoner

The company of Alödïm remained in the foothills of the mountains for another week, all the while maintaining a well-defended camp in the woods adjacent to the plain. Captain Makhai sent out scouting parties of tzëg riders into the lower passes twice a day, and kept a rotation of lookouts in strategic high places to watch for a return of the Erog.

As the days passed, Ashe paid little attention to such activity. After burying Lüfet at the base of a tall boulder outside camp, she slept heavily, exhausted by grief. Thian tried to comfort her, but he seemed equally weakened, the usual warmth of his presence gone. Ashe could not find her pouch of mip weed. Desperately, she wanted its soothing influence—numbness of her pain, escape when she could not sleep. A seed of rage grew within her. She began to toss violently in the night. Both her mind and body felt agitated—as if wrestling with a force fighting to be free. Memories plagued her dreams. Rising from her camping mat, clumsily walking around, even in the darkest hours of morning, did little to abate the tense energy. Nor could she will the images away.

Thinking her restlessness a result of grief, the Rök healer tried to console Ashe. "Your Erïeth will wait for you in the Shadow World. I am sure of it."

The Rök believed that the spirit of an animal with which one shared a special connection would reunite with its master in the afterlife; there, helping him or her pass through the Door of Zürük to the Great Mountain

69

Hall. Ashe hoped to see Lüfet again, but was not sure she believed it would happen. She had felt close to all her mounts. Would they all be waiting for her? She did not know what she believed. Most Chaléthians asserted that in death their spirits would return to Elím, a place of peace, until some period of reckoning. She could not remember anything more about it, and felt more drawn to the views of the Alöweans of Nemenelor, where the spirits of the departed would simply wander the world, tending to nature, perhaps even becoming like a Séoran. Considering Thian, this did not seem to be a terrible outcome, but Ashe preferred to not dwell on the subject.

The healer encouraged Ashe to return to a normal routine as best as she could, but acknowledged that it would take some time. While the injuries to her arms and legs were mending well, she needed to be careful not to overexert herself in terms of her broken rib. "I'm also concerned about your head," he added, examining her brow, having removed the dressing. "The stitches are holding nicely, but we've got to watch for symptoms of deeper head trauma." Stroking his grey beard, he regarded her Sky Rider's helm, the crown of which now bore a small dent. "It's good you were wearing this."

She received the helm, but then tossed it aside. With a thud, it landed next to her riding saddle, another item she no longer needed.

* * *

"It survived the fall with no apparent damage," Captain Makhai commented.

Standing next to him, Ashe observed the large iron cage at the center of camp, separated from everything else by a perimeter maintained by twelve Alödïm guards. Inside the cage, the silhouette of the Erog prisoner sat without moving. This was the closest she had really looked at one. It was larger than she had originally realized.

"That is, except for the talon marks left by your Erïeth," Makhai added, crossing his broad arms. "You did well to help capture it . . . I'm sorry for the cost."

"It serves neither of us to dwell on what has passed," Ashe replied, tightening her jaw.

"This Erog is unusual," Makhai said. "It's missing its right forearm, and all its horns have been filed down."

Where two straight horns should have protruded from behind its head, there were now only twin stubs. The same was true of its lesser matching horns, which jutted from its jawline and cheeks. Even without the sharp points, the size of the creature and its jagged facial profile were enough to remind Ashe of its formidable nature. She hated the creature.

"Why do you think it was alone?" she asked. "Is it their chieftain?"

"I don't think so," Makhai replied. "We slew their leader—the one with the face painted red. This one was too detached from the conflict to lead or be of any real use."

Damn. Had Lüfet died for nothing? "Well, you have your prisoner." Ashe turned away, not wanting to think about the Erog anymore.

The captain nodded grimly, and then strolled next to her. "My warriors are banged up and our supplies are limited. King Nodshek will want the prisoner brought to Ashkenaz, but in our condition, it'd take two weeks to arrive. We need to replenish our provisions and recuperate in a safer place. Unfortunately, most of our northern settlements have been abandoned to escape the threat of Erog raids, so the closest choice is Rínroth Outpost. Reinforcements from the Alödïm First Company should arrive tomorrow, but that's only a temporary solution to ensure our secure withdrawal."

It seemed strange for the Rök to abandon a field of victory, but Ashe did not feel like questioning the captain on the subject.

"Rínroth Outpost is three days away," Makhai continued, "We'll go there to reorganize."

"What about me?"

Makhai looked at her. "What do you mean?"

"I am an Alöwean Sky Rider without an Erïeth. There is nothing more I can do for you here."

"How long before you can get another mount?"

"None are readily available," Ashe replied, "not since the Illirium War. Capturing them from the wild demands significant skill, not to mention risk, and training one to a basic level requires months. I am one of the few trainers left in Illirium, but Nemenelor does not have the resources to acquire more Erïeth at this time."

"It seems to me that your leaders ought to reprioritize."

She was inclined to agree.

Makhai frowned, scratching the back of his head. "Best you come with us for now. We'll lend you a pony. We can decide more from the outpost. Goodnight."

"Goodnight, captain."

The prospect of riding a pony for days—ultimately weeks if she was to return south to Nemenelor—made Ashe's feet ache. She glanced back at the cage. Light from nearby fires revealed the Erog's wide, scaly face, and glinted on two round black eyes that watched her intently.

Defiantly, she stared back.

"You will not touch her again." I speak with as much confidence as a sixteen-year-old girl can muster against her father.

"Be silent, child," my father, Zaen, booms over his shoulder, his bare crimson back to me. With his right hand, he hammers a length of hot metal on his anvil, while the other hand manipulates the metal using tongs.

"No," I say. "Your abuse will stop."

Zaen's face is flushed and glistening from the heat of the forge. "Your mother likes to exaggerate."

"I have seen you do it," I press. "It is deplorable."

Zaen glares at me, setting down the tongs, wiping his hand on his dirty, faded brown apron. "It is not your business."

"She is my mother."

"And I am your father. You will respect my wishes, and not interfere."

"I will respect what merits respect," I counter.

He grabs my face with his left hand, pinching my cheeks against my teeth with his strong fingers. "I thought you were smarter than that. Maybe I have been too lenient with you."

I try to push him away, but he stands unyielding.

Beginning to chuckle, he adds, "You have much to learn, child. Relationships are complicated, and life can be unforgiving if you take it for granted. You think too highly of yourself."

"Let me go," I press, images of Mother's recent bruises and bloodied face fueling the fury rising within me. I sink my teeth into the soft flesh between Zaen's thumb and forefinger.

Growling in pain, he throws me down and swings at my face with the hammer. The small iron head strikes the side of my nose, blurring my vision. Landing facedown, my blood pours onto the stone floor. I touch my nose, but recoil at the pain.

Zaen places the bottom of his boot against my ribs and thrusts me onto my side. "Clean that up," he mutters, staring at the mess on his floor.

I am surprised by his actions, but also chide myself for not having seen it coming. It was only a matter of time before he directed his aggression toward me. I rise unsteadily and aim to punch him in the gut, yet he seizes my throat with his free hand.

"Remember your place, child," he says, his deep voice resonating.

I resist his grip, but struggle to see clearly, the pain in my nose is so great.

"Need I do more to remind you?" He releases my neck and snatches my left wrist. "You can still work with a broken finger." He pulls it to an adjacent table, begins to isolate my pinky while readying his hammer.

Struggling against his hold, I reach out with my free hand and grasp the tongs left on the anvil. Without thinking further, I stab his left eye with the tong's jaw slightly open, squeeze the reins, and pull. Zaen screams and clutches at his bleeding eye socket.

Released, I drop the tongs and run.

* * *

Ashe hated riding horseback, and could not remember when she had last been on a quadruped. Being grounded drained her spirit. The blue sky above looked so inviting. If only Lüfet was still alive. Spotting a sparrow, she envied Thian.

"Can you transform into anything?" she asked one evening, wondering if the Séoran could become an Erïeth.

"No."

"Why not?"

"My power is limited," he said. "So it has been since the beginning, by Elíbom Prímom's decree. Limitation encourages creativity as well as humility. I can choose but one mortal form in a land. Here in Illirium, I chose the sparrow because I am fond of them, and because it allows me flight. Even many of the great Séorans assume the guise of smaller animals, for it calls less attention to their passing. The largest I have seen is a buck."

"What about a mountain ram?"

He looked at her curiously. "Yes, that too."

Thinking back to the Upper Mountains, she wondered how many other layers of existence she had yet to discover.

With the Girgash Mountains behind them, the Alödïm followed a straight dirt road east across the plain. Progress felt slow. Mornings were often shrouded in bleak, damp fog, which took until the afternoon to be burned away by the sun.

At first, Ashe intended to ignore the pain in her feet by reflecting on where her next steps would bring her; however, she became increasingly distracted by images from her dreams that loitered in her waking thoughts.

She wondered how her mother was doing.

She wished she had mip weed to smoke.

Her Rök companions acted increasingly irritated. She overheard various arguments between individuals or small groups, and witnessed minor brawls while they were encamped—all over nothing of apparent consequence. The cost of battle on a soldier's mind was familiar to her, but this seemed strange. Most of the Alödïm were as seasoned as her, chosen for that very reason; yet, aside from troubled dreams, her own inner disorder did not manifest itself so blatantly. Had she missed something?

"Maybe it has to do with fighting an enemy they do not understand," she suggested to Thian one night.

The Séoran nodded ponderingly. "Perhaps." He did not seem convinced.

Every time she passed the cage with the Erog prisoner inside, she felt like she was being measured. It made her feel uneasy.

"Why did you try to stop me from attacking that Erog?" she asked Thian, but he remained silent. He seemed detached, lately adopting a habit of disappearing for hours each night. "Is something wrong?" she pressed.

Thian stared at the bustle within the Alödïm camp: two Rök exchanging punches, another lying facedown, passed out, presumably drunk. "Something is haunting this company."

"What?"

"I do not yet know," Thian said.

"You did not answer my first question," Ashe urged, "about the Erog. Why did you get in my way?"

Thian opened his mouth, but faltered. "You are not ready to understand."

"Tell me."

Sitting across the fire, the Séoran's black eyes met her gaze, seemed to search it, but he kept silent.

What do you see? Another question had been growing. "Are you able to hear my thoughts?"

He smiled faintly, but could not sustain it. "No."

"Then why do you hesitate?"

"I do not want to upset you," he answered. "I am for peace."

"Then why did you come?" Ashe stared at the fire. "You knew of my purpose here, and even talked about an Unseen War. Where is peace in any of that?"

"Peace begins with awareness," Thian said softly. "I am learning what I can, doing what I can, to protect you. That Erog . . . I believe he holds some of the answers."

Ashe straightened, furrowing her brow. "The prisoner?"

"Yes."

"It killed Lüfet," she protested. "What possible answers could it provide?"

"He is not your enemy, Ashe."

"How can you say that? What makes you so sure?"

"I have been conversing with him. That is where I go each night—to understand."

She stood, leaning on her war hammer, clenching its head. "Understand what, exactly?"

"His purpose." Thian's voice remained calm. "He has come from far away, and has still farther to go. The Erog are rational, intelligent beings like you and me, Ashe, with their own dreams."

What do you know about dreams? She tried to center her thoughts. "You actually talk with it—him, whatever it is?"

"Yes."

"And he sees you?"

"Yes. His sight is like yours."

Disbelief overwhelmed her anger. "What does he tell you?"

"His name is Raez," Thian explained. "He is not like the others. I discerned it from the start. He would like to speak with you, actually."

With me? "Why?"

"You also stand apart, seeing beyond what is seen."

"That does not make him my ally," Ashe countered.

Thian rose and motioned toward the center of the Alödïm camp. "Come see for yourself."

After a moment of deliberation, Ashe adjusted her hold of her war hammer and limped after him, breathing slowly, deliberately, trying to calm her indignation. She assumed a composed demeanor as she approached the cage, all the while perceiving the Erog watching her from the shadows within.

The guards eyed Ashe with suspicion. The first raised his hand. "That's close enough, Sky Rider."

Thian continued past, unseen and unabated.

Ashe addressed the Rök guard. "I just want to have a closer look."

"It isn't for spectators." The guard glanced back at the cage, and then at another guard. "Besides, the creature's dangerous."

"That does not trouble me," Ashe replied. "I am the one who brought it to you in the first place, and doing so cost me my mount and nearly my life."

She stepped closer to the guard, looking down into his wavering expression. "I want to know my enemy."

"All right," the guard conceded quietly, stepping back. "A few minutes is what you'll get."

She nodded and proceeded.

"Don't get too close, though," the guard added. "It can reach between the bars a bit."

"So can I," she replied.

Thian waited for her next to the cage. This was the closest she had come face-to-face with a living Erog. It was nearly twice her size. The soft glow of firelight flickered upon its body: rough yellow and brown scales, spikes and horns filed down, a missing forearm, and a pair of bulbous black eyes. Slowly, Ashe lowered herself to sit cross-legged, and placed her war hammer across her lap.

Boldly, she stared back at the Erog, though its presence left her in awe. Despite what she had witnessed of the battle, despite the cost of her first encounter with this creature, a part of her struggled to accept that it was real. The prisoner reminded her of the Illirium War, of other creatures that had forced their way into her consciousness so swiftly and brutally—names like Ülak and Küllka. For the time being, reminding herself of Lüfet's absence helped reorient her emotions, grounding her mind, while the hate of the Erog focused her resolve. Still looking at the prisoner, she pointed at Thian. "You see him?"

The Erog glanced at the Séoran then back at her.

She took that as an affirmative. "You wish to speak with me?"

"He does not understand your language," Thian commented. He then addressed the creature with strange intonations.

The Erog growled deeply, its timbre subtly rising and falling, punctuated by clicks that sounded like bone clattering on bone.

"He is Raez Het of the Thraz," Thian told her. "They do not refer to themselves as Erog, but by the name of their tribe. You may call him Raez. I have already told him your name and general history, including some context of the Alöwean presence here in Illirium, but he wants to know why you are specifically helping the Rök."

Staring into Raez's large black eyes, Ashe said, "For now, I am here to understand why you are here. The Rök call you a pestilence."

The Erog's voice rumbled and clicked once more.

"His people are hungry," Thian interpreted. "They defend themselves against their aggressors."

Everybody claims to be a defender against injustice. "Are you their leader?" she asked.

"Not in the way you imply," Thian said before translating. "He seems to be a kind of sage." He spoke to the Erog, who then responded. "He seeks the deeper truths about life, the stars, the Unseen. He seeks a great body of water across the world."

"Which body of water?" Ashe asked, looking at Thian.

"Oceanus."

An oddly simple aspiration. She looked at Raez. "Why?"

Thian interpreted then listened to the Erog's guttural speech. "He has seen it in a vision from the gods." The creature glanced at the Séoran. "Even now, he says, they move among us, guiding."

Ashe wondered if the Erog saw Thian as a god. "Well, we are far from the sea."

"Some kind of change is threatening the Thraz," Thian said. "I do not grasp what he means by it, but Raez claims that reaching Oceanus will give him the power to unify his people and restore peace, not only among his tribe, but with all, perhaps even neighbors like the Rök."

"What does that have to do with me?" Ashe asked.

Thian smiled. "He needs your help."

She looked at the Séoran incredulously. "He wants *my* help?"

"You and I can free him and show him the way," Thian answered, "This is an opportunity for real peace."

She shook her head. "After what his people have done to the Rök, after what he did to Lüfet?"

Raez's voice rumbled and clicked once more.

Thian nodded. "He is sorry for mortally wounding your eagle, but claims he had no other choice to survive. I tried to warn you, Ashe."

Ashe heard the footsteps of a Rök guard approaching. "Time's up, missy."

She stood, not looking at the caged Erog.

"Consider the possibilities," Thian urged with eyes full of fervor.

Ashe turned away with nothing more to say.

9

Outpost

The company reached their destination in the middle of the fourth day. Defended by a ditch and wood palisade, Rínroth Outpost jutted up from a flat featureless plain. Outside the walls, herdsmen tended to grazing livestock, while a larger gathering of Rök, including a few women and children, weeded among fields of crops. Many stared at the new arrivals, their eyes wide at the sight of the Erog prisoner in its cage.

Crossing a simple drawbridge, the company of Alödïm entered an open courtyard with a well at its center. Ashe longed for a bath. Dried sweat and dust clung to her skin. Her groin and inner thighs felt sore from days of abrasive riding. A flood of dizziness passed over her as she dismounted, forcing her to keep her hands on the pony's back. Once her head cleared, she walked around the courtyard a bit, leading the pony by the reins while stretching out her limbs.

The outpost's interior contained two barracks and stables, a clanging blacksmith's shop, and a few other structures. Between the two barracks, a gate opened to a lesser walled area, apparently reserved for stowing livestock overnight. A tall, narrow tower stood at the far end of the courtyard, built from a combination of wood and rough stones like those that littered the plain outside. The tower rose from what Ashe presumed to be the main hall and adjacent kitchen. She liked the simplicity of the place, but remained conscious of its remoteness.

Many of her Alödïm companions grumbled around her, cursing, tossing gear on the ground, and aggressively unclasping harnesses. Some eyed Ashe darkly. The ponies became increasingly uneasy.

Makhai looked around with a scowl on his face. "Where is everybody?" he growled to no one in particular. "Is nothing prepared for our arrival?"

"Captain Makhai." A brown-haired Rök strode from the tower hall. Two other Rök accompanied him. "Welcome."

"Captain Üsev," Makhai acknowledged, still frowning. "What's the meaning of this?" He motioned around him.

The other captain looked confused. "What are you talking about?"

"This," Makhai exclaimed, still signaling with his outstretched arms. "Where are the stable hands for our ponies, and servants to help my tired soldiers unload? Where is the rest of First Company?"

"Captain, your Alödïm are out riding a patrol. The—"

"Who gave that order?" Makhai interrupted.

Ashe did not understand the angry spectacle, especially with everyone to observe. It seemed unprofessional.

Üsev raised a brow and his tone grew firm. "I oversee the workings of this outpost, Captain Makhai, but I do not command your Alödïm. That was your arrangement with the king—against my advice, if you recall. We are here to accommodate you, but not to serve."

"Does our victory mean nothing to you?" Makhai said. "Good Rök have died to preserve this small plot of land. You disrespect them with such irreverence."

The two Rök standing behind Üsev glanced at each other with uncertain expressions.

"Our hearts grieve such losses," Üsev replied, keeping his tone in check. "We laud your recent success against the pestilence. However, for the survival of this outpost, including your two companies, we currently have to focus on preparing for the first harvest next month. Most of the garrison is needed in the fields. The barracks allocated to you and your Alödïm remains exclusively yours. Can you not manage settling in yourself?"

Walking up to Üsev, Makhai drew his sword and rested the flat of the blade upon his shoulder. Üsev's companions gripped their sword hilts, but he lifted a hand to calm them. "I do not understand this antagonism," he said. "If you wish, we can talk more after you have had a chance to unpack and rest."

"While here," Makhai said evenly, "I'm in command."

"That is not—"

"You'll do as I say without argument. Got it?"

Üsev's jaw tightened. He noted how many of the armed Alödïm had spread out in a semi-circle around him and his two soldiers. Returning his attention to Makhai, he said, "Let us know how we can help, captain."

Bewildered by the confrontation, thinking it a continuation of the strangely contentious spirit among the Alödïm, at least since the battle in the mountains, Ashe looked away. Through the outpost's second main gate, the road proceeded southward a hundred miles to the rugged cluster of the lower Girgash Mountains. Beyond those mountains waited friendlier possibilities. She wanted to leave Rökad as soon as possible.

Her second night after arrival, Ashe enjoyed talking with the blacksmith, Martum, about his work. He had heard of Khïrem's reputation in Ashkenaz, and considered him a master smith.

"Though I've yet to meet 'im in person," Martum commented.

"Would you like to?" Ashe asked.

"Aye, that I would. It'd be an honor."

"I would be happy to introduce you."

Admiring her knowledge of the craft and wanting to hear more news from the south, Martum invited her to join his family for supper. Ashe welcomed the time away from moody soldiers and discussions of military matters. Though Thian's company had helped at times, there was something substantial in human interaction that she missed. She preferred being with tradesmen and common folk; though generally more settled, which she was not ready to do herself, their lives made her feel wholesome and at ease.

As the sun began to set outside, its burgundy glow visible through the small kitchen window, the blacksmith's wife put their young daughter and son to bed. As she did so, Martum offered Ashe a drink. "Here now, try this."

It harbored a bitter tang, but the jolting aftertaste invigorated Ashe. "Well, hello there," she said to the drink.

Martum smiled in return. "It's something, isn't it?"

"I like it."

"Little better than piss," the blacksmith commented, "but I ken the brewer. He's trying, I'll give 'im that. There's little to work with in these parts. Be glad you didn't taste the first batch."

"Oh?"

Martum nodded. "Like a punch to the throat, it was." He chuckled.

"Is it difficult being a blacksmith in such an isolated place?" she asked. "I imagine that supplies are hard to come by."

"My family manages well enough, to be sure," Martum replied. "The soldiers keep me busy. We trust that the outpost'll grow into a proper settlement in time—once the region's secured. I've friends—"

A commotion sounded outside. The door of the home burst open, and in walked four Alödïm with a crazed look in their eyes. Fitted in plate armor, three bore swords while another held a spear.

Closest to the door, Martum stood timidly. "What's this?"

The spearman pushed the blacksmith back over the dining table with a crash, while the leader lunged at Ashe with his sword. She dodged to the right, but then the Alödïm behind him came forward and hastily swung his blade at her face. Leaning back to avoid the tip of the second sword and then moving into a crouched position, Ashe kicked the leader firmly in the side of the knee, knocking him off balance into the second soldier. Rising quickly from her lowered stance, she moved around the table to keep it between her and the assailants, grabbing her war hammer along the way.

Martum stood rubbing his head beside her.

Ashe gently guided him back with her left hand. "Protect your children."

"Aye." The blacksmith withdrew into the room where his wife stood rigidly in front of her children with a broom and knife in her hands.

Martum closed the door.

"We're not here for him," the Alödïm leader said, rubbing his leg and staring at Ashe. As he adjusted his helmet, spittle dripped from his mouth. He held his sword ready, flanked by the second soldier, and approached one side of the table while the other two began to make their way around the opposite side.

Ashe needed to get out of the tight space, so leapt over the table toward the entryway. The landing stabbed her feet with pain, but she gritted her teeth and dashed through the open door. Outside in the main courtyard, outpost soldiers and Alödïm clashed violently. A few bodies lay in puddles of blood.

A lone soldier came at Ashe with a poleaxe, swinging at her head, but he was not close enough. He moved unevenly, with eyes that looked vacant like a man inebriated.

"What are you doing?" she cried.

"Cleansing ourselves of the pestilence," he mumbled, drooling.

Had everyone gone mad?

"I am not your enemy," she protested.

It was useless to reason with him, however. The Alödïm soldier stepped closer while her four original attackers exited the blacksmith's house and began to encircle her position. Without further hesitation, she turned and seized the shaft of the spearman's weapon with one hand while driving the head of her war hammer into his face. Blood gushed from his nose as he stumbled back against the wall of the house.

Putting his sprawled-out body between her and the next soldier, Ashe moved as quickly as she could around the corner of the house into an adjacent alleyway and, holding her hammer with her left hand, swung at the soldier with the poleaxe to keep him back.

The alley was narrow, allowing only two to attack her at a time. A dead Rök lay at her feet. She knelt, slid her left forearm into the straps of his round shield, and sprung upward against a sword attack. Using the shield to deflect the blade, she slammed the hammer end of her weapon against the side of the swordsman's head and then parried the other soldier's poleaxe. Knocking the poleaxe further aside, she kicked the Rök's exposed chest and nearly collapsed from the pain of her foot contacting the breastplate. She could not dwell on it as the two remaining Alödïm swordsmen, one of them the original leader, pressed past the faltering poleaxe soldier and attacked. One blade stabbed over the top of her raised shield and cut her shoulder, but she blocked the one to her right with the metal-plated shaft of her war hammer. Coming closer, she then cracked the rightmost soldier's jaw with a thrust of the hammer, struck the leftmost swordsman's blade away with her shield, and then promptly dealt him three successive hammer blows: knee, elbow, and shoulder. Though each joint was protected by plate armor, the impact of the solid iron head brought the Rök leader to his knees with a groan. Punching his face with the rim of her shield, he collapsed.

Strides away, beyond the alley entrance, the Alödïm with the poleaxe had been engaged by two outpost soldiers. Behind Ashe, the alley ended at the palisade wall. Focusing back on the central courtyard, she cautiously walked up to the left corner of the alley. Glancing around it, she saw that the fighting had slowed. The Alödïm appeared to be winning.

"There you are," a familiar voice said. A sparrow soared down from an adjacent rooftop, spun and transformed into Thian's glowing figure. "Osré and Oshrémi could not find you. This chaos—"

"I do not know what is happening either," Ashe said.

"It is not that," Thian began. "The—"

"I need to get out of here," Ashe urged. "Can you help me?"

"I can show you the way." He strode out from the alleyway to the courtyard. "Come."

That seemed like the opposite way they should go. "Are you sure?"

He held out his hand. "Trust me."

Keeping her shield and war hammer ready, she followed the Séoran left around the perimeter of the courtyard. Back to the right, near the western gate, the fighting intensified. Presumably, Thian was leading her to the southern gate in a roundabout way to avoid the sporadic skirmishes in the courtyard.

Passing the second barracks near the outpost tower, Ashe found herself standing before the large Erog cage. Thian stopped and spoke with the prisoner before turning to her. "You must free him."

"What?"

"He can help you escape."

"It killed Lüfet," she protested. "Will it not do the same to me, if given the chance?"

"Alöwean," someone shouted from behind her.

Ashe turned to see Captain Makhai standing at the center of the courtyard, glaring at her. Other Alödïm gathered behind him, most splattered with blood. Spreading out, they advanced toward her.

"They mean to kill you," Thian said with an edge of urgency.

"I do not understand why this is happening."

"Now is not the time to explain," the Séoran urged. "Free the prisoner."

Ashe looked around. Could Thian somehow be the source of the conflict, manipulating the situation? She considered retreating alone up a flight of stairs, which led to the palisade wall walk, but various Alödïm were already clustering there. She had a better chance of overcoming them than staying to face Makhai and his numerous followers in the courtyard. An arrow whooshed past her face, and then another. Two Rök archers focused on her from the wall. She lifted her shield to deflect a third arrow, crouched and retreated behind the side of the cage, her war hammer held ready.

The creature inside muttered something.

Ashe's heart stopped a moment as she realized how close she was to the Erog. It could easily reach her through the bars of the cage, yet it just sat there calmly, unmoved, watching her.

Makhai raised a hand to halt the archers as he and his contingent approached within ten strides away.

"Now," Thian insisted.

Unable to think of anything else to do, while also wondering what the Erog would do if freed, she asked, "How do I open this thing?"

The prisoner held up an iron ring containing a single key. The ring dangled from the creature's thin forefinger, the claw of which had been filed down.

"How long have you had that?" Ashe cried in disbelief.

"Stop," Makhai shouted at Ashe, hesitating in his steps.

As the Erog appeared uncertain about what to do with the key, Ashe hastily took it and unlocked the cage door, which opened with a creak. The creature came out quickly and hissed at the semi-circle of armed Alödïm. Arrows struck its bare, scaly back from the archers on the wall, but did not hinder it. A rolled up black fur cloak was fastened around its waste. The creature moved on all three of its good limbs, its missing right forearm causing a slight wobble in its steps, which it tried to counteract with its tail. It growled at the Alöwean.

"Climb on its back," Thian said. He rose into the air and assumed his sparrow form.

With no more time to deliberate, Ashe leapt onto the Erog's wide back, which was not high, and positioned herself on her stomach while holding the two filed spikes at the base of the creature's neck. The Erog turned away from the Alödïm line and effortlessly sprang up the palisade wall, scattering its Rök defenders. With every movement, Ashe felt herself being scraped by the Erog's rough hide. After one step on the wall walk, with Ashe trying hard not to fall off, the creature climbed over the wooden parapet and then down onto the quiet grasslands beyond.

They fled into the night, a bright moon illuminating the expanse of the Rínroth Plain.

The Erog quickly slowed, its hobble progressively worsening. Glancing back, Ashe saw a line of glinting shadows rushing across the outpost's lowered drawbridge in pursuit. Her keen Alöwean eyes perceived Rök astride galloping ponies. A few of the riders bore torches. Looking ahead, a dark forest offered the hope of escape, but they would not be able to reach it before being overrun.

Stopping, the Erog said something to Ashe. It shook its back as if to indicate that she get off. She happily complied.

Thian appeared in his Séoran form beside her. "You must hurry."

"I cannot outrun ponies," she replied. The initial adrenaline of her engagement with the Rök had faded. In its place, she felt a nearly overwhelming pain in her side, likely from the rib healing from her fall upon

Lüfet, making it difficult to breathe. Her shoulder also stung. Reaching over, she found that her torn tunic was only slightly damp with blood, the wound already congealing.

"Raez will hold them back and then rejoin us after," Thian explained. Already, the Erog appeared to be bracing itself for the coming onslaught. Placing his hand on her wounded shoulder, which soothed it, Thian added, "I will do what I can to ease your feet, hopefully empowering you enough to run to the forest."

Run? "How far is it?"

"A little over five miles."

She had never run that far before. "I cannot."

"You can," Thian said, offering a faint smile. "I will help you."

The Erog hissed at the approaching Alödïm.

"We must go," Thian pressed. "Now."

Stiffly, Ashe began to jog west toward the trees. Shouts and a clash of arms sounded behind her, but she did not look back.

10

Choices

As she jogged, Ashe felt nimbler than ever before as warmth deeply permeated her feet and ankle joints. Pain still pulsated with each step, but to a duller degree than she was accustomed to—less distracting and inhibiting than the usual sharpness of her limitations. Thian ran alongside her, matching her pace, encouraging her with words. A thin layer of frost formed on the grass in his wake. Whatever the Séoran was doing to aid her progress, it seemed to be working.

When they reached the forest border, Thian did not slow, but directed her farther. She was about to protest, but quickly recognized the wisdom of retreating into the full concealment of the wilderness. The glow of Thian's body lit the way in the dark, helping Ashe navigate the rugged landscape. Near the zenith of a long ridge, he finally halted.

Recalling her recent journey with the Alödïm east from the mountains, she knew this forest to only be a few miles wide before dispersing into the continuing plain. The jagged silhouette of the Girgash Mountains marked the western horizon. Looking back eastward through the trees, she glimpsed the greater Rínroth Plain, but did not see any activity.

She wondered about the fate of the Erog prisoner. If it had survived, would it actually seek to find them? She doubted it, and did not care. Her body ached, weariness hanging from every limb like a weight. "I need to rest," she said.

Thian turned away from one of his sparrow scouts. "Yes," he agreed. The sparrow flew away. "Osré says that we are safe, and should be for the remainder of the night." He guided Ashe to recline against a large tree. "I will keep watch while you sleep. Here . . ." He sat beside her. "You may rest your head on my lap."

If only she could have retrieved her gear. Her winter cloak would be missed, for one, as well as her bow and quiver of arrows. With her pipe at hand, but no mip weed, she once again longed for its numbing effects. Laying her head on Thian's thigh like a pillow, feeling his warmth slowly cover her like a blanket, she closed her eyes and faded from consciousness.

Uncertainty is exhausting.

The outstretched wings of the black swan churn like smoke, rising from its form until the sky is blackened with soot. Below, a city burns.

Anaríl, our eastern capital, has fallen to fire. The enemy is too strong: cruel foes from across the Wasteland far away and an alliance of the twelve clans of men are poised to end our existence. We, the remnant in Hamrothél, stand as the last bastion of Nemenelor.

Yet, the enemy does not come. We wait, brace ourselves for death, but are merely watched from the other side of Lake Cüivenen. Soon after, they turn on each other, fighting on the Prothiläüm, the plain marking the southern entryway to Anaríl. Why do they turn on each other? Is it mortal nature or an unseen power coming to our aid at last?

Later, flying over the still smoldering ruins of Anaríl, I see the devastation. Already, I am numb to it, which began weeks earlier when I fought alongside Rök allies to defend our shared border against the Ülak army. So quickly, the mind grows calloused.

What would have happened had I been sent to defend Anaríl instead of the north, and why did I survive when so many others fell?

Chaos follows me wherever I go.

"I am here," the voice of the black swan echoes from the surrounding smoke.

"Be wary," the white swan answers.

Damp fog clung to the morning.

Groggy, Ashe sat up, bent forward, and extended her arms to stretch out the tension from her back. She wished for a dry bed, and the chance to sleep the day away. She missed Lüfet, and considered how easy it would be to leave Rökad if the Erïeth was still alive.

"How did you sleep?" Thian asked, still with her.

"Well enough, I suppose," she replied, slowly standing to further rouse herself. "What happened last night at the outpost?"

"What do you mean?"

"Why did Makhai and his soldiers turn against everyone?"

Thian's eyes lowered. "I do not know."

"You had nothing to do with it?" Ashe pressed. "You were the one who wanted to see the Erog prisoner freed."

The Séoran's voice remained subdued. He looked grieved. "Not like that."

Ashe rubbed her face. Recent events had happened so quickly, out of control. She felt tired.

"There is a stream down there, if you would like a drink and wash." Thian pointed.

"Thank you."

Using her war hammer for stability, she walked stiffly down from the ridge toward the sound of trickling water. There, she knelt down on one knee and drank a few mouthfuls using her cupped hand. The water tasted cold and refreshing, and splashing some against her face chased the drowsiness away.

A crunching and tearing sound caught her attention. Listening carefully, she realized that something was eating nearby. Stepping over the stream, she gripped the handle of her war hammer and advanced.

Around the bend of the hill, she came upon the Erog prisoner sitting with its back to her. It appeared to be eating a large piece of meat, holding it with its left hand. Bone and bloody fragments lay on the ground beside it. Not moving, she studied the remains closer, and recognized one as the head of a Rök connected to nothing more than an exposed spine. A helm had been discarded nearby, along with other pieces of cloth and armor. She spotted a boot attached to a single leg.

The Erog paused and looked back at her with its large black eyes. Blood stained its wide maw and rows of sharp teeth. Seeing her, it slowly lowered the stub of flesh in its hand and exhaled.

Ashe felt sick, unsure whether to flee or fight the creature. She stepped back into Thian, who placed an assuring hand on her shoulder, but recoiled from his touch. "What is this?"

"The Erog are carnivorous by nature," the Séoran said, "like you."

"We do not eat the flesh of our enemies," Ashe countered, frowning and shaking her head in disgust.

The Erog spoke.

Thian translated, "The Alödïm gave him little to eat since his capture. He needs meat to thrive."

"Stay away from me," she said, pointing her hammer at the Erog's gaze. She turned to walk away.

"Wait." Thian held her upper arm. "We must discuss our plans."

"I have nothing to discuss with that animal," she replied. "Nor you, if you intend to befriend it."

"You misunderstand," Thian said. "Raez wants what we want."

She faced the Séoran. "And what is that, exactly?"

"We can live in peace together."

Ashe scoffed. "They should have thought of that before invading Rökad."

"Please," Thian urged. "There is much you do not yet understand."

"I am not interested anymore." She withdrew her arm from Thian's hold and walked away, back up the hillside.

Sitting on a rocky outcrop at the crest of the ridge, Ashe felt overwhelmed by the extent of her solitude. She had no provisions, no mount, and remained far from any settlement. Rínroth Outpost was the closest, but had been contaminated by chaos. She hoped Martum and his family were safe, along with the many other innocent Rök civilians. Maybe they could aid her if she managed to sneak back inside; they could supply her with food and help her commandeer a pony. *No.* Doing so would place Martum and his family in an impossible situation, risking their lives. They deserved better.

What else could she do? She could not journey south alone in her current state. The only other option was to stay with Thian, which apparently meant the Erog as well. Thian was right—she did not understand. From the start, the Erog had put her into this situation. She would not forget that, especially not the death of Lüfet. Yet for now, maybe it would be best to hear Thian's plan and let him help free her from the current mess.

She returned to where they had spent the night, but the Séoran was nowhere in sight. Instead, the Erog sat nearby with its eyes closed, back erect, and left hand resting on its left leg. Wrapped in its black fur cloak, the creature was either sleeping or meditating.

"Where is Thian?" she demanded. Dusk approached.

The Erog did not move, but merely took a long, slow breath.

Ashe sat down across from it, keeping a good distance between them, and watched, noting its faded yellow, rough scales and the various filed horns adorning its head: one above each brow, one at the end of each side of its jaw, another three like a crown running back from its cheekbone around its head, and the two most prominent ones jutting up from the top-back. With its mouth closed, its expression looked like a perpetual frown. A firm intensity characterized its demeanor, but also a calm dignity.

A black vulture swooped down and landed on the Erog's shoulder, yet still the latter did not move.

"The bird's name is Ornithez," Thian commented, walking up beside Ashe. "He serves his master in a manner like my sparrows. Even after Raez was captured, Ornithez did not abandon him, but remained near and watchful."

"Tell me what you intend to do," Ashe said, not looking at the Séoran. "Tell me everything."

"Everything is too much for the present," Thian replied. "At this moment, the Alödïm hunt for you, and my allies cannot misdirect them from your trail indefinitely. Therefore, we must act quickly in the interest of keeping you both safe."

A set of calls resounded from above. Three large Erïeth glided down and landed on the nearby stone outcrop. Seeing them lifted the Sky Rider's spirit.

Thian smiled at her. "They come from the mountains."

"They are magnificent."

The Erog stirred with a hint of uneasiness, its eyes now open.

"I have spoken with their lord," Thian said, "who has given them leave to aid us for a time." Tenderly taking Ashe's shoulders, he directed her attention to him. "Having spoken long with Raez, I believe our futures are intertwined—yours, his, and mine. Forces beyond ourselves have brought us together. The success of his quest is connected to the Unseen War, and could influence the future of not only the Northland, but all of Illirium. We must help him reach the sea."

"But that is over a thousand miles to the south," Ashe protested. She did not understand why Thian was so enamored by the Erog. The creature was dangerous and revolting. She did not care about its quest, and still knew almost nothing about the Unseen War. What did Thian really want? "Even if we can safely get out of Rökad, we would still have to pass through Rodaním."

"Trust me," Thian said. "With wisdom, patience, and above all unity, we can overcome each barrier."

She was prepared to trust the Séoran a while longer out of necessity, but would not trust the Erog. "Tell that creature to keep its distance from me."

Thian nodded solemnly, and then motioned toward the three waiting Erïeth. "They have agreed to transport you and Raez across the southern Girgash Mountains."

Good. That would at least get her across the Rökad border. "No farther?"

"No." Thian brushed a lock of silver hair away from Ashe's face. "We can determine the next move along the way."

The Erog stepped forward and spoke in its deep, reverberating voice. Thian replied.

"What did it say?" Ashe asked.

"Raez is not keen on being carried by an Erïeth," Thian answered. "They have been known to hunt his people."

"The Erog need not come," Ashe suggested.

The Séoran frowned at her. "I have assured him that this is the only way; that these Erïeth will not harm him. The third is here as a substitute, for nearly two-hundred miles separate us from the southern end of the mountains. Raez is a heavy burden—at least twice your weight."

Ashe thought of Lüfet and their fall during the battle. *Forgive me.* She strode past Thian toward the outcrop and three waiting birds. "I presume they are ready to leave?"

"Yes." Thian followed noiselessly after her.

Having climbed up the rock, Ashe stared once more in admiration and a sense of familiarity at the three large eagles. One had white feathers tipped with grey, the second was mostly black, and the third brown with white accents. Closest to the white one, Ashe reached out to stroke its neck, but it flinched away and eyed her fiercely. The Sky Rider held up her hands to assure the Erïeth.

"They are a proud and independent race," Thian said, floating up beside her, "with their own language and culture." He made a series of whistle and piping sounds then bowed his head reverently. The white Erïeth nodded in return, and seemed to relax. Thian addressed Ashe once more: "I know you and Lüfet were close, but this is not the same. These three are here under the command of their lord. You are their guest, not their master."

"I understand," Ashe replied softly, feeling a bit foolish. To the white Erïeth she added, "Pardon me."

The giant eagle leaned back slightly, lifting its sizeable left talons toward Ashe.

She hesitated.

"You have nothing to fear," Thian said, guiding her to straddle the lower talon, its hallux, while the other three digits gently closed around her waist. "He will not let you fall, and I will be with you the whole way."

Across from them, the Erog crouched down tensely before the two other birds.

Thian smiled. "Time for me to help Raez."

As the Séoran drifted over, Ashe's carrier lifted its wings and, using its free right talons, leapt from the outcrop. It glided down swiftly from the ridge, for a moment shifting left with the Alöwean's weight. Ashe hastily brought her knees up, and then assumed a prostrate position, fearing that she would strike the treetops; yet the Erïeth stabilized, flapping its wings faster, and ascended high above the plain.

Feeling both helpless and exhilarated, Ashe watched trees and grassland pass by hundreds of feet below. Three small sparrows darted by her to the left. To her right, the Erog was being carried in a similar manner as she, though gripped at each side of his wider back. *A strange, unexpected course,* she thought about her life. Tilting her head up to look ahead, she felt a pang of relief as the distant southern arm of the Girgash Mountains gradually came closer.

11

Southward

"How did you find us?" The tall Alöwean looks at me warily, but with a hint of relief.

"Ramoth and Letroth told me where you might be," I say, dismounting from Lüfet, having already removed my riding helm. "I spoke with them in Pernor."

We stand atop a grassy knoll amidst the easternmost reaches of Wéswood. Moments earlier, by luck really, I had spotted movement among the trees. After circling back, a figure dressed in green and grey garb strode out to the clearing and waved me down.

Farther to the east, a portion of the Ilinoth Plain is visible. North, to the left, is the western fist of the Girgash Mountains. At the center of that fist, the ashen ruins of Pernor, the pinnacle of Nemenelor, lies on a quiet lake island. The previous day, I had flown over the region, having made my way west from Rökad after concluding my time with Khïrem. Fourteen years have passed since the Illirium War. The towers of Üth and Síon still stand at either end of the Wall of Pernor, a high rock cliff dropping from the southern shore of the lake upon which ramparts had been built. A waterfall pours out from a gap in the wall. The two stone towers continue to guard the mountainous bowl behind, but little more than a graveyard remains. That is, except for the two Alöweans I discovered living among the rubble.

"I do not know those names," the Alöwean comments, running his hand back through his long, white-blonde hair. I am transfixed by his azure eyes, how they

compliment his faint crimson complexion.

"I do," another man says. He removes his green hood and mask, showing him to be an Illiri with graying black hair that matches his beard.

"This is Theanor," the Alöwean tells me. I recognize the name, for Ramoth and Letroth had mentioned him. "He commanded Pernor's garrison."

"Before its destruction," the grim-looking Illiri says. Addressing the Alöwean, he adds, "Ramoth and Letroth are the brothers I mentioned, two of my best hunters. They are the ones who chose to stay behind to—"

The Alöwean raises a cautionary hand, glancing at me. He asks me, "So, what news from Pernor?"

"All is quiet," I reply. To Theanor, I add, "They await your orders."

"I am due for a visit," Theanor mumbles, more to himself.

"What is your name, Sky Rider?" the Alöwean asks.

"Ashe Pethus."

"I am Hectiliath," he replies. "What brings you this far west on your own? Last I heard—which, granted, was many months ago—all Sky Riders are concentrated around Hamrothél. How fares Lord Däne?"

"I am here by my own decree," I explain, having relinquished my role as a trainer in Hamrothél seven years earlier. "Däne has managed well enough as far as I know."

"Could you bring him a message for me?" Hectiliath asks.

I had not planned on returning to Nemenelor so soon. Shrugging, I reply, "I could."

Hectiliath's eyes narrow, apparently not appreciating my nonchalant tone. "It would benefit your Alöwean brethren here, Ashe, not to mention the Illiri who remain faithful to our cause."

"Oh? And what cause is that?" I ask, though I already suspect the answer.

"Do you not know?" Theanor replies.

"She knows," Hectiliath says, eying me. "We work to preserve Nemenelor's legacy."

"Having a Sky Rider among us would be useful," Theanor comments, staring at me.

"Nemenelor no longer exists west of the Emülath Sea," I counter. "What is left

here to preserve and die for? I am no proponent of Dwairian, but your so-called rebellion seems futile."

"Careful." Theanor's jaw tightens.

"We fight for many reasons," Hectiliath says calmly, "and for much that is meant to remain secret. If little is known about us beyond defying Dwairian's self-asserted kingship and expanding empire, then our efforts since the war have not been in vain. Nonetheless, if you will not help us, there is nothing more for us to discuss."

He turns away.

"Relax, captain," I say, offering a smile to lighten the mood. "I meant no disrespect. I will bring your message to Däne, and do what I can to coordinate provisions or whatever you need. I will not do so on a permanent basis, however, for I am done with the disputes of kingdoms and empires."

"Life is seldom so simple," Hectiliath comments. He indicates that I follow him into the woods.

Ashe could not comprehend why her dreams about the past were intensifying. At first, she figured it had something to do with the stress of supporting the Rök campaign against the Erog and then witnessing the violence at Rínroth Outpost. Yet, surely, the dreams were rooted in more than circumstantial triggers. After all, she had not felt emotionally invested in the Rök campaign. Maybe the dreams were simply a symptom of mip weed withdrawal.

One night, amidst their aerial journey across the Rökad border, she camped with Thian and the Erog in a wide valley high in the mountains. During such times, the three Erïeth left the companions on the ground while seeking more precipitous perches, likely for their own sense of security. Ashe studied the valley's descent to the large Dragos Plain, beyond which extended two hundred miles of forest.

Thinking more about her dreams, she dwelled on the elements that had not occurred in reality, such as the presence of the two swans. "What do you know about dreams?" she asked Thian. They had no means for a fire, so she sat next to the Séoran, accepting the warmth he offered by proximity.

Meanwhile, the Erog sat cross-legged nearby observing them, pulling his cloak closer to ward off the cold.

"What do you mean by dreams?" Thian asked.

"Thoughts, images . . . emotions experienced during sleep."

"I see."

Ashe recalled that he did not sleep. "Memories."

"To me, memory is history interacting with the present," Thian answered. "I can relive the past at will to some extent—not to make different choices, but to observe, recollect, and better understand. We are able to do so with greater clarity than you mortals. The closest you come to that kind of consciousness is in your sleep."

"You once said that you cannot hear my thoughts," Ashe commented.

"Indeed, I cannot."

"Can you perceive my dreams?"

The Séoran looked over at her. "I see fragments."

She did not know what to think about that. Was he the reason so many memories were finding their way into her dreams?

"I thought you knew," Thian added.

"How would I know?"

"You have seen me there."

"Have I?" She could not bring to mind such an encounter, but then wondered. "Do you mean the swans?"

He tilted his head. "You see more than one?"

"Yes," she replied, confused.

The Séoran looked away with a pensive expression.

"Why assume that form?" Ashe asked. "Are you trying to hide from me?"

Without returning her gaze, his brow furrowed, Thian answered, "Why would I hide?"

"That is the question. Why fluctuate between so many forms—this figure of light as you appear to me now, the sparrow, the swan? I thought you could only choose one."

"As I have said, I assume the form of a sparrow to more quickly navigate the tangible plains of this the Lower Kingdom, Illirium; yet in the Middle

Kingdom, what you call Alöwe, I chose to assume the form of a swan. My sister chose that expression for us . . . long ago. She admired the swan's elegance as well as its representation of love and faithfulness."

"Is that why there are two swans?" Ashe asked, wondering if one represented Thian's sister.

He straightened and stared at her. "I cannot say."

"What does that mean?" she asked.

Across from them, the Erog grumbled something punctuated by soft clicks. Thian responded, and the two conversed for a while.

"What is it?" Ashe asked after both quieted.

"Raez wanted to know what we are talking about, so I told him."

"He has something to add?"

"He is fascinated by the subconscious," Thian answered. "There are a few in his tribe, one in particular, who can communicate with the rest through their minds, even to the extent of influencing the tribe's collective vision and motivation."

Motivation? She thought of the behavior of the Alödïm. Had this Erog instigated what had happened at the outpost; and if so, did Thian know? "Does he have that power?"

"That is not clear to me," Thian said.

"Have you asked?"

"Yes."

"Well?"

"Among the Thraz, only a high sage called the Ezren can truly influence the visions of the entire tribe." He looked at Ashe. "Raez is not the Ezren."

"How can you be sure?"

"I trust him," the Séoran answered.

Ashe did not understand why. More harrowing, however, was the question of how honest Thian was being with her, including his translation of the Erog's speech. If the Séoran could tap into memories, and the Erog could influence her subconscious imagery, were they banding together to manipulate her? But then, if the Erog had stirred the Rök to violence, why had she not felt the same effects? No, this Erog could not be that powerful.

There was no hint of it. Thian was the greater suspect, though what had happened at Rínroth Outpost seemed out of character. Had she become paranoid?

Be careful. The words echoed in her mind.

Be careful of what? her thoughts retorted. Could she even trust her own intuition at this point?

"Is something wrong?" Thian looked at Ashe with concern.

She offered a faint smile. It was time for her to reassert her own agency with these strange companions. Thian claimed that her help was important for peace, but that was too ambivalent a motivation. His words and deeds were often too formless, like smoke hiding a deeper intent. As of yet, she could discern nothing sinister, but neither could she entirely trust him.

"Tomorrow, we will leave the mountains," she commented.

"Yes," Thian affirmed, watching her expectantly.

"At which time, our three Erïeth allies will depart."

"Yes," he said, and then addressed the Erog, presumably to interpret.

"We need to discuss our next step," Ashe continued, recognizing that the many miles of walking ahead left her few options. She needed to find a way to take control of the situation.

The Erog spoke.

"Are you willing to help Raez fulfill his quest?" Thian asked.

Ashe focused on the Erog's firm, scaly features, realizing that she had begun to view the creature looking back at her as no mere beast, but a conscious, rational being. "Is he still intent on reaching Oceanus?"

Thian's smile widened. "He is."

Raez spoke.

"What do you propose?" the Séoran translated.

"On foot we will be slow," Ashe replied, looking at both of them.

"Raez could carry you," Thian offered.

Remembering how quickly the Erog had tired during their escape from Rínroth Outpost, she shook her head. "We will have to manage on our own feet for now, at least to get out of northern Illirium. Norwood continues another few hundred miles beyond the Illüvatar River, and then there are another four-hundred miles of the Norwood Plain to cross before the coast." She shook her head again, more to herself. In all, it was a long way to travel in their current state. "There are too many potential problems that way." Passing through Rodaním alone would be risky, but she did not plan to go with them that far. Where and how she could separate herself from the Séoran and Erog, however, she could not say. It would be best if agreed upon by all, at least with Thian, for he had easily found her in Ashkenaz, and would likely be able to do so again if she tried to slip away. Would he let her go if she just asked?

"What of your people?" Thian inquired. "Can they help us?"

"Hamrothél is too out of the way," she replied. Moreover, Däne would have too many questions, especially concerning the events in Rökad. No, it would be best to avoid the entanglements of Nemenelor. Why did she need to be involved anyway? "Can the Séorans not aid the Erog?"

Thian's smile faded. "Their attention is elsewhere."

Of course, she thought bitterly. "The Unseen War?"

The Séoran nodded. "Yes."

More questions arose in Ashe's mind, such as whether Thian had any real influence among his people, but she decided to focus on her more immediate, practical needs. As acquiring a mount was not an option anytime soon, and would not change matters even if she could find one, she needed help from someone who was not only resourceful but open-minded. The answer quickly became obvious. *Fumond.*

* * *

After the three Erïeth left them on the southern side of the Girgash Mountains, Ashe, Thian, and Raez hiked on foot for ten days to reach the edge of Norwood. No paths ran along the feet of the mountains bordering the eastern end of the Dragos Plain. Every few hours of walking, the soreness of Ashe's feet would creep up her legs, requiring a break. Raez said nothing about this, possibly grateful for the rest himself, missing his right forearm, and Thian offered what support he could, easing some of the tension in Ashe's joints and muscles.

On the eleventh day, the Séoran scouted ahead in his sparrow form, leaving Ashe and the Erog alone beside a trickling creek. Ashe took off her boots and soaked her feet in the cool water, while Raez sat to her left with his eyes closed.

After some time, movement upstream to her right caught Ashe's attention. She stood, gripping her war hammer as four masked figures dressed in green, brown, and grey quietly approached. Three held loosely nocked bows, waiting at a distance as the fourth figure strode toward Ashe. Stopping a few steps away from her position, he gripped his spear with one hand, keeping it upright like a staff, and pulled down his mask to reveal a faint crimson complexion.

He addressed her in Alöwean. "Who are you?"

Glancing back, Ashe saw that Raez was also standing. She motioned with her hand, hoping the Erog understood not to do anything antagonistic. If only Thian was there to translate. Returning her attention to the Alöwean hunter, she replied, "My name is Ashe Pethus, and I am a Sky Rider. We are just passing through these lands on our way to the Emülath Sea. Our business has nothing to do with you, Nemenelor, or your fight against Siligen."

"I have heard of you," the hunter said. "A Sky Rider from Hamrothél gave us news a few days ago. Why are you not in Rökad, and where is your mount?"

"My mission changed," Ashe replied. So much would be different if Lüfet still lived.

Frowning, the hunter addressed Raez in the common tongue: "And what are you called?"

Raez eyed Ashe, but said nothing.

"He neither understands nor speaks our languages," she explained. "He is called Raez, and comes from beyond the Rökad Northland. We are here in peace."

"Captain Hectiliath will be the one to judge that." The hunter lowered the point of his spear toward Ashe and Raez and motioned for them to move.

"Come with us."

The Erog stepped forward, guiding Ashe behind him, and hissed. Was he trying to protect her? Whatever the reason, she felt a pang of admiration for him as well as fear of what he might do as the Alöwean archers drew their bows and the lead hunter gripped his spear with both hands.

"Wait," Ashe said, raising her hand, keeping her eyes on the lead hunter as she quickly stepped back in front of Raez.

"Tell your companion to stand down," the lead hunter said sternly.

"He is not mine to command," Ashe replied, keeping her hand up. She lowered her war hammer to the ground and raised her other hand. "Just let us go on our way, and all will be well."

Raez did not move, but glared at the hunters, focusing on the leader. Standing next to him, Ashe felt both small and remarkably calm.

"Stand down," the lead hunter demanded, pointing his spear at the Erog.

"If you value your lives," she said, "it is you who will stand down."

"I cannot let you pass through these lands freely," the lead hunter said.

"Captain Hectiliath knows me to be an ally."

"I will need to hear him say so," the hunter replied,

Ashe hesitated, wondering if going to Hectiliath could be her chance to be rid of the Erog's company. No, she would have to explain too much, which could lead to her being forced back to Nemenelor. Uncertain about the fallout of what had happened in Rökad, she could not risk it.

"Let me be clear about your two choices," she said evenly. "If you try to detain this creature, you will die. Your arrows are useless." She focused on the lead hunter. "Your spear will not be enough."

The hunters shifted uneasily, glancing at each other.

"Or," Ashe continued, "you can live by letting us go on our way."

"We will not be threatened," the lead hunter stated.

"I mean it as no threat," Ashe replied. "This is the reality of the situation. Be sensible."

Keeping his spear raised, the hunter hesitated.

Raez lowered himself onto his three limbs, as if preparing to lunge. *No.* Ashe placed a hand on his shoulder and met his eyes, willing the look to convey her plea with him not to attack. These hunters were her brethren, fulfilling their responsibility to protect Nemenelor. She did not want to see them die.

The lead hunter relaxed his hold on the spear, and brought it up beside him. "Go then," he said gruffly. Turning back to the archers, he motioned for them to disperse back the way they had come. "If you follow us, however, or linger in these lands," he added, glancing over his shoulder, "there will be consequences. We will monitor your progress."

"Understood," Ashe replied.

The hunters would also report what had happened to Captain Hectiliath, who could in turn decide to send a greater force after them. She had to risk it, figuring that Dwairian's forces would be perceived a greater threat and priority than a handicapped Alöwean and Erog just passing through.

12

Reunion

"It is good to see you again, Ashe." Uncle Cylas draws me into a firm one-armed hug. In the other hand, he grasps a long harness connected to his hooded Erïeth. The bird appears to be one of the species that inhabits the coastland, smaller than a mountain Erïeth like Lüfet.

"I missed you," I reply, hugging him back. He is a strong, lean Alöwean. I am surprised to now find myself as tall as him.

Still holding my shoulder, he takes a step back to look at me, shaking his head in amused disbelief. "It has been too long. Remind me, when did you leave Chaléth?"

"Over two centuries ago," I say, suddenly struck by how much time has passed. My attention withdraws into memory for a moment—so many memories.

"Two hundred years," Cylas murmurs in amazement, still gazing at me.

In the citadel of Nemenelor's eastern capital, we stand before the Door of Anaríl. The courtyard is quiet except for a few wardens, soldiers, and the privileged individuals permitted to pass through the Door. Weeks earlier, I had received word from Cylas that he would be coming by way of the Door, which linked Anaríl to Alöwe. He had been called to serve as the lead trainer in Illirium's Tower of the Sky.

"I can be of greater use here, I think," Cylas had commented in his letter. He mentioned how quiet life had become in Chaléth, how he was ready for a new environment and people.

The midday sun warms the stones of the Door, an archway about ten strides wide built in the citadel wall. Through the archway, a bright moon casts a faint hue on the battlements and rooftops of the city of Nïlök in Alöwe. The ability to instantaneously cross thousands of miles from one point to another, like walking from one room to the next, never ceases to impress me.

We turn away and begin walking across the paved courtyard, my war hammer tapping lightly as we go.

"How is Mother?" I ask as we approach Anaríl's Sky Rider tower, which is adjoined to a portion of the inner curtain wall.

"Shenïm is complicated," he replies quietly. "When did you last hear from her?"

After my violent confrontation with my father in his shop, I had since received only one note from her. "It has been a long while."

Having abruptly left home to live with my uncle in Alöwe's Tower of the Sky, it hurt to receive so little from my mother—no conveyance of affection, grief, or explanation. I dismissed the feelings quickly at first, thinking my mother's silence an affirmation of her passivity and a justification of my choice to leave. If she would not help herself then there was little more I could do. I had to look toward my own well being. Part of her silence with me is my fault, but I do not admit that to Cylas.

He exhales slowly. "I do not understand my sister anymore. I have tried to reason with her—again and again. She still refuses to leave your father."

I do not understand it either.

"Come." Cylas pats my shoulder and motions ahead with a nod. "I can tell you more in due time, if you wish. But first, how about showing me the best place for a hungry appetite in this city?"

Agreeing with a chuckle, I first bring him to the Sky Rider tower to leave his Erïeth. From there, we slowly make our way into the city proper.

"How is your foot?" Cylas asks, looking closer at my war hammer and limp.

"It does not stop me."

We talk about the best riding saddles and how, since my fall long ago, I have never again failed to double-check that my leg and belt harnesses are secure. He feels partially responsible for my accident, once again expressing his regret at not having kept a closer watch on me.

"I heard you were finally promoted," he says eventually.

I nod. "Forty years ago. My first command was a unit of the Northern Tower in the Kurshemnt Mountains. Two years ago, my request for reassignment was finally approved. I now serve in Hamrothél."

"From what I hear, Hamrothél is the more desirable post," he comments. "I look forward to getting to know this place." He looks around and breathes in the dry, warm air. "Illirium is so much larger than Alöwe."

"There are many beautiful places here," I say.

"Have you met anyone?"

"I meet many people," I reply, being intentionally evasive.

"I mean, is there anyone special in your life?"

The question evokes images of patrolling the Kurshemnt Mountains from the In them, another Sky Rider from Chaléth flies beside me. With an ache, I recall the feelings of tenderness claimed together during our downtime in the Northern Tower barrack. Gian, I miss you. If only I had been there. "He was killed during the Second Kurshemnt War," I say.

"So long ago," Cylas comments softly. "There has been no one since?"

I shake my head and direct our conversation back to my uncle and his new role, asking all the questions I can think of rather than dwelling on my past.

Ashe's senses awoke to the present. Her back ached. She shivered against the moist air, once again missing her cloak and blanket. Nearby, a bird whistled a somber refrain. Sitting up, she bent forward as far as possible, reaching her arms out, to ease the tension in her spine and shoulders. Rubbing her eyes helped her focus a little, yet her head continued to spin in a slow maelstrom of memory.

I wish I had some mip weed right now.

Whether in dreams or waking, concepts like family and belonging remained elusive. Uncle Cylas had become more of a father than her real one. Though she had learned to take care of herself effectively enough since she was young, she sometimes longed to be able to defer, if only briefly, to the leading of another—not just anyone, but someone she could trust who actually cared for her wellbeing and championed her success. Her uncle, Cylas, had been one of those few individuals—supportive without being patronizing. After his arrival to Anaríl, they met together only one other time, three years later at the Tower of the Sky. The Illirium War erupted only a few months after that. Having failed to find him after the war, she presumed him another casualty.

The sun had yet to light their camp, but had begun to color the treetops above. Smooth grey trunks towered around her. The nearby creek seemed to slumber on, a quiet murmur echoing from its lazy flow.

She sat alone.

Where had Thian gone, and where was the Erog? Their absence might have once concerned her, but after weeks of traveling south together through Norwood, she had abandoned the notion of any immediate threat. If Raez wanted to make a meal of her, he would have done so already. Needing less sleep than her, he was likely already out foraging. At least he was a creature with observable habits. The Séoran, however, remained unpredictable, his fluid presence both captivating and unsettling.

She noticed a pair of sparrows perched on a low branch watching her.

"Good morning, you two," Ashe muttered.

Osré and Oshrémi cheeped in response.

Gripping her war hammer, she stood unsteadily and walked over to the stream to splash her face. Hearing the rustle of damp leaves behind her, she turned to see Thian and Raez. The Erog held a basket of berries and roots. He made the basket from fresh twigs soon after their journey through the woodlands had begun.

"Breakfast," Thian commented, smiling at Ashe.

"Thank you." Sauntering toward them, she added, "You do realize that Raez is not the only one of us who appreciates meat."

"Yes," the Séoran replied, "Yet as we have already discussed, while you are in my company, benefiting from my relationship with nature, you will abstain from killing my friends." He indicated the basket. "These offer enough nutrients to keep you strong."

"Strong perhaps," Ashe commented, "but not quite satisfied." The Erog looked down at the basket's contents with a similar lack of enthusiasm. He sat and placed it between them. Meanwhile, his vulture sat on his shoulder also staring at the basket.

"How did you sleep?" Thian asked, sitting himself cross-legged in the air.

Ashe picked three berries from the basket and popped them into her mouth. Their tartness exploded on her tongue, sending a pleasant shudder down her body. Still not looking at the Séoran, she reached for more. "Do you not know?"

"If you would rather me not see your dreams," Thian answered, "you have but to ask."

"Why do you observe my dreams to begin with?"

"I want to know you better."

"That is all?"

Thian's black eyes met hers. "Yes."

She did not believe him.

Glancing over at the Erog sitting motionless with his eyes closed, she asked, "Is he going to have anything?"

"Raez has already eaten his fill," Thian said. "He brought this back for you."

A thoughtful gesture. "His idea or yours?"

Thian's brow tightened. "I do not understand."

"Never mind." She continued eating.

That afternoon, they reached the northeastern shore of the Emülath Sea. To the left, the wide Illüvatár River flowed into the clear, blue water, and in the far distance at the center of the lake, a hundred miles to the south, Ashe glimpsed the shape of a small island with a protruding tower. She knew it well, for upon that mound of earth stood what remained of the Tower of the Sky. She thought of her uncle, but then focused instead on how, at the southern end of the lake, the Elentari River flowed southward to their destination: the coast of the Menendros Sea—Oceanus. They would have to contend with the size of the Emülath Sea first, which was nearly three-hundred miles from its northernmost to southernmost tips, and well over a hundred miles from west to east.

Beside her, Raez stared at the water with wide black eyes, his mouth slightly agape. Noticing Ashe staring, he straightened and said something with a rumble and click.

"He has never seen so much water," Thian translated, beaming.

Recalling that the Erog's quest was predicated on a vision of a large body of water, Ashe wondered if the Emülath Sea itself might fulfill his task. She asked Thian about this, to which he exchanged words with Raez.

"He will meditate on the possibility," Thian said, "and search for a sign from the gods."

"How long will that take?" Ashe asked.

"The gods do not act on the whims of time," Thian answered without consulting the Erog. "For now, we shall proceed according to your idea."

Five days later, they reached the top of a tree-covered hill, which provided their first view of Fumond's Hut a few miles away. During the previous days spent crossing the river and wooded coastland of the lake, with Ornithez helping scout the way before them, Raez had received no word from the gods. Ashe considered asking him about them and their manner of communication, but discarded the thought. She did not feel like conversing about such a potentially complex subject through Thian's interpretation. The persistent ache in her feet also robbed her of the energy to do much else but grit her teeth and bitterly celebrate the accomplishment of every mile walked. There was something satisfying about overcoming the physical pain, though. She trusted that it made her tougher and more resilient.

Looking down at the familiar town, Ashe said, "It will be best if you both stay here out of sight while I am away."

"We understand," Thian said, having translated to Raez. "Do you really believe your friend will help us?"

If not him, I do not know who will. "Few are more connected than Fumond." She glanced at Raez. "I will return as soon as I can."

* * *

"It's a pleasure seeing you again, Ashe," Fumond said calmly with a mild grin. He stood from behind his desk, which contained organized stacks of parchment, a few books, as well as numerous foreign objects and trinkets. He motioned to one of the chairs facing his desk. "Please sit."

The simple wooden chair creaked as she relieved the tension in her feet and legs. In each wall of his second-storey office, a large window looked out over the town. Outside, the sky was a vibrant blue freckled with white clouds.

"Can I offer you a drink?" he added, brushing a tuft of graying black hair from his forehead.

"Do you have any Madai wine left?"

"I do." Fumond smiled mischievously at her. "I was saving it for you."

"No need to be shy," she replied, leaning back, trying to make herself comfortable on the rigid chair. "It has been too long since the fruit of the vine has caressed my tongue."

"Oh?" he replied, pulling out a dark bottle from an ornate cabinet and then opening it. "I'm glad to be of service, of course, and will readily provide whatever you need." He filled two glasses with crimson liquid.

"Thank you," she said, receiving one, watching the Illiri man with both affection and assessment.

"An excellent choice." He raised his glass. "To your return; sooner than expected, I'm happy to say."

"Proselé." She lifted her glass, clanged it gently against his, and took a sip after he took one from his own. The wine rolled over her tongue to her throat, arousing sensations in its velvety wake, leaving a refreshingly smoky aftertaste. Her stomach tingled with ease. She felt herself relax, but also wanted some real food.

Fumond strolled back around his desk, sat, drank another sip from his glass, and then focused on Ashe. "You look tired."

"I feel it," she replied, basking in the warmth of the indoors after being out in the wilderness for so long. "The last few months have been demanding."

"I heard you came on foot." He set his glass to the side, clasped his hands, and placed his forearms on the desk, resting his weight on them. "I'd like to hear everything." He nodded at her faded tunic. "Your clothes appear in need of mending as well. I'll happily provide fresh ones, if you'd like . . . and a bath."

A steaming bath sounded wonderful, as did clean clothes. "Do you have mip weed at hand?"

"Of course." He offered her some from a small wooden box. "Out already?"

She placed some of the dried mip weed into her pipe, lit it, and welcomed the calming sensation. "Something like that."

Meeting her gaze, he smiled. "You're welcome to stay as long as you like."

She looked forward to sleeping in a soft, dry bed. Staring back at Fumond, she also yearned for a warm, familiar body next to hers. "I would like that."

She had not told Thian and Raez how long she would be away. What would it be to them if she took an extra day for herself? They had forced her into this situation in the first place. They could wait a while longer.

Fumond's green eyes narrowed and he tilted his head. "You're not here for me, though, are you?"

"Not entirely," she admitted, focusing back on him. "I need your help."

He leaned back slowly. "What kind of help?"

"Passage to Winslöri."

He raised a brow. "Winslöri?"

"Yes," she said. "For my . . . companion." She was about to say *two companions*. Circumstances were more complicated than she preferred.

"Now I'm intrigued," Fumond replied, straightening. "Who is this mysterious friend?"

"Not a friend, exactly." How to explain it all to him?

Fumond rose and casually walked around the desk to stand behind her. His hands slid over her shoulders and began to massage them tenderly, including her neck. "Relax," he whispered, but it was hard for her to do so after weeks of stress, sleeping on hard surfaces, and enduring painful footsteps. "Tell me everything."

Without looking back at him, she replied, "How about that bath first?"

Fumond brought his lips down to brush against her ear. "Very well."

Late the next afternoon, feeling cleaner and more rested than she had since leaving Hamrothél, Ashe walked beside Fumond in his private garden. An exotic, multi-colored assortment of flora had fully blossomed, their fragrance tempting Ashe to continue dwelling on the present, delaying her purpose in coming. Knowing that further delay risked intrusion from Thian—if he was not spying on her already—and her growing curiosity about what would happen at the end of Raez's journey, while also wanting to be done with the Erog, Ashe told Fumond the summary of her recent travels, focusing on the Erog while leaving out the presence of the Séoran. It left many holes in her story, but thankfully Fumond's interest latched on to Raez.

"I've recently heard of the Erog," he commented, "from Rök merchants."

"Can you help him?"

"I think I can, but must meet this creature first. From there, and only there, will I decide."

She had surmised as much. "He is waiting outside of town."

As a warm dusk settled over the landscape, Fumond followed Ashe to the forest hill where she had left Thian and Raez. Fumond's personal bodyguards—Heben and an Illiri woman, both of them tall and broad-shouldered, wearing grey attire and armed with swords—accompanied them.

Walking a few strides ahead, Ashe first came upon Thian.

"It is all right," she said, noting his worried expression. She kept her voice soft, not wanting Fumond to hear. "He will help us. I am sure of it. He just wants to meet Raez first."

"It is not that," Thian said with his airy voice, staring past her. His posture remained tense.

"Is something wrong?" Fumond asked Ashe, coming up beside her. "Why have we stopped?"

"He is coming," she replied.

The Erog materialized from the darkening shadows of the forest. He approached the group walking low on his three good limbs, but at the sight of Fumond and his two bodyguards, removed his black fur cloak and stood on his hind legs to full height, nearly ten feet tall. The bodyguards shifted their footing, their hands reaching for their swords. Staring down at Fumond, Raez spoke in guttural reverberations and clicks.

As Fumond met the Erog's large, dark eyes, a faint grin formed at the corner of his mouth. "Magnificent," he murmured. He motioned for his two guards to stay back while he took a few steps closer.

Stepping aside, Ashe quietly engaged Thian once more. "What is wrong?" She did not understand why the Séoran looked so troubled.

Thian ignored her, however, merely translating what Raez had said.

Disregarding the Séoran's behavior for the moment, Ashe focused back on Fumond. "Raez thanks you for coming, and would welcome your aid in his quest."

"I'm happy to provide what I can," Fumond replied, still staring at the Erog. He bowed his head in reverence. "I'm honored to meet you, Raez." Lowering his voice, he asked Ashe, "How do you understand his speech?"

She had already prepared a response. "We have formed a special connection . . . of the mind." Recalling what Thian had shared about the Thraz high sage, she still wondered if her answer was closer to the truth than she dared realize.

"I'd like to learn more about that," Fumond said, "but first, know that there's a merchant ship that can take you south to the coast, to Winslöri. It leaves in a few days. The captain is a friend of mine. Yet, there is a cost."

"What cost?" Ashe chided herself for not discussing the topic with Fumond beforehand. He was a businessman; of course he would require something. She wondered what they could barter with, having nothing of real monetary value on hand.

"I don't need coin." Fumond continued to study the Erog. "I'm interested in the transcendent." His male bodyguard approached and spoke quietly in his ear. Fumond nodded.

"What do you mean?" Ashe asked. Fumond had a penchant for the dramatic, which she usually found amusing, but it now threatened to annoy her.

"I have three demands," Fumond said, stroking his bearded chin, meeting

Ashe's gaze. "Two are of a practical nature. The first is that you must go with him."

Ashe had hoped to conclude her involvement with Thian and Raez that night. "Why?"

Fumond looked taken aback. "Are you not his friend? Do you not wish to see his quest fulfilled?"

"It is not so simple," Ashe replied, not wanting to explain her reservations about her unseen third companion, Thian.

"It will be good for you," Fumond said, grinning. "See the journey to its end. But more importantly, Raez needs someone he knows and trusts to go with him—who can speak for him."

That was reasonable enough, Ashe thought, especially considering that Fumond did not know about Thian. Moreover, if she was honest with herself, there was a part of her that had grown curious about what would happen to Raez. There was something about him that garnered respect.

"My second demand is that my man"—Fumond motioned to Heben—"also accompanies you to the coast."

That complicated things further. "To what end?" Ashe asked.

"He'll ensure my investment is not wasted, and give me a full report when he returns. I want to know about this sign that Raez will receive." Fumond's green eyes glinted shrewdly. "I too would like to hear from the gods. That brings me to my third demand." He took a step forward. "I'd like a taste of the . . . special connection you two enjoy." His eyes rose to the Erog. "Do so, and you'll have all you need to reach Winslöri."

Ashe looked at the man in disbelief. "Fumond—"

"Explain to Raez my terms." Fumond kept his eyes fixed on the Erog. "Let him decide."

Ashe glanced back at Raez, and then at Thian. They had been quietly conversing throughout the whole exchange. Ashe felt disconnected and powerless between the two positions of negotiation—Fumond and his bodyguards, and Thian and Raez.

Coming closer to Raez, as if intending to speak in private, she asked Thian, "What will Raez do?" She had no idea how they could fulfill the third demand.

Thian looked at Ashe then glanced past her with narrowed eyes. "We should part ways with this man as soon as possible."

"We need his help."

Raez spoke to Fumond.

Thian translated. "Trust me," he added after. "Trust Raez."

Ashe returned her attention to Fumond. "Raez agrees."

Fumond smiled. "Splendid."

"Such a connection is not without risks," Ashe said as a last effort to deter the man, not sure what was going to happen next.

Fumond's smile faded, replaced with an expression of resolve. "I accept the risks."

Ashe stepped aside so that Fumond and Raez could face each other more directly. The two bodyguards watched with somber curiosity, their hands resting on the hilts of their swords, as the Erog lowered himself from his upright posture and brought his large, scaly face a few feet from Fumond's. Fumond twitched slightly, as if countering an inclination to withdraw. Ashe was still impressed at the Erog's size. It would take little effort for him to bite Fumond's head off.

Fumond and Raez stared at each other as the last light of the sun dipped behind the eastern hills. The air began to cool, which made Ashe grateful for the new wool coat Fumond had given her. She noticed his chest rising and falling more quickly, could hear his increasing breath, though his demeanor remained calm. He began to blink without cadence.

Something is wrong. She looked to Thian, but his attention appeared to be elsewhere.

Raez stepped back, almost stumbling, and sat down with a weary posture. Meanwhile, Fumond stood motionless, his face pale, subtly shaking his head to himself, as if to ward off a thought. He turned his back to the Erog; the usual vigor in his voice was gone as he told Ashe, "Join me in town, and we'll make final arrangements."

Using her war hammer for support, she followed after Fumond, but struggled to match his stride. "What did you see?"

"I saw enough." He frowned slightly, but not without a spark of calculation in his eyes. "If you want to continue doing business with me, however, you'll be a help to Heben and return with him once the Erog's quest is done."

13

The Elentari River

Ashe did not argue with Fumond. He could think what he liked, but she would be indebted to no man—certainly not to him. Reaching the coast seemed so close and yet so distant. She needed time to think.

At first, her heart sank at the prospect of losing Fumond, or, more specifically, a reliable place to retreat—a refuge from busyness, confusion, her past. Yet, she also knew that Fumond was little more than a temporary distraction, and that she was likely no better than that to him. The conclusion left her feeling adrift in a deep current surrounded by fog. When they reached the coast, where should she turn? Would coming back to Fumond's Hut be so bad in the short term? Determining a place to go daunted her less than considering a person to be with. Khïrem was her closest friend alive, but she could not return to Rökad—not anytime soon.

Chiding herself for such meandering thoughts, she redirected her attention to the practical needs of the moment. There was work to do.

The next evening, she helped Fumond and his bodyguards smuggle Raez through town in a large wooden crate. It was best, Fumond thought—and Ashe agreed—to keep Raez's presence as hidden as possible. Raez expressed wariness about being placed in the crate, but Fumond assured them that it was the only way. Having contracted a carpenter earlier that day to hastily build the crate, Fumond showed the Erog that he could rest comfortably inside, though it barely accommodated his size and did not provide enough space for him to sit up and shift positions easily. Straw was placed inside to provide some padding, and one of the sideboards could be removed, offering a subtle means to pass the Erog fresh food and water.

"What if an inspector demands that the crate be opened?" Ashe asked.

"That won't happen," Fumond said. "Heben will make sure of it."

As Ashe conversed with Fumond, Thian spoke quietly with Raez, seemingly more than interpreting. Not knowing what was shared between them, Ashe once again felt like an observer with little say in the matter.

Another concern took root in her mind. When she had an opportunity to speak with Thian privately, thinking of what happened a month earlier, she asked, "Are you sure that what happened at Rínroth Outpost will not happen again here?"

"These circumstances are different," Thian said. "For one, Raez is not a prisoner."

"That is not my point."

"We do not know if Raez caused the conflict."

"Have you asked him again, pressed him for the truth?"

After a pause, Thian answered, "Even Raez does not understand the full extent of what transpired."

"You believe him?" Ashe asked.

"Yes." The Séoran's eyes narrowed. "What does knowing the answer matter now?"

"That depends on the truth," Ashe replied. "The death in that outpost was needless, and I can see no other reason for it than to help Raez escape."

"That does not mean that Raez instigated it," Thian countered. "There are larger forces at work in this world, Ashe. Not even I can fathom them all."

"You said that you discerned something haunting our company," Ashe said, suddenly remembering. "You never discovered its source?"

Thian looked at her pensively. "Whatever it was, it did not follow us into the Rök outpost."

"What are you hiding from me?" Ashe asked. "Friendship cannot thrive on secrecy."

"You are my friend," Thian assured with a faint smile. "But some things are not meant for the mortal mind. What I choose to share or not share is for your benefit. Can you trust me about that?"

Ashe wanted to believe him. It would be simpler that way. Still, doubts remained. "What will happen when we reach the coast?"

The Séoran's smile widened, though his eyes looked tired. "That is the question we all share."

At the western end of Fumond's Hut, a shipping dock extended from the shore over the shallows of the lake. Various boats were moored alongside the dock nearest the shore, and larger vessels were anchored farther out on the water. The group went to the end of the wooden walkway where a merchant ship waited, a hundred feet long from bow to stern. Its two masts held lateen sails, the main mast crowned by a crow's nest.

"The ship's called *The Liberty*," Fumond commented to Ashe. "Its captain is Lallél." He pointed to a tan-skinned Illiri woman standing on the quarterdeck. The woman, a bit younger-looking than Fumond, wore a slim coat reaching down to her ankles. Sun-bleached brown hair braided at the back of her head was partially covered by a drooping rimmed hat. "She's originally from Peleg," Fumond added as they reached the gangway, "in eastern Rodaním. She knows the route between here and Winslöri better than most."

With the help of some crew members, they brought the crate onboard and lowered it into the hold through a hatch in the main deck. Meanwhile, the captain leaned against the railing of the quarterdeck stairs with her arms crossed, her eyes focused on Ashe. "You made no mention of an Alöwean," she muttered to Fumond.

"She'll give you no trouble," he replied, wiping his hands together.

"The Tärm Tower guards may think otherwise," Lallél pressed.

Fumond turned to face the captain. "My man, Heben"—he clapped the broad shoulder of his Illiri bodyguard—"will ensure that you have no trouble from Siligen. Trust me."

Lallél scoffed. "I'll trust that you've secured your investment, anyway."

"Come now, Lallél," Fumond said, grinning. "We know each other better than that."

"We do indeed," the captain retorted. She glanced sullenly at Ashe. "Therefore, considering the circumstances, as well as our history . . ." She returned her attention to Fumond. "My rate just went up. Consider it my insurance."

"Oh?" Fumond raised a brow. "I'm already covering your fee to cross the Elentari Falls, and have guaranteed expedited passage through Tärm Bridge."

Though neutral grounds, the falls were under the jurisdiction of Rodaním, to the east of the river, while the bridge was controlled by Siligen, the kingdom of Dwairian to the west. The two kingdoms maintained an uneasy truce over control of their river border. Fumond worked hard to keep good rapport with both powers. Ashe suspected there to be more involved than amiable business relations, especially regarding Dwairian's domain, but had not inquired about it with Fumond. He was a clever man, and resourceful.

"If you want no more questions," Lallél replied, "that's my price." She crossed her arms.

Fumond stared back at her for a while then smiled. "I can be reasonable." He took her aside to speak further.

As he did so, Ashe noted the faces of the ship's crew. She counted twenty-eight Illiri men. Many were relatively young, yet a few older than Lallél worked among them. Most did not show interest in Ashe, but instead went about their business of preparing the ship to set sail. *A good sign*, she thought.

Nearby, two sparrows perched on the main sail gaff of an unattended lesser vessel. High above, a vulture soared. Ashe presumed that Thian was currently with Raez in the hull, keeping him informed of the situation.

"All right." Fumond stepped up beside Ashe, speaking in a subdued voice. Heben joined them. "Lallél and I have an understanding."

"I thought you had arranged everything beforehand," Ashe commented.

"This isn't uncommon," Fumond replied. "It's part of the game, really."

"As long as we have no more trouble from the captain," Heben said in his deep voice.

"There will be none," Fumond assured. "Most of her business involves transporting goods to and from Fumond's Hut, and I've been more than generous. I reminded her about what's at stake." To Ashe, he said, "Stay out of trouble." To Heben: "You know what to do."

The burly man nodded sternly.

Ashe thought it a refreshing change to cover miles without having to walk or ride. On the Emülath Sea, *The Liberty* averaged about a hundred miles a day. Enjoying fair winds, they reached the headwaters of the Elentari River two days after leaving Fumond's Hut. The Elentari River was the largest in Illirium; partnered with the Emülath Sea, it served as the only waterway joining the south and north. Traveling downstream to the coast was an additional advantage, despite crewmen having to keep on the lookout for sandbars or other dangers in shallower portions of the river. Fortunately, water levels were still high from spring snowmelt.

To stay out of the crew's way, Ashe sat against the railing of the quarterdeck while Heben kept to himself on the forecastle deck, sitting and oiling his short sword. Ashe's gaze wandered from him to *The Liberty* pilot steering the quarter-rudder, and then down to the swelling waves left in the wake of the ship. Eastward, the shore of the river was characterized by banks of green grass stretching miles across the Norwood Plain. Ahead, the horizon looked like a blank, flat line.

Pulling out her pipe, she filled it with ground mip weed and began to smoke. Fumond's demand for her to return with Heben did not sit well with her. It felt too submissive. What kind of power did he think he had over her? What would he do if she refused? Surely, he did not think he could force her. Losing ready access to mip weed would be an adjustment, but not insurmountable. She could live without it if need be. Looking down at her pipe, thinking of the difficult weeks without it in the north, however, she was not so sure.

I could stay with Thian, she thought, wanting to focus elsewhere, *at least for a while.* She recalled her time in the dell with fondness. It seemed so long ago, a simpler time. Yet, a distance had formed between her and the Séoran since then, and he now seemed more interested in Raez's quest. Did he mean to stay with the Erog after they reached the coast? Could she join them? Did she want to?

Going south plagued her with somber questions. At least they would not have to venture near the Kurshemnt Mountains in the southwest, for she had resolved never to return. *Had I not left the first time, though*, she mused, *Gían might still be alive.* So eager to rise as a Sky Rider commander, she had abandoned the only man to truly love her as an equal. They had found joy in each other, free and at ease. When she had finally acknowledged to herself how much she loved Gían, it was too late. She had already left, and not long after that he was killed. Thus a part of her had been left in those mountains with him. Should she go back and try to find it? So many years had passed. *What are you afraid of finding?*

For most of her life, she had felt passion and purpose serving as a Sky Rider. It officially began in the Northern Pass of the Kurshemnt Mountains, where she met Gían, until she seized the opportunity to transfer to Illirium's Tower of the Sky. Within the next year, which would prove to be the final year of the Second Kurshemnt War, Gían was dead. At first, focusing on her ambitions as a Sky Rider helped distract her from her grief, patrolling the Emülath Sea and acting as a courier in its surrounding landscape for one hundred forty years until finally being given her first command. Yet, as the assignment brought her back to the Northern Pass, memories of Gían haunted her anew. When she was finally transferred to Hamrothél two decades later, her enthusiasm for her work had been drained. The violence of the Illirium War that followed only further eroded her spirit. Since then, she knew neither what to do nor where to go—not with any lasting meaning, anyway. All diversions, regardless of where or with whom, had proven fleeting.

She realized that it had been days since she dreamed. What had changed? If Thian and Raez had been the ones influencing her dreams, had they discovered all they needed to know from her? Or was this some new form of manipulation?

The roar of a waterfall increased ahead.

The crew stirred.

Lallél stepped out from her quarters. "Prepare to transition," she called.

The pilot steered the ship portside toward a small inlet. There, a channel of the river had been dammed, creating a staging area for ships to wait their turn. Atop the dam and adjacent shore of the channel, Illiri workers used wooden cranes with pulleys to transport cargo and ultimately the vessel itself, emptied of all excess, including sails and rigging, from the top of the Elentari Falls to a side pool and channel near its base. Meanwhile, the ship's crew could rest in a nearby inn, passing the hours sleeping, eating, drinking, and swapping stories. Once the vessel was lowered to the base of the waterfall, crew members would descend a steep, winding stone path to reload their cargo and prepare the ship for the next stage of its voyage. Ashe thought it a outstanding system.

"Wait here," Lallél commented after they dropped anchor in the cove. Heben joined her as two crewmen rowed them to shore in *The Liberty's* longboat.

As the sun beamed low over the hilly western shore, Ashe went below decks. Checking that she was alone and unwatched, she whispered through the boards of the crate. "How are you?"

The Erog did not answer.

Sitting next to the crate, her arms around her knees, she began to feel clearer minded and at ease. There was indeed something calming about the Erog's presence, which she had begun to notice while venturing through Norwood together. Furthermore, with both being far from their homelands, lacking a present sense of belonging, perhaps they understood each other better than she had originally admitted. Sliding the side panel of the crate open, she saw the Erog stir and look at her with his large dark eyes.

"I envy your dedication," she said softly. Despite all that had happened, Raez remained committed to his quest, to a single purpose. She did not understand his ways, but discerned a depth of wisdom in his quiet attentiveness. "Could the sign you seek guide me as well?"

Raez responded with a low murmur and click.

Spurred by a strange impulse, she grinned and placed her hand, palm up, on the bottom ledge of the crate's opening. Not knowing if the Erog would understand the invitation of the gesture, she was startled when he placed his large hand on hers. Raez's fingers were long, the yellowish skin rough and scaly to touch, the claws filed down. Tightening her own fingers around what she could of his hand, she recognized how much still separated them. His confinement was physical, while hers was mental. There was also a chance that he was just mindlessly mirroring her action. It was dangerous to project sentimental interpretation on his actions.

Careful now, she told herself, and prepared to stand and close the panel.

Thian appeared beside her at that moment, glowing white with ripples of crimson and gold underneath. "Raez needs to stretch his limbs and breathe fresh air."

It would probably be days before the Erog had another chance. "What do you propose?" she asked.

"We wait attentively for an opportunity."

Opportunity came that evening.

"*The Liberty* and its cargo will not be moved until morning," Heben explained to Ashe, his tone matter-of-fact. "Captain Lallél has decided that she and the crew will spend the night ashore. You and I will remain onboard."

"Is that her idea," Ashe replied, "or yours?"

"Mine."

"Lallél agreed?"

"I convinced her," Heben replied, his voice still calm.

"And what about moving the crate tomorrow?" Ashe pressed.

"I'll make sure it goes smoothly," Heben said. "You needn't worry."

As crew members gathered their belongings and intermittently went ashore using the longboat, Ashe considered what would happen if Raez was discovered during the transition. She imagined that few Illiri had even heard of an Erog, so would not know how to respond at the sight of one. There might be fear, but what could anyone do? She preferred to avoid the hassle of such a confrontation, but felt some relief recognizing that the safety of her own position did not necessarily depend on keeping Raez hidden. Her being an Alöwean may be deemed a more immediate threat, in fact, particularly to Siligen, so she would have to be careful when they reached Tärm Bridge.

In the meantime, with the ship vacant and still anchored away from the shore, she perceived no danger in letting Raez out of the crate. Not wanting to draw unnecessary attention, however, she agreed with Heben that they would light no lamps.

Free from the crate, Raez stiffly climbed up to the main deck where he appeared to savor the cool night air with slow, steady breaths. Pale moonlight formed shadows across his firm features, his filed horns illuminated white.

Ashe watched him with little thought, concentrating more on the earthy taste of smoking her pipe while she reclined against the bulwark of the main deck. While Raez ate some fresh food provided by Heben, Ashe found a wood board with a rope attached to each side—a seat likely kept for one to work on the hull—and suspended it from the starboard side of the ship. She then lowered herself down, sat on the board, and dangled her feet in the river. The cold water felt soothing.

Floating through the air in a prostrate position, Thian joined her, gazing into the glassy darkness of the river. "So much life beneath the surface," he commented, "so much unseen."

"Yes," she said.

Raez stuck his head over the edge of the ship, and climbed down far enough to reach the surface of the river with the stub of his right forearm. He stared at the water sliding from his limb. He looked at Ashe and said something with a low rumble.

"Water is an immense gift," Thian interpreted, "not to be taken for granted."

Ashe nodded blankly as the Erog returned to the main deck.

"I have seen your dreams," Thian commented.

"I know," she replied. "What about them?"

"Why do you try so hard to bury your pain?"

"The past is dead," Ashe replied. "Why leave it out to rot?"

"Your heart and mind seem to be in disagreement," Thian said. "One still grieves while the other denies."

"It is not your concern. Stop spying on me."

"I care about you."

"If you care, you will respect that I mean to keep some aspects of my life private."

Thian sat upright in the air. "Lasting strength comes from facing your pain."

"What do you know of pain?" Ashe said. "You live a step detached from the world."

Thian's expression grew solemn. "There is much that you do not know, Ashe Pethus."

"Tell me then."

"Look around and listen closer. There is peace in stillness and solitude."

There is peace in forgetting. "I have been alone enough," she said.

"Yet you do not trust yourself."

"I trust myself," she countered.

"Then why does discontentment cling to your dreams? What do you want in life?"

Want? She looked at Thian. "To begin with, stop acting as though you know everything about me. I may have shared with you stories from my past, or you may have glimpsed them in my dreams—maybe exhumed them yourself—but those provide only a portion of the truth."

"What is the truth then?" Thian asked with an uncertain expression.

Ashe did not really know, nor could she grasp what she ultimately wanted. Besides, did such questions really matter? She had been doing fine without them. "I do not need your concern. It is not why we are here." Pointing up toward the deck, she added, "We are here because of him—unless there is more going on than you have revealed to me."

"Circumstances seldom remain simple," Thian said.

What does that mean? Ashe pulled herself back onto the main deck. "I am tired." Heben sat across from her, leaning his back against the port bulwark with his legs extended. He appeared to be resting his eyes. If he had been listening to their conversation, without hearing the Séoran, it must have sounded incoherent.

Retrieving the cloak Fumond had provided her, Ashe withdrew to her quarters to rest.

The laboriously systematic transition over the Elentari Falls went as Heben had promised. Nonetheless, Ashe was glad to venture onward. In three days, they would reach Winslöri, and she felt increasingly ready to be done with it.

About halfway between the falls and coastal city stood Tärm Tower, which guarded the only bridge across the river and served as the main gate between Siligen and Rodaním. The fortifications and tall stone bridge adorned with the flags of Siligen flapping in the wind—a gold lion standing with mouth agape in a blue field lined with white—reminded her of the war. Tärm Tower had once belonged to Nemenelor.

Her stomach tightened.

"Try not to call attention to yourself," Heben whispered to Ashe as they approached the bridge.

She pulled the hood of her cloak over her head and remained seated at the corner of the quarterdeck gallery.

A barrier of rusting chains had been lowered like a net from the downstream side of the bridge, and extended to each bank of the river. The bridge contained four abutments, the two arches at the center being large enough for vessels like *The Liberty* to pass through. A few archers stood ready atop the bridge while more watched from behind the adjacent battlements that protected the towers overlooking each side of the bridge. Dwairian had expanded the defenses since the war's end. A lesser tower and surrounding wall with its own gatehouse access to the bridge now protected the east bank.

Soldiers directed *The Liberty* to one of the available docks jutting out from the western shore. There waited a slender man with a book tucked under his arm. Five soldiers dressed in blue brigandine and armed with spears and swords accompanied him.

"Hello, inspector," Lallél greeted from the main deck.

"Good afternoon, captain," the man replied dryly, opening his book and glancing down. "Your manifest, if you please."

Heben strode up beside Lallél, motioned for her to lower the book held ready, and stepped off the ship to talk privately with the inspector. The latter looked startled by this, but motioned the soldiers back. As Heben and the inspector spoke, the disposition of the latter shifted to deferential.

Still watching from the quarterdeck gallery, Ashe whispered to Thian, "Do you know what this is about?"

After concentrating on the situation on the dock, the Séoran replied, "Heben has pulled a document with an ornate seal from within his cloak, and is presenting it to the inspector."

"A document?" Apparently, she could neither see nor hear as well as the Séoran.

"Heben is now introducing himself as a Reminax." Thian glanced at her. "Do you know what that means?"

Ashe had heard of the Reminax from Captain Hectiliath when they met in Wéswood years earlier. Special agents of Dwairian, the Reminax were said to pursue various clandestine missions, from infiltrating rebel units to spying on Nemenelor. Did Fumond realize that Heben was one of them? Ashe did not know which answer she preferred. More importantly, whose idea was it for a Reminax to supervise their voyage to Winslöri—was it Fumond or actually Heben? Questions mounted, as did her suspicions.

"We will have to be more careful," she whispered to Thian.

Heben stepped back onto *The Liberty* and addressed Lallél: "No further inspection will be necessary."

"Is that so?" the captain replied.

The bodyguard nodded.

"Mind explaining how you managed that?"

"An explanation wasn't part of the bargain," Heben said, expressionless, and then casually stepped past her.

Meanwhile, the chain barrier of Tärm Bridge began to rise.

14

The Coast

Cold caresses my skin, piercing to the center of my being.

My heart flutters, breath faltering with the surge of a tempest's windy vanguard as I drop from a high, blue vastness toward rigid shapes of grey and brown below. Attentive, squinting my eyes, I lean back, pulling the reins while my thighs squeeze against the saddle—against diving down further toward immovable barriers and death.

So close.

The stirring in my stomach recedes. Glancing right without turning my head, I find that I am not alone. Another Sky Rider glides in front of me, calling me to safety. Gian. The muted mass of abstraction below is a mountain range with rocky ridges, crevices, and banks of snow. Shadows lengthen across its wilderness.

No, not there. Not again.

My winged mount shifts upward, paralleling my companion—my lover. I cling to the reins, and must not let go. Sensations diminish to a gentle rise and fall across the air—a touch of warmth lifting us up in slow spirals. I realize that I am not flying an Erïeth, but a large black swan. Gian rides one that is white.

Darkness is beneath, fading light above, and ahead a crimson glow behind a jagged, mountainous horizon—like the sharp teeth and fiery throat of a dragon. Leading to the worm's maw is a sandy plain: the Desert of Oblivion. Gian flies across it toward the horizon.

No, not there.

Does he hear me?

Do I follow or turn back?

Below, cloaked figures ride in a line across the wasteland. All are on horseback. Their leader removes his faded black hood and looks up at me, revealing a familiar face.

Ashe opened her eyes to a sky shrouded in damp mist. For a moment, she could not remember where she was. But then the creak of wood underneath, the splash of a fish, and the bright clang of a bell reminded her that she was onboard *The Liberty.*

Rubbing the sleep from her eyes, she looked over to see Thian sitting beside her, smiling affectionately. Though she still found his mannerisms unsettling, his proximity did not surprise her. "Keeping me warm again?" she asked dryly, sitting up.

"I saw you shivering in the night," the Séoran said.

Wrapped in her cloak, having fallen asleep on the quarterdeck gallery, Ashe stared at the grey water of the river lapping gently against the side of the ship. "Do you know where we are?"

Thian gazed ahead. "The sea is not far. I can smell the salty air."

Ashe could detect no such scent. "I did not know you could smell."

"We are more alike than you think," he replied. "Though my senses are less inhibited than yours, we do share the same essential nature: sight, smell, hearing, taste, and touch."

"You are a peculiar individual," Ashe said. She was not sure if she envied his heightened senses. Without them, a kind of detachment from the world could be justified.

Thian's smile widened. "You mortals live with so much tension and constraint that I wonder if you experience life with greater focus than we Séorans. Are you not more eager or desperate to draw from present moments?"

"Perhaps," she replied.

"Who was the Alöwean you saw in your dream?" Thian asked. "The one in the hooded cloak leading riders across the dunes."

"Still intruding upon my subconscious, are you?"

"I merely seek to learn."

So you have said. "About me or something more?"

"I care about you," the Séoran answered, looking taken aback.

"And Raez?"

"Can I not value you both, and more?"

Ignoring the question, she asked, "Why do you want to know about my recent dream?"

"It was a memory?" Thian asked.

She hesitated. "Yes."

"If so, you may have witnessed more than you realize. The Illirium War, like so many wars, has links to the Unseen War. Even the undercurrent of Raez's quest may flow in the same direction. I know more about your people and their history than even you, and I am trying to piece together some last fragments for the betterment of all. We are allies, Ashe, you and me. But more so, are we not friends?"

It would be better that way. Who was she, anyway, but a small part in the larger narrative? Indeed, what might she know that an immortal Séoran did not? She felt tired of misgivings. She wanted to move on. Did that not require a semblance of faith in all that Thian had said and done for her? Though questions remained, he had continued to show her good, never expressing doubts about her. More importantly, he had saved her life—presumably without knowing anything about her. What could she really lose by trusting him, at least for while longer?

"We are friends," she acknowledged. "I will tell you what I know about my dream." She considered the face she had seen. Spotting the contingent during a patrol at the western end of the Kurshemnt Mountains had really happened. Gían had been there too. It was her first post as a Sky Rider. "The Alöwean rider," she began, "was Brother Ësal, a member of the Twelve, the Council of Pernor."

Gían had urged her to report the matter to their commander. She had hesitated at first, but Gían persisted. The Sky Rider commander of the Northern Pass ultimately dismissed the news, however, explaining that he was aware of the situation: "It is not for us to dictate the movements of the Twelve."

Thian furrowed his brow. "Do you know why they were crossing the Desert of Oblivion?" Ashe shook her head, surprised by how unsettled Thian suddenly seemed. He added, "Do you know what lies in the mountains beyond the desert?"

Ashe shrugged. "Why does Ësal matter now? He was killed in the fall of Pernor."

"The memory makes you uneasy," Thian said solemnly, "the echoes of the war still heard, and the tremors felt."

"I would rather not dwell on that time of my life."

"It is not only that," the Séoran pressed. "Your discernment is deeper than you acknowledge."

"What is to be gained by looking closer?"

Thian grinned. "Looking closer could guide you to a renewed sense of purpose, confidence . . . even trust."

She looked away, focusing on the river ahead. For now, she just wanted to reach the coast and see what Raez would do.

By midmorning, the sun had burned away the mist. Ashe welcomed the warmth and cherished the fragrance of flowers blooming along the riverbank. Sitting at the bow of the ship on the forecastle deck, she noted seagulls flying about.

"There is another matter of which we must speak," Thian said, startling Ashe as he poked his head above the bulwark. Keeping his head below the topmost railing, he sat in the air alongside the port hull of the ship, acting as though he wished not to be seen.

"What is it?" Ashe asked, slightly annoyed.

"We should separate ourselves from Heben as soon as possible," the Séoran stated. "He is more aware than he lets on."

She glanced around to locate the bodyguard, but could not find him. "What do you mean?"

"There is another Séoran," Thian answered, his voice low and quiet. "I first encountered her at our meeting with Fumond. She reappeared last night to speak with Heben."

"Wait," Ashe said, "can Heben see you as I do?"

Thian slowly shook his head. "Not that I can surmise."

"But the other Séoran knows you are here, and that you speak with me and Raez?"

"I cannot discern the extent of her perception," Thian answered, "but she does know who I am. We even spoke."

"Why are you only telling me this now? Is this other Séoran a threat?"

"Yes."

"Why is she here?" Not for the first time, Ashe wondered if she had underestimated the extent of Fumond's ambition and prowess.

"I cannot say."

"Meaning that you do not know or will not tell me?"

Thian tilted his head. "I do not understand."

She did not have the patience for this. "What do you think we should do about it?"

Gripping the edge of the bulwark with his hands, Thian's black eyes looked around as if to make sure that no one was watching. "Oshrémi will give you a signal at the opportune moment. At that time, keep Heben away from Raez." He lowered his voice to an airy whisper. "I will contend with the Séoran."

* * *

Quiet settled over the port city of Winslöri as the last glow of a violet dusk faded in the west. *The Liberty* glided into a large marina, located at the western end of the city, built within the east bank of the estuary where the Elentari River ran into the Menendros Sea.

Before the ship docked, Captain Lallél called Ashe and Heben into her quarters. "I am well known here, so we shouldn't have any trouble from the inspectors."

"That is good," Ashe offered, glancing uncertainly at Heben.

"Indeed." Lallél raised a brow at Heben. "Rodaním's laws are less strict than Siligen's in this respect. Being that my manifest says nothing about a certain crate, and cargo is only inspected once it's unloaded, you'll wait until my crew's done with its business and left for town before you remove your item. I still don't care what it is. I just better not see you or it onboard in the morning. How you proceed from here is your own affair."

"We understand," Heben replied dryly.

"Good," Lallél said. "Port guards patrol at all hours, but will be fewer in the dark of morning. I suggest you use that time wisely. If you're questioned while still aboard my ship, I'll deny knowing you. We don't take kindly to thieves."

"Understood," Heben said.

As a Reminax, whatever authority Heben had in Siligen would be useless in Rodaním, probably even dangerous if exposed. Ashe wondered if that could be used against him if need be. Though not as confrontational as Siligen, Rodaním had harbored a tenuous relationship with Nemenelor since the Illirium War. Therefore, as an Alöwean, Ashe doubted she could evade suspicions herself if problems arose. Far from her homeland, she had to be careful not to get entwined with anything else.

Though tired, she struggled to sleep while Lallél's crew unloaded their main cargo. She had not seen Thian for the remainder of the day, and had not interacted with Raez since the Elentari Falls. With Heben keeping close to her, Ashe recognized the precariousness of her position. How did Thian intend to evade the bodyguard? And was Heben really a threat? So what if he had his own Séoran companion?

A couple hours later, Heben nudged Ashe on the shoulder. "Time to go."

Using her war hammer for leverage, she clenched her teeth against the stiffness in her foot and stood. They walked from the quarterdeck gallery to the main deck where two grim-looking men waited.

"They'll help us remove the crate," Heben explained.

Strapping her war hammer across her back, Ashe helped the other three lift the crate from the hold, carefully walk it across the gangway to the dock, and set it down as quietly as possible on the back of a cart waiting in a shadowed alleyway. At first, walking on firm ground felt imbalanced.

The two men left after Heben handed them each a coin. Turning to Ashe, he said, "Let's get this done with. The coast isn't far."

"Now?" Ashe asked. She looked at the cart, which was harnessed to a mule. "Will this not be loud, drawing too much attention to us at this time of night?"

"You have a better idea?" Heben replied calmly, drawing a heavy tarp over the crate.

A sparrow fluttered past Ashe's face, cheeping once as it went. Heben noticed it pass, and frowned.

Now? Ashe's heart faltered for a moment. Trying to retain a casual tone, she said, "I could use a drink first. Some establishment must still be open, for I warrant that the thirst of sailors is never quenched."

Facing her, his back to the cart, Heben did not move; nor did his solemn expression change.

"What do you say?" Ashe asked. "Standing about here waiting for a patrol will do us no good."

Thian appeared behind the bodyguard, and stuck his head through the tarp and crate, saying something to Raez. The mule whimpered as the cart shifted. Alerted, Heben looked back at the cart. Not knowing if he could see the Séoran, and not able to think of anything else to do, she gripped the shaft of her war hammer and brought the flat end down against Heben's head.

He blocked the strike with his right forearm. Ashe heard a crack, and figured the blow had fractured the man's bone; but before she could respond further, Heben delivered a firm punch into her stomach with his other fist. She gasped in pain. The bodyguard then drove his right knee into the soft inner side of her own knee, causing her to collapse. Clenching his teeth and exhaling painfully under his breath, he seized Ashe's war hammer with the hand of his damaged right arm while the left hand clutched her neck, using his weight to drive her back against the wall of a nearby building. She released the war hammer, gripping Heben's right hand with both of hers in an attempt to pry it from her throat. He lifted her up from the ground.

She kneed him in the chest, and then elbowed his hurt arm. Grunting in response, he pulled her away from the wall and slammed her back again.

"I thought you might be troublesome," he growled, his eyes fierce, as if trying to control both pain and anger.

Ashe pulled a knife from her belt, sliced at Heben's left forearm and then at his chest. He dropped her, but managed to avoid her second blow.

"Enough," he said.

A deep, rumbling voice spoke, interposed by dull clicks.

Heben turned to see Raez standing a few steps away, free from the crate. Thian stood beside him, but Ashe was still not sure if the bodyguard could see the Séoran. For the moment, she just fought to breathe normally again.

"What are you doing?" Heben asked, addressing the Erog. "We made a deal."

A white light flashed between them, forcing Ashe to shield her eyes. When she could see again, she saw Raez lifting Heben up with his good arm, his large hand gripping the man's chest. The Erog tossed Heben against the wall, picked him up again, and then threw him out into the water of the marina. Ashe was impressed by the show of such strength, for Raez had thrown the man well over a hundred feet.

Across the marina, Ashe spotted a patrol of five soldiers rushing toward them.

"We have to go," she urged Raez.

The Erog turned back toward the cart, grabbed his black bearskin cloak, wrapped it around his body, and began to run down the alley away from the marina. Ashe retrieved her war hammer and ran unevenly in pursuit.

What are we doing? The Erog could not run blindly through town with a hope of success. She called to Raez, motioned that he join her down a wider street, after which they turned left, using another alleyway until they reached an empty, open-air stable. "Here," she whispered sternly, pointing in.

The Erog followed her inside where they crouched and waited, trying to slow their breathing. A few voices echoed down the street from which they had come, but were unaccompanied by the sound of thumping boots or clinking armor.

Where was Thian?

Noting the position of the moon, Ashe determined the direction of the coast. Waiting until she could hear no sign of activity, she slowly stepped out from the stable, and motioned for Raez to follow.

Carefully, they walked the streets of Winslöri.

In the east, the sky began to brighten as they came upon the city's south gate. Observing it from the shadows of a narrow alleyway, Ashe saw that the gate was already open. Numerous Illiri soldiers oversaw those coming and going.

A sparrow flew down and landed on Raez's broad shoulder. Another perched on the edge of a nearby roof away from the direction of the gate. The one on the Erog chattered at its companion, flapping its wings, to which the second replied, turned, and flew away. Seemingly urged on by the sparrow on his shoulder, Raez walked in the direction of the second.

Why not? Ashe trailed them without protest.

Soon, they reached an unoccupied portion of Winslöri's outer wall. With his back to her, Raez turned his head and said something. Brushing aside a portion of his cloak, he indicated the filed spikes on his shoulders, which she interpreted to be an invitation to climb on his back. Since the incident at Rínroth Outpost, she had hoped to never have to do so again, but conceded. Once she was as secure as possible on his back, gripping the spikes for stability, the Erog climbed the wall and dropped down on the other side with little effort. They then quickly moved through a field of sagebrush toward the sound of crashing waves. Osré and Oshrémi led the way, while Ashe spotted the vulture, Ornithez, flying higher up.

A mile later, as the first rays of sunlight were expanding across the landscape, they came upon Thian. He stood at the edge of a cliff overlooking the vast, glimmering sea. The brilliance of his usually white light had faded, and there were claw marks on his chest and neck, but he smiled at them. "Welcome, friends."

Raez straightened, staring at the sea. Tall storm clouds lined the horizon, before which shone a rainbow like a gateway. Inhaling the cool, damp air seasoned with salt, gazing out upon the boisterous green and blue water, Ashe's thoughts wandered beyond the Menendros Sea, across Oceanus to another ocean: the Brödinathíanic. At its center, in a region called Chaléth in southern Alöwe, amidst the Gulf of the Sky, the island of her birth waited: Lemnas. She imagined walking its sandy beaches, basking in the warmth of the sun after swimming in the clear depths of its surrounding waters.

Raez spoke with Thian.

Eventually, the Séoran turned his attention to Ashe. "Raez intends to cross Oceanus to Alöwe." He indicated a boat resting on the beach below.

"Has he received word from the gods?" she asked.

"They beckon him onward." Thian stepped closer. "Come with us."

"To what end?"

"The clarity of revelation. I can show you places you have never seen, Ashe Pethus. We have but to commandeer that vessel and return home."

Shifting her gaze to the brightening crimson clouds illuminated by the dawn, Ashe reviewed her options, trying to identify what she really wanted. Looking down at the boat, she wondered about the likelihood of success crossing Oceanus in such a small craft. Did Thian have the power to make it possible? Part of her wanted to return to Alöwe, but a stronger instinct found the sentiment to be deceiving. Thinking of her father, more pain awaited her in Chaléth than happiness. The pull of Illirium felt stronger. "So, you will abandon your dell in the Upper Mountains?"

Thian's eyes lowered. "I do not want to part with you, but the only way forward for me is across the sea."

She could not imagine them surviving. "It took my people over sixty years to cross from Alöwe to Illirium."

"I know," Thian answered. "I was there. But that was a different journey."

There were just too many variables, too many impulsive choices already burdening her past. She had an opportunity to change the course of her behavior. It simply did not feel right to return to Alöwe, not yet. It would be like stepping too far back into a past from which she had long tried to escape. *I am not ready.*

"Perhaps we will see each again one day," she said.

"Please," Thian urged. "Come with us."

"My place is here," she replied, confidence in her decision mounting. The uncertainty of staying compelled her more than the possibilities of going. She turned to the Erog. "May you find what you are looking for."

After a sigh, Thian spoke to Raez. The latter bowed his head respectfully, and, looking at Ashe, responded in a guttural murmur.

"He says to keep strong," Thian translated.

"I will." Ashe offered a grin. *Always.*

Leaning on her war hammer, she watched her two companions slowly navigate past the surf. The Erog handled the oars clumsily at first, but somehow managed to wield both.

She sat down, placed her war hammer to the side, and pulled out her pipe. About to light it, she hesitated as the image of a grey mountain pass captured her thoughts—memories that touched every emotion: rage, grief, happiness.

"Lasting strength comes from facing your pain," Thian had said.

Focusing back on her pipe, she put it aside, took her pouch of mip weed, and on a whim emptied its contents to the wind. Of all the questions that remained, there were some she could still answer, or at least explore without outside influence. To move forward, she would have to go back. It was time to return; not to the beginning of her pain, her family, but to a place where the pain had, like a bog, truly ensnared her spirit.

I will go, she thought, bracing for whatever might come of returning to the Northern Pass in the Kurshemnt Mountains. "I will go," she told herself out loud, afraid yet resolute. She would have to find a new Erïeth first, perhaps one from the coast.

I will fly again.

In the meantime, she chose to cherish the quiet solitude of the moment: the breeze cool with ocean spray, the beauty of the rising red sun, and the curious sight of an Erog with a vulture on his shoulder, sitting in a row boat across from a black swan and two small sparrows.

II

RAEZ

1

Warrior

Raez's consciousness glided over a hushed desert landscape.

"What dost thou see?" Züd's rumbling voice echoed from afar.

"The Pa'dëm have assembled," Raez replied calmly, withdrawing the visionary link with his black vulture, Ornithez. Of his tribe, Raez was one of the few able to maintain such a connection, which enhanced his ability to see the world, if only briefly, through the bird's eyes.

"How many?" Züd asked.

"They outnumber us by fivescore."

Züd grinned with a trace of bitter resolve. "Good."

Züd, the Aditám, chieftain of the Thraz Tribe, wore a helm made from the skull of a giant serpent; the two long fangs of its upper jaw protected the front of his wide face, while the separated lower jawbones with their lesser teeth framed his lower maw. Ribs from the same snake comprised his breastplate, fastened close together in overlapping layers. Züd was more than a leader to Raez; he was his surrogate father.

The two Thraz, Aditám and son, stood halfway up a rugged mountainside. Ahead, to the west, the desert plain remained washed in grey and mauve hues. Though the sky had begun to lighten from the night, hours remained before the sun would heat the plain—time enough for the Thraz to make their claim.

"There." Raez pointed to a dark line in front of a sag pond, the only source of water for miles. Little water remained in the shallow circle of earth, but in the desert such water helped define authority. "They know we are here and wait for us. I did see no archers in their ranks."

Züd hissed with satisfaction. "Then shalt we meet them directly."

Walking on all four limbs, each using his tail for balance and mobility, Raez and Züd descended the mountain to where the host of Thraz waited, five-hundred strong. Most bore tall rectangular shields made of wood paired with black stabbing swords fashioned from glassy stone. A unit of archers waited toward the back. Few Thraz wore additional armor, each finding that his thick scaly and spiked hide provided adequate protection. A number of veterans wore the bones of slain foes or prey, predominantly enemy tribesmen. A couple elites had even adapted the metal armor and weapons of defeated Dwarves to their liking. The youngest and fastest Thraz, held in reserve, tended to fight using nothing more than their sharp claws, teeth, and horns. Like them, Raez preferred the greater mobility and temperature regulation of wearing nothing, but since Züd had put him in command of a frontline unit, Raez decided to use a long-handled battle hammer.

"Brothers," the Aditám greeted, standing before the host. "Today we end the plague that is the Pa'dëm."

The army stirred in anticipation. Raez not only observed, but could smell the rising aggression—like sun-baked stone. He could even perceive the beating of their hearts.

The tribe's Ezren stepped out next to Züd, with three young acolytes following in the dust of his passing. The Ezren, Hand of the Gods, wisest and most powerful of the Thraz, lifted his right arm, which lacked a forearm. "Remember," he said with a husky voice. "Victory is granted to the tribe that battles not as scattered rocks, but as a mountain." His bulbous black eyes examined the line of warriors. Two curved tzëg horns fixed together adorned his neck, and a grey fur cloak hung from his shoulders. "Quiet sleep awaits the faithful," he continued, adjusting his grip on the staff, the top of which was decorated with rows of vulture skulls. "The Spirits of Life feedeth our collective strength." He lowered his stub of a right arm toward the host. "Do you hunger?"

The Thraz murmured their affirmation.

Raez looked at his two friends in the second column, standing next to each other—Meris and Enyo. They smiled with determination and nodded.

"As one," Züd called, stepping forward. He pointed his hammer north to where the Pa'dëm waited. "As a mountain."

The Thraz marched toward the enemy.

Raez had fought in many battles. As he went, an unfamiliar voice, like a whisper, intruded upon his concentration: *Look beyond.* Bewildered, he observed the surrounding landscape, searching for the source of the voice. He was suddenly struck by how beautiful it appeared, how much its tranquility contrasted what was about to ensue on the plain. An urge to separate from the host and bask in silent meditation, pondering the details of his environment, both vast and intimate, tugged at his desire.

"Keepeth up," Züd called back.

Raez shook his head against the distraction, and increased his pace alongside his unit of warriors. He strode up next to Meris and Enyo who each led a column.

"What troubles thee, brother?" Enyo asked Raez, keeping his voice low.

How could he explain it to his friends? Instead, he re-centered himself with images of hunting together—slaying a large black bear in the mountains, while Meris and Enyo cheered him on and helped carry the carcass back home. "'Tis nothing more than a passing weariness," he replied.

"These warriors look to thee," Meris commented. "If thy focus is clouded—"

"I am here," Raez assured, "and shalt lead our brethren to victory."

Smiling, Meris clapped Raez on the shoulder. "We are also here with thee."

"All of us," Enyo added. "None doth battle alone."

Thump. Thump. The lead Thraz warriors began to beat their shields in unison with the pommels of their stone swords. Others started a continuous, reverberating chant with intercalated grunts and hoots, evoking the sense that the earth gods themselves were rising up to encourage their advance.

Ahead, the army of the Pa'dëm Tribe waited, tightening their shield line. The pounding of Raez's heart intensified in his chest, shuddering with the rhythm of the shield chorus. So he perceived the hearts of his brothers around him.

Thump. Thump.

A hundred strides away, the Pa'dëm did not move. Raez could see their features—the firm lines of their wide scaly faces; the short spikes protruding from their brown-yellow cheeks and brows; and the two great horns at the back of their heads, with lesser ones crowning the base.

Thump. Thump.

Fifty strides away . . .

The front Pa'dëm ranks raised their shields and crouched low, protecting their more vulnerable undersides. Those behind expanded their girth to intimidate, roaring their own war song.

The Thraz slowed to a halt.

Züd motioned for his archers to begin loosing their arrows, and some darts found their mark in the eyes of the enemy. No arrows were returned. Suffering further from another volley, the Pa'dëm came forward.

Twelve strides away . . .

Both sides hissed at each other in defiant fury.

Six . . .

The Pa'dëm shield line surged forward with alarming speed, crashing into the Thraz like rockfall. The Thraz held firm against the onslaught and soon began to drive the enemy back.

Raez saw the Pa'dëm line expanding to the right, presumably to hook the Thraz flank, which he commanded. He extended his thoughts to Meris and Enyo's columns, held in reserve, and ordered them to engage the enemy with a fresh battering of shields and sword thrusts. When his friends arrived, Raez charged with them. At the enemy line, he swung his hammer downward, cracking a Pa'dëm's skull, and then another's with a sideways stroke, but the impact of a third caused the shaft of his weapon to snap in two. Letting go of the hammer, he picked up a shield from a fallen brother whose neck had been cleaved by a sword. Meris and Enyo appeared at either side, the first protecting him with his shield while the latter kept back another attacker with the point of his blade.

"Advance," Raez cried, both verbally and with his mind, squatting among the tightening line of Thraz, putting all his weight against a shield he had picked up.

"Come on, brothers," Meris shouted.

"Advance."

The Thraz columns rallied and grunted together, moving ahead with determined steps in cadence with Raez's calls: "Advance."

The Pa'dëm's left flank began to deteriorate.

Holding back from the shield line for a moment, Raez's thoughts called for a second wave of reinforcements, directing them to rush around the Pa'dëm host's broken flank and pierce the main body, hopefully to shatter their resolve like brittle stone.

With his clawed right hand, Raez tore the throat from an enemy soldier. As blood sprayed upon his face, a tremor of exhilaration rose from his heart and sharpened his concentration. His Thraz brothers equally reveled in the exchange.

Ahead, a Pa'dëm warrior leapt into the air and landed on Meris' shoulder, clawing at one of his eyes while biting into his neck. Seeing Meris go down, Raez rushed to his friend's aid, driving the attacker away with his shield. It was too late. The life quickly vanished from Meris' gaze.

No. Gritting his teeth, Raez dropped his shield, tackled the Pa'dëm perpetrator, and clawed out the warrior's eyes. The latter screamed in agony and became limp in blinded defeat, his fear pungent like sulfur.

A shadow passed across Raez's third eye—a light and heat sensor at the base of the back of his head. Instinctively, he sprang forward, flipping around as he did so to face the new assailant. A Pa'dëm chieftain swung at him with a crude battleaxe, but was not close enough. Raez stepped back on his hind legs, tripping over a dead Thraz as he did so. The chieftain promptly strode forward, but Enyo appeared and bit into one of his arms while seizing the chieftain's torso with his claws.

Raez hastily rolled onto all fours. After retrieving an abandoned shield, he saw the chieftain pull out a long knife and stab Enyo multiple times in the softer flesh of his chest and stomach. Raez slammed into the preoccupied chieftain with his shield braced against his shoulder, knocking the other onto his back. Lifting the shield up, Raez drove its end down on the chieftain's neck and face, repeating the action again and again, battering the life from the Pa'dëm.

At last, gasping for breath, he glanced around. The bodies of the dead covered the sandy ground, which was already absorbing pools of blood. A few skirmishes remained, but numerous isolated Thraz were already beginning to search the carnage. Others bound and gathered captured Pa'dëm into a cluster at one end of the battlefield, while the Ezren and his three acolytes approached with pleased expressions.

Sunlight now warmed the plain. They would have to move quickly to escape its destructive heat. Though the dead Pa'dëm provided enough meat to feed the Thraz Tribe for at least a month, the Thraz would not be able to salvage all the bodies in time.

Looking at Enyo's lifeless form lying nearby, and Meris not far beyond, Raez dropped to his knees and tossed his bloodied shield aside. The Thraz had suffered few defeats in recent years, but the satisfaction of conquest for the sake of survival no longer felt like enough. *Thus, we survive, but for why?* The gods promised a quiet sleep after life, but was that really all the Thraz fought for? Perhaps wisdom was better than weapons of war.

Coming next to him, Züd clapped him affectionately on the shoulder. "Thou hath led and battled valiantly, my son. We sup from the hand of victory."

Looking at the dead and dying, Raez felt no such triumph. "I thanketh thee, Father."

"Come," Züd said. "We must hasten before the day is too advanced." He straightened and gazed out upon the battlefield. "Our toil has barely begun."

2

Prescience

Before rising to the status of warrior, Young Brothers of the Thraz Tribe spent years completing the more mundane tasks necessary for a thriving settlement. This they did dutifully, for all Thraz learned the value of serving the collective whole. While warriors were the most glorified, comprising the majority of the adult populace—courageously sacrificing to defend or expand territory, which often affected access to food and water as well as protecting the tribe—they meant nothing without the foundation sustained by the youngest.

All Thraz were male save their mother, the Frynosoma, Voice of the Gods. Her name was Thraz, thus the tribe acted as a manifestation of her will. The Aditám, strongest of her offspring, determined and reinforced by periodic physical challenges or duels, was charged above all with the Frynosoma's protection and provision. In that, he and the Ezren safeguarded the location of her dwelling place, a private sanctum removed from the tribe. Once a year, during the Amplexus, the Aditám would ritually mate with the Frynosoma in her hidden pool. It was said that she could produce two-thousand eggs each year, which in time would grow into Soleps, infant offspring not yet ready for sunlight and a waterless existence. Eventually, the Frynosoma would direct her Soleps away from the pool to the outdoors where they would be received by the Ezren who was responsible for guiding them to the tribe.

Many Soleps died along the way, usually from getting lost or eaten by predators. Only the survivors were deemed worthy members of the tribe. During the journey, the Ezren imparted the language and cognitive connection that formed the basis of Thraz society. Once the Soleps arrived at the tribe's dwelling place, they were claimed by or matched with an adult for further life instruction, such as hunting, gathering, building, and surviving. At that time, they stopped being known as Soleps, and became Young Brothers. Thus each Thraz came to understand his place in society, including what was required for its preservation.

A Thraz contingent of Young Brothers had witnessed the victory against the Pa'dëm. In time, those who lost a surrogate father would be adopted by another. Watching from afar, protected by a unit of warriors, the Young Brothers were called forth at the battle's end to first help remove the bodies of their slain brethren. Pulling crude carts in pairs, they worked quickly against the rising sun; for at its zenith, the sun's heat could roast a Thraz within an hour.

In the first passing of the carts, Raez directed a pair of Young Brothers to pick up the bodies of his friends, Enyo and Meris. As the dead were periodically taken away—about a third of the original host—Raez helped his fellow warriors gather their other fallen. He thought little while working, nor wanted to, but simply prepared body after body to be carted away. The metallic smell of blood permeated the air. The fading pulses of the dying, like receding echoes of the Thraz beating their shields only hours earlier, added to the sensory excess. *Thump. Thump . . . thump . . . thump . . .* Fatigue seeped up from his feet. His limbs ached.

Young Brothers also brought barrels to fill with water from the sag pond. Moving on all fours to the shore, Raez lowered his head to a puddle, formed a bowl in the mud with his clawed fingers, and drank. The warm water relieved his dry throat and enlivened his concentration, but left him wanting more.

Looking back at the field of dead, he sighed. *We fight for scraps.*

A whiff of smoke alerted his attention to an aggressive presence. In his left periphery, Raez marked the approach of another Thraz warrior.

Halïrez stood a head taller than Raez. A long-handled hammer, its stone end bloodied, rested casually across the length of his broad shoulders and behind his neck. "The Pa'dëm near broke our right flank," he commented with a hint of derision.

"And we paid them for it," Raez replied wearily. "Oft is victory a matter of close margins."

"Yet, all the while, thy resolve doth appear to wane," Halïrez said. "Our brothers begin to take heed."

"Now thou speakest for them?"

"A time cometh when—"

"Not at present," Raez interrupted, straightening to stare firmly into the other's eyes. He indicated the fallen around them. "Here lie our brothers, calling not for contention but conclusion. Let us honor their memory and leave questions of competence for another hour."

Glaring back at Raez, Halïrez's jaw tightened and his hand's grip on the handle of his battle hammer shifted. Raez also noted the other warrior's rising heart rate, and subtly adjusted his footing. Halïrez's aura, like the churning heat of the sun, gradually calmed, however, and he nodded. "A time cometh," he echoed, and then turned away.

Once the Thraz dead had been removed, the survivors turned to hauling away the spoils of battle: the Pa'dëm. The few captured Pa'dëm—for none surrendered willingly, knowing their fate if they did—were forced to help. Their fear was nearly palpable, reeking like sulfur, but also visible to Raez as a faint blue aura shuddering from their forms. Thraz consciousness was bolstered by heightened olfaction and pallesthesia, but with concentration Raez also benefited from the ability to perceive and interpret the heat emitted from another like light. Why he and a few others had the skill, while most did not, none could say. The Ezren ascribed it to a gift of the gods, over years teaching Raez and those like him how to focus the unique sight. Now, Raez felt barraged by the many sensations.

By the time the blazing sun reached its apex, most of the corpses had been taken away, and Raez, his mind exhausted, followed close behind the last departing carts.

To escape the fluctuating temperatures of the desert, the Thraz dwelled under the eastern mountains in caverns either found or crafted with their own hands. Out of respect for the creation of the gods, they preferred to use what the land freely offered. Excellent stone masons, they reinforced the carefully guarded entryways and interior spaces of their settlement with ornately carved stones. Wood was a rare commodity, and not to be squandered.

Passing through the stone archway that marked the main entrance of Süretuwam, home of the Thraz, Raez welcomed the feeling of cool underground air. Guards and Young Brothers nodded to him as he walked by on all fours, following the straight wide course of the tunnel to the heart of the mountain. A large chamber marked the center of Süretuwam, illuminated by pale beams of light coming down from shafts engineered in the ceiling. Cubical structures carved from the solid stone and earth of the mountain lined the chamber walls, each accommodating members of the tribe. The highest and largest structure at the back housed the Aditám.

Slowly, Raez made his way up to his home. There, he scraped the dirt and dried blood from his body, and then rested while the night's feast was being prepared elsewhere by the Young Brothers. Most of the salvaged Pa'dëm bodies would be skinned and preserved for later use, but some, including the dead chieftain, would be enjoyed as meat fresh from victory. The choice portions, the living prisoners, would be blinded and brought by Züd to the Frynosoma for her own consumption—and by association, that of the gods—but first she would reverently dine on the carefully prepared bodies of her slain offspring.

Similarly, before victory could be celebrated, the Thraz would mourn the lost.

At dusk, Raez stood beside Züd and the Ezren to oversee a farewell ritual for their fallen brothers. The Thraz congregated in a large dell high in the mountains, a natural bowl that was said to have once held life: a lake of glistening blue water. The sacred ground could only be accessed from one of Süretuwam's interior tunnels. Cliffs rose steeply from every side of the dell except its eastern end, which opened to a sharp drop and view of continuing peaks, beyond which waited the land of the Dwarves.

At the center of the bowl, a pyramidal mound of stone shelves had been built and added to over time from the base up. The shelves faced outward, and contained the heads of dead Thraz dating back to the establishment of Süretuwam. The centermost stacks of shelves were the tallest, comprising the pinnacle of the mound, most of their contents now hidden from view, while the shelves farther out on the mound were less stacked. When the old ones were full, new shelves were built and added to the mound. Thus the Mountain of the Fallen gradually grew. The Ezren and Het, his three acolytes, oversaw the care of the monument.

Soft amber light filled the sky. As the sun withdrew behind the eastern ridges, the temperature swiftly dropped. Raez pulled his cloak closer, appreciating the heavy hide of the black bear he had killed in the mountains as a youth. The other Thraz wore cloaks as well, most made from grey tzëg or brown rel hide, or some from other desert or mountain animals they had hunted. Once again, he remembered how Meris and Enyo had shared his triumph over the bear. Their absence left him feeling more alone than he thought possible.

Züd wore a white cloak, the neck and front lining made from the fluffy brown tail of a rel. A pair of slightly curved rel horns hung from his neck. Standing on his hind legs, he stepped forward and raised both arms to hush the crowd. "Let us honor our fallen with silence and attention." He nodded to the Ezren and stepped back.

"The Spirits of Life speak," the Ezren began, coming forward. "Through the rock, earth, water, plants—through all, they humble our assumptions and draw our attention to what is to come." He motioned toward the freshly added shelves that contained the heads of the dead. "Though the bodies of these our brothers shall soon return to their mother, the place of their beginning, their knowledge remaineth with us. Thus, find we power in their sacrifice."

Raez stared at the heads, lingering on those of Enyo and Meris. In about ten years, their flesh would decompose entirely, leaving the anonymous vacant glare common to the inhabitants of the Mountain of the Fallen. Collectively, the eyes looked out north, west, south, and east, forevermore watching the world on behalf of the tribe. The Ezren claimed to know all that they had known, and through their eyes to better see the realm beyond the visible world.

Doth they deserve our envy? Raez wondered. Was a quiet sleep all that awaited them in the afterlife, or would it be an eternal vision more real than his current wakefulness? Thinking of the whispering voice from the battle, assuming it to have come from the gods, he pressed: *Is it that our deaths have no value to thee?*

Treacherous brothers were punished—sacrificed to the tribe and devoured as no better than their enemies. In death, there would be no rest for such individuals, but instead slavery to the gods. Though the Span, the land of the gods, was not a place sought by the living, more than ever before Raez felt drawn to its mystery.

During the evening feast, he decided to approach the Ezren to speak in quiet audience. The Ezren dined alone on a high stone platform overlooking the central courtyard of Süretuwam. Below, the rest of the tribe sat in groups and conversed amiably, enjoying the sustenance of victory. Countless star beetles buzzed or crawled lazily about, casting a soft golden glow throughout the cavern.

Halïrez spoke quietly with one of the acolytes, apparently in confidence. Seeing Raez approach, the other warrior promptly stepped back and strode past Raez with a glint of suspicion and defiance in his round dark eyes.

Raez ignored the sense of challenge for the time being, focusing instead on the Ezren. Though he was the son of the Aditám, Raez was not allowed through by the three acolytes until the seer permitted it.

"Come sit," the Ezren said, finally, with a motion of his hand indicating that the acolytes let Raez pass. Carefully guiding some star beetles out of the way, he motioned for Raez to occupy the place next to him.

"I thank thee," Raez replied, reclining on his stomach next to the seer, appreciating how the Ezren emitted a calm scent like warm sand. He remained baffled, however, about how clouds like a churning sandstorm concealed the seer's aura. Was that a kind of controlled concealment?

"Thou foughtest with valor today," the Ezren commented, offering a faint smile, though to Raez it seemed a polite formality. "All aspire to emulate thee. The Spirits of Life have blessed thee."

"My every action, I do for the benefit of the Thraz," Raez said, meaning it.

"So it hath been since thy birth. Thou art unique among us." The Ezren looked calmly into Raez's eyes. "But what dost thou wish to speak to me about, Raez, son of Züd?"

Raez hesitated, not for the first time questioning the correctness of voicing his thoughts to the seer. He glanced down at the congregation. For the sake of not only himself, but his brothers, he had to find some answers. "Why do the gods maintain such distance from us?" There were so many intermediaries: the Ezren spoke on behalf of the Frynosoma, who spoke on behalf of the gods, and even certain individual gods acted on behalf of the rest, such as, perhaps, the unknown voice from the battle.

"There is much the Spirits of Life must do to nurture the roots and support the branches of this world," the Ezren replied. "If no boundaries existed, our petty lives would distract them and risk the eventual decay and collapse of all things."

"Yet the gods are all-powerful," Raez pressed. "Is it that our actions might truly thwart their will?"

"They are powerful," the Ezren agreed, raising the stump of his right arm, "but not omnipotent. Like us, they need each other to flourish."

"I desire to know them more."

The Ezren raised a brow. "What dost thou mean?"

"I think often about the unseen world, the Span, and the stories of a great body of water."

"Oceanus."

"Yes."

"Large subjects for the son of the Aditám." The Ezren leaned closer, speaking in a hushed tone. "Ever since thou first left the Frynosoma, thou hast known greater strengths than most. These matters have led me to wonder about the future."

"The future?"

"The future," the Ezren acknowledged, with a mildly calculating expression.

"What future dost thou see?"

"I see thee," the Ezren said.

"Me?" Was the seer changing the subject deliberately?

"And more." The Ezren lowered his voice further to the point that Raez had to turn his ear toward the seer. "Thou art destined to one day lead us, and the time for this draws near."

The answer disappointed Raez, for he already knew that he would soon have to fulfill his duty by overthrowing his father. The current Aditám would not yield easily, though; for combat between father and son was meant to be a test of not only the potential successor's strength, but the legacy of his father in preparing him. If the father defeated his surrogate son too easily, the tribe might question his leadership and increasingly challenge him. Yet, if the Aditám yielded to his son without a true effort, his resolve to prepare for the future of the tribe, training its next leader, would also be mistrusted. Challengers of the new Aditám would follow. The pressure, therefore, was on both participants to fight with everything they had, and without reservation. The Aditám needed not only personal strength, but the support of the majority to thrive. Already, rumors of other challengers like Halïrez had reached Raez's ears.

Considering his mounting doubts and distractions, Raez wondered if he was truly meant to be the next Aditám, or more to the point whether that would be enough to satisfy his restlessness. The Ezren's unique access to the mystery of the gods held greater appeal.

"I have witnessed it in my visions," the Ezren continued. "As the future Aditám, know that there are also signs of coming destruction: Frynosoma of every tribe imprisoned and dying whilst our brothers are gathered under an unfamiliar power."

"A power outside the realm of the gods?"

"It is unclear."

"Then the gods are warning us," Raez offered.

"Perhaps," the Ezren replied. "Visions reveal a hidden landscape that few can explore without eroding their minds. For this reason I oversee and guard the threshold between waking and sleeping—to maintain Thraz order and cohesion—for the Spirits of Life manifest most clearly in such a space. Thus, I perceive shades of the past, present, and future. What I see could already be happening, might yet be, or may never come to be."

"If such a threat is to manifest, what canst we do to repel it?" Raez asked, wanting to focus on more tangible solutions.

"Fulfill thy duty."

Once again, Raze found the answer unsatisfactory. "Is that all?"

"Tis what helps our people survive," the Ezren replied.

"Raez," a strong voice called.

Raez turned to see Züd standing before the three acolytes who barred his path, one looking back at the Ezren for instruction. The Aditám was larger than the acolytes, and could easily overpower them, but respected the Ezren's authority and deferred to his wisdom.

The Ezren raised a hand, suggesting that Züd wait a moment longer. Keeping his voice low, he said to Raez, "I advise thee against sharing our discussion with thy father."

Raez nodded and stood.

"We shall speak again soon," the Ezren added, looking away.

Walking on all fours, Raez followed his surrogate father up a series of ramps to the war room, a stone hall built beneath the Aditám's living quarters. Two of Züd's personal guards led the way, while two more followed a few strides behind. Upon reaching the entrance of the war room, at a nod from Züd the guards stayed outside and closed the doors made from dried cactus.

The room's ceiling was dotted with glowworms that emitted soft blue light like shooting stars. With his back to Raez, Züd stared at a map painted on the wall that depicted Thraz territory and surrounding lands. "Be wary of the Ezren," he said.

"He is the Hand of the Gods," Raez replied instinctively, though heard a diminished conviction in his words.

"He hath his own agenda." Züd turned to face his surrogate son. "Though the Ezren serves as the vision of our tribe, the Aditám is at its heart, empowering its limbs for action. Without action, the Thraz will die. Therefore, I advise thee to preserve some distance from the Ezren's whisperings."

Stories were told about a few isolated attempts in Thraz history to overthrow an Ezren. All attempts had happened before the lives of anyone currently alive, and had failed due to the seer's unrivaled supernatural power. Raez was not sure about the extent of such power. It was widely assumed that he enjoyed the protection of the gods—something to do with his missing right arm—therefore, no Thraz warrior, not even Züd, dared challenge him. Granted, the Ezren was the main purveyor of such tales, which to Raez prodded additional questions.

"Thou hast much else to consider and prepare for," Züd continued. "The tribe is ready to embrace thee for its future. Today, thou proved thyself worthy beyond doubt."

"I thank thee, Father." Raez felt honored by the affirmation, but also troubled. *Do I desire such a role as it stands?*

Züd returned his attention to the map. "For now, the nuisance that is the Dwarves persisteth in driving the tzëg herds and rel farther from the mountains, depriving us of important resources. We cannot tolerate this affront; yet without an aggressive far-seeing strategy, we may not survive it. Tunneling with our allies shall continue, for one, opening points from whence to attack and reclaim what is ours, whilst also sheltering our brothers from the dangers of crossing the high country."

Raez thought of the frequent snow and freezing cold of the eastern mountain passes, even in the summer months. He thought of the giant birds of prey that also dwelt there, readily swooping down upon isolated Thraz if given the chance.

"Victories like today," Züd continued, "though rewarding are costly and cannot be relied upon alone. The Thraz need more than a strong warrior;

they need a leader of cunning forethought, free of mind and with the will to do that which is necessary—that which is tangible—in the present." He looked at Raez. "Art thou ready, my son?"

3

Acolyte

Dry bones cover a barren desert valley. My feet are buried beneath them. I cannot move. Thraz skulls with hollow sockets stare up at me. I am too late to save them. The thump of hearts echoes all around, fading, ever fading.

Ahead, the sunrise maketh the horizon ripple like water. From it, a slender figure in a hooded white cloak advanceth.

I cannot move. The bones still cling to my feet.

I cannot look away.

Raez shuddered awake to the urgent blast of a tzëg horn reverberating through the caverns of Süretuwam. *The alarm.*

Rising hastily from within his bed of sand, he shook off the excess, retrieved his black stone sword, and left his private chamber in time to see Züd depart the residence surrounded by personal guards. Already, the Aditám gripped his battle hammer.

"What dost thou know?" Raez asked, jogging up beside him, still feeling disoriented from his vision.

"Nothing yet."

As they descended ramps toward the central courtyard of the settlement, cries erupted from the direction of the main tunnel entrance. Looking that way, Raez lost a breath as he saw a large shadow, long and menacing, slither in.

No.

"How did it get inside?" Züd demanded of an approaching commander, Lün.

"I know not, Aditám," Lün replied. "All gates were secured at nightfall."

From their vantage point, still high above the center of Süretuwam, they saw the giant serpent knock a unit of armed Thraz aside and make its way along the periphery of the settlement toward a side tunnel.

"It moveth toward the Wocron," Raez said. The Wocron housed the Ezren.

"Direct thy force to protect the Ezren," Züd urged Commander Lün, who turned promptly to the right down another ramp. To Raez, Züd said, "We will trap it inside the Wocron tunnel. It will not leave Süretuwam alive."

Raez nodded grimly.

Injured Thraz, some with limbs bent in unnatural directions, and others struggling against the pain of their broken ribs, lay in the wake of the intruder. A host of warriors gathered at the courtyard, most wielding stone-tipped pikes, awaiting the Aditám's instruction. Ahead of them, a loud hiss echoed from the Wocron's entrance tunnel, overpowering the shouts of the Thraz warriors within.

"Move brothers," Züd urged, motioning for the host to follow him toward the tunnel. He exchanged his hammer for a pike held ready by a Young Brother.

Raez declined the offer from another, deciding instead to keep his sword. He also picked up a shield.

Striding down the tunnel toward the Wocron, they passed a few more crushed Thraz, most still alive. Brief images of the serpent striking out at surrounding Thraz permeated their thoughts. *Hasten*, the Ezren's voice echoed in Raez's mind, affirming that the seer was still alive.

Soon after entering the tunnel, Raez slowed and directed three lines of shield warriors to block the way out behind them. Meanwhile, Züd advanced with the main host, quickly moving out of sight into the Wocron to drive the serpent back toward the tunnel. Glimpses from the Ezren's vision showed Commander Lün's contingent to be scattered but unflinching in its attempt to surround and jab at the creature. The serpent itself was a hundred yards long, black with speckled stripes of yellow. It coiled in warning against the Thraz, lashing out at those who dared come too close.

Raez wondered at the creature advancing so deeply into Süretuwam. A thought struck him that the serpent might not have come with bold malice, but rather a desperate confusion. It could have unintentionally wandered into Süretuwam for shelter, not realizing who dwelled within.

There was no more time to speculate. Raez envisioned the serpent rapidly breaking through Züd's newly formed perimeter in the outer sanctum of the Wocron, and returning to the tunnel. With his present eyes, Raez spotted one of the Ezren's acolytes fleeing toward the shield line, calling for help. His first instinct was to rush forward to protect the acolyte's escape, but a suddenly stronger instinct held him back. The serpent came into view, seized the acolyte by his back left leg, and violently tossed him aside against the wall.

Seeing the Thraz shield wall and its warriors swelling their bodies in intimidation, the serpent stopped, but could not retreat with Züd's force continuing to attack its tail. In the narrower confines of the tunnel, it could also not easily turn around or coil tight enough for any long-range attack.

Opening its large jaw, revealing two rows of solid, conical teeth, it hissed loudly and reached for the nearest warrior, biting down on his shield. In that moment, Raez glimpsed fear in the creature's round, black eyes. Its quivering azure aura confirmed as much. Without hesitating further, Raez took three steps forward, his shield held up protectively, and drove his blade up through the center of the serpent's chin. The creature stiffened and writhed, pulling the sword from Raez's grip, and then collapsed. Raez watched it twitch for a moment longer, but seeing the point of his blade sticking up through the top of the serpent's head, knew it had been mortally wounded.

Though he felt his body ease with victory, the sight gave Raez no satisfaction. Instead, he felt sick as his brethren cheered and proceeded to hack the creature into pieces. Trying to ignore the sounds, including the serpent's abruptly quieted heartbeat, Raez turned away and walked out of the tunnel into the central courtyard of Süretuwam. Little light filled the space, but his keen eyes could discern the shapes of buildings and the movement of Young Brothers and other Thraz tending to the wounded.

The urge to breathe outside air and feel the expanse of space around him drove Raez to the Mountain of the Fallen. There, a half moon shone just above the western ridge, illuminating the mound of dead with pale blue.

The night felt bitterly cold.

Gazing at the faces of the fallen, he wondered, *Didst thou foresee this?* Stars filled the indigo sky. He thought of the gods. *Where art thou?*

Meandering to the eastern end of the dell, he sat and stared blankly at the jagged mountain silhouettes, trying to imagine what lay beyond those mountains.

Sometime later, a deep gentle voice interrupted the silence. "Thy thoughts are weighted with questions." Wrapped in his grey fur cloak, the Ezren sat down beside him.

"I am glad thou art safe," Raez said, glancing at the seer. "We would be lost without thee." A part of him still believed that. After all, the Ezren helped maintain the cognitive cohesion of the tribe.

"The time for my passing will come," the Ezren commented. "Thus it is for all."

"How many were lost tonight?" Raez asked, wanting to change the subject.

"Less than thou might expect. Most of the wounded will recover after care and rest." The Ezren exhaled slowly. "One of the Het hath been killed, however."

"I am sorry." Raez considered his lack of action to aid the acolyte.

"He proved himself unworthy," the Ezren stated, "his fate sealed when he abandoned the Wocron. More than this, the Aditám, your father, is enraged by the negligence of the gate wardens. It was reported that one abandoned his post before the serpent appeared. All four wardens shall be executed for waywardness, and their bodies discarded in the Valley of Bones."

"Enslavement by the gods awaits such failures," Raez muttered.

"Yes," the Ezren said softly. "Why hast thou come here alone?"

"I seek the voices of the gods," Raez replied.

"What doth thou hear?"

"Nothing but the stir of the wind."

After a pause: "And what doest thou see?"

"Little more than a dark landscape lit by the moon."

"Then there is much to hear and see," the Ezren said, looking out at the view.

Thinking of the slain acolyte, Raez had at first assumed that his motive had been to punish him for abandoning the Ezren, or the fact that he had been the one talking with Halïrez during the feast; yet Raez realized that there was another reason—something more personal. The gods decreed that there always be three Het serving the Ezren. The third would now have to be replaced, and Raez wanted to be the one to replace him, thereby stepping toward a future of his own choosing—closer to the Frynosoma, Voice of the Gods, and thereby closer to the gods themselves. "I wish to understand the truth behind such signs."

The Ezren placed an affirming hand on Raez's shoulder. "And so shalt thou."

"Let me serve thee as the third Het," Raez added, wanting his request to be clear.

The Ezren's smile faltered. "An intriguing but unusual prospect."

"Yet possible?"

With calculating eyes, the Ezren replied, "It shall be for the Spirits of Life to decide."

* * *

Züd paced the war room while Raez stood to the side, having just shared his intention to become the third Het.

"The future is at hand," the Ezren commented, standing in the middle of the room. His two surviving acolytes waited behind him, one with a broken arm in a splint. Both conveyed pale green auras, a persisting arrogance toward the Aditám and his surrogate son.

Days had passed since the attack. Repairs of Süretuwam's minor structural damage caused by the serpent were well underway. The wounded were being cared for, the honorable dead had been added to the Mountain of the Fallen, and the blamed wardens put to death. Afterward, the tribe had feasted on the flesh of the serpent, its freshly prepared skull presented to Raez by Züd as a reward.

"Thou art destined to be the next Aditám," Züd said to Raez, ignoring the Ezren. "Thy slaying of the serpent hath surely secured the confidence of the tribe. It must be a peaceful transition of power unlike any before, especially with warriors like Halïrez ready to challenge me—or you, if given the chance. Why sacrifice that with this foolish notion of becoming a Het?"

"Peace need not be sacrificed," Raez countered, though knew there could never be a peaceful transition as long as current Thraz traditions were maintained. After all, to become Aditám he would still have to overthrow his father, let alone contend with the likes of Halïrez. "I could establish a new legacy, become an Ezren Aditám, both warrior and sage. Consider the possibilities. Through me, the Frynosoma might birth a more powerful generation."

"That is much to ask of one Thraz," Züd murmured, running his fingers along his firm, scaly jawline, which culminated with a spiked protrusion at each side.

"Tis a grand vision," the Ezren added, "but that matters not. Raez is too old, and the time for the Het to stand before the Frynosoma is fast approaching." He addressed Raez: "The Spirits of Life have already directed thy purpose. I know thee to be different from the other Thraz; since thy rise as a Solep, after thy father's first Amplexus, thy strength, resilience, and awareness have set thee apart for unique deeds. When the time comes, thou shalt lead the Thraz well. Yet, the choice of Het, let alone Ezren, is not so simple as a matter of individual will."

"And what of thy will?" Raez asked. "Is it already set?"

"My will matters not," the Ezren replied, "but that of the Spirits of Life. What thou asks is impossible."

Impossible to the gods, or impractical to thee? The swift response to Raez's request raised doubts in his mind as to whether the gods had even been approached on the matter. The way forward seemed so clear to him; the

Ezren and Aditám's imaginations were just too limited to grasp it. Granted, he was pushing for an aggressive change in a short amount of time, but had the Ezren himself not warned about an impending threat? What if the failure to act on Raez's sense of divine prompting made the tribe more vulnerable to that threat? Or was the failure to act the threat itself? Either way, now was the time for action. The gods could be testing Raez's resolve. For the sake of the Thraz, a change had to be made.

* * *

When the Ezren announced that no one had been chosen to replace the fallen Het, many Thraz were surprised, but all trusted his word—all but Raez. Not wishing to displease Züd further, or to stir confusion among the ranks of warriors who looked to Raez as the future Aditám, Raez did not share his thoughts with anyone else, and determined that he would no longer confide in the Ezren. If the seer could not be entirely trusted, being part of the threat to the future of the Thraz, Raez would look to the gods directly. Surely, they would honor his faithful intent.

Nights later, he crept down the entrance tunnel of the Wocron, evading the guards. If caught in the inner sanctum ahead, he could be executed; but there was only one way forward—the gods drew him thus. He had to find a way to reach the Frynosoma, for she could provide some of the answers he sought. Soon, the Ezren would bring the Het to her, and Raez would follow.

Leaving the tunnel, he entered the outer sanctum of the Wocron, and gazed up at its mighty tree. The Wocron was less a cave and more a space hollowed out around the tree's gnarled root system clinging to every side of the cavern, carefully reinforced by stones. The top of the tree reached a hundred feet high through a gap in the cavern ceiling that showed a starry night sky.

A shallow stream trickled out from the left side of the chamber, and continued right into the earth. The water provided the Thraz a minimal source of drink. The brothers showed respect to the gods by leaving small gifts along the stream's banks, but that was as close as they could come to the tree. Not even the Aditám was permitted across the stream inside the inner sanctum. The Wocron was a sacred place of meditation, and thought to be a tangible threshold of the Span.

Carefully, Raez leapt across the stream and navigated the unfamiliar passageways of the tree, following the reverberations of a single voice. Eventually, a small hole in a wall of dense roots revealed what he presumed to be the main, innermost chamber of the Wocron. There, the two acolytes sat cross-legged before the Ezren.

"Tis important to recall a whisper of what has passed before we turn our gaze to what is to come," the Ezren was saying. "Each of thee"—he closed his eyes and inhaled slowly—"gather thy thoughts into a cluster."

In the silence that followed, Raez waited intently.

The Ezren proceeded: "Now place that cluster onto a space before thyself, focusing instead on the air enriching thy blood with every breath."

Raez concentrated on his own breathing, relaxing his limbs, feeling the tension in his body disperse. If this activity was necessary before facing the Frynosoma, he would be ready.

"Remember," the Ezren said, "this meditation can protect thee and those in thy proximity from the chaos of the external, to find root in each day. Now . . . open thine eyes."

Raez focused on the dark gaze of the seer.

"Before I became Ezren, I was called Antha. Until the next Thraz Ezren is declared, the fourth of our tribe's history, ye shall not utter my true name beyond these walls. At that time, I will withdraw from the world and return to my original identity. But first, and soon, ye will be brought to the Frynosoma to begin thy holy quest. I do not know what vision the Spirits of Life will offer each of thee through her, but trust that what they show is meant to guide not only thy purpose, but the future of the tribe.

"Ye have heard it said that only one Het returns to his tribe to assume the role of Ezren, whilst the others are slain. That is not always true, though a Het who returns having failed to fulfill his quest will certainly be killed. Some, however, simply choose not to return. In my own journey, for example, before I returned to Süretuwam, I stumbled upon an old Het living high in the mountains. Wrapped in heavy furs, he studied the stars and the movement of the earth, and toldeth me that one of the Spirits of Life kept him warm. He said little else, but for many days I sat with him and learned the gift of silence."

"In thy quests," the Ezren continued, "ye shall seek a sign from the Spirits of Life. I cannot speak to the nature of what each of thee wilt see or find, but thou shall discern it when tis revealed. Mine was the first Thraz encounter with the Dwarves—a lone warrior dressed in shining armor, carrying strange weapons. The Ezren before me, Häbe, brought back the seed of a great tree from the west, which he planted here, letting it grow into the Wocron. Each sign not only brings thee into closer communion with the Spirits of Life but enhances the future of the tribe. The Ezren is above all a servant, directing his people toward new horizons. The lives of your brothers depend on it."

And to what horizon doth thou bring us, seer? Raez thought, once again eager to find the Frynosoma.

4

The Voice of the Gods

In the dark before sunrise, Raez carefully followed the Ezren and his two acolytes from the Wocron. The Ezren had blindfolded the other two, loosely tying them together in a line at the waist, to be led at last to the Frynosoma.

"This is the last ye shall gaze upon each other," the seer explained to the Het, as he secured the line. "Remove not the blindfold until instructed to do so. The one whom the Spirits of Life choose to replace me as Ezren will learn the truth of the Frynosoma's dwelling, but no other. Until that declaration, each of thee shalt walk by faith and not sight. Thus, we begin."

A stairway had been fashioned around the trunk of the Wocron Tree, accessible from the main inner chamber by a passageway between the roots. It led them up out of the cavern to the open air where a narrow path wound high along the steep canyon that divided the eastern end of the mountain under which Süretuwam existed and the next mountain.

There, Raez was glad to discover that he was still within cognitive range of Ornithez, resting at home within Süretuwam. Keeping a safe distance from the Ezren and his acolytes, Raez connected with the vulture and guided him to his position. Not knowing where the seer was leading them exactly, where the Frynosoma dwelt, Raez felt better having another set of eyes to help monitor his surroundings. For now, he kept the bird perched on his shoulder.

They walked north for hours along a gradually rising path, reached a windy height on the mountainside, and then descended to another canyon. Walking on all fours, Raez felt the grit of dry earth against his hands and feet, heard the soft crunch of each step. The crisp aroma of sage enlivened his nostrils. At the bottom of the second canyon, which had brought them eastward, he slowed, mindful of how his footsteps echoed off the rocky cliffs. Soon after climbing out of the canyon, the Ezren proceeded for a few hours through the cool, hushed darkness of a tunnel. Raez wondered when it had been made, for it was not part of the network used to venture east against the Dwarves. Leaving the tunnel, his sense of direction temporarily disoriented, Raez welcomed the heat of the sun on his scaly skin. The mountains were far colder than the desert, but so far the insulation of his bearskin cloak kept him warm enough. He hoped their journey would not lead to the snowcapped peaks visible over the next set of rises. One peak looked familiar, like one observable from the Mountain of the Fallen. Had they returned south, closer once more to Süretuwam?

More so, he wondered if he was ready for what was to come. The other Het had spent their lives with the Ezren, preparing for this day and the prospect of leading the Thraz as the Hand of the Gods. *Hath my fervor been premature?*

Scaling a steep rocky way, the Ezren's progress slowed while he had to tell each acolyte where to step and hold. As he did so, dusk darkened the landscape. The air cooled, and wind stirred more frequently. Using Ornithez's sight, noting that the three others had stopped on a ledge facing the mouth of a cave, Raez climbed to the right as far as he could before continuing his ascent. Ornithez helped him spot a level cluster of boulders where Raez could be close enough to hear and observe the Ezren, while also remaining concealed.

"Ye have reached the Threshold of Thraz," the seer said, his voice raised against the wind. He guided each blindfolded Het to sit. "Each of thee, in turn, will be brought before the Frynosoma to hear from the Spirits of Life. Ye are the gifted two. Soon, the veil will be removed from thine eyes, enabling ye to see anew. Be reverent but attentive, humble but bold. Such traits will help guide ye to thy quests' ends. Yet, only one of ye wilt rise as the next Ezren—if the Spirits of Life will it."

The seer led the first Het into to the cave, while the second remained outside.

Hours passed.

Reclined against a rock, wrapped in his bearskin cloak, weariness crept into Raez's consciousness, drawing him into sleep.

I cannot see. The ground is so bright—glimmering like a star-covered plain. It even moves, rocking me to and fro; I struggle to find balance in its rhythm.

Looking down, I realize the earth is transparent. There is movement beneath. Filling the murky depths, white Thraz skeletons crawl through the blackness. They look up and reach for me with bony fingers.

The troubling mood of Raez's vision lingered with him throughout the next day. In the morning, the second Het was taken away by the Ezren, leaving Raez alone to the quiet of the nameless mountainside. What had happened to the first acolyte, he could not say. An instinct told him that it was too soon to follow. Should he wait for the Ezren to return from the cave and go back to Süretuwam? What if the seer did not return? How long should Raez wait before entering—another day, a week?

He did not mind the waiting, but wished to rid himself of the images of the dead. It deepened his resolve to find another way forward for his people—that which readily gave life instead of death. He thought once more of Oceanus, the idea of an endless expanse—water, the essence of being.

The scarcity of water divides us, he mused, unable to count how many battles had been fought merely to secure a source of drink. *What if we all had it in abundance?* Could that not bring the tribes together? Could it not strengthen them against any greater threat?

What did the Frynosoma know?

Floating up from the ground, I approach the stars. They art countless, twinkling. Radiant forms like illuminated clouds of sand—the hands of the gods—caress the greater celestial shapes: warming, cooling, and setting them into motion. The depths beyond such nebulae art blue like sapphire. So much color and light, and yet my heart lies heavy in mine chest.

Why? Why doth emptiness accompany such vast beauty? What do I not see? What should I do?

With his thoughts still spinning from yet another vision, Raez rose and discovered that the Ezren had returned. The half light of the clouded sky made it difficult to determine whether it was the start or end of another day.

The seer was not alone. Three pale warriors stood before him, their scent smoky with hostility. Raez did not recognize them and, thinking they were from another tribe come to harm the Ezren, was about to intervene when he quickly realized the seer was talking to them.

"There hath been no trouble, then?" the Ezren asked the leader of the three.

"None, my lord. The first hath already been resettled." The leader's voice was unusually high for a Thraz.

"Good," the Ezren commented. "Thy loyalty will be honored by the Spirits of Life."

"What of this life?" the pale leader asked. "Must we toil only for some future paradise?"

"All is coming into place as intended," the seer replied. "Continue to fulfill thy charge, and soon ye may return to Süretuwam."

The pale warriors departed, making their way north along the cliff, away from the cave and Raez's position. Not long after, the Ezren descended the way he had originally come with the Het—from Süretuwam in the west. None but the Ezren and Aditám were permitted access to the Frynosoma's sanctum. What were the pale warriors doing there, and who had they resettled? If the Frynosoma had been hurt, Raez resolved to personally tear out the Ezren's bowels. The three pale warriors were a problem, but less of an immediate concern than the wellbeing of Thraz. He could follow them, but decided to first see what had become of the Voice of the Gods.

"Stay near," he instructed Ornithez. "I will return."

The vulture launched from Raez's shoulder and glided up with a draft out of sight.

Focusing ahead, Raez entered the cave. The sound of the wind withdrew immediately, while the echo of his feet on rock grew louder. Utter darkness settled over Raez's perception. The air warmed. A faint golden glow began to shine ahead, drawing him forward.

That which is invisible can come to be seen, a whisper caressed his thoughts, *the given received back with new meaning. Thus shall a gift reveal its true power.*

I do not understand, Raez thought.

Patience, Raez Het, the voice replied. *Soon shalt thou see with new eyes.*

Encouraged by the voice acknowledging him as a Het, Raez pressed ahead. He did not know how long or far he ventured deeper underground, but eventually felt lost in silent blackness. The golden glow had vanished. On all fours, he carefully shuffled forward until he caught the sound of dripping water somewhere ahead, its resonance suggesting a large cavern. Moisture filled the air, carrying a strong earthy scent—a hint of flowers, but also moss and fungi.

Something stirred nearby, like the clatter of many bones.

"You are bold to enter here, my son," a soothing voice echoed around Raez, startling him. Its timbre was lighter and yet more commanding than any he had ever heard.

"Who art thou?" he asked.

"You know who I am," she replied.

The Frynosoma, Voice of the Gods. He had found her at last.

"Why have you come?" she asked.

"To know the gods and convey their will," Raez replied without hesitation.

"To be the Hand of the Gods is to be the wisest and most powerful of your tribe," the Frynosoma said. "To do so, you must first embrace that which seems most foolish and frail."

Raez dared not move.

"Do you know of what I speak?" the voice pressed.

Raez considered all that he had witnessed and learned. "Does it begin with questions and doubt?"

"Go on."

He thought about the Ezren's missing forearm. "Is there also sacrifice?"

The bones clattered softly once again. "Open your eyes, Raez Het," the voice said, "and look upon your beginning."

He concentrated ahead, and soon the darkness withdrew like a curtain. Before him were many small pools. Light shone from within each emerald depth, softly illuminating the tan walls of a large cave. Beyond the pools, a creature like Raez, but twice his size, materialized from the shadows: Thraz, mother of the tribe. Four horns protruded from the back of her head. Standing on her hind legs, she wore a heavy robe of rib bones decorated with dried flowers, and upon her head sat an ornate crown made from a coiled spine. He could detect neither her smell nor aura in that place. Even her heartbeat was difficult to discern, absorbing echoes in the cave like the slow gusts of a soothing wind. She was unlike anything he had ever encountered, stirring vague sensations like those associated with falling asleep or waking—calm, warm, mind full of memories: rising from a watery depth, crossing a desert plain, hunting in the mountains, friends, enemies, hopes, uncertainties.

Two pairs of round black eyes observed him. "Come closer," she said, indicating a way between the pools.

Raez obeyed and followed the Frynosoma to a small chamber lit by blue glowworms. She sat on a throne, its back decorated with Thraz forearm bones and hands. Blood still stained the surface of two forearms, one set at each side of the throne's back.

"Do you know what must be done?" she asked.

"The Het is destined to undertake a journey to prove himself worthy," Raez replied, "and return with a sign of the gods' favor."

"Yes," the Frynosoma said, smiling. "First you must sacrifice a portion of your past, returning it to the origin of your life." She brought her face close to his and lowered her voice. "Do you trust me, Het?"

For a moment, Raez hesitated. Mentally, he could acknowledge that the Frynosoma was his mother, and comprehended a kind of connection therein, but at the same time he felt distant from her. After all, she had been little more than a mythic idea all his life.

"What are you waiting for?" she asked, smiling, showing her sharp teeth.

"What must I do?"

She pointed to his right arm. "Sacrifice your assurance."

His stomach sank. "How?"

The Frynosoma brought forth a black knife, its blade long and wide. "To become the Hand of the Gods, you must entrust yourself to their hands."

Raez took the knife and stared at his right forearm, thinking about the Ezren's missing right forearm. Noticing a flat, bloodstained stone next to him, he placed his right arm on it. His heart began to pound as he positioned the blade just below the elbow where the joint was softest. Trying to control his breathing, he glanced back at the Frynosoma.

She nodded slowly. "When you are ready."

The given can be received back with new meaning, a voice in his head whispered. *Walk by faith.*

His heart beating furiously, Raez began to sweat. Gritting his teeth, fighting back nausea, Raez gripped the knife hilt tighter, shifted his eyes away from his arm, and pressed down as hard as he could.

He was surprised by the lack of resistance, the ease with which the blade cut through his limb. *Unnatural,* he thought with some relief, but then felt a surge of pain coursing up his arm, overwhelming his senses. He pressed his bleeding elbow against his stomach, trying to slow the blood and distract himself from the agony. Vision blurring, he leaned against the cutting stone and shakily lifted his severed right forearm as an offering to his mother. She took it and bit into the flesh.

Wanting to shut out the sound of the meat ripping, Raez cradled his elbow with his left hand. The room began to shift unsteadily, out of control, faster and faster until he collapsed.

Darkness dissolveth into white light.

A shining figure standeth before me, alike to me in form, but translucent as golden clouds of sunset. His eyes are black like the night sky speckled with stars. He smileth at me, beckoning me forth with a gesture of his hand while his other pointeth toward a vast churning landscape.

"Oceanus," the figure says, his voice like the rumbling roar of the waves below. "It waiteth for thee."

"Where?" I ask.

"Cross the mountains to the east," the figure states, "and I will show thee the way."

"And when I reach Oceanus?"

"What dost thou desire?" the figure asks.

"An understanding mind to lead my people," I answer after some thought, "to discern between good and evil."

Something is behind me. Looking over my shoulder, I see menacing black smoke billowing from the ground. White shapes crawl within the darkness—bony apparitions of the fallen.

"There is little time," the figure says, coming next to me on my right, "but thou wilt not face the future alone."

A glow below my periphery catches my attention. Glancing down, I see that my right forearm hath been restored, only now translucent with bronze light.

The smoke hath nearly reached me.

The Frynosoma standeth at my left. "Resist the darkness and it will flee from you."

I brace myself, widening my stance, and press my palm against the wall of dark soot.

Swirling shadows withdrew as Raez opened his eyes. At first, he could not tell what he was looking at or where he was. Dim blue light filled his vision, and then a vaguely familiar face.

"Can you hear me, Raez Het?" Thraz, the Frynosoma, asked. Blood dripped from her lips and jaw.

After staring at her for a while longer, he mumbled, "Yes."

He reached up to rub his eyes and was shocked at the absence of his right hand.

"The fog will fade," Thraz said, leaning back. A freshly cleaned arm adorned her throne. "You have overcome the most difficult task. That which you have given has been returned in greater form." She pointed to his right forearm.

Sitting up and looking at his limb once again, he saw the same glowing forearm as in his vision. Moving it felt normal enough, yet when he reached for it with his left hand, he could feel nothing.

"You have touched the Span," the Frynosoma said. "Your arm will never again be what it once was, and it will take time to get used to having that part of yourself connected to the unseen world. You now hold the power to serve as the Hand of the Gods. Fulfillment of your quest will prove whether you are worthy of such a gift."

"Didst thou see what I saw?" Raez asked.

The Frynosoma nodded.

"What figure was that?"

"The Spirits of Life can assume different forms, but I discern that was Ekrath Namor who stewards the Northern Mountains. It is through him that I comprehend the mysteries of the Span."

"Ekrath Namor is one of the gods?"

"He is," Thraz replied, smiling.

"I understandeth not why the gods remain so distant," Raez said. "If they wish us to fulfill their will, why not show themselves in the flesh, and address us more directly?"

"They do so to honor our freedom to follow or not," she replied, "yet also to preserve our sanity, for the mortal mind is limited. Most of us can only gradually learn to see beyond this tangible plane to the fullness of the Span. You have been given new eyes, Raez Het, but the extent of your sight will take time to focus, as with the power of your right arm to touch the immaterial fabric of this world. Moreover, be wary. There are those in the Span who abandoned their roles long ago, who resist the will of the Spirits of Life. Rogue entities can look akin to the spirits who have remained faithful."

"How am I to distinguish betwixt the two?"

"You have keen insight, Raez Het. Trust it. Your brothers will need that to survive the coming threat."

Another indirect answer. "What of all the tribes?" Raez asked. "Can they be united? What of their Frynosomas?"

"Long have I anticipated the new age," Thraz replied. "Whether it will be built on the preservation of the current age or rise from its ruin, I do not know. The groans of my sisters can already be heard. Destruction has begun, and the Thraz are not strong enough to resist its power alone. You are a harbinger of what could be, but is not yet certain, Raez Het. Succeed in your quest, and you could be the one to establish a lasting future. Yet, know that by following such a course you also choose to abandon Züd, your father. Without a ready successor, his enemies will be emboldened."

A pang of guilt shuddered through Raez. Had he left Süretuwam too hastily? "What of the current Ezren? Is he a foe?"

"Each mover fosters his own vision for the good of the tribe," Thraz said, "which outcome is best will be determined by the Spirits of Life. Aspects of their will elude even me."

"Am I in error pursuing the gods in this way?" Raez pressed. The path forward suddenly felt so uncertain.

"It is not a matter of right or wrong, but a conscious choice. Every choice bears consequences, for ill or good."

I have come so far already. Too much had been sacrificed. Because the Ezren had already spoken on behalf of the gods against Raez's appointment as the third Het, the seer could simply deny the legitimacy of Raez's claim as a Het. Raez would also be readily condemned for having discovered the way to the Frynosoma's sanctum before being named Aditám or Ezren. He wondered if waiting to succeed Züd would have been wiser, for at least as Aditám he had lawful access to the Frynosoma.

It matters not, now, he realized. He had made his choice, and the gods had recognized it. In embracing the identity of a Het, giving his right forearm to Thraz, Raez could not go back to his tribe without having fulfilled his quest. Thus, all immediate routes back to Süretuwam led to death. He could do nothing more for his surrogate father except pray that he survive the maneuverings of all challengers.

Forgive me, he thought.

"Time is precious," Thraz commented. "You must go."

5

Torn

The Frynosoma showed Raez a different way out of her lair. Exhausted by his ordeal in her sanctum, stepping out from its warm shelter to the side of a windy ridge shook him back to alertness. More jarring was the flurry of heightened sensory details: small snowflakes whirled around him, cold and glowing like star beetles, their moisture tickling his skin; or the soft, churning texture of the clouds, and the deep rumbling of rock plates far beneath the earth. He closed his eyes, trying to focus on his breath alone, his thudding heart, slowing, steady, strong.

Drawing his cloak tighter against the chill required more concentration and fumbling than he anticipated, for his glowing right hand was gone, reduced to a stub above where his elbow had been. *Damn.* Not only would he have to adjust to the missing limb, but learn to control the plethora of external information barraging his senses like never before. *Gifts from the gods,* he mused, frustrated by their persistently indirect and unexplained manner of engagement.

Extending his thoughts toward Ornithez took longer than normal, but he was relieved to find that the vulture was not far. Connecting to the bird's vision, Raez saw that the storm dissipated not far to the south. From that vantage point, the sun could be seen rising above the eastern horizon. Identifying it oriented him to his position and the direction he must go.

"Cross the mountains to the east," the god had said in his vision.

South on the ridge, lower down its eastern slope lit by brightening sunlight, he spotted movement. Still connected to Ornithez, Raez directed the vulture to circle back for another look. There, he saw the three pale warriors from days earlier. They stood close together, looking over the body of the second Het who had entered the cave. One warrior held a bloodied black sword, wiping it with a dirty brown cloth. The other two warriors lifted the body and began to carry it eastward down the mountain.

If the first Het had met the same end, leaving none to return to Süretuwam, the Thraz would assume that the gods had rejected each as a successor. New ones would be chosen, starting the cycle all over again, for as long as the Ezren decreed it necessary—according to the gods, of course. Why would the seer have the Het secretly killed if not to ensure the preservation of his power?

Villain.

Though weakened from the loss of his right arm, Raez would not let this affront go unpunished. Rage churned within him, reinvigorating some of his strength. He disconnected from Ornithez and strode forward, but then immediately stumbled without the use of his right forearm. Cursing, he stood on his hind legs, which, though slower, gave him a sense of familiar stability. With his left hand, he seized a large rock and then proceeded.

His mind reached out to Ornithez: *Be ready.*

He ran along the crest of the ridge with increasing speed, feeling remarkably fluid as he did so, and when above and perpendicular to the position of the departing pale warriors, turned left to charge downhill into their flank. The leader with the sword, walking at the back, noticed Raez's approach when he was three strides away, but it was too late. Raez leapt and kicked him in the center of his chest, knocking him roughly into the other two. Dropping the body of the Het, the warrior to the right managed to catch his fall with his arms; but as he prepared to rise, Raez slammed the rock down hard upon his right eye. The impact was met with a crack and grunt. The warrior pressed his hand against the bloodied remains of his eye and writhed in pain.

Raez regained his footing and stepped back just in time to avoid a slice from the leader's blade. Raez threw the rock at the other's face and, as the leader blocked it with the lower end of his sword, came closer. Keeping the pommel of the sword away with his scaly stub of a right arm, Raez used his momentum to drive the leader to the ground. Enduring the leader's right-handed punches to his ribs, Raez focused solely on reaching his neck, just managing—as he was losing the initiative—to tear the other's throat out with the claws of his left hand.

As the leader tensed, grasping at his neck, blood spraying all over Raez's face and left hand, a blow against his right shoulder sent him spinning sideways to the left. Without the aid of his right hand, he hit the ground harder than intended. He turned to see the third warrior lifting his battle hammer for another strike when Ornithez swooped down and gouged out his eyes with its talons. Raez quickly rose to a crouched position, retrieved the leader's abandoned sword, and drove it through the other's unprotected stomach.

With two of the pale warriors dying on the ground, Raez returned his attention to the third who now stumbled away half blind and whimpering. Heading south along the ridge, the warrior had already managed to put a good distance between them, but his course appeared unsteady, putrid with fear. Raez would catch him easily; and when he did, questions would have to be answered before the warrior was permitted to die.

Keeping the sword at hand, Raez began to follow the last pale warrior when a large winged mass swooped down from a rocky prominence at the far end of the ridge and plucked the warrior off the ground. The warrior's shriek echoed across the mountainside as the giant eagle secured its grip, ascended, and flew southward around the outcrop. Alert to new danger, Raez hastily scanned the sky and, spotting the silhouette of another gliding eagle high above, crouched as low as he could, retreated a few steps to the bodies of the slain, and exchanged his sword to use the leader's twitching form as a shield. The eagle dove toward Raez, and yanked the corpse violently from his grasp.

Seeing the bird ascend with its prey in its clutches, and having quickly confirmed that no other predators were gliding about, Raez ran as fast he could further down the ridge to the shelter of the nearby trees where Ornithez had already taken refuge.

Though he had been unable to learn more from the pale warriors, Raez felt certain about his initial assessment. Nonetheless, he chided himself for not asking the Frynosoma about the pale warriors, wondering if she had known about them. What if she and the Ezren were in league with one another, together manipulating the tribe's understanding about the gods' will? No, the Ezren had to be acting alone. Raez could not accept that Thraz herself was involved.

He did not know what the Ezren intended for the future, but could expose his treachery to Züd and the rest of the tribe. Yet, doing so now would also stir immense chaos. The tribe relied upon the leadership of the Ezren, and was not ready for such a drastic measure without clear evidence from the gods who they feared most. Only when Raez was strong enough, and not before his quest was fulfilled, could he return to challenge the seer.

Raez felt more isolated and vulnerable than ever before. To trust the gods felt like his only foundation. Recalling the vision of his glowing right arm in the Frynosoma's sanctum gave him some hope, but since leaving the cave the arm had vanished.

I have much to learn, he thought dourly, stroking Ornithez's feathered chest with the knuckle of his left forefinger. *And far to go.*

6

Harbinger

For days, the vision of Oceanus permeated Raez's thoughts and nightly visions. Assuming he could reach such a place, he wondered if it would be the end of his quest or only the beginning, and what kind of sign the gods might provide. The Frynosoma had suggested that Raez held the means to unite the tribes against a looming threat. He wanted to see his brethren joined in strength, but achieving such a goal began to feel both lofty and intangible. Who was he to bring about such outcomes?

Change begins with me, he reasoned, *and dissociating violence from strength.*

He, therefore, began to saw off his horns and file down his claws and the spikes protruding from his face and shoulders—anywhere he could reach. Using the rock of his environment, fashioning a piece into a jagged blade and another into a rough file, he slowly made progress. No more would he present and define himself merely as a warrior. He had to be more. The idea of an Ezren Aditám continued to intrigue his imagination.

He missed his right hand, recognizing how much he had taken having two hands for granted. At times, especially while resting, he even forgot its absence. The ghost of half his right arm haunted not only his body, but his mind. In sleep, the arm's bright replacement plagued his sense of possibility, while waking without it felt like a mockery.

For a week, he navigated his way through the mountains without a specific trail to guide him. Instead, aided by Ornithez's aerial sight, Raez found his own routes down steep cliffs, across deep canyons, and over high passes, all the while maintaining an easterly course. He came to rely more on his feet and legs, adjusting his center of mass accordingly, building a new level of strength in his left arm while figuring out uses for what remained of his right.

"Cross the mountains to the east," the god had said, "and I will show you the way."

The unknown beckoned him onward.

Time will yield clarity. Alone in the mountains, unsure of what awaited him on the other side, the mantra sometimes felt like a meager attempt to sustain his resolve. Would time indeed yield clarity? Glancing down at his missing right forearm, he reminded himself that he had stood before the Frynosoma and encountered the gods in a vivid way; that change was happening. He had but to remain patient and attentive.

Time will yield clarity.

* * *

He could not remember how long it had been since he had last felt rain. Welcoming the sensation, drinking in the cool moisture, he nonetheless shivered against the damp cold. Once soaked through, his black bearskin cloak did little to ward off the chilling mountain winds.

As the early light of a new day revealed a grey, misty landscape, Raez glimpsed a vast green land beyond the mountain peaks. He followed a ridgeline, staying in the shadows of rocks below its apex to avoid providing an obvious target to predators, especially giant eagles. Movement in the canyon down to his left caught his attention.

Stopping, he crouched low and observed a hundred warriors emerging from a hole beneath a rocky overhang. Raez recognized their chieftain. They were not Thraz, but the Hysmïnai Tribe. The Hysmïnai contingent separated into three contingents. The smallest, comprised of only five warriors, went eastward along a creek cutting through the canyon floor. The largest contingent moved north, apparently following a narrow trail up around the mountainside, while the third contingent disappeared into another cave across the creek to the south, which presumably delved through the mountain upon which Raez watched.

He decided to follow the first, paralleling the canyon creek.

An hour later, the mountainous terrain opened to a rocky crest, the end of which dropped steeply to woodlands and a grassy plain. Using Ornithez's vision for a fuller perspective, Raez had never seen so much green. The sight and scent of damp earth and vegetation renewed his spirit in a way he had not thought possible. Disconnecting from the vulture, Raez focused on his immediate surroundings. Nearly a thousand feet below him was a small brown meadow full of grazing tzëg with curved horns and long grey fur. He had never seen so many of the creatures gathered together in one place. He relished the clapping of their hooves on rock and the friendly bleating of their calls. Spotting a few Dwarves tending to the herd, Raez lowered himself onto his stomach amidst a cluster of boulders near the edge of the cliff. He recognized the Dwarves because a few prisoners had been brought back after Thraz raids over the years. They were difficult to capture and not as flavorful as other game, but were prized for their distinct armor and weapons.

The five Hysmïnai that Raez had been following approached the unsuspecting herd. A glint in Raez's periphery to the right drew his attention to an armed host of Dwarves concealed behind a rocky escarpment at the eastern end of the meadow. An ambush? Though the Hysmïnai were not of his tribe, they were still his brethren by race. The path toward unification began by recognizing that. He had to warn them.

Before he could act, the five Hysmïnai attacked the herd. Soon after, a large eagle swooped down over the field, startling Raez with how close it had been perched to his position. A figure rode atop the eagle, but Raez could not tell what kind of person it was—the rider looked too tall and slender to be a Dwarf. Moments later a unit of Dwarves mounted on rel surged down the mountainside against the flank of the Hysmïnai skirmishers. Meanwhile, the eagle circled above, its rider shooting arrows down at Raez's brethren.

His stomach tightened. Instincts pressed him to descend and fight alongside his people, but he wavered as a horn reverberated from the forest to the north. Relief washed over Raez as, after some confusion among the ranks of Dwarves, the largest contingent of Hysmïnai emerged from the forest and scattered the enemy like wind blowing sand. The third contingent also appeared, except from a gully to the northwest. Combined, the two contingents provided an admirable pincer assault. Surely, the battle had been turned, for the Dwarves could not defeat so formidable a host of Hysmïnai.

The feeling of a glorious, imminent victory soon faltered, however. Recalling the Thraz battle against the Pa'dëm, Raez pondered the point of such conflict—a few more meals, tribal pride, expanded borders?

Ornithez swooped down and landed on his shoulder.

"What do you see?" a voice startled Raez's attention.

He turned around to find a small brown sparrow perched on a rock, studying him. The creature was no common bird, for it emitted a faint white light. Moreover, Raez could not smell it, nor detect the rhythm of its heart. It seemed more an extension of the landscape—the shudder of rock, the whisper of grass, the hush of the breeze.

"Thou speakest my language," Raez said in disbelief.

"Yes," the sparrow replied with a bright, friendly tone. "I know all manner of speech. I have spoken with your companion here, Ornithez."

"Art thou a messenger of the gods?"

The sparrow tilted its head curiously. "This is a dangerous place for you."

"What dost thou mean?"

"Flee," the sparrow said urgently, darting to the right.

Following its flight, Raez's heart shuddered at the sight of the giant eagle flying toward him.

Go, he urged Ornithez.

As the vulture took flight, Raez ran low on his three good limbs away from the cliff, dashing around and over rocks toward the shelter of a deepening canyon to the south. With his third eye, he sensed the eagle almost on top of him and promptly ducked. Something pinched the back of his knee as the eagle passed, causing Raez to stagger. Glancing back, he saw an arrow jutting out, lodged in one of his scales. He pulled it out with his left hand and continued to run on his hind legs as best as he could.

Ahead, the eagle turned back toward him. Gaining speed, with its wings straight, its rider bent close over the bird's back, Raez guessed what would happen next. Once again, he lowered himself as close to the ground as possible. If it had been sand, he could burrow into it for added protection and concealment, yet this was stone.

The eagle lifted its wings, slowing, and extended its large talons. All the while its aura glowed bronze like sunlit desert sand, full of courage. The flutter of each feather resounded in Raez's ears. Its pulsating heartbeats struck at his nerve to keep his eyes fixed on the rapidly approaching predator.

I will not die here.

At the last moment, Raez rose on his hind legs and bloated his body. The talons caught him awkwardly in the chest, and struggled to maintain a steady grip as the eagle fought to gain back elevation.

Still, it managed to pull Raez off the ground. "Release me," he growled. Hoping to deescalate the situation, perhaps by reasoning with the rider, he shouted, "I am not for war."

The eagle's talons tightened, digging into Raez's ribs. Clenching his teeth, he hissed in pain. He had no weapon or sharp claws with which to further discourage the eagle, leaving him once again doubting his choices. Looking down, his desperation increased as the landscape dropped over a thousand feet to the carnage of the meadow below.

Raez punched his left fist up into the eagle's chest, but in response it tightened its hold around his torso. He then seized one of the bird's talons with his left hand, trying to both lift himself up and prevent the talon from digging any deeper. With his face near the creature's chest, not knowing what else to do, realizing he at least still had his mouth, Raez bit away a layer of feathers, spit them out, and then continued to bite until his sharp teeth found the bird's flesh.

The eagle cried out. A wing went limp while the other flapped to keep itself upright. Still, the talons held Raez fast. His vision blurred as they spun toward the ground below, faster and faster.

A brown sparrow rushed past him, and then another one. Light grew in Raez's periphery. Looking over, he saw the original bird glowing gold with undulations of white and red underneath. "Do not be afraid," it said with an airy voice.

Yes, this had to be one of the gods.

Warm air rushed up as if harnessed by the sparrow's flapping wings. The speed of their fall slowed, though not entirely. Raez braced himself for impact and felt air burst from his chest as he struck the ground. Stars flickered before his eyes. Darkness swirled around him, burning his nostrils like smoke. Different whispering voices battered his mind: *Fear. Flee. Fight. Fear. Flee. Fight.*

He was not sure how long he lay there partially underneath the eagle's weight, but as he regained full consciousness and tried to move, he found that his legs were pinned. Able to sit up, he saw the eagle's rider slouched forward limply, facedown. The eagle itself was still awake, but its eyes struggled to focus. It nipped at Raez's face, but the effort was weak. Raez knocked the beak aside with the stub of his right arm, and then struck it on the side of the head with his left fist until the bird quieted.

Feeling the eagle's talons finally ease from his torso, Raez crawled out from underneath and rose on his hind legs. Checking himself, he was surprised to find nothing more than superficial damage—mainly scratches and a few shallow punctures from the eagle's talons. He stood at the edge of the battlefield. As he spotted armed Dwarves swiftly approaching his position, their auras blazing with rage like the hot midday sun, the voices returned: *Fear. Flee. Fight. Fear. Flee. Fight.*

Raez considered resisting. A spear lay on the ground within reach, and the initial rush of Dwarves could be easily beaten.

"No," a voice urged. The first sparrow, returned to its normal form, landed on the back of the eagle rider's helm. "Be at peace," it urged, "and be not afraid."

The Dwarves surrounded Raez and readied their weapons against him. The leader wore armor made from the hide of one of Raez's brethren. He said something, but Raez did not understand.

Hissing a warning at the soldiers, Raez's eyes shifted back to the sparrow. "Is not this a moment of slay or be slain?" He would not let himself be captured and eaten, and wanted to at least make short work of the Dwarf leader.

"This is not the end," the sparrow replied.

The Dwarves tightened their circle as well as the hold of their weapons.

"How not?" Raez asked.

"I can help you," the sparrow said.

At that moment, it expanded its size once again, only this time transforming into the radiant form of a Thraz—not of flesh, but a softer, more transparent essence like the shadow of a Thraz. To Raez, this was the figure witnessed in his vision. This was the god calling him toward Oceanus.

"Art thou Ekrath Namor?" Raez asked, thinking of his vision in the Frynosoma's cave.

"I am called Thian Darhe," the god said, smiling warmly while gazing at Raez's right arm. "You have a gift."

Looking down, Raez realized that his right arm had returned, glowing bronze once more.

The god continued to smile. "Yes."

Was this some kind of test? The smile seemed genuine, yet what control did the god have over the vengeful Dwarves now only two steps away? Moreover, the Dwarves seemed to only focus on Raez. Could they not see the bright being also standing before them?

"There is much we might discover together," the god said. "These people will not stand in the way for long."

Uncertain, but wanting to demonstrate strength as faithfulness to the gods—to the path set before him—Raez extended his arms and hands to indicate compliance. While most of the Dwarves kept the tips of their weapons pointed at him, three approached from behind, covered his head with a blinding sack, and bound him with chains.

Fear. Flee. Fight.

7

Observer

Raez sat in a cage of cold metal. Through the bars, surprisingly robust despite their slenderness, he studied unfamiliar faces speaking an unfamiliar language. What needed no translation, however, was an underlying aura of rage emanating from each Dwarf, blazing like the sun through a thinning veil of clouds. Rage was inescapable, uncontained by boundaries—geographical, racial, lingual. As with the Thraz, it seemed to feed upon violence; and though violence could empower survival, if they survived only to preserve a culture of hostility, was that not another kind of imprisonment?

For days, the host of Dwarves remained at the foot of the mountains. For days, Raez sat quietly, attentive to his environment. He admired the surrounding forest of swaying trees, so green and lush, and the temperate climate, amazed and thankful to not be scorched by the midday sun. The Dwarves' excessive wood burning, however, which flooded the camp with smoke, stinging Raez's nostrils and eyes, giving him a headache, became hard to ignore. His stomach also grew tight with hunger, worsened by the flavorful fragrance of tzëg nearby, or even the Dwarves themselves.

Noting the number of guards and their routines helped distract him to an extent. One guard, in particular, shorter and broader than the others, with curly brown hair, enjoyed periodically prodding Raez with the butt of his spear. The tone of his speech suggested derision, but his smell and shuddering blue aura exposed fear.

Thy time shall come.

From what Raez could observe, the Dwarves were a physically frail race. Greater numbers and sophisticated weaponry were the only explanation as to how they had defeated the Hysmïnai in battle. That the Dwarves left the bodies of their defeated foes to rot, neglecting to feast on their strength, only baffled him more. Could a people be so dishonorable?

He did not fear them, but among them felt isolated and partially blind. Ornithez was gone, lost or killed. Searching the thoughts of his captors, whether awake or asleep, proved disorienting; there was an indecipherable resistance, an agitation. Sometimes Raez found it difficult to distinguish his own consciousness amidst it. The glimmering sparrow god appeared at times in his visions, yet remained at a distance—a detail in the background easily overlooked. Sometimes, instead, there was the presence of an elegant black bird with a long slender neck.

What doth it all mean?

One night, he discovered the god in Thraz form just outside his cage, floating in a casual sitting position. The sudden appearance unsettled Raez, especially being unable to gauge the god's deeper state via scent or aura.

"How wilt thou aid me?" Raez asked, growing impatient.

The god smiled. "Tell me your name."

The god's voice reminded Raez of wind echoing in the recesses of an empty cave. He was not sure what to make of such an elusive response. Ever since the god had revealed himself, he had worn ambiguity as a cloak. Was the god testing him?

"I am Raez Het, son of Thraz."

"You have come far?"

"My journey has only begun."

The god tilted his head. "What journey is that?" His interest seemed sincere.

"Dost thou not know?" Raez asked, mindful of how much he shared.

The god's smile widened. "We have met before, though not in this world."

Raez recalled his vision in the Frynosoma's cave, but this could not be the same god. Or had she been mistaken about the presence of Ekrath Namor?

Perhaps this sparrow god simply referred to being present in Raez's more recent visions. "So it seems."

"You seek the invisible?" the god asked.

"I seek Oceanus," Raez said.

"That is far from here," the god commented, glancing up at the moon, "at least in mortal terms." His black eyes returned to Raez. "How do you mean to reach it?"

"Thou promised to help me."

The god's brows rose. "Did I?"

Raez's stomach tensed. Without thinking, he seized the god by the neck and pulled him roughly against the bars of the cage. "Mock me not," he growled, surprised by his strength, but more so by his ability to move the god in the first place. Glancing down, Raez realized with amazement that he had done so with his glowing right hand.

"Rest assured, Raez Het," the god urged, smiling anew. "I want to help you and will do what I can. Yet, it cannot be accomplished alone, for my power is limited in these lands."

Limited? He released his hold of the god's neck. "What lands are these?"

"Illirium," the god answered. "We are at the northwestern border of the Kingdom of Rökad."

Neither name sounded familiar. "What shall I call thee?"

The god gripped the bars of the cage with his hands, bringing himself closer. "I am Thian Darhe and come from across the sea—across Oceanus. I steward what life I can here, tasked by the Creator, Elíbom Prímom."

More unfamiliar titles. The Thraz dared not name the gods themselves, believing that doing so would be irreverent. The Ezren taught that the gods were a collective power, not a hierarchy to be dissociated into individual entities, and that such thinking led to disunity and ruin, long ago dividing the tribes into warring factions like the Thraz, Pa'dëm, and Hysmïnai. The Frynosoma's identification of Ekrath Namor as the god of the northern mountains had been the first divine name Raez had ever heard. Now, in a matter of weeks, he knew three. The old world was being buried like bone under sand.

"What must I do to be free of this cage?" he asked.

"Be patient," the god calling himself Thian answered.

Surely, Thian was a lesser god than one such as Ekrath Namor. As the gods favored strength, Raez decided that he needed to show a greater level of assertion with this one. "Tis thy duty to aid me."

"I will guide you," the god assured. He looked over his shoulder to where a Dwarf chieftain conversed with a taller individual who had long silver hair and a crimson complexion. Raez had noted her at various points since his imprisonment. "But we need the help of another," Thian added, returning his attention to Raez. "One who sees as you do. She does not yet understand, but leave that to me."

"She canst see thee as I do?" Raez asked.

The other grinned. "When I choose."

"And feels not threatened by thy form?"

"She sees me similar to her own likeness," Thian explained, "as do you."

Raez observed the woman closer while she also looked at him.

"You met once before," Thian commented, "though in a manner I had hoped to avoid."

The eagle rider. Raez clenched his teeth. *Of course.* "So she survived the fall."

"Her mount succumbed to the wounds you inflicted." The god sounded remorseful

Good. Raez felt no grief at having defended himself against such a menace to his people. "The eagle rider is thine ally?"

"Yes."

Raez would not trust such a rider, and he was not sure he could follow a god who did. "Is she the mother of the Dwarves?"

"She is an Alöwean," Thian explained. "Her people dwell hundreds of miles south of here and are allied with the Rök."

"The Rök?"

"That is what the Dwarves call themselves. They refer to your kind as *Erog,* a word that implies an unwanted, invasive force—a pestilence."

Who is the true pestilence? Raez mused, considering the antagonism of the

Dwarves. "They have no mother?"

"In Rök society, there are many mothers, though few are given the same care and respect as your Frynosoma."

"And they do not see thee?"

"No."

"Why?" Raez pressed.

"They do not seek to reach that which is beyond the tangible."

Raez focused back on the Alöwean eagle rider now turning away with the Dwarf chieftain. "What do they think to do with me?"

"They intend to bring you to their king," Thian answered, "though I will not let it come to that. They are afraid of you, Raez Het, and of the shifting age. So it is with all unfamiliar things."

"I am not afraid of change," Raez said, "but time is valuable. Wilt thou show me the way to Oceanus or no?"

"Soon," Thian said, offering a fresh smile. Raez could not yet decide if it was genuine.

The god offered him his right hand. Receiving it instinctively with own right hand, Raez was once again surprised to feel the god's touch. Warmth coursed through his body. He looked down at his illuminated right arm.

Thian's smile widened. "Already, you cross the bridge to the Unseen. To succeed in your quest, however, we will need the Alöwean's help."

For the moment, despite lingering misgivings about Thian and the eagle rider, Raez would trust that the gods had guided him to Thian for a purpose. "Bring her to me," he said.

* * *

When the Dwarves finally broke camp, Raez's cage was placed on a crude wagon pulled by four ponies. Kept under close guard at the center of the marching columns, he watched the mountains slowly shrink in the west while to the east a green plain opened. The plain appeared full of movement—thin strands of whispering grass, murmuring pools of water, clusters of creaking trees. The air warmed, but the wind remained bitter.

One night while encamped on the plain, stars shining brightly above, Thian brought the Alöwean before Raez. It was then that Raez noticed the Alöwean walking with a limp, leaning upon what looked like a thin battle hammer. He presumed it to be an injury sustained from the impact of their fall.

Thian spoke with her before addressing Raez. Hearing their speech reminded Raez of the echo of water rushing across rock. All the while, the Alöwean's fierce gaze remained fixed on Raez. She emitted the smell of warm sand and dried wood—a calm curiosity. Her aura, resembling the last glow of a crimson dusk, reinforced this interpretation. A smoky tinge also clung to her, which, along with a slightly tremulous heartbeat, led Raez to note how the woman retained a mixture of anger and grief.

She said something to him. When he did not reply, she spoke again. Thian conversed with her further before turning to Raez. "This is my friend, Ashe Pethus."

"Thou art perhaps too liberal with the term, 'friend,'" Raez replied, still holding the Alöwean's gaze. "Hast thou told her who I am?"

Thian said something to the woman, she replied, and then he nodded.

Raez addressed the eagle rider directly: "This cage doth not hold me permanently. When next we meet in battle, thou shalt not have thine eagle for protection. May thine limp serve thee as a reminder."

After another brief discourse with the Alöwean, Thian translated, "She wants to know why you are here."

"I seek the realm of the gods."

"She does not understand," Thian said after further conversation with the woman.

"Hast thou not already explained what I told thee?" Raez asked Thian, annoyed. To Ashe he said, "I intend to find Oceanus, from whence the gods will reveal what is to be done. I will do this with or without thy help." It would be simpler without her; he had enough challenges already.

"To what end?" Thian asked, presumably for Ashe who had spoken.

"Strength in unity," Raez replied. "For my people."

Ashe talked, but Thian focused on speaking with her in her own language for a long while. Raez wondered if something was being kept hidden from him, not liking the implications. If this eagle rider thought to use him, she was mistaken. Willing to wait no longer, he pressed Thian, "What doth she say?"

Thian looked at him, but then proceeded to talk with the Alöwean. Shortly after, one of the Dwarf guards approached and spoke to Ashe. She stood and, without looking at Raez, walked away, not even acknowledging Thian as he called after her.

Raez considered the interchange to have been pointless. Still skeptical about whether he could even rely on Thian, he resolved to find a way to break free on his own.

8

Chaos

Meditating helped Raez find some solace, not only by dwelling on memories of living among the Thraz in Süretuwam, but also by pondering what he had so far witnessed. He felt alone, missing the cognitive connection with his brothers. The thoughts of the Dwarves, in contrast, remained confused and restless, though Raez felt compelled to delve deeper with the hope of understanding them. The experience of doing so with the Thraz felt akin to walking around a featureless plain under a dark amber sky, which always left Raez empowered and refreshed. Navigating that of the Dwarves, however, felt like trying to wade through a sandstorm.

More intriguing yet, and strangely calming, were the dreams of the Alöwean eagle rider, Ashe. Hers were clearer than the Dwarves' dreams, though the mood was usually as painful, such as one where she confronted a tall man wielding a small hammer. Such clarity of comprehension mystified Raez. It had to be the will of the gods. Could his interaction with Thian be opening his eyes to the world in a new way, or was this some form of manipulation? Raez was not yet sure how to distinguish between the two. In one of Ashe's recurring dreams, she sank in a dark pool shrouded with mist, and from that mist came the black bird with a long slender neck, and then one vividly white. Were these images meant for Ashe or for Raez, and what did they mean?

After days traveling east, he suspected that his cognition was having a harmful affect on the Dwarves. They had become unusually restless and confrontational with each other. Why their temperaments responded in this way, he could not say. At first, he felt guilty about the negative affect, but his captors' continued practice of not feeding him and prodding him with the butts of their spears through the cage numbed his compassion. Hunger pulled on his gut, irritating his focus.

Curiously, the Alöwean did not appear affected by Raez's cognitive exploration. She was either better at keeping the caverns of violent anger within her closed or was somehow protected from the adverse affects of his mental probing. As the nature of connection was different for Raez with his Thraz brothers as opposed to the Dwarves or this Alöwean, perhaps it was simply a matter of race.

"She will help you," Thian said one evening at camp.

"Art thou certain?" Raez asked.

"Give her time," the god answered. "Trust me."

For how long? Though Thian assured him that he would not be harmed or remain a prisoner, Raez stayed skeptical. How much power did Thian actually have over the situation, and where were the greater gods? *Why doth ye remain silent?*

Interest in the Dwarves' tangled dreams evolved into a targeted stratagem. If Raez's presence in their subconscious could indeed disrupt the host's unity, that could work to his advantage. If he could somehow intensify their paranoia, that they were being watched—that all were suspect—perhaps they would turn on each other, and in their distraction offer an opportunity for him to escape.

On the fourth day since leaving the mountains, the company reached a small, frail-looking fortress. The opulent use of wood surprised Raez, but he had observed plentiful trees in the region. The height of the palisade implied that the Dwarves more commonly fought enemies of smaller stature than his tribesmen, and less apt at climbing. Furthermore, though the stonework of the base looked sound enough, he doubted its structural integrity compared to the pure rock of Süretuwam. Twenty Thraz warriors would make short work of such a place.

Other Dwarves worked in the fields surrounding the settlement. Many stared at him as the caravan passed, their eyes wide and auras pale blue. *Is it that they all fear me?* Sitting calmly in the cage on the cart, he stared back at them. To him, their community was equally strange, though in it he perceived a cohesion of everyone working together to survive.

Unfamiliar sounds also captured his attention: the high-pitched cries of the smallest Dwarves—their Soleps and Young Brothers, he guessed—and a persistent clanging from within the fortress ahead. Passing through the main gate, he saw that the ringing came from a sturdy looking Dwarf beating his hammer against bits of metal.

What we could achieve with the knowledge of such craft, he thought. Whatever threat was mounting against the Thraz and their neighboring tribes in the north, could they be stronger if allied with a people like the Dwarves? As long as he remained caged and the Dwarves continued to steal essential resources from his people's land, and as long as desperation drove both races to violence, little progress would be made. Raez acknowledged his own part in agitating the minds of his captors, but also that some level of confrontation was necessary to regain his liberty.

Halting in the central courtyard of the fortress, the arriving Dwarves exchanged what sounded like contentious tones with their hosts. The stench of rage, like smoke, filled the air. If his cognitive influence on their emotions had been effective, perhaps his opportunity would come soon.

It came quicker than he anticipated, and more violently. The next night, the Dwarves who had captured him rose against those of the fortress. Raez felt some satisfaction at seeing them destroy each other blindly, and surprise at how effective his cognitive disruption had been, but also knew that he was to blame and that a meaningful lasting coexistence could never be won this way.

First, he had to be free. *Let future storytellers judge.* Better yet, let the gods shoulder some of the responsibility, for where were they in fostering peaceful outcomes?

As the skirmish unraveled, the five guards stationed around his cage shifted restlessly, clearly unsure what to do. Raez thought he glimpsed the Alöwean eagle rider across the courtyard surrounded by Dwarves, defending herself. As the fighting intensified, the cage guards found themselves engaged by an opposing force of Dwarves. They fought brutally, hacking down their adversaries. Four fell. Close to the cage, the fifth, the curly haired one who had tormented Raez the most, managed to kill his last attacker with a knife in close combat.

Swiftly reaching through the bars, Raez seized the Dwarf by the neck and pulled him back against the cage. The guard's eyes widened. Raez grinned with satisfaction and spoke into the Dwarf's ear, "Resist and I will snap thy neck."

The guard did not move, except for a faint trembling. He stank of fear.

"Release me," Raez urged.

The Dwarf's heart rate intensified.

Raez recalled hearing some kind of clicking mechanism when the cage door was first shut. There was a small, solid portion of the door with a hole in it. He glimpsed something like a thin, straight metal twig dangling from the guard's belt, pulled it free and pushed it into his hand. "Open the door."

As Raez loosened his hold of the Dwarf's neck, the latter began to turn as if to comply; yet slipping away from Raez's grip, he tried to bolt away. Raez grabbed the Dwarf's beard and promptly yanked him back to the cage.

Raez bared his teeth.

The guard passed out.

Useless wretch. The swiftness by which the other had succumbed to fear disappointed Raez. Retrieving the metal object from the Dwarf's limp hand, he stared at it and was about to try fitting it into the hole when a voice interrupted him: "Raez Het."

He quickly concealed the object from view and looked up to see Thian approaching with Ashe at hand, her heartbeat heavy but controlled. Her scent was not clear, but the faint crimson aura emanating from her form suggested that calm self-sufficiency retained mastery of her actions.

"We have come to free you," the god said.

Raez was about to ask how when the god spoke with the Alöwean who looked resistant despite the storm of rage closing in around her. Complicating matters, a unit of Dwarves led by the chieftain who wore the hide of one of Raez's tribesman gathered in the courtyard facing them. They were covered in blood, and looked crazed.

Thian said something urgent to Ashe. She looked around, and just in time brought her shield up against a barrage of arrows. As she took cover at the side of the cage, crouching within reach, Raez considered taking hold of her to coerce her to action.

No, he reasoned. Thinking of the frailty of the Dwarf, he would try a different tactic. "Tis time we help each other," he suggested.

Thian presumably translated, during which Raez offered the Alöwean the metal object, trusting that she would know what to do with it. She took it without hesitation, slid it into the hole of the cage door and turned it with a click. The door creaked open.

At last. With the Dwarves drawing dangerously close, Raez rushed out of the cage on all three of his good limbs and hissed at them in warning. He felt an arrow strike his back, lodging in one of his thick scales, but paid it no heed. The Dwarves did not worry him. He needed to depart this madness—these weak, conniving beings—but recalled that beyond the fortress walls was a cold, unfamiliar landscape. Thian had promised to help him, but did they really need the Alöwean to succeed? She would only slow them further.

Thou owest her nothing, Raez told himself. She had tried to kill him—not even directly, honorably, but with one of the giant eagles.

"Climb on my back," he demanded, lowering himself, ignoring an inclination to tear off her face. Gritting his teeth, he cursed her for the indignity of needing to become her mount. "Hurry."

Thian said something more to Ashe and then transformed into a small brown sparrow. "Follow me," he called to Raez.

As Ashe leapt onto Raez's back, the lightness of her weight surprised him. An impulse shuddered through his body to shake her off and leave her behind; but without further deliberation, he turned away from the approaching Dwarves, quickly climbed the nearby fortress wall, battering aside its archers with his firm head as he passed, and descended the outer side of the wall to the dark plain beyond.

The cool, moist grass tickled Raez's hide as he ran. A bright moon lit the way. It was not long, however, until he felt himself tiring, joints stiff and muscles cramped from days contained in the cage and cold environment. It had also been too long since he had eaten. *Damn.* He did not like the thought of having to rely on the god and Alöwean.

Slowing to a stop, he muttered to Ashe, "Get thee off." When she hesitated, he shook his back.

She obeyed.

Raez glanced down at his missing right forearm, wondering what good its renewal was and why it never manifested at opportune moments.

Thian appeared beside them in his glimmering Thraz form, and spoke to Ashe. The god's persistent prioritization of communicating with the Alöwean annoyed Raez. He remembered the Alöwean's limp. Both being handicapped, their current escape would prove to be a futile gesture if they did not act quickly. Glancing back in the direction of the fortress, no longer visible, Raez saw the flicker of a few approaching torch lights. The Dwarves were coming.

With a bleak sense of resolve, Raez knew what he had to do. To Thian, he said, "I will hold them back. Guide the Alöwean to safety, and I will find thee both when I may."

Thian nodded and spoke to Ashe.

Meanwhile, Raez fixed his eyes on the coming lights and lowered himself in the grass. With practiced control, he inhaled calmly and deeply. The Dwarves were closing in fast. Already, he could make out their features, twenty of them, all riding ponies. The smell of blood and flesh churned his stomach anew. Soon, he would eat heartily. He focused on the Dwarf chieftain. *Thou wilt be the first and the last to die.*

As the god and Alöwean had not moved, but continued to deliberate, Raez hissed at them. "Flee, fools."

He did not watch them go, but instead listened to the rumble of the approaching riders, nearly upon him, all the while concentrating on the Dwarf chieftain.

In his mind, the beating of the hooves slowed to match the thumping of his heart.

Wait.

Wait.

Wait.

At last, Raez rose from the grass to his full height and, with his large left fist, pummeled the chieftain's face at the eyes. The force of contact dismounted the Dwarf, suspending him for a moment in midair still connected to Raez's knuckles, until he dropped to the ground blinded.

The sensation of time resumed its hasty pace as the other riders halted in alarm and turned their mounts against Raez. He felt no confusion, but absolute presence, trained instincts taking mastery. He seized the head of a Dwarf to his right and slammed him to the ground, bringing his pony down with him. The impact crushed the rider's skull, leaving him motionless. Exhilaration coursed through Raez's being. Taking the dead warriors' spear, he thrust it into another Dwarf attempting to charge at him, releasing the weapon as it lodged firmly in his stomach, sending him backwards off his mount. With his one good arm, Raez grabbed the now riderless pony by the neck, which was too thick to grip well for long, and launched it clumsily into another rider, knocking him over.

Raez reveled in the pain he inflicted.

He needed another weapon. Retrieving a discarded Dwarf longsword, more like a regular sword for a Thraz, Raez wielded it with his left hand, cutting down assailant after assailant, callous to whether his strokes killed or maimed. Fury stirred throughout Raez's body, inundating and invigorating, abandoning reason. Survival reigned. This would not be the end of his journey.

Quickly looking away from a Dwarf he had just beheaded, anticipating another attack, not sure how long it had been since the skirmish had begun, Raez found himself at the center of a bloodied field. His sword arm ached slightly, but more with anticipation than weariness. There was also disappointment at the contest being over so easily. A circle of grass was flattened underneath the bodies of Dwarves and their mounts, or where combatants had trodden. One pony still bleated faintly, but soon quieted from suffocation, its ribs crushed under another mount. The cacophony of heartbeats echoing around him faded to quiet.

All accept one.

Nearby, the Dwarf chieftain crawled weakly on his stomach away from the dead, trying to contain his moans. Blood stained his face, mostly coming from his eyes.

Raez came within a few steps of the chieftain. "Thou wast blind in thy actions before—in attacking my people and in betraying thine own. Now shalt thou learn to see with new eyes and know prudence."

He removed the chieftains' helmet fashioned from the skull of one of Raez's brethren. He stripped the Dwarf of his armor, keeping the hide layer while tossing aside the rest. The chieftain whined bitterly, but did not resist.

"Hush," Raez said scornfully. "Thou wilt survive."

Leaving the unworthy opponent to his sightless misery, Raez returned to the center of the battlefield, stabbed the longsword blade down into the ground, and hung the hide upon it like a banner—a testament to Thraz strength.

Desperate for nourishment, he fed upon the raw flesh of one of the dead ponies. Fresh life returned to his limbs. It was a shame to have to abandon the other bodies, armor, and weapons—enough to supply a unit of Thraz—but Raez had no choice. He considered taking a weapon, but then remembered his resolution in the mountains to explore other solutions. Change would be more difficult than he imagined. He placed the chieftain's skull helm under his right arm, pressed against his side, took the ankle of one of the dead Dwarves and dragged the body away in the direction that the god and Alöwean had fled.

* * *

The cloudy sky began to brighten as Raez tracked Ashe to the edge of a forest. There, mist clung to a tree-covered hillside, leaving the top visible—a ridge stretching miles to the north and south. Raez welcomed the damp veil's concealment. He also needed to rest, drink, and eat some more.

Stepping into the forest, he noticed a sparrow staring at him. It was not the same as Thian, but seemed somehow similar.

"Who art thou?" he asked.

The bird chirruped, and then darted away. Raez watched as it circled back, cheeping as it passed, and then did so a second time. He followed it a ways up the hill until he reached a trickling stream. There, the sparrow sat perched on a branch jutting out from a rocky cliff. The water flowed from somewhere above, dripping down the stone face until forming a small pool and stream. Raez let go of the Dwarf body then approached the cliff. In a crevice near the source of the water, he reverently placed the skull helm, the vacant eyes looking eastward toward the plain.

"Here may thou rest," he said softly, stepping back to look at it after making sure the skull helm would not shift or fall, "and act as lookout on behalf of our people."

Kneeling down next to the pool, leaning on his elbows, he drank his fill. Clarity of mind began to return. He found it incredible how much the gift of water could offer. Satisfied for the moment, he returned to the body of the Dwarf and dragged it away from the stream, eager for further sustenance and to honor, even if undeserved, those who had fallen.

Dwarf flesh was a rare delicacy to the Thraz, and one that Raez had never before tasted. The meat was leaner than he had imagined, full of rich new flavor, more juicy and tender than any tzëg or beast he had dined upon. *Delicious,* he thought with surprise, savoring every bite.

Nearly an hour later, with only a leg remaining next to him, Raez felt his appetite abate. He nibbled further on the remains of the calf of the first leg, determined not to waste anything. Footsteps sounded behind him, too soft on the ground to be a Dwarf. Astonished to be caught unaware, Raez looked back and met the Alöwean's small blue eyes staring back at him as she readied her slender battle hammer.

9

Opportunist

The Alöwean stepped back into Thian who had appeared behind her. The tone of their conversation was edged with tension, mainly from Ashe, but throughout Thian glanced at Raez with mild disapproval. Once again, Raez felt frustratingly detached from their exchange. He hated the lack of control, the vulnerability. "What is wrong?" he asked at a lull.

Thian did not answer, but spoke further with Ashe. Raez focused on controlled breaths while the other two deliberated. Precious time was being lost, not only to fulfill his quest, but to put more distance between them and the Dwarves.

At last, as Ashe brusquely walked away, Thian returned his attention to Raez. "I am glad you are safe," he said.

"What didst thou and the Alöwean discuss?"

"It is not important now," Thian answered. "Come, we must prepare for the next stage of your quest."

"Wait." Raez did not like the god's continued evasiveness. He needed more answers. He deserved more. "What dost thou intend to do?" So far, it had been minimal at best.

Thian's expression suggested that the answer was obvious. "I will bring you to Oceanus."

"And the Alöwean?"

"Patience is needed to broaden both of your perspectives," Thian said, his voice like the wind echoing off a mountainside. "Only then will the truth be unveiled."

"What dost thou mean?" Raez pressed.

Thian smiled. "Come and find out."

Tightening his jaw, Raez abandoned trying to learn more for the moment. He buried what remained of the Dwarf, carefully laying out the warrior's helm and pieces of armor upon the small mound as a memorial, at which point Thian, who had been observing the process, placed his hands over the mound and drew up white blossoms that looked like drops of snow. Raez felt a touch of awe at the sight, remembering that Thian was not some powerless being. More would be needed for the future of the Thraz, however, than charming garden displays.

The god motioned for Raez to follow him up the hillside. "I struggle to comprehend the reliance on violence for resolving disputes," he commented as they walked, "though, alas, even my own people have succumbed to it. War is an ever-willing mediator, it seems, and one that too readily disregards the consequences."

Raez was inclined to agree. "Tell me more about thy people."

"Our story began before the formation of the world," Thian answered. "We were first named *Séorans*, servants."

"What about the Span?" Raez asked.

"I have heard none but you call it that," Thian answered. "Once, we Séorans inhabited every corner of the world, but conflicts throughout the ages have scattered us into isolated assemblies."

Raez remembered the Frynosoma's warning about wayward gods. "What brought thee alone to these lands?"

Thian's narrowed black eyes suggested calculation, and he smiled faintly. "I came in support of Ashe."

"Why alone, though?" Raez asked. "Where are the other gods?"

"Some of us are tasked to work alone," Thian answered, "like a scout, with aid seldom far should we seek it."

In a way, Raez could relate to that, seeing himself as a kind of scout—leaving the collective strength of his tribe to explore a better future. "Thou once said we have met before."

"I did."

"Where, and when?"

"You know the answer," Thian said. They reached the crest of the ridge, stepping out onto a clearing partitioned by heaps of boulders. "After all that has happened, why do you still doubt?"

Raez did not know what the other was talking about. "I seek clarity not more riddles."

"There are no straight paths to meaningful outcomes," the god answered. "That is why trust is important—being sure of one's hope in the face of the unseen." He pointed up. "An old friend approaches."

Raez saw his black vulture gliding down toward him. As the bird landed upon his outstretched left forearm, he felt a pang of relief. Ornithez symbolized an important link to the familiar, to the Thraz, and to Raez's sense of autonomous strength. Gently, he stroked the bird's neck. "I did not think to see thee again."

"Ornithez did not stray far," Thian commented, grinning. "He would not abandon you. Also, allow me to introduce two of my trusted companions." With his hand, the god indicated the two sparrows that had landed on his shoulders. "Osré and Oshrémi have aided me since the beginning. I understand that you have already met Oshrémi."

Recognizing the bird from earlier that morning, Raez nodded.

"Together with Ornithez, they will keep watch while I am away."

"Where art thou going?"

"I will not be gone long," the god assured. "Farewell."

Thian lifted from the ground, leaning forward while bringing his knees up to his chest, and in a rush of silent wind and whirling golden light transformed into a brown sparrow. He flew from Raez's sight a moment later.

✳ ✳ ✳

Inhale calmly, controlled. Hold and ponder its power inside thy chest.

Now exhale slowly, focusing on the action, the moment, the cleansing.

With each steady breath, savor the fragrance of all that grows around, below, above—damp earth, flowers, pine.

Embrace the breeze brushing against thy scales. It whispers, soothes, stirs. A beam of sunlight caresseth the landscape and warmeth thee.

Staccato birdsong: whistles, cheeps.

Dried cones and needles crunching underneath feet.

Without opening his eyes, Raez recognized the Alöwean walking toward him—not only from the nimble steps, but the distinct rhythm of her heart—strong, unhurried—and the smell like warm sand that she generally emitted.

Simultaneously connected to Ornithez gliding above, Raez examined the landscape, noting the serenity of the forest, the somber mountains to the west, peaks shrouded in clouds, and the expanse of rippling grass to the east. Ashe said something, but Raez did not move. Instead, he continued to focus on breathing slowly, while taking in the features of the landscape as it came closer, including the sight of the Alöwean sitting across from his own form. Ornithez flew down and landed on his shoulder. Raez retained the connection as the vulture stared back at Ashe.

Thian strode up beside her. As they talked, Raez continued to observe through Ornithez's eyes. If the god and Alöwean thought him helpless, they would find themselves gravely mistaken.

The cries of giant eagles caused Raez to stiffen. As Ornithez flapped away to the shelter of the woods, with his own eyes Raez witnessed three large birds—one white, another black, and the third brown with accents of white—land upon a nearby rock formation. The black one stared at him with fierce yellow eyes. The auras of all three shone bronze like sunlit desert sand. Subtly, not wanting to draw attention to himself, Raez shifted his sitting position to where his feet were planted on the ground, ready to retreat—the image of the two pale warriors snatched from the mountain ridge vivid in his memory.

He called to the god. "Hast thou brought these creatures?"

"They are of the noble line of Girgash Erïeth," Thian answered calmly, "and have agreed to bring you and Ashe across the mountains out of Rökad."

"I am eager to depart," Raez said—he had been ready for days—"but trust them not."

Ashe interrupted. Thian presumably explained. Afterward, the Alöwean left the small clearing and began to climb the rock to where the white eagle waited.

"All shall be well," Thian said to Raez. "The greater threat is not the Erïeth, but the cohort of Rök who are now within a day's ride of this place. Oceanus is over a thousand miles south from here as the bird flies, and these Erïeth will only carry us a hundred. Every opportune gift should be accepted, Raez Het. Such is the journey of faith. It is the only way to complete your quest."

Raez began to wonder how often the gods used the call to faith to coerce their followers.

"You cannot do it alone," Thian urged.

With all the delays, including his imprisonment, Raez's doubt of the god's capabilities had not diminished. Yet, he could not outrun mounted Dwarves and likely did not have the strength to repel multiple attacks. He was stuck in a foreign land, and did not know how to reach Oceanus without more guidance. Despite his misgivings about Thian, Raez recognized that the god did openly champion his quest—or acted like it. Where were the other gods—the voice in the desert or Ekrath Namor? Each had directed him toward a future path, but then just as quickly abandoned him to navigate it alone. Thian at least remained, though his leadership had proven less definitive. Raez still wanted to trust that they had been brought together for a purpose. "What about Ashe?"

"After the Erïeth bring us across the border of Rökad," Thian said, "Ashe will show us the safest route to the coast. She knows southern Illirium better than me."

Whatever was to come, Raez wanted to avoid additional entanglements like that with the Dwarves. There could be no more delays. "Very well," he said.

Thian's grin widened. "Come."

Raez followed the god to where the brown and black eagles waited upon the rocks.

"They will carry you," Thian explained, and then floated up to a higher stone perch where Ashe stood before the white eagle. Eventually, she allowed herself to be held by the bird's intimidating talons.

All appeared to go well, but the eagles were not known to feed on Alöweans. Raez lowered himself cautiously before the two other eagles. Though their heart rates and auras were calm, briefly probing their minds revealed glimpses of his kind being eaten. He was food to them, and would have to remain alert. "Let us bridge the chasm between our two races and be at peace," he said. *Betray me, and ye shall not fly again.*

Standing erect, the black eagle's yellow eyes narrowed. It nodded its head. There was more than hunger in its mind. Its thoughts exuded focus and purpose, suggesting a creature that did not let base urges dictate its actions. This surprised Raez, but time would prove whether the impression was accurate.

Nearby, the white eagle leapt from the outcrop with Ashe held in its clutches.

Before he could brace himself, both sides of Raez's jagged back were gripped by the brown eagle. The talons held him firm, but did not tighten uncomfortably. His stomach lurched as the eagle soared out over a vast green land, higher than Raez had ever been or wanted to be. The sensation of immense space below and the prospect of falling were nothing like seeing the world through Ornithez's eyes. Raez did not like being carried, and continued to read what signs he could of the eagles, ready to fight as he had done with Ashe's mount.

Three sparrows fluttered by. Raez spotted Ornithez following their progress from closer to the ground. To his left, the white eagle carried Ashe, while the black one soared above them to their right. Ahead, many miles away, loomed a dark mountain range, and somewhere beyond that waited Oceanus.

Or so Raez dared to hope.

10

Memories

Raez missed the desert heat. Rising high at the mercy of the giant eagles, the temperature dropped, chilling him to the core. His bearskin cloak provided inadequate protection, and descending each evening to make camp in the mountains offered little respite. The cold lingered, as if permanently absorbed by his scales. It became difficult to think. He just wanted to burrow into the earth and sleep away the discomfort; yet sleep, when it came, only added to the torment.

Raez found some relief in perceiving no immediate hostility from the eagles. Daily, he gauged their wills as best as he could. They might fundamentally see him as food, but there was no evil intent in their mannerisms or cognitive states. Somehow, Thian had convinced them to deny their nature with Raez. In this, the god had finally demonstrated a trace of competence. The eagles were cunning creatures, however, and ever watchful. Raez would feel better once they parted company.

Early one morning, he woke dizzy with the images of what he had seen and echoes of what he had heard in his sleep. There was some relief at the touch of firm earth beneath him and the familiar sight of the mountain pass observed the previous evening. The nearby peak, its crevices still packed with snow, now glowed red from the sunrise.

Ashe rested nearby, curled on her side, and Thian sat next to her, his hand placed tenderly upon her brow. Raez had yet to understand their relationship, which at times seemed distant while at other times suggested a deeper intimacy. Meanwhile, the eagles did not spend the night with the three companions, but instead departed each evening after bringing them to a place to camp, usually on or near some precipice from which the birds could readily land and take flight.

Thian stared at him. "Your thoughts are restless, Raez Het."

Raez rubbed his eyes, trying to remove the images of his most recent vision: sinking down as though earth and rock were made of oozing black tar; beneath, in the heart of the mountain, a labyrinth of passageways and caverns. Wandering among them, suffocating, trying to find a way out, yet still cold, he had stumbled upon a space full of metal cages. Inside each cage, a Frynosoma sat hunched over, her body thin and sallow, groaning faintly.

"Help us," they said.

Even his mother, Thraz, was there. Shadows surrounded her, binding her with clanking metal chains. As her eyes met his, white feathers sprouted from her scales. She cried out. Raez fled, all the while chased by the reverberation of her pleading voice: "Hurry."

He did not wish to speak with Thian about the vision. "How far to Oceanus?"

"Soon, we will have crossed the Girgash Mountains," Thian answered with his airy voice. "The way will be far from there, and far from certain."

Time remaineth mine enemy, Raez mused. He returned his attention to Ashe's slumbering form. "What art thou doing with the Alöwean?"

With a furrowed brow, the god tilted his head in confusion. "Doing?"

"Ever thou linger close to her, especially in sleep. Why?"

Looking down at Ashe, Thian shifted his hand to settle on her shoulder. "I keep her warm. It is a small mercy I can offer . . . after all she has endured."

"Dost thou glimpse her dreams as I do?" Raez asked.

"Yes."

"Art thou present in them?" Raez pressed, discerning that somehow the black bird with the long slender neck was connected to the god.

Thian nodded slowly. "Ashe carries the past like a weight upon her back, though she tries to keep it concealed. For you, it is different; the burden is not the past, but the future." His black eyes, depthless like a starry night sky, looked at Raez. "You are afraid."

"The diminishing breadth of opportunity vexes me," Raez countered. He had to find something—some meaningful, lasting sign—to bring back to the Thraz. Yet, beyond the notion of Oceanus, he had no idea of what to look for. It was unlikely to come from this god. Why was the quest of a Het so ambivalently designed? Where were the other gods; were they toying with him and his kind? A burst of wind caused him to shiver. "And the cold is unyielding."

"I can help." Removing his hand from Ashe's shoulder, Thian extended it toward Raez.

The air stirred like a soft breeze. A path of frost formed on the ground between the two of them, crackling lightly, surrounding Raez, though it did not touch him. Instead, he felt an unseen wave of warmth cover his body. Too quickly the heat dissipated, but Raez felt renewed enough to endure the cold for a while longer—until the rising sun warmed the pass.

"Forgive me for not offering it to you sooner or for longer," the god said. "I did not realize to what extent the cold can breach your physical defenses, by my estimation so much sturdier than an Alöwean. Alas, I have not the strength to keep you both warm. However"—he indicated Raez's right arm—"I warrant that you have the potential within yourself."

Raez looked down to see his right forearm restored, glowing with dull bronze light. "I understand not why it always cometh without warning."

"It resonates the light of the Unseen," Thian said, "and is always present to my eyes." He looked confused. "You do not always see it?"

"I do not."

Thian appeared to ponder this. "Learning to see with new eyes requires patience and wisdom."

His interest piqued, Raez asked, "What is wisdom to thee?"

"Reverence of the Creator, Elíbom Prímom, is the beginning of wisdom," Thian began, "and turning away from evil is understanding."

"Yet, how might one perceive evil when it oft comes cloaked in shadows?" Raez met the other's eyes. "Or even light?"

"Elíbom Prímom is my light," the god answered, "and that light is peaceful and good. Anything else is but an imitation or deception. A harvest of peace is sown by those who revere Elíbom Prímom, by those who make peace as servants of all."

"I know not Elíbom Prímom," Raez said. If a hierarchy among the gods did exist, Thian seemed to be of a lesser kind. The role of servant was not ignoble, however. Leading the Thraz as an Ezren Aditám would require a similar attitude.

"Seek and you shall find," Thian answered.

"For one, I seek to control this," Raez said, holding up his right forearm.

The god stroked his chin. "I have never seen anything like it with a mortal. How did you come to attain it?"

In basic detail, Raez recounted the ritual with the Frynosoma.

"Remarkable," Thian commented in response, shaking his head. "You have been given a unique gift, Raez Het."

"It hath brought me more confusion and hindrance than blessing," Raez replied dourly.

"The way of Elíbom Prímom is often mysterious," the god said, "even to me. Though I do not have the same limitations as you, what I do perceive from my time among you, including Ashe, is that seeing begins with looking, and looking is focused by a mind open to believing, exploring, and ultimately knowing in the intimacy of understanding."

Thian's tone made it sound simple, yet the concepts remained vague.

"If your arm is made of a matter similar to mine," Thian continued, "there are ways for it to redirect small measures of life, such as with the temperature of the air or the course of water." He studied the brightening sky. "Even light." Dark clouds drifted over the northern reaches of the mountains, rain falling beneath like a thin curtain. "My sister, Phedra, had such power."

"Thy sister?"

Thian continued to study the view. "My twin. She was the stronger of us."

After a lasting silence, Raez pressed: "What burdens thee?"

"Nothing." Looking down, the god frowned for the first time that Raez had seen. "We all carry some portion of pain from the past."

Thinking of Ashe, how visions of her past intruded upon his sleep, Raez wondered if there was something unique about her race that caused this, or if it was orchestrated by Thian instead. *To what end?* he wondered. *To draw us closer in unity?* There would be some sense in that, akin to what the Ezren offered his tribe.

Focusing on his glowing right forearm, Raez tightened his fingers into a fist, noting the sensation. Touch triggered little more than a numb feeling, but it was something. He tried to grip a pebble between two fingers, but failed as though his hand were no more than light. Brushing his fingers through the air, he felt traces of invisible currents, like a draft, only with an elevated comprehension of detail. He willed himself to draw a portion of the air into his hand like he had once done with grains in a mild sandstorm. To his surprise, the air responded. Concentrating on his selection, he felt his palm begin to warm.

"Yes," the god said, watching with a smile. "That is it, Raez Het. You begin to understand."

The moment vanished, and Raez's hand cooled anew. This disappointed him at first; but then, staring at his right arm, he reminded himself of what he had just done. *Yes*, he thought. *Tis a beginning.*

An hour later, as the three companions waited for the arrival of the eagles, Raez approached Ashe who sat staring out at the mountains. He took a seat beside her and concentrated on the rumble of the rock beneath their feet, the slow movements of the earth, the swirl of blue and gold light in the air, the burning fingers of the sun. After a while, overwhelmed from trying to absorb too many sensations, he focused on the Alöwean.

Who art thou, crimson warrior? "I desire more knowledge of thy homeland."

Thian had joined them. "She comes from across the sea." He spoke with Ashe for a while, during which Raez discerned in the Alöwean's demeanor a kind of casual aloofness. "She does not want to speak about it."

"Why not?" Raez asked.

"Each of us copes in our way," Thian answered. "As you may have guessed, she works hard to conceal the scars, physical or otherwise."

Raez nodded, surmising it to be so with every warrior. He had been no different until recognizing that he had to face his pain to heal and nurture the determination to press ahead. The Thraz were able to do so, in part, by joining their minds in a communal subconscious. Memories and visions could then be shaped by the wisest among them, the Ezren, who worked on behalf of the Frynosoma channeling the will of the gods. If Alöwean society was anything like that of the Dwarves, however, Ashe's seemed an isolated and divided existence.

Granted, while the Thraz enjoyed general unity as a tribe, tribal divisions in the desert had only been intensifying in recent years. *Are we any more cohesive as a civilization?* So far from familiar lands and people, feeling alone, Raez remembered that his identity among the Thraz was also under debate. Thian was right: the future held Raez's greatest attention. That was his quest. *Why, then, do my thoughts still wander in confusion?* Once again trying to concentrate away from his own uncertainties, he asked Ashe, "What dost thou seek?"

Thian answered without consulting the Alöwean. "She wishes to live unburdened by the past and future."

"To what end?"

"I think that is the point," Thian said. "The end matters less to her than drawing all she can from the present."

They stared at Ashe. Noticing them, she raised a brow, and then surprised Raez with a nonchalant grin before standing and walking away as if to look closer at the surrounding landscape.

Soon after, the eagles appeared.

11

Vision

Reaching the southern end of the mountains, Raez looked out in awe at the vast green landscape covered in countless tall trees. There were so many unfamiliar, soothing smells. Colored flora speckled lush, grassy fields partitioned by streams. Animals roamed. He had never imagined that such a wealth of life could exist. Surely, the gods dwelt in such a place.

On a rocky rise overlooking the edge of the forest, the eagles departed, their task fulfilled according to Thian. While Raez appreciated their help in escaping the land of the Dwarves, he did not mind parting with them and hoped to never again have to fly.

The three companions traveled south on foot. A part of Raez wanted to go slower, to tarry at various places of beauty—to look closer, breathing deep every scent, learning to distinguish the origins, all the while meditating on the wonder. Nature felt more alive, almost looming, than anywhere he had ever been. Yet, he reminded himself that his brothers were waiting for him, their survival possibly depending on the fulfillment of his quest. After all, could not Oceanus offer the secret to bringing such living wealth to them? He had to press on.

Yet, what if this land was the sign he needed from the gods? What if he actually did need to slow and show greater attentiveness? Ahead, in the form of a Thraz, Thian glided smoothly through the trees, following some invisible path. Did this god hold any more answers? And what of Ashe?

Thian said she knew the lands of southern Illirium better than him. Now that they were free from the immediate threat of the Dwarves, who in their company was really in control and how could Raez claim that authority?

The time has come to lead.

Along the way, at any opportunity, he talked with Thian about the Span—or the Unseen, as the god liked to call it. The realm of the gods was intrinsically linked to the mortal world. They were essentially the same, overlapped, except that the boundaries of possibility were enhanced in the Span. With care and conscious effort, one could wield nature in distinct ways—ways that Raez wanted to better understand, especially concerning water. He needed to master the potential of his right arm not just for the fulfillment of his quest, but to ultimately challenge the Ezren. Moreover, if circumstances proved treacherous with Thian, Raez needed a way to subdue or at least repel the god. The brief display of power against Thian in their early encounter, while Raez was imprisoned in the cage, encouraged Raez that it could be so. That it would be necessary to fight seemed unlikely, considering Thian's amiable behavior so far, but Raez would not be caught unprepared. Though Thian had so far not seemed a formidable appointment, there was much about him that remained hidden.

The Alöwean concerned Raez less, for he perceived in her small stature no tangible threat. He had glimpsed her prowess as a warrior, yet she could not run quickly, and seemed more vulnerable without her eagle mount. If a confrontation occurred with her, he could easily defeat her. He did not desire such an end, but would be ready for it as well.

* * *

Crouched low to the ground, his scales mimicking the brown and green hues of his environment, Raez waited. Before him, about ten strides away, a small creek trickled through a dell in the shadowed forest. Eventually, the sun would rise, but for now grey clouds blanketed the sky and rain drizzled down.

As the hours passed, dim blue light gradually revealed his surroundings.

A few birds began to stir, but most remained quiet. The land slept a while longer, while the creatures that rose early to drink and feed in the greater concealment of predawn began to come. Evidence of their frequenting the creek was everywhere. Seeing them grazing along the way, he asked Thian what they were called. "Deer," the latter said. Their smell was distinct. Judging by their physique and the strong pulses of their hearts, one of them would make a good meal.

Having thoroughly rolled in and rubbed damp dirt and pine needles over his body, as well as positioned himself downwind from the creek, Raez hoped to be undetected. Though unfamiliar with the game in these woodlands, he trusted that his skills as a desert hunter would be enough. Ornithez perched on a branch nearby, also watching. At times, Raez connected to the vulture's sight to scan the area from the higher vantage point.

The Dwarf had been Raez's last meal of substance. While some roots, nuts, and berries offered by Thian provided brief relief, the emptiness in Raez's stomach deepened. Away from the god's scrutiny, Raez had caught a few rodents by himself in previous days, but he needed more. Concentration became difficult. He felt irritable.

Conscious of the adverse impression his dining on the Dwarf had made on his two companions, Raez deemed it simpler to satiate his hunger away from their strange sentiments. He did so to respect them, but if it came down to a choice he would prioritize his health. *Let them think what they will.*

Rustling in the bushes alerted his attention. A glance through Ornithez's eyes confirmed approaching shapes: four adults, none with antlers, with three young.

Slowly, quietly inhaling, Raez held his breath, pressed himself closer to the ground, and fixed his eyes on the creek as the deer came.

Wait.

One of the deer appeared to keep watch while the others drank.

Wait.

Gradually, the other deer turned away while the sentry stood erect, her eyes scanning the area. Ears perked up as she suddenly looked directly at Raez. Lifting her front foot up, she stomped the ground.

The others stopped.

Quiet.

Nothing but dripping rain could be heard.

Minutes passed, and then eventually the deer moved once more, their heartbeats still elevated. The sentry relaxed and lowered her head to drink.

Now.

Though missing his right forearm limited his speed, Raez could still swiftly cover short distances. The sentry turned to run, the other deer already dashing away in fright, but with a leap from his hind legs, Raez managed to seize the deer's left haunch with his good hand and bite the other with his powerful maw. The deer stumbled, crying out, and resisted; however, Raez's grip with his claws and teeth could not be dislodged. Using all his strength and weight, clenching his teeth, Raez managed to adjust his handhold, grab the deer's neck, and pull it back. He then let go with his jaw and, clinging to the deer by the neck, slammed its head against the trunk of an adjacent tree. The action stunned the deer, but did not kill it.

Not wanting to prolong the pain of his prey, Raez instinctively reached to secure his hold with his right hand, thinking to break the hapless creature's neck. He suddenly glimpsed a bronze glow from his right forearm. The hand could not clutch the deer, but seemed to pass through it. With his thoughts bent on a quick, peaceful death, Raez suddenly felt a rush of heat against his right hand. With his hand still in the chest of the deer, he heard the creature gasp, felt it stiffen and then collapse. Raez almost lost his balance with the shift in weight. Quickly withdrawing his lucent right hand from the deer's chest, he was amazed to see no mark or indication of having penetrated the creature's hide—again, as though his new limb was little more than light. Opening his right fist, a gust of warm air burst up from his palm, knocking him back.

Raez lay still for a moment, wondering if anything more would happen. As nothing did, silence returning to the dell, he sat up, stared at the dead deer, and then focused on his right hand. Its glowing form appeared unchanged.

He had somehow drawn the breath from his prey.

Above, the sky was rapidly brightening. Soon, if not already, Thian and Ashe would rise and wonder where he had gone. Raez had no time to speculate further, so reverently placed his right hand on the head of the deer, thanking the gods for such provision, and dedicated its spirit to the Span before beginning to eat.

* * *

Cresting a ridge one afternoon, they looked out upon an immense body of water to the south.

"Oceanus?" Raez asked, captivated.

"No," the god said, chuckling. "It is called the Emülath Sea, or Mirror Lake to some." He explained that it was predominantly fed by two large rivers, one of which came from the hill and mountain country to the east, while the other began far away in the western highlands.

Raez had never seen so much water with his waking eyes. Its blue surface glimmered with a thousand stars. Reaching its shore an hour later, the scent of cool moisture, damp earth and living organisms further saturated his senses.

"It is vast," Thian said, "but merely a pool compared to Oceanus."

Barely able to see the far end of the lake, Raez struggled to comprehend anything larger. "How much farther to the coast of Oceanus?"

"We have traveled halfway from where we began," Thian answered. "Hundreds of miles still stretch before us."

So far to go. The notion of returning home from his current location overwhelmed him on its own. Had any of his people ever come this far south? Focusing on the lake once more, he said to Thian, "I shall meditate on my options."

"As you wish."

"Wilt thou not give me guidance?" Raez asked. "Art thou not a god?"

Ashe stood nearby, watching them. She said something to Thian, starting a brief conversation, during which the god's expression appeared calculating. At last, to Raez he said, "It is not for me to provide the sign you seek, but only to show you the way."

"And the way thou offereth?"

Thian pointed across the lake. "Onward."

For days, they ventured south along the lake's eastern shore. At every point of rest, however long or brief, as well as each morning before departing camp, or each evening before sleep, Raez separated himself from the others to absorb his environment. Sometimes he simply closed his eyes and listened; at other times, he quietly walked along the shore, watching twilight settle over the water, noting various night birds and bats swooping down to catch bugs buzzing above the surface of the lake; or he just admired the fading radiance of the sunset, the tranquil lapping of water, and the stillness of the land. Never before had he felt such peace, yet his isolation from the Thraz remained a small, but ever present ache.

"Where are ye?" he whispered to the gods. "What am I to do?"

His right arm glowed, but did not emit real light as darkness settled around him. It drew his eyes, but did not reveal anything beyond himself. In a way, it made it more difficult to see. The silhouettes of rolling hills surrounded most of the lake, while the water itself reflected the dimming sky.

Water, full of life and light, a voice whispered in his thoughts—the voice from the desert. *To flow as water is to learn the way of truth and an undivided heart.*

"Who art thou?" Raez asked, but only silence answered.

"Then there is much to hear and see," the Ezren had once said. There had to be truth in that, Raez thought.

Kneeling, he dipped his left hand into the water, cupped some, and drank. *Life.* He did the same with his semi-translucent right hand, impressed as the portion of water held in his open palm radiated a soft bronze glow. Somehow, the water interacted with what was not tangible, with the unseen. *Light.* He stepped out into the lake until the water reached his waist. Closing his right hand into a fist, he inserted it beneath the surface and watched a sphere of illumination reveal the rock, sand, and green grass of the lake floor.

Remarkable.

He withdrew his right hand, returning the water to shadows, but then stuck it back in, once more illuminating the underwater depths. Repeating the action a few more times, he smiled to himself, discerning a new level of power and possibility. *Yes*, he thought. *Life and light.*

* * *

Connected to the soaring vision of Ornithez, Raez wondered if he was the first to spot the town. The settlement reminded him of the fortress of the Dwarves in the north, only larger and less fortified. He could not understand why people would leave their homes so exposed to the elements, not to mention possible aggressors. Nature's bounty was the only reason he could ascribe to how such a civilization had lasted this long.

"It is a place of trade," Thian explained. "'Fumond's Hut', Ashe calls it. Its doors are open to all, one of a few such places left in Illirium."

The Alöwean said more.

Thian looked mildly bewildered. "She wants you and me to stay here in the cover of the woods while she seeks out a friend in the town. Differences are welcome here, but only familiar differences it would seem."

Raez shrugged at the irony. He did not mind waiting in silence. He wondered, however, what kind of friend Ashe meant to find and to what end, once again resenting his companions for not including him in their plans. *Soon, that shall change.*

Ashe returned the next evening with three companions. Their features looked similar to her, only they lacked pointed ears and had fairer skin, tan as opposed to crimson, and their stature was slightly shorter. Thian had called their race the Illiri. The one in the center strode with the confidence of a chieftain, but his demeanor reminded Raez more of an acolyte than Adítam—conniving and physically unremarkable. Moreover, while the man's heart pulsated calmly, Raez was unfamiliar with his smell and light. He emitted a scent that reminded Raez of a dry stone tunnel, and his faint aura was like looking into a deep grey well. Was Raez expected to put his trust in such an empty being? The other two Illiri, by contrast, had broader physiques, which, partnered with their sternly attentive demeanors and the short swords sheathed at their hips, looked far more formidable as adversaries than the leader. Raez figured that they were his bodyguards, and found some consolation in the fact that they, at least, provided normal sensory information. Still, he had expected more from friends of Ashe. What could two average warriors and an acolyte offer that Raez, Ashe, and Thian could not already do themselves?

All the while, concern lined Thian's expression. He rose and approached Ashe in conversation while Raez remained hidden in the shadows. The three Illiri did not appear to be aware of the god.

Eventually, Thian returned to Raez. "That man"—he indicated the leader—"is named Fumond. He governs the town and, according to Ashe, can help you reach the coast."

"How doth he mean to aid me?" Raez asked.

"First, he requires a meeting with you."

"Is he aware of thy presence?"

Thian looked distracted. "I am not sure." He waved the thought aside. "Come. The sooner we resolve this, the better."

Once more, the god was not sharing all he knew. "As you wish." Walking on his three good limbs, Raez followed Thian.

Upon seeing Raez, the two bodyguards gripped the hilts of their swords. In response, he rose to his full height, towering a few feet above them. He did not wish to fight, but neither would he be deemed a weakling. Meanwhile, Fumond remained calm with the trace of a grin on his face. Another power suddenly coursed through the air like ripples of water. Raez thought it came from the Illiri leader at first, but now he was not sure in the face of a mist-like shroud surrounding both the leader and his two bodyguards. Could Fumond be more than an acolyte, but a seer or even a demi-god?

Meeting the man's gaze, Raez said, "I am Raez Het of the Thraz. I herald peace from Süretuwam, and request safe passage across thy lands."

Fumond motioned his guards back as he stepped toward Raez. He spoke in what sounded like the same language as Ashe, but Raez simultaneously heard a feminine voice rumbling like distant thunder: "Don't be afraid, traveler."

The voice was different than the one first heard in the desert. Surprised, Raez met the man's green eyes. "Who art thou?"

"Patience." Fumond's grin widened, though he had not spoken. "I can help free you from inferior companions," the female voice continued while the man addressed Ashe.

"Of what do they speak?" Raez asked Thian.

Uncertainty continued to shadow the god's disposition. After Raez repeated his question, Thian shook his head, as if to ward off a trance. "They are negotiating the terms of transporting you south in a ship."

Raez was tired of being excluded from the planning. "What manner of transport is a ship?"

"A vessel that glides across water," the god answered hastily. "It shall spare us not only time and effort, but various dangers. Fumond will ensure that it is so, but requires that one of his bodyguards, Heben, join us." He indicated the larger of the two guards.

"Dost thou trust Fumond?"

After studying the man for a while, Thian said, "I trust Ashe."

Fumond took another step toward Raez, quieting Ashe with a raised hand.

"Trust in strength," the female voice said. Fumond stared at Raez, saying something that he could not understand.

Ashe came next to Raez, standing between him and Thian, and spoke softly. Thian translated: "In addition to sending his bodyguard with us, Fumond requires a sample of the connection you have with your brethren."

A strange request, Raez thought. "What doth he imply?"

"A glimpse into the Unseen, perhaps," Thian answered. "Do this and he will bring you to Oceanus."

Focusing back on Fumond, wondering if his mind would be resilient like

Ashe's or fractured like the Dwarves, Raez said, "I can fulfill thy wish, but I caution thee: some are driven to desperation and madness as a result."

As Fumond and Ashe conversed, the voice returned. "I'll show you where true strength lies."

"Fumond accepts the risk," Thian interpreted.

"Dost thou hear the voice?" Raez asked quietly.

"What voice?" The god looked at him intently.

There was no time to clarify. Ashe stepped aside, providing space between Raez and Fumond. As she did so, Raez lowered himself so that his face matched the man's eye level. The other tensed slightly, despite what appeared to be his best effort to hide uncertainty.

"Yes," the voice whispered. "Do not fear your power."

Raez had never directly entered one person's consciousness, having only done so indirectly or with many at once, such as the contingent of Dwarves. For the Thraz, connection usually happened in the subconscious, in the visions of sleep, or else as a kind of collective echo of inspiration. Undeterred, and curious about discovering the source of power churning around Fumond, Raez focused on the green depths of the man's eyes and felt himself drawn in as though entering a mossy cave.

A rapid blur of images and sounds rushed past: a man and his son in a wooden vessel floating atop a large sea, fishing . . . the same man drifting lifelessly down into the deep . . . Fumond standing before two women, one leaving . . . the one who stayed leaping from a great height and violently striking the surface of a river . . . a group of roving Illiri, Fumond among them . . . the latter departing their company and meandering to the coast of Mirror Lake where a large creature stirs in the murky depths, its many limbs uncoiling like snakes to ensnare Raez.

With a shudder, Raez opened his eyes, not realizing he had closed them.

"Yes," the voice said, sounding pleased. "The water calls all . . . and binds all."

"What did you see?" Thian asked.

Raez stepped back, nearly stumbling. Was the vision connected to the mysterious voice or at odds with it? Were the gods trying to warn him?

"Be wary, Raez Het," the Frynosoma had said. "There are those in the Span who abandoned their roles long ago, who resist the will of the Spirits of Life . . . rogue entities . . ."

231

12

Cargo

The next night, having left Raez and Thian in the woods once more, Ashe returned with Fumond and his two bodyguards carrying a large wooden crate. Using Thian as an interpreter, Ashe explained to Raez that he was to get inside and be smuggled through town to a waiting ship. Raez did not like the idea of returning to confinement, nor did he feel comfortable with the persisting theme of hiding. He was a champion of the Thraz, son of the Aditám. He cowered before no one and no circumstance. "Is there another path?" he asked.

The Alöwean said something to Fumond who stepped forward and spoke.

"He assures you," Thian translated, "that this is the safest way to reach the coast. You will be provided regular food and drink. Fumond thinks, and Ashe agrees, that it is best for you to remain hidden from the ship's crew. Of those onboard, only Ashe and Fumond's bodyguard, Heben, will know of your presence."

"Why doth Fumond aid us?" Raez asked. "What doth he want?"

"I cannot say for certain," Thian answered. "Ashe says that Fumond sometimes values and trades insights over material goods."

Raez wondered at the absence of the voice from the previous evening. Had he imagined it, or was it now watching silently? He was not sure which prospect troubled him more. "So be it," he said to Thian. "I shall do their bidding. But I ask thee, how long must I remain in this wooden cage?"

"The journey will take many days," answered the god. "After crossing the Emülath Sea, the ship will follow a river downstream to the Illiri coastal town of Winslöri."

Fumond motioned for Raez to enter the crate, offering what Raez guessed was meant to be an assuring grin.

"All will be well," the god said as Raez crawled into his new confinement. *So sayest thou,* Raez reflected, *but time shall reveal all truths.*

* * *

It took a while for his stomach to adjust to the motion of the ship. Having never traveled on water before, he felt some disappointment that his experience had to be restricted to a small lightless space. The creak of wood sounded all around him, with the murmur of water beneath; above him the voices of the crew spoke in a language he could not understand. Their speech seemed muffled as though removed by an additional barrier beyond his cage, which left him feeling even more detached and at the mercy of strangers. Meditation only slightly helped contain the sensory excess as well as direct his thoughts away from a looming doom—some power he did not understand ready to pull him down into the fathomless deep.

He thought about Süretuwam, and wondered if his father was still alive. Raez's departure from the settlement left Züd without a direct successor. Further emboldened by Raez's absence, Halïrez had likely already challenged the current Adítam. Surely, Züd was strong enough to defeat the younger Thraz, but if the Ezren had secretly allied himself with the challenger, thinking him an even better pawn than Raez might have been, who knew what level of treachery was possible. The Ezren had gone so far as to have the Het murdered outside the tribe's knowledge. The seer would only continue to corrupt the strength of the Thraz. Guilt hammered at Raez's conscience. If the Ezren overreached his authority, thereby making the tribe vulnerable to external enemies, it was partly Raez's fault. He had made a choice to pursue the call of the gods. To protect the future of the

Thraz, he had little left but to return with a sign of the gods' favor and strength.

To rekindle a semblance of agency, Raez practiced maintaining the manifestation of his glowing right forearm. Moving his fingers and interacting with his environment became increasingly natural. The right hand's ability to interact with all tangible matter remained elusive, yet he became increasingly adept at comprehending the elements that comprised such material—the simplicity of the dried grass cushioning the crate's interior, or the fibers of the wood structure surrounding him on all sides.

Another remedy was to connect to the vision of Ornithez who paralleled the ship's progress from the safety of the shore. Outside, the hills of northern Illirium subsided to flatlands covered by tall green grass and patches of gnarled trees. The ship itself was unlike anything Raez had seen, with many features he could not describe. He wondered at its capabilities, and at the thought of a society not only having access to an abundance of water, but being able to use such a resource for swiftly covering long distances. Not wanting to hurt the minds of the crew and risk further delays to reaching Oceanus, Raez meditated regularly and limited his connection to his vulture.

Fumond's bodyguard, Heben, brought him supper each evening, sliding open a panel at the side of the crate. Morsels of meat were included in the meal, among other things Raez did not recognize. Some of it tasted strange, but at least temporarily quelled his deepening hunger. As his stomach remained tense from the movements of the ship, it was probably just as well not to eat heavily.

Of greater interest to him was Heben. His presence reminded Raez of their first encounter in the woods outside Fumond's Hut. A grey shroud concealed the bodyguard's emotional state, but Raez discerned him to be keenly attentive to his surroundings. The rhythm of the man's heart was also unusually slow.

"My thanks," he said to the bodyguard one night after receiving his daily ration of food.

Through the open slit, Raez glimpsed the man nod. Had he understood? Heben moved to close the panel, but Raez pressed his face near the opening.

"Wait."

Heben hesitated.

"Dost thou understand me?" Raez asked, quieting his voice, remembering that his presence on the ship was meant to remain a secret.

The man did not move.

"Wert thou the one I heard at our first meeting?"

Still nothing.

"What is thy true purpose here?"

Heben slid the panel closed then walked away.

Hours later, the voice returned while Raez meditated.

"Your perception is strong, son of Thraz." As before, the female voice rumbled like an approaching storm. "It's rare for a mortal to wield such power without more . . . direct influence."

"Who art thou?" Raez asked, now sure the voice had not come from Fumond. "I am a faithful servant of the gods. Show thyself to me."

"Peace, acolyte. Revelation comes to those who fulfill their potential with both courage and wisdom. You're well on your way, yet the gods you look to cannot help. Small-minded and weak, they're unworthy of your dedication. Faith in them only holds you back."

"They have not yet abandoned me," Raez countered, but recognized the lack of conviction in his tone.

"All while your fellow tribes fall, one by one enslaved, their leaders imprisoned and consumed. The Thraz won't elude the same destruction."

Indeed, Raez had long carried such doubts, their weight only increasing the longer he ventured with Thian. Yet, aside from a lack of understanding where his quest would lead him in the end, he could identify no real reason to mistrust the god's motives. There was only suspicion, but could that not be part of his spiritual refinement? He recalled the warning of the Ezren about a looming threat, and his own vision of the Frynosoma bound by shadows, calling for help and urgency. Something had to be done, but was he not trying? "What wouldst thou have me do?"

"Alone," the voice said, "you can gain nothing."

"What help dost thou offer? Canst thou give me a sign to empower my people against the rising menace?"

"I can help unite your people," the voice replied quietly, "but first, you must demonstrate greater prudence by leaving Thian Darhe."

"He hath proven true enough thus far."

"Thian Darhe uses you," the voice echoed with fervor. "Without you, he'd drift like an autumn leaf—dried of substance, though color remains on the surface. Don't be misled by it."

This fed Raez's suspicion. "If thou knowest so much and wilt help me, tell me this: what doth Thian intend to do?"

After a moment, the voice replied more gently: "He seeks she who abandoned him long ago."

Raez recalled something Thian had said. "His sister?"

"I don't know how he intends to use you to find her."

"Nor, it seems, canst thou offer me a greater reason to trust thee," Raez retorted. "Thian hath demonstrated worthiness through his presence and action. What provision maketh thou of equal or greater value?" Cramped in the crate, Raez understood his vulnerable position—that he may be going too far in questioning what might be another god—but he needed more definitive answers. Enough time had already been wasted.

"I'm a Sentinel," the voice said. "Call me Berech. Very soon, I'll reveal myself . . . but not yet."

"When?"

"When the ship reaches Winslöri, be ready."

"For what?"

"A reckoning."

The voice did not return. For days, Raez ruminated on the words of Berech. Were they full of truth, partial truths, or lies? Could this be just another god manipulating him? He was getting fed up with divine ambiguity. Yet, the thought of abandoning the gods felt more overwhelming; for without them, who was he and what was he even doing so far from home? His quest was defined by finding a sign that the gods had chosen him to be their next

Hand, the Ezren. He would not return with nothing to offer. If what he had foreseen was true, their future depended on his success. *I must not fail them.*

The thought of abandoning the Thraz brought Raez to the edge of a world too vast to comprehend. In isolation, he would be devoured. No, that was not his path. *I must endure whatever is to come, however long it may take.* He prayed that his quest was nearing its end, and that reaching the coast would resolve at least some of his questions. In the meantime, he would withhold judgment of Thian as well as Berech. If they were indeed greater beings, let them prove themselves for a change.

* * *

Ashe sat outside the crate whispering to Raez.

He wished that he understood her language; that they could speak privately, without Thian's mediation. What might they learn from each other, and what kind of connection, perhaps even friendship, might be fostered? Ashe and he were veterans of war, and both were outsiders from their society. While Ashe appeared to bury her pain and uncertainty, Raez sought to engage and learn from them, gaining wisdom and thereby power. He wanted to offer the Alöwean that kind of perspective, and to know what she had learned on her journey. He did not have all the answers, and would readily admit his own struggle with resolve. Berech's statement about how triumph rarely partnered with lone ambition echoed what the Ezren had once said: "As with us, the Spirits of Life need each other in order to flourish." Thus was Thraz culture defined. Ashe carried herself with such calm self-assurance. What could he learn from her about being more present, about freeing oneself from the burden of the future?

The side panel slid open. Looking through the gap, the space in which the crate was stored remained dark, but Raez still caught the glint of Ashe's brown eyes and the outline of her smooth crimson features. Sitting next to the crate with her arms around her knees, her expression appeared unusually pensive while her heart beat louder. *Yes,* Raez thought, there was more depth within her psyche than she readily conveyed. Her choices were likely less about concealment than protection.

Staring ahead, away from Raez, she said something more. He was suddenly struck by how soothing her voice sounded, like flowing water—a contrast to the guttural reverberations of his own tongue.

"I desire friendship between us," he said.

Without turning her head, she glanced at him. Slowly, a grin formed, but it bore the trace of sadness. She began to lift her left hand toward the crate, hesitated, and then continued, ultimately gripping the bottom ledge of the panel opening. After another moment, she rotated her hand and opened it to expose the palm. Without thinking, Raez carefully placed his own hand on hers; and as he did so, she tightened her fingers around his. Her hand felt small and soft. He realized with a pang of both happiness and grief that this was the first time he had touched someone without hostility since his quest had begun. In truth, it was the first time he had connected with anyone this way. After so many weeks of tension and stress, he wished to rest a while in such tranquility. He realized that it was the kind of future he desired for himself and for all.

Ashe's eyes narrowed as she looked at him. The grin faded, she withdrew her hand, and nodded her head slowly to herself. Murmuring something, she then stood and was about to close the panel when Thian appeared, glowing a dull white with ripples of gold and crimson underneath.

"How are you managing down here, Raez?" he asked with his airy voice, sticking his head through the sideboards of the crate.

"Where hast thou been?" Raez asked, annoyed not only by the god's appearance, but his intrusion on an intimate moment.

"Forgive my absence," Thian answered. "An invisible presence concerns me."

Raez thought of Berech. "Dost thou foresee a threat?"

"We should be cautious," the god said. "I know not what it wants, or the extent of its capabilities, but suspect that it is another Séoran, perhaps one of the Fallen."

Ashe said something to Thian. He responded, to which she departed.

Returning his attention to Raez, Thian added, "Soon, you will have a chance to stretch your limbs and breathe fresh air again. It may be the only opportunity before reaching Winslöri. Oceanus is not much farther, my friend. We shall reach it in less than four days."

13

Oceanus

My ears are deaf beyond the pounding wind. Swirling sand stings my flesh; to open mine eyes means blindness. Bent double against it to survive, though sand banks rise and hold me fast, how much and for how long might I endure? Slowly, buried by each testing moment, my resolution suffocates.

Suddenly there is quiet, and I feel nothing.

Shielding mine eyes with my one remaining hand, I dare to look. Dunes surround me, staring down at my lone form. Shaking off the sand, I ascend the tallest mound. A vast desert revealeth itself, heated by an unseen sun. The sky is black, yet somehow brightness glows over the barren expanse.

To my right: a line of mountains like jagged teeth. To my left: a taller range. And there within that cluster of mountains lurketh a presence, menacing and watchful. Towards it moveth a column of cloaked figures. They ride mounts of a breed unknown to me—similar to ponies, but larger. The riders cross the desert in a column approaching an invisible barrier. I see it not, but I discern its power. Is it meant to keep the riders out or something else imprisoned?

I should not be here.

A soft voice whispereth in my ear: "Welcome to Oblivion."

I look around but see no one.

The voice is familiar, yet not my own. It remindeth me of the Frynosoma, only sinister.

"Who art thou?" I ask.

"You know who I am," the voice sayeth.

Two large birds soar across the sky. One is black, the other white—not eagles, but the birds I have seen before, though not in waking. I spot Ashe riding the black one, clinging to its long slender neck.

"She does not see you," the voice declareth with a hint of amusement. "She does not hear."

I return my attention to the scene at my left, and realize that one rider hath separated from the column and approacheth me. He removeth his hood, revealing himself as the bodyguard, Heben. "I am here." The man offereth his hand, yet his mouth moveth not. "Come."

"Berech?" I say.

Heben smileth at me.

The clouds of doom that had gathered in Raez's visions shadowed his waking, making him feel exposed. The imagery no longer reflected only Ashe's memories, he surmised, but suggested an intrusion into the present. It was not Thian. Though the god often cloaked himself in a layer of mystery, appearing in some visions, his presence had never felt antagonistic. No, something else had entered. *Berech.* Was the figure of Heben merely some kind of disguise? If a god, what did she—or he, or it—intend, and what did she want with him? Or was Berech's real interest directed elsewhere, leaving Raez an onlooker?

If the gods were divided in their loyalties to the point of conflict as the Frynosoma had suggested, Raez did not want to be trapped between them. The presence in Raez's recent vision reminded him of the nameless threat against his people. Could Berech be the source of that threat, or was she merely a messenger? Where did Thian's loyalty ultimately lie? By comparison, Ashe seemed a ready friend. The language barrier remained a problem, but felt less formidable than the prospect of having to contend with the will of the gods. Could he free himself from the gods and remain allied with the Alöwean?

Free myself from the gods, he mused, chuckling bitterly to himself. *Folly.* Yet, if the gods would not help him, at least not without manipulation, who else could Raez trust? The Thraz survived not by individual heroism, but unified purpose. He missed his brothers. Isolation was the greatest danger.

"Can you smell it?" Thian asked, suddenly appearing in the crate. His body glowed softly, revealing the featureless interior where Raez reclined.

"Smell what?" Raez asked.

The god inhaled with an expression of satisfaction. "The sea."

A sulfuric, tangy aroma filled Raez's nose. At first, he could not decide if he liked it, but thinking of it in association with Oceanus filled him with some hope. "How much farther?"

"Your servant, Ornithez, can already see it."

Connecting to the vulture, which currently circled over some carrion near the bank of the river, Raez glimpsed a blue-green horizon to the south. At its edge stretched a flatland of grass and shrubs. Even closer, along the shore of the river, was a settlement.

"We shall reach Winslöri within the hour," the god added.

Raez detached his consciousness from Ornithez and saw Thian smiling at him. "What then?"

"When the time is right," Thian answered, "this crate shall be taken ashore with you still inside. From there, Ashe will determine the best way to get you out of the town."

"What of Fumond's bodyguard?"

The god's smile faltered. "Heben has nearly served his purpose. He may be a problem."

"What nature of problem?"

Thian tilted his head. "Do you not already suspect?"

Trying to maintain a calm respectful tone, all the while agitated by the god, Raez pressed, "What dost thou know?"

"There is indeed another Séoran among us." Thian's voice remained hushed above a whisper. "Of that, I am now certain. Last night, I spied her speaking with Heben. I do not know if she meant for me to see, to defy me, or whether there was another reason."

"Who is she?"

"She is not a servant of Elíbom Prímom."

Raez hesitated. Should he tell Thian what he knew?

The god narrowed his eyes. "You once asked me about hearing a voice. Has she spoken to you?"

"She names herself Berech." Revealing that kind of detail seemed worth the risk. Raez needed to learn what he could from Thian.

Crossing his arms, Thian withdrew so that only his face appeared in the inside wall of the crate. "I do not know what else she has told you. As she has concealed herself from my eyes, so also she has apparently muted her voice from my ears. . . . I suspect her to be one of the Fallen."

"She hath called herself a Sentinel," Raez offered.

Thian's eyes widened. "Has she?"

"Canst thou not also veil thyself from her?"

"I can, and have been doing so to the extent of my power since we reached Fumond's Hut—since our first encounter. Yet, that has its limits."

So, Thian had known since the beginning. Raez needed more to make a choice. But first: "What is a Sentinel?"

Thian sighed, his light diminishing. "The Sentinels have a complicated history. They aspire to create their own kingdom autonomous from the original order—from that of Elíbom Prímom."

The gods are indeed at war with each other.

"Their cause was devastated in the Illirium War," Thian continued. "Most were slain, having sought to expand their influence by partnering with mortals like the Alöweans and Illiri. Those that remain are scattered, their loyalties divided. There are chaotic powers at work in Illirium. Too well do I know such grief."

"Thinkest thou Heben is in partnership with Berech?"

"It is likely."

"And Berech is one of the chaotic powers?"

"Yes." Thian looked up. "The desert you saw in your recent vision is called Oblivion, and the region beyond is known as Seeregüm. Most of what you saw was actually a glimpse of history. Ashe served for a time patrolling that desert. If Heben was one of those who crossed the Divide then danger is close."

Raez did not like how much the god knew of his visions. A storm of questions gathered. "Thou alludest to ancient conflicts, but what have they to do with me and my brethren? We fight not in the wars of Illirium, and I am still a Thraz Het."

"Think not so lowly of yourself," the god urged, some of his vigor returning. "Remember your quest. The power once kept behind the Divide is now unbound, seeking to poison every source of order and peace in the world—as far as can be reached, including the Northland where your people dwell. Your presence here, along with your rising engagement with the Unseen, provides either an ally or enemy to it."

Thus, Berech had sought Raez first as an ally. "What can I do to resist such a power?"

"Remember all that you have seen and heard," Thian answered. "Remember your quest. You stand at the threshold."

"What lies beyond?"

"Corruption . . . or liberation."

Raez decided that if Heben threatened Ashe, he would come to her aid. Yet, if Heben or the power behind him only challenged Thian, Raez would see who came out the victor. The gods owed him a clear answer. One way or another, regardless of which god showed him the way, Raez would reach Oceanus.

* * *

Raez heard voices outside, including those of Ashe and Heben, and felt himself moved in a series of efforts, presumably to the shore. As they went, light flickered through the seams of the crate, fresh air seeped through, and the temperature cooled. He drew his bearskin cloak closer. Once the crate was set down, the earth seemed to still sway like water, jarring his equilibrium.

Connecting to Ornithez confirmed Raez's whereabouts. Night had settled over Winslöri. The crate sat on a cart harnessed to a grey, four-legged creature similar to those Raez had seen in his recent dream, only slightly smaller. The cart reminded him of the Young Brothers removing the dead from battle. Heben drew a heavy tarp over the back of the cart, casting Raez in shadow once more.

Outside, Ashe and Heben conversed with each other.

"It is time," Thian said, peeking his head into the end of the crate closest to Raez's feet—the end comprising the way in and out. A scuffle sounded outside. "Hurry," he urged, indicating where the crate door could be slid open.

Hastily, Raez reached down and did so, and then crawled backwards out of the crate into the cool evening air. Various small lamps lit the settlement to his right. Nearby, water lapped against boats of differing sizes. He did not dare escape into the river at his left, for he would surely drown, but also felt intimidated by the tall, labyrinthine structures comprising the town. Escaping alone was not yet an option.

"Time to choose," Berech's voice interrupted Raez's thoughts. Echoes like unintelligible whispers suddenly surrounded him, swelling into a crescendo.

Disoriented, Raez saw Heben pressing Ashe against the side of a nearby building, gripping her neck. Why were they fighting?

"Free yourself," the voice said.

"Berech is here." Thian stood next to Raez, his voice clear through the din. His eyes focused on something beyond the bodyguard. "Help Ashe."

"Shut out the deceivers," the voice continued.

The Alöwean appeared to need no assistance, having separated herself from Heben by means of a knife; yet traces of fear and rage emanated from her form: shuddering blue and blazing amber.

"Cross the threshold," the voice urged.

"And thee?" Raez replied, struggling to concentrate as he felt increasingly agitated from the voices in his head. He was concerned more about Berech than Ashe, for he could find no sign of the god, discerning only a watchful presence looming nearby, growing. "Wilt thou do nothing?" he asked, whether to Thian or Berech or some other power, he could not say. Were the gods weaker than he thought?

"Do whatever must be done with Heben," Thian said grimly, still gazing ahead.

Meeting Ashe's eyes as she gasped for breath, Raez felt a momentary clarity. Whoever Berech was, her elusiveness posed a more immediate danger than what he knew about Thian. *One doubt at a time*, he thought. *One conquest.*

Facing Heben, Raez removed his cloak. "Let her be," he ordered. The man looked back at him and said something. His heart rate had elevated, but his inner being remained otherwise concealed by a misty aura.

In Raez's periphery, Thian's form brightened white with undulating shades of gold and crimson, his form gathering currents of air toward him. "Focus ahead," his voice boomed among the rising chorus. He surged forward in a streak like lightning.

Raez did not look away fast enough to avoid being temporarily blinded by the light. Trying to ignore the black spots hovering across his vision, letting instincts take mastery, he rushed forward on his hind legs and seized Heben with his left hand. The bodyguard's eyes widened as he did not have time to resist being picked up and thrown against the wall.

Feeling unbalanced, having not used his legs for so long, Raez rubbed his eyes with his right hand to refresh his equilibrium. The voices vanished instantly, and he was surprised to feel his sensory confusion dissipate like smoke drawn from his mind. Glancing at his right hand, now radiating with bronze light, he realized with mounting confidence that he had expelled them himself.

Before him, Heben rose unsteadily to his feet, his countenance less commanding than Raez had ever seen. The sulfuric stench of fear began to rise from his body; his aura was no longer concealed, but revealed a confusion of churning black. Nearby, a whirlwind of dust burst from the side of a building. Where was Thian? What was happening?

One challenge at a time, Raez reminded himself. He grabbed the bodyguard once again, lifting him with little effort, and hurled him into the center of the river. The ease of doing so amazed him, until he reasoned that his right arm, a gift from the gods, had infused the rest of his body with a new level of strength.

As fast as her crippled foot allowed, Ashe ran past Raez, speaking and waving for him to follow. The cause of her haste appeared to be five Illiri soldiers approaching their position. They did not worry him, but neither did he wish to further escalate the situation.

As his visage was certainly too conspicuous for an Illiri town, even in the cover of night, Raez retrieved his cloak from the ground, wrapped it around him, pulling the hood down over his face as much as possible, and ran ahead of Ashe toward one passageway. He tried to connect to Ornithez, who would be able to provide a helpful aerial view of the labyrinth, but failed. *Strange.* The vulture was near, but Raez found himself struggling to breathe and his energy waning. Whether it was from malnourishment, days of immobility, or drawing power from his renewed arm, he could not say.

Ashe called to him, indicating that they go right along a wider way.

After a few false turns and briefly hiding to catch their breaths, they reached a gate. Dawn approached. The gate was open, but many armed guards stood attentive to those passing in and out. They did not intimidate Raez, but he preferred to not fight his way through—not if it could be avoided. Advancing in peace began with him, yet that kind of self-control required more energy than he felt. Considering the number of guards, the risks were too great anyway. He had Ashe to also think about. She stared at the scene with a firmly set jaw, her eyes fierce but bloodshot. Neither of them could afford such a gamble.

"Hurry," a soft whistling voice said.

Startled, Raez looked up to see one of Thian's sparrows, Oshrémi, perched above them on the edge of a roof. The other sparrow, Osré, swooped down and landed on Raez's shoulder. "Follow," he said faintly.

Putting aside his surprise at beginning to understand their speech, Raez tracked the movement of Osré as he flew up and rejoined his brother, both of whom fluttered from perch to perch, ensuring that Raez and Ashe could keep up. Raez even glimpsed Ornithez higher above, and guessed that his vulture was helping scout the way with the sparrows.

At last, they reached an unguarded portion of Winslöri's outer wall, at which point, with little deliberation, Raez carried Ashe over as he had done at the outpost of the Dwarves many weeks earlier. Tired of captivity and escaping foreign settlements, he resolved to maintain better control of his circumstances. No more cages and crates, for a start.

Having descended the other side of the wall, they followed the birds across a field of dense brush toward the sound of soft thunder. The rumbling did not crack like real thunder, but carried with it a majestic kind of tenderness.

Thian stood at the edge of a precipice ahead, his inner light dimmed. He smiled weakly upon seeing them, beckoning with one hand while the other pointed toward a glimmering horizon. "Oceanus," he said, voice rising above the crash of waves below. He looked weary, and tried to cover marks on his chest and neck with his forearm and hand. "It waits for you."

The words were familiar. The scene was familiar. Raez recalled his vision in the presence of the Frynosoma, Voice of the Gods. Slowing at the edge of the cliff, he gazed out at Oceanus. Ornithez glided high above, riding a gentle air current. Mustering the strength to temporarily connect with the vulture's vision, Raez looked out at an endless expanse of water. Not even Ornithez could see its end.

The multitude of shimmering green and blue hues, the roaring depth of such a mass, stirred both delight and fear in Raez. The salty air elicited additional feelings of strength and freedom; the sound of the waves was like the voice of a god greater than any he had yet encountered. Looking beyond the visible, Raez witnessed a maelstrom of white light rippling with the calm of a crimson dusk and the hardiness of golden desert sand.

To flow as water is to learn the way of truth and an undivided heart.

That so much water could exist in the world—Raez struggled to absorb the sight. While at first he felt exhilarated by the beauty and possibilities, the sentiment soon sank into a well of emptiness. Was this it, the end of his quest? Recalling the vision from Fumond of the creature reaching for him from the deep, he wondered if he should step any closer. Had the imagery been a warning from the gods or merely his own fear trying to stop him?

"Beyond that horizon," Thian said, smiling, pointing south across Oceanus, "is my homeland, the dwelling place of Elíbom Prímom."

The Span, Raez thought, *land of the gods.* "Can it truly be reached by mortal kind?"

Thian grinned. "Yes." Still pressing his hand against the lacerated flesh of his upper chest and lower neck, he looked down to where the waves crashed into the shore. On the sandy bank waited a small wooden vessel.

"Be that a boat?" Raez asked. His vulture, Ornithez, swooped down and landed on his shoulder.

"Yes," the god replied.

Surely, the vessel was too small for crossing such immensity. Besides, Raez knew nothing about navigating water, and the god appeared to be hurt.

Where is the sign?

Or did the gods once again call him forth in faith, in being sure of his hope and certain of what he could not see?

"What happened betwixt Berech and thee?" he asked Thian.

"Berech will no longer be a problem," the other answered.

So be it. The gods had chosen.

The east blazed with golden rays, like the fingers of the divine. Was there a preeminent deity, a ruler of the gods, as Thian had said? Who was this Elíbom Prímom, and if such a being beckoned Raez onward, could it be trusted more than the rest? Standing on the edge of the cliff, no good option other than journeying forward presented itself.

The time has not come to turn back. Was that his own notion or had it come from the other voice?

Something called from across Oceanus, some power that he trusted could help him lead his people. Raez felt a rising certainty at the prospect, but also a lingering trepidation.

Enough.

He could no longer let feelings dictate his identity and purpose. Feelings could inform the present, but the time for merely envisioning himself as the Ezren Aditám was coming to a close. Glancing at his glowing right arm, he knew that he had to start living like one, not only seizing every opportunity and trusting in the gods, but also trusting himself. "I will cross," he told

Thian.

"I will join you," the god said.

"No," Raez countered. "This shall I do alone."

"But how will you navigate Oceanus?" Thian urged. "I know the currents better than most, and can show you the way to Elíbom Prímom."

The sudden trace of subservience in the god's tone and posture pleased Raez. The god had proven himself useful enough, and Raez had to think practically. Focusing on a path winding down to the shore and boat below, Raez said to Thian, "Come."

III

THIAN

1

Awakening

Nothing.
  Until darkness
  churns in the void, slowly filling
  a brightening mass: light
  illuminating black mist,
  floating tendrils of texture,
  particles,
  matter—
  the world.

Stirring
  the sea
  of currents rising
  before new sky
  bounds unravel, contract, set
  apart by celestial bodies,
  revolving shapes of substance,
  movement,
  life:
  the span of Oceanus.

"Awake, oh sleeper. Arise to the sun."

Sensations: a myriad of discoveries that begin with the soft caress of water, cool then warm. From the depths of murky shadows, we swim over rock to sandy floor, clutching each hold, pulling ourselves up toward breath. The murmur of currents nudges us onward. The waves applaud our coming. A shining surface awaits—so close, we can almost touch it.

At last, emerging from the hands of water and frothing foam, we stand—shakily at first—eyes blinded by new daylight, and then step forward invigorated, delighted, ready.

"Welcome to Rühílawé," the voice says.

Peace.

"Who are you?" we ask.

"I am." The voice emanates from the ground below and heavens above. "Power." Warmth surrounds us. "Presence." A figure materializes. "Unity." Her long white hair shimmers, framing tan skin, her form clothed in translucent silver. "Breath." She smiles, offering her hand. "Alíndor."

The one who sees.

"I am the manifest spirit of the Creator, Elíbom Prímom," she says.

"And who are we?"

Alíndor's smile widens, her eyes vibrant like the green foliage now tickling our feet, rapidly growing up to our knees. Everything is growing, filling the reaches of the land—trees expanding toward the sky like pillars, rivers carving paths through the earth, mountains swelling with shifting underground pressure. Soon, fish that swim, birds that glide, creatures that hum, and animals that run populate every corner.

"You are Séorans," Alíndor says, "sibling servants of Elíbom Prímom, your names shall be Darhe, 'the beautiful intimate'—Thian and Phedra."

Glancing at Phedra, meeting her eyes, which are white like tufts of clouds on a sunny day, I feel known and beloved. Looking back at me, she reflects my joy with her smile. For the first time, I let go her hand and study my own, seeing that our forms are alike; only her skin is a darker shade of indigo than mine.

"What do you desire of us, lord?" Phedra asks Alíndor.

Alíndor motions around us. "On this island and the mainland beyond, you are to steward the splendor of life, especially the smaller variety of plants and birds." With her palm held open, she lifts her hand, upon which a pair of brown sparrows land with a cheep of greeting. "These two shall be your helpers, Osré and Oshrémi."

The birds flutter over to us, Osré landing on Phedra's shoulder and Oshrémi on mine. In a series of chirrups, they share about what they have seen and heard.

There is so much to discover.

We laugh together, and with Alíndor's blessing, begin our task. Phedra and I stick our hands into the earth, feeling the tremors of its speech and the flow of its water and substance. Seeds form in our palms, their roots tickling our fingers. Soon, bright green shoots burst from the soil, drinking in the sunlight and rain. We do not create life, for only Elíbom Prímom has such power, but rather nurture its growth with the freedom to shape much of its expression.

"More color," Phedra urges me, smiling, kissing the leaves and blossoms, invigorating them with her breath and voice. She focuses on giving the plants strength and resilience, while I embellish their expression. We call the smallest birds to enjoy the shelter of the leaves, to build nests among their branches and feast on the succulent berries.

Other Séorans tend to their own charges, whether the trees, mountains, waterways, or some manner of creature. We all bask in the handiwork of Elibom Prímom, finding in it nourishment for each day. The most prominent sign of his sustenance is the Balmwéa Elïf, a tree with rich brown bark by day, white like the moon at night, and its ongoing harvest of golden fruit with leaves and blossoms of changing colors. Ever learning, exploring, and expanding our artistry throughout Rühílawé, Phedra and I know only harmony and bliss. So it is with all creation.

* * *

I am no warrior, but that does not mean I am helpless. I have come to

255

understand that the enemy preys upon fear, ignorance, and division, its influence more potent against mortal kind than those of us still loyal to Elíbom Prímom. If I am bold and swift, I may prevail. Violence is not my way, but I know of no other means by which to be free from this hostile presence. I do not wish to kill Berech, a fellow Séoran, but nor will I let her do as she pleases with Raez and Ashe. Yet, in choosing to fight her will I sever myself irreparably from the goodness to which I was born? Does that goodness still even exist?

I send Osré out to find aid, and pray that it comes in time.

As evening settles over the city of Winslöri, with the rumble of surf only a few miles away and the scent of the sea fresh in the air, Raez is brought ashore still concealed in his wooden crate. Fumond's bodyguard, Heben, oversees the process, and has the crate placed on a cart covered by a tarp. Ashe is present throughout.

In my sparrow form, I observe from the shadowed corner of a rooftop, trying to keep hidden. Berech takes refuge within Heben's being; the Illiri bodyguard appears to welcome her presence while also retaining some autonomy. This suggests that Berech's hold over Heben is limited, providing a gap by which to break them apart, saving me from having to conquer Heben to get to Berech.

Still, doubts try to paralyze my initiative. Lacking confidence about the outcome is difficult enough without the added sense of not knowing what I am doing. What if I fail to contain Berech? What if I succeed? If, in the end, I must choose between my life and hers, will I have the fortitude to do what is necessary to survive?

Focus. I must not dwell on all the possibilities. I do this for Phedra; she is my priority. I fight for Raez and Ashe only so far as they can help me reach her. I care for them, but I care for Phedra more.

While Ashe distracts Heben, his back to the cart, I glide down and resume my Séoran form.

"I told you to stay out of my way," Berech's voice startles me. I see her pale blue figure wearing Heben's form like a transparent garment, though she presently faces the opposite direction as the man.

Trying to ignore her, I hurriedly motion for Oshrémi to give Ashe the signal while I poke my head into the crate, encouraging Raez to get out. Looking back outside, my heart falters when I see Heben clutching Ashe by the throat.

"There'll be consequences to your meddling," Berech comments. I cannot tell how much she controls Heben's actions. Within the shroud of Heben's form, she turns to face the same direction as him, but then glances back over his shoulder. "You can have what's left of the Alöwean, but Raez Het comes with me."

Raez stands next to me. "Berech is here," I tell him. I do not think he sees the other Séoran, for his eyes are fixed on Ashe. "Help Ashe."

"And thee?" he asks me. "Wilt thou do nothing?"

"Do whatever must be done with Heben," I urge.

Stepping forward, I gather all available light between my palms, expanding it in an energy sphere as bright as sunlight upon water. As it envelops me with warmth and clarity of vision, I step fully into the Unseen, extend my translucent wings from my back, and surge forward. The force of impact with Berech is not as painful as I anticipate; slamming my shoulder into her torso, she loses contact with the ground and with Heben. I drive her back, her legs and arms flailing, against the dimly visible grey wall of the nearby building. The wall does not break, but the impact hurts Berech enough to cause her to gasp. Dissociated from the presence of Elíbom Prímom and the Balmwéa Elïf for so long, her form has drifted from the Unseen toward the mortal realm. Thus are the Fallen doomed to the corporeal dimension and all its limitations.

She is no weakling, however. She pushes herself from the wall with one foot while the other finds traction on the ground, and digs her clawed fingers into my back. Her mouth opens wide with rows of sharp, uneven teeth. I cry out as she bites into the base of my neck.

Her hold weakens as I punch her lean stomach. I further separate myself from her by pressing my other forearm up between our chests and pushing myself free. Now separated a few strides, we begin to circle each other.

The space around us is a blur of shadowed grey and brown shapes, mostly stone and earth, with glimmers of dim light from nearby lamps. To my right, the river radiates swirling blue with small silvery shapes of fish and green lengths of plants stirring within. Ahead, the faint crimson glow of Ashe is followed by the bronze brightness of Raez running away from the fight. Heben is no longer in sight. Berech does not notice them. Her eyes glow dimly red. Her limbs are now longer, as are her clawed fingers. She licks her lips.

"I've missed the taste of Séoran flesh," she says, smiling, her voice grating like the sound of metal scraping over metal. "You're out of your depth, curator."

She swipes at my face with her claws faster than I anticipate, barely missing. I manage to block a subsequent attack from her other fist, and then rapidly lose ground as I try to deflect blow after blow. A solid kick from her heel into my thigh makes me stumble. She seizes my wrist and pulls me down to her, pressing her feet into my midsection, and launches me back over her head.

Swiftly I turn over, stand, and ram into her from behind as she returns to her feet. With my right hand clinging to the back of her neck and the other gripping her upper left arm, I drive her to the nearest wall, slamming her head against its cold stone aura again and again. Black blood splatters from her battered forehead, but her body does not slacken. Her right elbow comes back into my eye. Blinded, I let go of her and stagger back.

When I recover my sight, Berech is crawling up the side of the grey building like a spider. Extending my wings, I leap into the air, transforming into a sparrow, and when I am above her on the rooftop, dive down upon her in my Séoran form. A tangle of limbs, we reel down the side of the roof and plummet to the ground with me on the bottom. The impact robs me of breath.

Still atop me, Berech reaches for my throat. My left hand holds her back just enough, but my right arm is pinned by her knee. The claws of her second hand dig into my chest. The pain becomes overwhelming.

But then her weight is gone.

Coughing and clutching my bloodied chest, I sit up. Osré lands on my knee, chirping.

"Find Oshrémi," I say, coughing again. "Guide Raez and Ashe to the coast. I will follow."

Looking past my sparrow servant as he departs, I watch three helmed Séorans in bright silver armor hold Berech against the faint grey mass of the building wall. Their lucent wings fold back and vanish from sight. One pins Berech in place with a spear tip stabbed firmly in her side, keeping her compliant, while the other two hold and bind her with chains of fiery light.

"You have no authority here," Berech protests, though her voice sounds weak. She has reverted to her more humanlike Séoran form, her black eyes wide with alarm.

"We have all authority," replies the female Séoran fastening the chains.

"The margins of Illirium are changing," the spearman adds. Once the prisoner is secured, he withdraws his spear point, raises the visor of his helm, and looks at me.

"Thank you for coming," I say, nodding in respect.

"Your sparrow was adamant," he replies, "and we are tasked with watching the river for signs of the enemy." Focusing on Berech, he states, "By decree of Captain Lachímel, the Fallen are to be brought to him for questioning." Returning his attention to me, he adds, "Continue to be vigilant, curator, for the servants of Üzmaveth are on the move."

"I don't serve Üzmaveth," Berech protests.

"Quiet," the first female Séoran warrior says. Stepping back, she draws a sword and places the edge of the blade against Berech's neck.

"Has Alíndor finally come?" I ask. "Has the Restoration begun?"

The Séoran spearman looks at me without expression, though his grey eyes suggest calculation.

The third Séoran, his visor still covering his face, says nothing, but keeps a firm hold on the occasionally squirming form of Berech.

"You should come with us," the female swordsman says, keeping her blade against Berech's neck. "The more that we who are still loyal to Elíbom Prímom join together in this war, the less this world will suffer."

"My purpose is elsewhere," I say, thinking of my mission.

"It is unwise to venture alone these days," the female swordsman comments.

"I am not alone," I answer.

"Then may Elíbom Prímom guide you," the spearman replies. He nods, brings down his visor, and turns to his two companions who lead Berech away by the chain while he follows a step behind with his spear lowered and ready.

Watching them go, my thoughts shift to Raez and Ashe. I fly for a while in my sparrow form, but find myself too tired to maintain it. Just beyond the walls of the city, therefore, I land and continue on foot in my natural state. My eye aches, and my neck and chest sting. Soon, I reach the cliffs overlooking the sea, but find Ashe and Raez nowhere in sight.

2

Boundaries

Eventually, history is understood as a progression where one can glance ahead or look back as though standing on a single road. That is the way of humanity, at least. Most of us Séorans dwell at either side of that path, able to examine and cross it at will, though not to the extent of actually venturing backward or forward in time. We are limited by time, yet our memories are clearer, and our ability to consider the history of the earth more like a sphere than a line. Life is less about future and past, but an ongoing, integrated present.

In the beginning, Elíbom Prímom created the land of Rühilawé. As other races are brought to life, as lands shift and borders are set, two kingdoms emerge: the Upper, retaining the name Rühilawé, where Elíbom Prímom dwells as Alíndor, and the Middle, Triönym, predominantly inhabited by the Elphadém.

Elíbom Prímom forms the Elphadém from the earth, shaping them to be distinct from the rest of corporeal kind, with greater awareness and wisdom. Their form—voice, hands, and feet—are said to be an echo of his essence. They look similar to us Séorans, but are made of a more vulnerable matter, and less luminous, their skin pigmented like one of the many shades of soil, with variance between groups—some lighter while others are darker. The First Born, as some call him, is Fréalwë, whose care for nature—more reaping than sowing by my estimation—holds sway over the health of the earth. With his partner, Evelën, Fréalwë ventures north into the Upper Kingdom and builds a city around the Balmwéa Elïf, the tree that bears the fruit of immortality. For years, the Upper and Middle kingdoms remain thereby linked, their spaces and inhabitants ever mingling.

I go to the city only a few times at Phedra's beckoning, but prefer the quiet stillness of the southern wilderness. I seldom turn my attention to matters beyond my charge. I would rather bask in the sun, float with the breeze, or glide as a bird across the heavens. The sparrows delight me, but I am most transfixed by the swans.

To dwell more tangibly in the world, particularly to fly, Phedra and I sometimes assume the forms of swans—Phedra with white feathers, me with black. Though navigating physical temporality that way requires greater energy, it enables us to fly and interact more directly with certain aspects of the visible world. I find the Elphadém to be the most wondrous and complicated of the mortal order, yet prefer to observe them from a distance. It is simpler that way. They are not our responsibility—leave that to the Séoran commanders. Phedra and I are curators of nature's smaller details.

"Shall we return to the northern lakes?" I ask Phedra one day. We often travel with the swan bevy across northern Triönym.

She shakes her head. "Not this time."

Ever since the Elphadém came, Phedra's interest has been divided between studying them and fulfilling our responsibility. She laughs less.

"Does it no longer bring you joy?" I ask.

"Too much is happening here," she replies.

I fly north, but it is not the same without her.

* * *

When Ashe brings Fumond and his two Illiri bodyguards to where Raez and I wait in the forest, I discern the presence of another being from the Unseen. It veils itself from my sight, leaving me suspicious of its intent. As

Raez connects with Fumond's mind to share in so-called revelation, I place my hand on the man's shoulder to glimpse his subconscious state and what they are sharing, also hoping to discover whether or not the presence is associated with him.

When I touch Fumond's shoulder, I find myself standing next to Raez who observes a stormy sea from a high cliff. A black mass stirs in the gloomy depths below, its limbs breaching the water's surface like tentacles. They reach for us, wrapping around our bodies, and pull us down. Overwhelmed by my own shock, I do not see what happens to Raez. All I know is that I crash through the waves and am brought into the deep to the body of the creature. Instead of some monster, however, I am faced with a dim visage of Phedra. The tentacles protruding from her back wrap tighter around me, drawing me close to her in a horrifying embrace. She smiles, revealing a large mouth of long, crooked flat teeth.

It cannot be you. I try to cry out, but cannot make a sound.

"The water calls all," she says, her voice like the dull thunder of waves above, "and binds all."

I do not know what that creature was. The imagery slithers through my thoughts, most prevalently when I am alone. It could not have been Phedra, for why would she appear to me like that now? Was this some mockery of me? Was it a warning?

When the ship sails from Fumond's Hut with Raez and Ashe safely aboard, my apprehension only intensifies. The presence lingers, and I gather that it has something to do with Fumond's bodyguard, Heben. Generally, I stay out of the humans' way in the form of a sparrow, a step dissociated from the Unseen, but the effort tires my already weary state. For a Séoran to remain too long in the physical plane risks becoming trapped in it. The exact threshold has proven to be different for each Séoran, presenting another challenge. Being away so long from Rühílawé and the Balmwéa Elïf, I cannot risk it. I have not the strength. What has happened to Phedra must not happen to me.

At times, the invisible presence feels distant, and I wonder if I worry unnecessarily.

Not wanting to lose sight of my purpose, I speak with Ashe, continuing to nurture the possibility that she come with me across the sea. After all, she should return to the place of her birth. It will lift her spirit in a new way—I am sure of it, or at least aim for it to be a compelling argument. If for some reason Raez decides that his quest goes no further than the coast, I need Ashe to bring me across. I thought about stowing away on another ship, from Winslöri or elsewhere, but have heard that no one sails across Oceanus anymore—not like the Elphadém and Alöweans once did; not since the creation of the Doors, though they are now shut. I can think of no other way but by Ashe or Raez.

At night, the presence draws closer. That Raez has heard a voice as well leads me to wonder if the presence is actually here for him. Could it be trying to turn him away from his quest? I must work harder to discover the source.

Raez and Ashe have each confessed to me their uneasiness about Heben. This is good, for the shared mistrust keeps us closer together. I have the Illiri bodyguard watched more closely by Osré. Ashe suspects Heben is an agent of the new Illiri king in the west, Dwairian—the lord who allied with Üzmaveth in the Illirium War. In a vision, Raez witnessed Heben riding in a cloaked company across the Desert of Oblivion toward the Divide, the barrier that once contained Üzmaveth. If Heben is allied to an agent of Üzmaveth, danger is close.

Raez tells me that the presence has identified herself as Berech, and calls herself a Sentinel. *Curious.* Most of the Sentinels were slain during the Illirium War, having partnered with forces that resisted Üzmaveth. Comprised of so-called repentant Fallen, the Sentinels had the misguided ambition of establishing a kingdom autonomous from both Elíbom Prímom and Üzmaveth.

The world has become so fragmented.

I finally catch Berech speaking with Heben. It is late in the night. Sitting as a sparrow on the tip of the ship's main topmast, I observe her separate like a shadow from the man's body to face him. Alas, I cannot hear what is said. Apparently, Berech can conceal her voice from me at will. Meanwhile, the bodyguard only listens to her and nods.

The cry of a bird startles me. I glance out into the dark beyond the ship, notice a black crow flying away, but when I return my attention to Heben, Berech is gone. The Illiri bodyguard sits on the edge of the boat, rubbing his eyes, and then departs to his quarters.

"Do you ever tire of cowering in the shadows, curator?" a female voice says.

I nearly fall back as Berech appears, balancing herself in a crouched position on the tip of the ship's fore topmast a few breadths across from where I sit. Her eyes are black and her skin is pale blue, all light receded from her being. A subtle grin forms at the corner of her mouth, while at the same time her eyes convey weary sadness.

"Who are you?" I ask.

"You know my name," she replies. "Raez Het has told you."

"What do you want with him?"

"He's no longer your concern," Berech says. "Leave the seer to his destiny."

"What destiny is that?"

"The Northland will grow stronger."

"That is why we are here," I say, "to fulfill his quest, to bring a sign back to his people."

The mockery of Berech's smile increases. "Illirium is no place for small minds. Go back to wherever you came from, curator. The world no longer belongs to Séorans such as you. Think of Phedra."

I did not anticipate this. "What do you know of Phedra?"

"She is in Lïmbol," Berech replies calmly.

This is the second time I have heard Phedra associated with Lïmbol. It seems I must indeed find a way to explore that land, though it is now controlled by the servants of Üzmaveth. "You claim to know much, but what proof do you offer?"

Berech looks at me evenly. I do not like holding the gaze of her lightless eyes. "I once also served Üzmaveth."

"Once?"

"Now I serve another," Berech replies. "Be wary of the call to Lïmbol. It tends to welcome one with false promises."

"What do you suggest?"

"I don't care what you do," she says. "Just stay out of my way."

I want to press her on the subject, but she vanishes.

To trust one of the Fallen invites confusion, yet I cling to the notion that Phedra could truly be in Lïmbol. Whether she is there as a prisoner or by choice, I will need the wisdom and strength of one far greater than me to succeed.

I do not know the nature of Berech's loyalty, power, or what she intends to do once we reach Winslöri, but she will not deter me from my present course. Phedra challenged me about passivity, about too often letting hesitation ensnare my actions. I should have been more attentive and done more to protect her. I will not repeat the same mistake with Raez and Ashe—for their own sakes, but most of all for what I need at least one of them to do.

3

Unrest

That all Séorans are not created for the same purpose or with the same authority has never troubled me. Some are empowered for unique roles, such as a warden, guide, or protector. Most of us Séorans are curators, limited in ability, but charged with caring for the various subtler aspects of nature, whether plant or animal. Without our stewardship, the natural world would fall into decay.

Endowed with greater perception and influence than us curators, though fewer in number, regents oversee our work to preserve the health of regions, whether a mountain range, forest, plain, or river. Furthermore, soldiers help protect the strongholds of Alíndor and execute her purposes while serving her commanders who are the most powerful Séorans of all. Alíndor originally names three commanders: Gathírel is the greatest, Captain of Rühílawé and Herald of Alíndor; second is Lachímel, Lieutenant of the Séorans, who maintains order among our race; and finally there is Üzmaveth, Protector of Triönym and the Elphadém.

Out of the three, I interact most with Lachímel, but Phedra is drawn to the company of Üzmaveth. She tells me that he has convinced some Séorans that the unique sensual gifts experienced by the Elphadém can be shared; that through the Elphadém, we Séorans can produce offspring of our own.

With all the life we get to cultivate, this prospect does not interest me. "If Elíbom Prímom meant it to be for us," I say, "it would have been so from the beginning."

"What if he waits for us to discover our potential?" Phedra replies. "Think of the wonderful array of colors you help draw from the flora, for example—how captivating it all is. Do you not want that for yourself?"

I had never considered my own potential in that way. "It is not about any one of us," I say, "but nurturing the potential of all life."

"All life except us," Phedra retorts. "Anyway, life does not need us to survive."

Her firm, almost dismissive tone discourages me. "Our work is about a thriving world," I urge.

She snickers bitterly. "According to whose terms? Alíndor limits our reach while letting the Elphadém explore the fullness of being. I want that freedom too. Many of us do. I thought you were more open-minded."

My heart aches at the sense of distance growing between us. "What do you mean to do?"

"I mean to explore the bounds of possibility."

Soon after, the Alöweans are born.

In human terms, Séorans are neither male nor female. Only the Elphadém women joined with a Séoran ultimately conceive; the Séorans partnered with Elphadém males do not have the same outcome. Fréalwë does not approve of this mixing, calling it a corruption, but nor does he reject the Alöweans. Remarkably, it is Alíndor who is said to advise him thus. Once the offspring are old enough, Fréalwë gives the Alöweans and their Elphadém mothers land in Chaléth in southern Triönym, the Middle Kingdom.

Since the beginning, Phedra and I have dwelt on an island off the coast of Chaléth. We frequent the rich forests on the mainland, and are among the first to welcome the newcomers. Though I am wary of the change, I come to think of the Alöweans as another bridge between our race and the Elphadém. To Phedra, the Alöweans are more—"a sign of wondrous opportunity," she tells me. She begins to neglect her work with the birds and plants to study the Alöweans. Her rising obsession with them concerns me, but I do not want another confrontation between us to drive her farther away from me. In an increasingly shifting world, she will need my loyalty and focus more than ever, and I need her resilience.

Alíndor declares the Séorans who bonded with the Elphadém to be fallen. Their power is reduced, and they are sent across the sea to redeem themselves by helping care for a place called the Lower Kingdom. I grieve their departure, but trust that Alíndor is just. That Phedra is not banished with them gives me some relief, for it confirms that she was not involved in the Corruption.

Strangely, Üzmaveth is not banished to the Lower Kingdom, though he is the instigator of the Corruption. Instead, he is barred from Rühílawé and must serve the first Alöwean settlement for seven years, after which time he will spend another seven years caring for Limbol, the uninhabited land to the west. While Üzmaveth lives in our corner of the world, I stay away from him, finding his presence volatile and his ideas perplexing. I do not like the deviance of his vision, and believe that Alíndor should have placed him in greater restraints.

"It is not for us to judge him," Phedra comments. Though she does not admit it to me, I suspect that she still finds a way to speak with him. This increases the pull of separation I feel between us. "Üzmaveth only wishes to develop our potential," she adds. "We can be so much more."

"But what more do we need?" I press. We sit beside each other on the beach. A warm night wind brushes through nearby palm trees. The sky is resplendent with stars and galaxies. Somewhere beyond, through the mist of space, is the Lower Kingdom. To reach it, I am told, requires crossing Oceanus, the great boundary waters of the inner sphere. Does another, one of the Fallen perhaps, sit on some beach on the other side looking up at us?

"Elíbom Prímom has empowered the Elphadém with choice," Phedra comments. "Now, by association, the Alöweans have the same. What about us? What real choices do we Séorans have to direct our future?"

"We have everything we could ever need"—I motion to the celestial sky and the swirling milky depths of the sea glowing blue with bioluminescence—"beauty all around us, purpose in enhancing it, and meaning. The Séorans who chose another way have been expelled from Rühílawé."

"Perhaps they are the stronger ones," she replies softly.

"Our people are now divided as a result of choice, strength, or whatever you want to call it," I say. "What about the benefit of the whole?"

"All I see," Phedra replies, standing and approaching the bubbling surf, "is that the so-called benefit of the whole predominantly benefits the one: Alíndor. To thrive in this world, dear brother, begins with recognizing individual power and how it rises over the complacency of the collective."

"We are strongest when together," I say.

"That may have been true in the beginning," Phedra comments, "but this world is no longer such a simple place."

"Phedra—"

"I know you mean well," she interrupts. "And honestly, I sometimes wish I retained your innocence and optimism. Yet, the reality is that unity is nothing more than an idea defined by the one in authority." She meets my gaze. "One day, I trust that you will understand that."

* * *

Sitting on the long branch of a beech tree, I watch my companions, Ashe and Raez, sleeping on the forest floor below. With the help of the Girgash Erïeth, we have escaped the chaos of the unsettled Northland and begun our journey south toward central Illirium.

I have brought them this far, but recalling my conversation with Phedra, wonder if it is for their benefit and that of our fellowship or mine alone. Both of them seek meaning in some way—some kind of purpose, perhaps even freedom. Phedra came to think of freedom as independence, but it consumed her. Contrarily, I have trusted freedom to be rooted in the harmony of all things, each fulfilling their role with an outward focus; yet for too long I have found myself isolated and alone. What has happened to this world? Why is goodness fading?

If I must continue to neglect my underlying responsibility in order to be reunited with Phedra, what will be the consequences? Will my connection to the Unseen diminish further? Will I become like one of the Fallen? Do I even do it for her?

At first, I sought Phedra out of some notion of comfort and familiarity; yet those sentiments were crumbling well before our actual separation. What about the strength we once shared? No, even that feels distant. Change, I now realize, is unavoidable.

4

Impetus

The Alöweans are rebelling against the Elphadém. One of our own kind, Helëna, is said to have sparked the conflict, but I do not understand how it has come to be. My attention is consumed by burning forests and fields, and people slain, young and old. Séoran unity is also fractured anew, some wanting to aid the Elphadém while others empathize with the Alöweans. Séorans even slay each other. The Second Unrest.

"I will not stand by idly," Phedra says. "Not this time."

"We need not choose one side," I urge, struggling to comprehend such needless destruction, "but can help anyone wounded or dying." After all, our power is rooted in giving life, not taking it.

Together, we navigate the butchery of war. Throughout, I am surprised to discover a new form of personal strength in comforting the suffering of mortals—calming their breaths, easing pain, warming vitality. It is not unlike aiding a struggling plant, only now more complex and with graver stakes.

"This is not enough," Phedra says, holding the hand of a dying Alöwean who is bleeding out upon a muddy field.

"What more can we do?" I ask, cradling the body of an Elphadém woman whose eyes wander in and out of consciousness. I am trying to keep her warm until more help arrives. I see a group of Elphadém approaching from the smoke not far away, so remain optimistic about her survival.

"I am not yet sure," Phedra replies, "but it cannot continue like this."

Empowered by Alíndor, Fréalwë ultimately restores order by capturing Üzmaveth who is revealed to have been behind the conflict. Other Séoran accomplices are also condemned, the greatest being Helëna who is banished to the Lower Kingdom. While once again Alíndor's mercy astounds me, I am bewildered by how divided creation has become. Are there wounds that cannot be mended? *How did it come to this?*

Most of the Elphadém decide to depart Triönym, the Middle Kingdom, by setting sail across Oceanus in search of a new home. Though they hold a greater claim to Triönym, their pioneering spirit drives them onward. With Alíndor's blessing, Fréalwë approves of this choice. He even gives them a seed from the Balmwéa Elïf along with one of its white branches. The seed is to be planted at the center of their new civilization, nurturing health and long life, while the branch will provide a touch of Alíndor's power.

"It will keep you connected to the spirit of Elíbom Prímom and the Unseen," Alíndor explains, "and also serve as a guiding light by which to return to Rühílawë." Though her voice is tranquil, it bears a hint of grief. She selects Lachímel and his sister, Äelmich, to go with the Elphadém as protectors. A few other Séorans will be permitted to join them.

"Let us journey to a new world as well," Phedra implores me upon hearing the news.

My heart sinks. "But why? Our place is here."

"A new age is beginning," Phedra presses, "and with it new opportunity. I want to see what else is out there for us. You heard it yourself: Alíndor has given us a choice—a real choice at last. We must not ignore it. The Elphadém need us."

Phedra has not shown concern for the Elphadém in a long while, so I do not understand her sudden fervor. "You mean to abandon what we have always held dear?" I ask. "The lands have grown lush and expansive, and there is so much left to do. And what of the Alöweans?" I think of her desire to nurture their advancement in Chaléth.

"We have done all we can for them," she replies without hesitation. "The future is with the Elphadém, as it has been since the beginning."

I do not know what else to say.

"If you are set on remaining," she says, "you should stay."

This prospect stabs the deepest. "You would leave me?"

"It need not be permanent," she says cheerfully. "I will return when all is established in the new world."

Tenderly, I place my hand around the back of her neck and draw her forehead to mine. The thought of being separated from her drains my fervor. "No," I say softly. I could not survive such a parting. "I will go with you."

* * *

Why is it so difficult to evade contention?

Helping Ashe and Raez flee the chaos of Rínroth Outpost, I instruct Oshrémi to enlist the aid of the local wildlife—ferrets, sage grouse, and even some pronghorns—in concealing the signs of our passing. Why the Rök turned against each other so violently baffles me, but I cannot dwell on that now; my priority is to secure the survival of my two companions. For now, necessity forces them together, but it will not last indefinitely. Only together will we succeed; I have but to convince them that it is so—to show them what that can mean. I perceive the way ahead like a series of stones across a rushing stream. Ashe and Raez provide the means to take each step. If one of them departs, a vital stepping stone will be lost, leaving me stranded. This is my chance. Once the two are settled in temporary safety on a wooded ridge bordering the Rínroth Plain, I fly further west in my sparrow form.

As I near the northern Girgash Mountains, a white Erïeth with grey feathered wings appears, marking my progress. She glides high above me, ready to swoop down at any moment. As a sparrow, I am at her mercy, and pray that she recognizes me for what I truly am.

Ahead, the range looms like the high wall of a massive fortress. I have entered Saurish, the largest kingdom of Erïeth in Illirium. I spot other winged forms taking flight from a tall granite pinnacle ahead. One Erïeth dashes past a hundred feet below me. A black one passes my left and then circles back to fly close to my right. He directs me to land on a large, flat protrusion high up the side of the pinnacle. I readily comply.

There waits the Lord of Saurish. With stern yellow eyes, the giant eagle watches me land. His white head crowns a body of large ochre and umber feathers. He is flanked by two Erïeth guards. The black one stands behind me.

"Welcome, Thian Darhe, servant of the Wind Maker, Elíbom Prímom," the Lord of Saurish begins in the language of his people, which is conveyed through his posture and eyes, supplemented by what others like Ashe would think sound like whistles and peeps. "I am pleased that you come to us once again."

"Greetings, Lord Saliq," I say. Returning to my natural form, I bow reverently to one knee and lower my head. "I am glad to have come."

"Do you bring news from the lowlands?" Saliq asks.

Maintaining my kneeling stance, I answer, "There is little that the Lord of Saurish does not know. Many in the lowlands are still healing from the Illirium War. Only in Siligen in the west and Rökad here in the north have there been violent stirrings of late."

"Indeed," Saliq says. "What errand brings you this far from your home below the Upper Mountains then? I did not think you an ally of the Rök."

"I have come on behalf of two friends, neither of Rökad." I meet his eyes. "We humbly request your help."

Saliq raises a brow and tilts his head. "What manner of help?"

"My friends are called Ashe Pethus of Chaléth and Raez Het of the Thraz. They need swift passage out of Rökad. They are being hunted by the Rök."

"The Rök tend to keep to their own affairs," Saliq comments. "What have your friends done to attract such hostility?"

How to explain the complications of the last days? "It is Raez who is in the most danger. He is a sage of the Thraz, a people who are at war with the Rök. Ashe, an Alöwean Sky Rider, and I helped him escape Rök imprisonment."

Looking at me grimly, Saliq straightens. "There is much in your reply that is troublesome. Foremost, we do not consort with the Alöweans, especially not Sky Riders who steal our young, enslaving them to their warlike purposes, driving our communities deeper into the recesses of the Mountains of the Crescent Moon. That you have allied yourself with one of them displeases me, Thian Darhe. But, what is more, we know of the horned desert dwellers, or 'Erog' as the Rök call them. They are an inferior race, violent and ignorant, however satisfying in sustenance."

I should have remembered that Raez's people are sometimes Erïeth prey. This will be more difficult than I anticipated. "I understand your caution, Lord Saliq, yet Ashe and Raez are not like the others."

The Erïeth present murmur to each other.

"Raez is on a sacred quest to unite his people in the Northland," I continue. "To do so, he must venture south to the coast, to the Menendros Sea and beyond across Oceanus to Rühílawé."

"What purpose does he have in uniting the tribes of the north?" Saliq asks. "Another invasion, another war? We do not associate ourselves with the squabbles of the lowland races, except to protect our kingdom and defend the sanctity of the wilderness."

"Raez is for peace," I urge, "as is Ashe. What is more, unlike most of their kind these days, they see me—they see glimpses of the Unseen. Their eyes are akin to yours." I look around at the Erïeth watching me. "Working together, we could offer the world a new vision of unity, including a hope for restoration. With your support, we could come closer to living as equals."

"Aside from you Séorans, the civilizations of Illirium have never offered us peace," Saliq replies.

Much to their loss. "For you to take the first step would be to model the greater strength," I say. "You can show them what is possible, which can begin now by helping them cross the mountains to the Plain of the Crescent Moon. If not for them, I ask it for myself. With these two, I can find answers to some riddles long plaguing Illirium." The Erïeth respect Elíbom Prímom, so I must use this to my advantage. "I intend to bring them to Elíbom Prímom to further learn the truth of the Unseen and be able to guide their people toward an age of harmony with all life. The long-term advantages are myriad."

For a while, Saliq remains silent. His eyes shift beyond mine to observe the wide landscape behind me to the east: the Rínroth Plain and bordering forest, and farther still the faint blue silhouettes of the Upper Mountains. "Your ambitions are commendable," he says at last, and then looks at me shrewdly. "Yet, I doubt the extent of their influence."

"What I say is possible," I reply, trying to keep my voice calm. Without help from the Erïeth, Raez and Ashe have no hope of escaping Rökad.

"Where then is Lachímel?" Saliq asks. "If what you say is true, and the current of the future could be redirected, should it not be he, your captain, who stands before me now?"

Lachímel's focus is too narrow. "He is needed elsewhere," I say, "and has entrusted this mission to me. As with all significant movements of power, it cannot be achieved by one alone. That is why I come to you myself, as a friend, offering Saurish a place at the forefront of authority for the future. The effects could alter the course for not only you, but generations of free Erïeth to come." I bow my head once more. "Please, I ask that you join me in marking a new way forward in this world."

5

Agency

As we depart the shores of Triönym, the Elphadém declare the start of the First Age. To them, the future is as full of possibilities as the depths and breadth of Oceanus. The journey is full of wonders too numerous to recount. Phedra attends little to these moments, however, for her gaze is ever forward.

"Look ahead," she urges me, smiling, basking in the warmth of the sun and the spray of the sea.

To me, the unfamiliar horizon both intimidates and inspires. Phedra is my deepest connection to the cosmos, but then she has been slowly drifting away from me—even as we stand next to each other. I go with her now to maintain that link; more so, I seek to rebuild and protect it—to protect her from further distraction and wayward thinking. The prospect of a new world offers a fresh beginning, uncontaminated by the corruption seeping into the roots of Rühílawé. With that, there is the energy of my own possibilities in helping transplant Elíbom Prímom's original vision for Rühílawé. His spirit goes with us, evident in the seed and branch of the Balmwéa Elïf given to the Elphadém.

The currents and winds of Oceanus ultimately bring our ships to the shore of an immense land. Here, nature appears underdeveloped—like the early years of the Séoran awakening. I come to learn that Elíbom Prímom breathed life into a few Séorans beyond the bounds of Rühílawé, and that there are other races beside the Elphadém and Alöweans.

Phedra and I, along with the other Séorans who have come with the Elphadém, quickly begin our work, introducing ourselves to and partnering with the native creatures and plant life, enriching the coastal region—alone, nearly the size of Rühílawé—by drawing water up from deep within the ground, by stewarding a diversification of flora and trees. I revel in the moments of connection, growth, and harmony.

As years pass, the Elphadém disperse into four settlements led by four chieftains. A city is established inland next to a convergence of tiny springs; it is declared the new Elphadém capital, and the new world is called Illirium. The Elphadém measure their time by the cycle of the stars and their history by physical deeds. In nature, things grow, wither, withdraw, and renew, yet there seems to be no regeneration like that for the Elphadém.

"Their light is fading," our Séoran captain, Lachímel, says.

Ever since the violence of the Second Unrest exposed them to death, the Elphadém have become more cautious. The shift is subtle, most evident in the increased hope placed upon their offspring and legacy. We Séorans who are with them have no progeny and do not die—at least, not by the passing of time—but the Second Unrest proves that we too are susceptible to being slain, raising questions about how long our people will last if violent conflict ever returns.

"That is why we are here with them," Lachímel's sister, Äelmich, tells me, "to keep the civilization of the First Born rooted in the truth, and to guide its members back if they ever wander astray."

I cannot imagine what would cause the Elphadém to abandon us.

"Séorans like Äelmich and Lachímel represent an old order," Phedra says later as we walk along the cliffs of the sea. "They do not care for change, for the freedom of possibility. They wish to keep everything within tight barriers, including us."

"I just want to help beauty grow," I reply, not interested in getting involved in questions of command. "And I am here for you, to continue what we began together in Rühílawé."

"That world is behind us now," Phedra replies quietly.

I begin to wonder if I am the reason she is withdrawing. My focus seems to agitate her, and my loyalty is increasingly treated like a strangling vine. Am I to accept change if it rips us apart? I cannot accept it. It cannot be good. But then what am I supposed to do?

The sea has been crossed, a new land reached and settlements established. Yet, despite all the blessed work we have achieved in Illirium, I perceive my hold of our original gift slipping. My power as a curator is diminishing. Lachímel explains that it is a natural consequence of being farther from the Balmwëa Elïf and spirit of Elíbom Prímom, but that it is only a minor loss and will not last. "The branch of the tree, the White Staff," he says, "will sustain us until the seed of the Balmwéa Elïf takes root here in Trïesch, the Elphadém capital. In the meantime, be careful about venturing far and for too long from it."

When I fully enter the physical dimension, I no longer assume the form of a swan, but rather enjoy the smaller, subtler expression of the sparrow. In part, I do this because I have seen no swans in Illirium, and therefore do not want to call attention to myself. Osré and Oshrémi also appreciate my choice. Phedra does not join me in this, however, but retains her guise as a white swan. Her attention to curating grows more inconsistent, marked by periods of absence.

"Where do you go off to alone?" I ask her one evening as we walk amidst the green fields bordering Trïesch. The grass whispers with the breeze. The clouded sky radiates azure and amber light.

"I search the corners of Illirium," she replies, not looking at me.

"For what?"

"Lasting opportunity."

I motion at the life flourishing around us. "Does opportunity not abound here?"

"Under Lachímel's supervision," Phedra says, "the Elphadém are merely recreating the Middle Kingdom. I did not come here to rebuild the past."

"You said the Elphadém need our help." I do not understand her discontent. "Our efforts are yielding bountiful fruit. Even the seed of the Balmwéa Elïf has taken root. Do these gains not offer meaning and purpose for us here?"

"There could be more, so much more." She steps back, gazing westward at the setting sun. Gradually, the sky darkens to violet. Phedra's form reflects the fading light, glimmering like water even as the shadows of night deepen. "It has already begun," she continues, watching where the sun had been moments before, but is now gone behind a flat horizon. She glances at me. "Have you not heard?"

I shake my head.

"You must become better engaged with the world, dear brother."

"Has something happened?"

"The Alöweans have asserted their independence from the dominion of Elíbom Prímom," she replies. "Fréalwë is dead, and Alíndor has closed access to the Balmwéa Elïf."

What? The separation of the Upper and Middle kingdoms seems impossible. "That cannot be permanent. Without the tree, the Alöweans will be vulnerable to mortality. What do they intend to gain?"

"Immortality is not everything, Thian, when it lacks the power to shape one's future." Phedra glances away and her voice quiets. "Üzmaveth understands this. He always has. He is here, in fact . . . in Illirium."

Astonished, I stare at her. "What?"

"As are the Séorans who once dared to dream, the ones condemned as the Fallen. Illirium is not some anonymous land, Thian. It is the Lower Kingdom."

I now feel more suspicion than surprise. "How do you know this?"

"I have spoken with them," she replies. "Those that roam more openly in Illirium, watching us, assume various physical forms. It does not entirely veil their presence, but it does disguise their light from other Séorans."

"If they are here, Lachímel must know."

"It may be that he knows," she comments. "The more intriguing question, then, would be why he has said nothing about it, and why Alíndor encouraged the Elphadém to sail across Oceanus to begin with." Her demeanor darkens. "Could it be that Alíndor cares little for the wayward ones? When the Elphadém resolved to depart Triönym, was their fate not sealed?" She smiles with an edge of bitterness. "I gather that Alíndor did not foresee the death of Fréalwë, her greatest ally among corporeal kind. Nor did she foresee the strength of the Alöwean race in alliance with Üzmaveth, who still has power in the Middle Kingdom. The hierarchy has thus unraveled further, loosening the original bonds of creation. I came here for a new world, and a new world is indeed being formed. Soon, you will have to determine your role in it."

"What kind of world? What other role is there for me to fulfill?"

"It is about true authority, dear brother. You will have to decide who to follow."

* * *

Phedra's words haunt me. She sought the freedom to choose, but is the choice simply about who to follow? Dare I follow her to Lïmbol, if that is indeed where she is? What if it is another trap, and who am I to save her anyway? I am the reason she is gone.

It no longer matters, I try to tell myself. *The future will not be the past.*

I am here now, evolving, but on my own terms. A new course has been set. No matter the size of the waves or the gusts of wind, though the horizon remains shrouded in fog, I will press ahead. To what end exactly, I am not yet sure, but courage is not rooted in knowledge.

Presently, I am at a crossroad in the guise of Rínroth Outpost. Raez remains a prisoner, and I have promised to free him. I have delayed only because I need Ashe's help to succeed. Yet, she needs me more, so exposed is she to the increasing tempests. Neither knows what is really happening around them. None of these mortals know.

It seems that the essence of choice is not who to follow, but what course I can make for myself. I have the power to direct Ashe and Raez's paths; it has already begun. Ashe has led me to Raez, and Raez points to Oceanus, the way back to Rühílawé and perhaps even a course to Lïmbol. I wish there was another way, less reliant on these mortals' whims, but I do not have the luxury of many options. Ashe and Raez look to me for now—they need me—and I can use that to my advantage.

No more delays.

6

Fog

Phedra leaves for days at a time. This cannot be good for her, and it is certainly not good for us. Does Lachímel know? Dare I ask? It is not that she is harming anything, as far as I can tell, but I worry that by distancing herself in this way she is venturing too close to the threshold of the Fallen.

I cling to the assurance that we are stronger together, she and I, and cannot fathom what it would mean for us to be separated. If Lachímel banishes her from our society, if he has that kind of authority . . . *It must not come to that.*

"Let me come with you," I say to Phedra one evening as the sun sets.

She looks at me with a hint of suspicion, but stronger in her expression are eyes brightened with interest. "What do you mean?"

"To wherever you go outside the domain of Trïesch," I answer.

"Lachímel also explores beyond the Elphadém borders," Phedra replies curtly, "As does his sister, Äelmich, or others more directly under their charge. It benefits them to know what is happening throughout the Lower Kingdom. So it is with me."

"Then I want to know what you know," I press. "Please."

"Very well." A faint grin forms at the corner of her lip. "It will be good for you. It will open your eyes."

As sparrow and swan, we fly west across the great river, Elentari, chasing the sinking sun far from Elphadém civilization. As night settles with no moon yet in sight, jagged snowcapped mountains come into view ahead.

"The Kurshemnt Mountains," Phedra comments.

The range is quiet and somber. Brooding clouds hover over the peaks. The air is cold and restless. All vibrancy is gone. Nothing moves in this land. Here, life seems asleep or in hiding. Phedra does not slow as we fly through the range, confidently navigating misty valleys and passes. Clearly, she has been here before.

Landing on a rocky outcrop at the western feet of the mountains, below the clouds, we face a wide desert. I have never seen a place so barren of life.

"It is called the Desert of Oblivion," she tells me. "Do you see the Divide?"

Looking out, I notice a wall, translucent like glass reaching up to the heavens, splitting the wasteland. It is difficult to spot amidst gently blowing dust and sand. "Yes, I see it."

She points to a second, smaller mountain range beyond the desert. "There dwells Üzmaveth."

It is as I feared. "You have seen him then?"

"No," she replies softly, "not yet. He cannot cross the Divide, for Alíndor formed it to be a prison cell."

"I have not heard such news."

"You have not been attentive," Phedra replies. "Lachímel knows, as do, I suspect, some of the Elphadém leadership."

"I am a curator," I say. "My duty is simple."

"Look around you," Phedra retorts. "To engage what is happening in the broader world is to better protect the life you strive to nurture. It is time for you to stop hiding in the shadows. No more excuses."

"But why do you come to this place, so full of shadows?" I ask, wanting to focus on what is immediately before us. This place unsettles me.

Phedra's eyes shift to something behind me. "To speak with her."

I turn to see a woman standing a few strides away, watching us with black eyes. She is a Séoran, but her light has faded. Her pale blue skin looks human, but bloodless and almost frozen. A ragged brown hide hangs from her shoulders. Jutting up from the neck of the cloak, framing her head like a crowned hood, are sharp antlers. Her voice is raspy. "I'm glad you have come."

I look at Phedra for an explanation, but she just stares at me.

"Don't be troubled, brother," the woman says, coming closer to me. Mist swirls up around her as though from the train of her cloak. "You're here with Phedra, and are stronger together."

Uncomfortable with the woman's proximity, I step back. "Who are you?"

"I'm Rïven," the woman replies. She glances at Phedra. "I bring good tidings."

"What tidings?" I ask.

"Liberation is coming."

"What kind of liberation?" I press.

"Just listen to her," Phedra urges.

"A day is coming when all kingdoms will be united, from the Lower to the Upper," Rïven continues. "Üzmaveth will make it so."

"A truly new world," Phedra adds, smiling, "No longer held back by the whims of Alíndor."

"You mean to trade one ruler for another?" I ask, unconvinced. "Where is your autonomy in that? Üzmaveth has never demonstrated a desire for unity, but thrives on disruption. The ways of Alíndor may be mysterious, but they are always merciful and just."

Rïven scoffs. "The folly of blindness."

"Do not fear your own strength, dear brother," Phedra says, placing her hand on my shoulder. "Üzmaveth means not to rule, but to free us from the shackles of the old world."

I slip away from her touch. "You do not know what you do."

"It's you who doesn't understand," Rïven comments.

"To release everything from its intended purpose is to embrace chaos," I say.

"I have explained it to you before," Phedra says calmly, stepping toward me. "You must choose who to follow. Will you continue to follow Alíndor, whose hold of the world is weakening, or turn to Üzmaveth who grows stronger? He offers us a new beginning."

Ever the promise of new beginnings. It does not make sense.

"There'll be order, make no mistake," Rïven adds, "with bounds that transcend the petty divisions of the seen and unseen."

"There will be creation," Phedra presses, "like in the Early Years."

"Üzmaveth cannot create new life," I counter, "no Séoran can."

"The birth of the Alöweans proves that you're wrong," Rïven says, also stepping closer to me. "We're capable of achieving so much more."

"It is not right," I protest. I will not trust the promises of Üzmaveth or his servants.

"It is what I want," Phedra says, "what I hope for. Join me, Thian. Please. I want to share the future together. Your faithfulness would be a valuable asset."

I suddenly realize that Phedra's eyes have faded from white to grey. How did I not notice them before? The white cloak usually luminous around her body has also dimmed. My heart shudders at how much of a stranger she has become. "I must go."

"Every action bears consequences," Rïven states. "Have you considered yours—what it will mean to leave Phedra?

Wanting to ignore this woman, I focus my attention on my sister. "Come back with me. This is not who you are. This is not where you belong. Can you not see it?"

"It is you who does not see clearly," Phedra replies.

How can I make her see the truth?

Fog encircles us. I can no longer tell which way to go. I can no longer see Rïven. Even Phedra's form, so close to me, seems to fade. "Phedra," I call, but my voice sounds muffled. "Come with me." I offer my hand to where I last saw her standing. "Together, we can overcome this fog."

"It's too late for that," Rïven's voice whispers in my ear.

Startled, I turn around, but see no one.

"Phedra," I call again.

I hear her voice, but it sounds far away. "Thian."

"Where are you?" I shout, stumbling. Does she choose this? Is this really what she wants? No, she has been deceived. I must help her. I must bring her back.

I try to concentrate on gathering the air around me, hoping to press back the gloom, but find it difficult to breathe. My legs become unsteady. I do not understand what is happening. I have to resist it.

"Thian," a voice calls, still distant.

"I am coming." Turning to my right, in the direction of the voice, I stumble along a narrow, rocky ridge. The atmosphere darkens. I can barely see.

Shrieks reverberate around me.

Black shapes rush up both sides of the ridge. One lands in front of me, crawling on four limbs tense with black muscle rotten away from the hands and feet to expose sharp bony digits. It jumps at me. Though startled, I manage to keep my footing, standing fast. The creature's bare skull is black; where eyes should be are only deep indentations. A large and menacing maw with crooked flat teeth stained with dried blood and green saliva snaps at my face. I push the creature back and, horrified, notice that its chest is empty but for a spine and ribs like an open cage. Also coming from the spine is a pair of spiked digits seeking to ensnare me like a spider's legs.

The other creatures are quickly closing in. I direct all my energy to leaping up, spinning as I go, extend my invisible wings and transform into my sparrow form. My reduced size and quickened speed manages to evade the rush of three more attackers. I fly straight up, desperate for air, for light, for escape. All the while, howling resonates from the swirling grey mist below.

"Thian," a voice calls. Is it one of longing or mockery?

Phedra, forgive me.

* * *

The Rök company departs the mountains to go to their outpost in the Rínroth Plain. All the while, Ashe grieves the loss of Lüfet, preferring to keep her own company. I do not mind the space, for my failure to save Lüfet tugs at my soul. I feel so powerless in the face of real need. Phedra was the stronger one.

Forgive me.

To repel troubled thoughts, I focus my attention on Raez. Ever since our first encounter above the battlefield, when I spotted his glowing arm, when he could see and hear me, he has captured my imagination. He tells me about a quest, about wanting to reach Oceanus, which leads me to consider what we might achieve together. His presence in Ashe's dreams is also curious, suggesting a mind even more attentive to the Unseen than the Alöwean's. Yet, most inspiring is the persistent presence of the white swan, which Raez also seems to see. This can be no coincidence. First with Ashe and now with Raez, they point to the original world—they point to Phedra. Whether it is a sign from Elíbom Prímom or a beacon from Phedra herself, I am not yet sure.

Meanwhile, the Rök ranks have grown agitated. I discern an antagonistic force stalking the borders of our camp like a predator. It must be the source of restiveness. Raez's imprisonment already complicates matters; I cannot contend with more. So, one night I withdraw fully into the Unseen to learn what I can of this new threat.

The Unseen is a land of light and shadows, the spirit of all things and the space between them. Tangible matter fades as I enter, leaving in its place only impressions of what exists in the visible world. The sky's atmosphere is drawn back like a thin curtain, showcasing a heavenly expanse of revolving colored spheres at various distances. The universe is so vast; it baffles my mind to consider what realms might exist beyond the inner canopy.

I focus back on my immediate surroundings: the shimmering strands of yellow and green that mark veins of grass, the slowly pulsating brown conduits of the trees and flickering emerald of leaves; and then deeper through the textured layers beneath my feet—the earth and its shifting crust, mantle, and farther below a fiery core. I cherish such beauty, but should not revel in it now.

Walking amidst the Rök camp, the fabric of the tents practically transparent, I perceive the forms, whether asleep or awake, of the soldiers, their ponies, and any other creature nearby. The spirit of each Rök glows grey and silver like the rock of the earth. With my hands outstretched, I extend my consciousness as broadly as possible, searching.

At first, there is a cacophony of whispering voices. Fleeting images arise: Rök dreams and memories of those living and dead, or things imagined but not yet seen with the waking eye. Without touching an individual, it is impossible for me to step in and observe his or her dream with any clarity. The glimpses suggest that all is as it should be, yet the invisible spirit of heightened agitation persists.

My attention is drawn to a bright bronze light at the center of the camp. It comes from the right arm of the Erog sage, the brilliance burning away the dimly visible black bars of the cage. Raez sits in serenity, his mind roaming. He seems to also be exploring the Unseen, though with a limited range.

I move to check on Ashe who is at the outskirts of camp. My thoughts brush aside the Rök tents between us like steam, leaving a clear space. I am relieved to find Ashe sleeping quietly. Whatever is disrupting the spirit of the camp, she appears to be unaffected. It may be that, having originated from us Séorans, an Alöwean's consciousness is better protected.

Coming closer, gently touching her brow with my forefinger, I enhance my vision of her dream state. Whether the imagery is from one specific memory or an assortment blended together, I do not know. At last, her spirit glides happily, longingly, across a vibrant blue sky speckled with clouds. Yet, it is not Lüfet that she rides, nor any Erïeth, but rather a large white swan.

With a shudder, I remove my hand from Ashe as the bird separates from the dream, wings outstretched, and lands before me. At that moment, the swan transforms into the visage of a woman with pale blue skin and black eyes, and her wings become a cloak of faded white. "Be wary," she says, her voice muffled as though heard through a wall.

Her aura is not entirely clear, but the voice and appearance are familiar. If this is Phedra, her inner light has gone, leaving her looking like one made of flesh and bone. Except, her eyes do not seem right. "Who are you?" I ask. "How are you manifesting through Ashe's dream?"

"Be wary," she repeats. She looks tired.

"Of whom?" I ask.

"Of you."

"Me?"

She looks around at the hazy shapes of sleeping mortals. "They do not understand what you are."

"I remain but a humble Séoran curator," I answer.

"It is not about who you were," she says, "but who you can become."

"I do not understand."

She grins with condescension. "You never do."

I should have done more to save her. "Phedra, is it really you?"

"What do you think?" she asks.

Whoever this is, she is not present here as I am. Something is different. Something is wrong. "Where are you now?"

"I am nowhere."

"Please," I urge, beginning to suffocate with guilt, "If you are Phedra, speak plainly to me. Tell me where you are, so I can bring you home."

She tilts her head in bewilderment. "Home?"

"At least tell me if you are alive."

"Has life or death ever really defined us?"

I fall to my knees. The wound that never mended in my soul tears open. "Why have you only come now?"

"To show you the way once more," she says.

"The way to what?"

Her tense expression hints at a pain that she is trying to repress. "The next stage of our evolution." She walks up to me and lifts my chin so that our eyes meet. The chill of her touch and the black abyss of her eyes make me tremble. I cannot hold her gaze. "Still afraid, brother?"

My periphery catches the shining bronze light of Raez's arm to my right. To my left, I glimpse Ashe's crimson aura. "No," I answer. "Hope still burns within me." Its white light brightens from the center of my being. It comes not from me, however, but something deeper and richer. "I have been looking for you."

She considers me for a while, as if trying to read my thoughts. "I am beyond your hope."

"No one is beyond hope," I counter.

Stepping back, she narrows her eyes. "I am waiting for you." She continues to walk back.

"Wait," I say. "How did you find me?"

Looking at Raez, she says, "This Thraz does not realize what kind of tremors his searching creates throughout the Unseen. Like amplified calls, it opens ways normally shut to a mortal. Few are capable of such a feat, so be careful. Your connection to him drew me to you like a beacon." She looks at Ashe's sleeping form. "Moreover, this Alöwean retains a trace of spiritual connection to her Séoran forefather, one of the Fallen, which provided a pathway here—frail, but a pathway nonetheless."

"I have been searching for you so long," I answer, unable to comprehend the implications of all she says.

"I am not who you think I am," she replies, "and this world is more complex than you know. You should better guard the passageways of your mind, brother; otherwise, you leave yourself vulnerable to more hostile encounters."

She turns away.

"Wait." Still on my knees, I reach my hand out to her. "Are you a prisoner?"

"Be wary," she says, lifting her arms in her cloak, transforming them back into wings. "Escape would cost you too much." Her voice suddenly sounds clear. "Go back to what you know, and care for what you can before it is too late—before all fades in fire and ruin. It is better that we remain apart."

"Wait," I cry out, still reaching for her as her form vanishes. "Tell me where you are."

"It does not matter anymore," she says. "I am lost."

"Tell me."

"There is a cave," she begins, her voice again muffled. A grin forms at the corner of her mouth. "In Lïmbol you can find me."

Lïmbol, the land west of Triönym, the Middle Kingdom—a land now occupied by Üzmaveth's forces. "Is there no other way?"

"Every way demands a cost," her voice calls, receding like a passing wind. "Be wary."

She is gone.

7

Tremors

Phedra, did you know what would happen?

Rising above the clouds sooner than I anticipate, I soar as a sparrow, turning east using the half moon as my guide. Eagerly, I put distance between me and the Kurshemnt Mountains, especially the menace of Rïven and her demons.

Winter snow covers the plains below, a fresh canvas for life. If only spring could come sooner. If only the sky did not suddenly feel so empty and vast.

I am alone.

Returning to Trïesch, I go directly to the Birithani Tree, offspring of the Balmwéa Elïf that has grown into a mighty tree at the city's center. Its bark is white, and its leaves are gold. It helps sustain the health and longevity of not only the Elphadém, but the power of us Séorans here in Illirium. There dwells Lachímel.

"Let him pass," he instructs the Séoran guards encircling the base of the tree.

Floating up to the middle of the tree, I kneel before Lachímel, his radiant blue form cloaked in translucent amber, and tell him what I have seen and heard. His sister, Äelmich, is there with him.

When I am finished, Lachímel remarks, "The situation is more serious than you realize."

"Rïven's mother, Helëna, is the one who helped incite the Second Unrest,"

Äelmich adds, "when the Alöweans rose against the Elphadém in the Middle Kingdom." To her brother, she says, "It seems Üzmaveth is using the daughter as he did the mother, only here to spur division among the Elphadém and all that we have labored to build."

"Indeed, there has been increasingly contentious talk among the mortals," Lachímel replies, keeping his white eyes fixed on me. "That Riven may be the source only confirms my suspicions. We will be on the lookout for her and her allies. As to the creatures that attacked you, they are the Ophidi, Holders designed to take over the minds and bodies of mortal kind."

"Could they do that to a Séoran?" I ask, disturbed by the thought.

"I think not," he replies with a grim expression, "but nor can I be certain. Much is swiftly changing. We have already had to repel these Holders from breaching our western border on multiple occasions. A number of Elphadém have died as a result. So far these instances have been kept quiet."

Is hiding this conflict from the Elphadém wise? I wonder, recalling Phedra's suspicion of Lachímel's motives.

"Where do such creatures come from?" I ask.

"We believe they are born of Be'hälemoth, concubine of Üzmaveth," Äelmich explains, "though how two Séorans spawned such creatures . . ." She shakes her head in disgust. "It is as my brother suggested: our enemy is ever evolving."

"The Lower Kingdom is cursed," Lachímel mutters. He walks out upon a thick branch, staring at the stars. "To have thought we could settle peacefully among the Fallen was naïve. Alíndor's choice to imprison Üzmaveth here confounds me."

"Much can still be preserved," Äelmich offers, focusing on her brother. "Doors remain open to us. Remember that it was not so much a matter of imprisoning Üzmaveth as containing him within the land he had already occupied."

"Alíndor should have invaded instead," Lachímel retorts, "and ended this conflict for good."

"What happens now?" I ask, feeling increasingly buried by matters beyond my purview.

"Tension has long been mounting," Lachímel says. Standing on the branch of the Birithani Tree, he gazes out upon the city of Trïesch. "War is inevitable with Üzmaveth."

"What about Phedra?" I ask.

"It seems that she is lost to us," Äelmich replies.

"There must be a way to save her," I press.

"She has made her choice," Lachímel states. "If we are to preserve our way of life, everyone loyal to Elíbom Prímom must now rally together."

* * *

I have seldom been this far north. The landscape of Rökad, as with Rök culture, feels too secluded and aggressive for my liking. Even Ekrath Namor, the Séoran regent who oversees the Northern Mountains of the Girgash, gave me that impression when I once wandered here long ago:

"Who are you?" he demands upon discovering me crouched next to a barren canyon creek. His human-like figure emanates grey and black like billowing smoke, and his voice rumbles like an earthquake.

I tell him my name and ask, "Do you know of a Séoran called Phedra Darhe?"

Expressionless, he continues to stare at me. "You do not belong here."

"True, I am originally from Chaléth," I explain, trying to sound amiable.

"Go back to Chaléth then," Ekrath Namor says. "You are not suited to such a harsh land as this."

"What do you mean?"

"We are at war here." A burst of red, like lava, brightens his eyes. "Too many of our kind have already been lost, either to death or treachery. This is no place for gardeners and peacemakers."

"Peace is the way of Elíbom Prímom," I counter.

"I do not expect a curator like yourself to understand." He scowls at me. "Much must transpire before the Restoration." His red eyes narrow. "Return to Chaléth and disturb these lands no more. Your presence threatens to undermine all that has been accomplished. Do not forget your place in the intended order."

I still do not know my place, not in geographical terms anyway. Yet, I will not stop nurturing peace wherever I go. For one, Ashe sees me and is receptive to my presence. That is a significant opportunity for change, our meeting a harbinger of the restoration possible—for everyone, but especially those like Phedra who have been deceived or ensnared. Elíbom Prímom works in mysterious ways.

I am glad to learn from Ashe that the Rök company does not intend to venture farther than the border of the Rínroth Plain, for the mountains beyond—to the north and west—mark the edge of Ekrath Namor's domain. The Rök commonly use the term, "Erog", in their conversation, and I have come to understand that it refers to those who dwell west of the mountains. The race has no collective name for itself. I recall briefly observing them before my encounter with Ekrath Namor. I perceived the Erog to be more attentive to the Unseen than their Rök neighbors, yet their ceaseless tribal warfare and violent practices discourage me from wanting to investigate their civilization further. In truth, it has been so with every human race in Illirium.

When they speak about the Erog, the Rök mention theft, murder, and escalating conflict by force of arms. Why do civilizations always turn to war for resolution? By being here, is Ashe affirming that approach? That was my initial thought, but then she also expresses a desire to be rid of its influence. I am coming to recognize that Ashe is a survivor more concerned with what meets her immediate needs. Perhaps there is something to be learned in that. I am happy to offer her what I can, but must not lose sight of why I am here with her in the first place.

Once again, I feel reduced to being a bystander of larger events. The Rök army disperses around a field at the foot of the mountains. Nature tenses in anticipation. I can feel it in the air, the rock, and the trees. Riding atop Lüfet, Ashe patrols the area from the sky. We have been unable to speak much lately. There is more I need to learn from her dreams, particularly the nature of the white swan, and so must make sure that she stays safe.

When the Erog finally come, the damage inflicted by both sides is sickening. I look away, but cannot shut out the rage, desperation, and pain echoing across the currents of space and time. Bloodied flesh, torn and battered, stains the earth. I am not powerful enough to stop it. *Is there no end to this madness?* At least Ashe is able to stay detached from the thick of it, though I grieve at the sight of her contributing with loosed arrows. In her compliance, even Lüfet is not innocent.

Where are the rest of my kind—those with authority to intervene? Where is Alíndor? I have asked these questions before, as far back as the First Age. The Lower Kingdom seems to have been abandoned to the inevitability of these mortals' independence. It is part of the reason I lost Phedra. In a way, Ashe is like her—the same kind of adventurous, free spirit. Mistakes must not be repeated.

I am about to fly out from my rocky perch to confront Ashe when Osré lands beside me. A black vulture follows after him, of a kind I have not seen since the early days of creation in Rühílawé. This bird, like Osré and Oshrémi, is a progenitor of its race, partner to the Séorans. From his calm, focused gaze, I discern that he too knows me for what I am, though I maintain my sparrow guise.

Still mindful of the battle below, with a pressing sense of urgency to direct Ashe away, I quickly ask the vulture, "What is your name?"

Through its eyes, mannerisms, and vulture form of speech, he says his name is Ornithez and that he serves Raez Het on a hallowed quest to find Oceanus, and that his master is the future of the Thraz Tribe.

Oceanus. My hope is kindled anew. I think of my homeland, and of Phedra. Events do not happen randomly. Elíbom Prímom promises that it is so, and seems to have guided us here at just the right time.

This Thraz sage is nearby, alone, Ornithez explains, also mindful of the clash of combat below. He is not here for conflict, however, but counsel.

Glancing out, I spot Ashe still safely atop Lüfet, soaring above the melee. "Keep watch," I tell Osré.

Maintaining my sparrow form, I follow Ornithez along the rocky ridge to where a large figure cloaked in black fur lies among a cluster of boulders. The figure's presence exudes a higher level of consciousness. More than that, his right arm glows bronze, bright like a Séoran, emanating the energy of the Unseen. *How can this be?*

As the Erog does not notice my arrival, I wonder if his sight is not as strong as I first thought. "What do you see?" I ask.

Startled, the sage turns to me in a crouched, defensive position. Seeing that I mean him no harm, he eases. "Thou speakest my language."

While I have heard Erog speech before, this dialect is different. Talking further, I gather that this sage is not connected to the battle below. Curiously, he considers me a god. "This is a dangerous place for you," I say.

Questions well within me, especially about his arm, but before I can inquire further, Oshrémi and Osré appear, cheeping a warning: Ashe is flying directly at our position. With her keen eyes, Lüfet must see me, so why does she not discourage her rider? With a twinge of trepidation in my heart, I remember how dutiful the eagle is to her Alöwean master. Ashe must view the sage as just another Erog, part of the fray—an enemy.

"Flee," I tell the sage.

Not delaying a moment longer, I dart out toward Ashe.

"No," I cry, flying back and forth across her view. "Not this one."

Ashe swats me aside, sending my vision spinning in a blur of grey and then black when I strike the ground. Returning to my Séoran form, I sit up dizzily. Such a blow would not usually affect me, but as a sparrow it is different. I must be more careful.

Nearby, across the meadow contaminated with death, the Rök appear to have defeated the Erog. Composing myself further, preparing to ascend as a sparrow once more, I look up and see all my hopes plummeting toward me. Ashe clings to the reins while Lüfet grips the Thraz sage with her talons but has lost the use of one of her wings.

Quickly lifting my hands, I use all my strength to shift the currents of the air up toward them. My body rises from the ground as I do so, but until I return to my sparrow form, I will not fly higher. The directed currents are not enough to slow them, and transforming will limit my power, but I must get closer. As my body shrinks into the brown-feathered creature, my wings twitch against the strain of upward wind. Swiftly, I ascend; when I reach them, I return to my primordial form, trying to redirect the currents anew, in part to stabilize Lüfet's fall.

Pain shudders up my legs as I am the first to strike the ground, but I am more disoriented than hurt. Looking around, I see Ashe slouched forward, unmoving. Lüfet cries as she lies sprawled out on the rough-backed mass of the Thraz sage. The sage promptly crawls out from underneath her, apparently unharmed. His back is to me, his attention on the Rök soldiers quickly surrounding our position. They do not see me, but focus on the sage.

"No," I urge, noticing the sage looking at a weapon lying nearby on the ground. "Be at peace, and be not afraid."

I must not lose this gifted being to needless violence. From what I can surmise, the Rök intend to take him as a prisoner. Let them. It will gain us time to assess and reorient. I flutter over to land upon Ashe's helm, relieved to find that she is still breathing.

Meanwhile, I perceive Lüfet's life draining from her. "Help me," she says faintly.

"Surrender," the Rök captain demands of the sage.

The sage hisses at the soldiers, but looks to me once more for guidance. I assure him that this is not the moment of his death, tell him my name, and say that I will help him navigate the way ahead. To provide an additional sign of encouragement, I return to my Séoran form, praying that he sees me in a friendly light.

Staring at his glowing right arm, I offer, "You have a gift." *Do not squander it.* Thankfully, he seems to accept this, glancing down at his arm. "Yes," I assure him, smiling. "There is much we might discover together."

While he is being bound in chains, I turn back to Lüfet, caressing her head, trying to numb the hurt coursing through her body. My limbs are trembling. Weariness creeps in. I used too much energy to slow their fall.

No. Closing my eyes, I press my brow gently against Lüfet's head. "Forgive me," I say, still willing a last portion of strength to pass from me to her. If only I could stop her pain. If only I was not alone. Where are the other Séorans charged with overseeing this land? Where is Phedra? Our power was only complete when we were together. My hands fail to bind the Erïeth's wounds. Blood seeps through her feathers and my fingers, hot and abandoning hope.

8

Rift

Civil war erupts among the Elphadém, in part over control of the Birithani Tree. I stand with Lachímel and his forces in trying to protect the tree, but the devastation that ensues—the loss of lives, Elphadém and Séoran, and the death of the Birithani Tree to fire—drains me of strength and hope. I cannot comprehend the waste. If this is the way to preserve our dominion, the spirit of Rühílawé, perhaps Phedra was right. Perhaps the vision of a unified peace has deceived us all along—a means for control.

Nevertheless, I strive to comfort and aid anything that suffers. What else can I do amidst such needless violence?

I wonder if I will see Phedra again, and search among the ashen wreckage of Trïesch.

"She is not here," Lachímel says, coming beside me. "Her betrayal has become her death."

Death.

Other Séorans still loyal to Elíbom Prímom search the dead. Among them are the Elphadém who have decided to remain in this region and rebuild. They now think of themselves as Rodaním. The other three clans—Arizaleth, Siligen, and Sabtah—have departed farther west and east.

"Did you kill her?" I ask.

Lachímel's white eyes meet my gaze. "No." He looks around at the smoking skeleton of the Elphadém capital. "Yet, she rose up against us, against Elíbom Prímom. That choice only leads to one place. In death, everyone is welcome to return to the Upper Kingdom. Äelmich offers to guide them, but not all choose to follow. There are other paths carved into the Unseen—ways of isolation."

"Where is Phedra?" I press. Had she managed to return to the Upper Kingdom? Could I follow her there? I must speak with Äelmich.

"Phedra is lost to us," Lachímel replies. "Why can you not accept that?" He turns away with a tired expression and examines the carnage littering the ground. "We who remain faithful must now rebuild what we can, though most of the surviving Elphadém want nothing to do with us."

"What will you do then?" I ask.

We stand next to each other in silence.

"I will guard what Alíndor has entrusted to me," he says at last. "Much is destroyed, but not all. The White Staff, branch of the Balmwéa Elïf, is still safe. The power of Elíbom Prímom can live on here in Illirium, even if only as a whisper."

What am I to do?

My resolve is depleted. My limbs tremble. I cannot believe that Phedra is dead. I will not. If she is lost then she can be found again. I will find her somehow, even if it requires abandoning my duty. Life has been set in motion; though it may lose its vibrancy, it can survive without me. It is Phedra's resilience that the smaller forms of nature cannot live without, so it will be my fault if they perish. I must try harder to bring her back, to convince her—to prove myself worthy.

The time has come to separate myself from the confusion. Lachímel will not help me, nor will any of my people. They all stumble over the rubble, weighed down by their own measures of disillusionment. I am friendless. Our society has broken apart. Each of us has but to preserve what he or she can.

My sparrow companions, Osré and Oshrémi, meet me on the plain outside Trïesch. Chirruping, Osré inquires about my wishes. He too wants to find Phedra.

To the south churns the depths of Oceanus, which I have no way to cross on my own. To the west journey the Elphadém survivors of Siligen and Arizaleth, neither of whom I want to follow; I feel the same about the people of Sabtah to the east. They have embraced the Lower Kingdom—a new, diluted heritage.

"We shall begin in the north," I murmur.

* * *

Since the end of the First Age over a century ago, Illiri and Alöwean awareness of the Unseen has vanished. Their forgetfulness of us followed the abandonment of our fellowship after the Elphadém Civil War. Now, there are only a few accounts of mortals gifted with original sight—the ability to glimpse the Unseen. It is as though most have become nearsighted, unable to comprehend beyond their main five senses. Ashe is one of those gifted few, which nurtures my hope that the Restoration will one day come.

As a sparrow, I touch the fetters of mortality. Reduced to such a small size, with its hindered vision and stamina, I am nevertheless able to track Ashe and Lüfet's progress. Osré and Oshrémi help me, without whom my task would be more precarious. It is not that they are stronger than me, but rather are better accustomed to such physicality. Though they are also immortal, the sparrow form is all they have known, while I have danced across the stars and delved into the deep of the sea. Though my power is limited in Illirium, especially in this animal state, it is not to the extent of a normal bird. It is a necessary, if imperfect, disguise, the limitations of which have their advantages, such as helping veil me from other Séorans. The most attentive of my race would be able to differentiate me from a regular sparrow, yet this unassuming form should draw no interest in my passing. It will have to suffice.

I have been to the Rök stronghold of Ashkenaz only once before. Falling under the shadows of its neighboring mountains as the sun begins to set, the place conveys a spirit of cold isolation. Predominantly carved from solid bedrock, the city is nonetheless an impressive feat. I appreciate the Rök desire to use what the land naturally offers as opposed to simply uprooting, cutting, and building upon it as the Illiri and Alöweans more commonly do.

Ashe's room is on the second floor of a building full of Rök soldiers. Perched outside her window, Osré waits, keeping watch.

Having landed on the outside windowsill, I suddenly hesitate: *Be wary.*

Dare I enter?

Dare I risk losing everything again—friendship, purpose, hope?

There will be a cost. There is always a cost to crossing a threshold. Yet, if I had followed Phedra sooner, crossed that barrier of unfamiliarity, might catastrophe have been avoided? Ashe could be my second chance, our meeting an opportunity for redemption. If I do not risk, I do not gain.

Resuming my Séoran form, I pass through the glass into Ashe's chamber. Alone in a foreign land with an unknown adversary to face in the days or weeks ahead, she will need my help. That is the reasoning I will use with her, anyway.

She trembles for a moment, pulling her blanket tighter about her body. Mindful not to wake her, I come near, drawing the warmth of the air together over her sleeping form while settling myself in the space next to her head.

She sighs, but does not wake.

Gently, I place my fingers upon her brow. In her dream, soft shadows frame Ashe's body as she lies nestled in the arms of an Alöwean man. Both are serene in their intimacy. They speak, smiling tenderly, but I cannot hear what is being shared. At first, I feel like an intruder, but then search beyond the immediate for some clue from the Unseen—from Phedra. There is a trace grief in this moment—another of Ashe's memories, I presume. Her body remains motionless, but I discern her spirit reaching, as if for something lost. Perhaps this man has also been lost.

I know your sorrow.

Withdrawing my hand, I decide to simply watch Ashe from the tangible world. *Patience.* Ashe's eyes are closed, body completely relaxed, and remains so for the rest of the night. When dawn approaches, Osré and Oshrémi begin to sing their morning song, but I quickly hush them, not wanting to disturb Ashe's rest. Too late it seems, for she stirs, stretching out her arms.

"What do you want?" she asks languidly.

I am not sure if she speaking to the sparrows, me, or is still dreaming. "I asked them to watch over you," I offer.

She shudders and sits up, glaring at me. "What are you doing here?" I try to explain, but she interrupts: "You should not spy on me. A friend does not do such a thing."

She is clearly upset, but that is not entirely unexpected. I must be careful about what I share, about preserving her trust as a friend. I tell her that I want to keep her safe, and that her mission to the Northland is dangerous. "You do not know what may be at stake," I say. Though I do not understand the extent of her mission with the Rök, the allies of Üzmaveth are rumored to be assembling anew, including in the north. Ekrath Namor said as much, as did Lachímel and Äelmich. "I can ensure your safety."

To convince her to accept my aid, I must open her eyes to some of the broader aspects of the Unseen War without getting ensnared by the minutiae. Recalling the inspiration of how the Séoran, Nora, partnered with the Alöwean, Adáren, I add, "I will be your guide, providing clarity when your eyes fail to see past the limits of mortal perception. With my help, you will be stronger."

"Is there a cost to accepting such aid?" she asks.

"No cost," I answer, recognizing that my greatest need from Ashe is time and proximity. Yet, I am also not discarding the potential impact our alliance could have on the future restoration of Illirium, the Lower Kingdom. "Simply the presence of a friend."

After some thought, she replies, "Very well," and offers me her hand. "It will be nice to have the company of a friend."

Keep calling to me, Phedra.

"I am glad," I reply, offering my own smile.

I will find you.

9

Connection

Being away from the power of the Balmwéa Elïf for so long—with its lesser offspring, the Birithani Tree, now destroyed—I feel my strength diminish anew. I offer what I can to the small animals and vegetation I pass, but can no longer nourish all. Travel becomes easier in the form of a sparrow, so much smaller in size while also calling less attention to my passing than in my primary form.

I do not know how long I search for Phedra, investigating every portion of Illirium. Even if she is dead, her spirit must be somewhere. Yet, when I am honest with myself, I wonder if I really believe I will find her—or even want to. After all, I avoid the Kurshemnt Mountains where I last saw her—where she is most likely to be. I fear the Ophidi and whatever else guards those mountains; but most of all, I fear the idea that Phedra is one of them, and that I will once again fail to help her, whether to free her from bondage or convince her to return.

I am so tired.

With Osré and Oshrémi, I meander back to the northeastern corner of Illirium, flying toward the snowcapped peaks of the Upper Mountains. It is quiet here. The silence fills me with dread at first, but I come to recognize its tranquility—that silence is a gift. Though I am alone, at least I am no longer barraged by external contentions.

I discover a dell at the base of a mountain. Little grows in the dell except a stream trickling down from the mountains with delightful applause. Much could grow here if given attention. Osré and Oshrémi agree.

"We shall rest here then," I say.

Sitting on a rock that juts out from the cliffs overlooking the dell, I study the shadowed landscape as another mortal day concludes. Memories of Phedra fill my thoughts, exposing all my inadequacies, leaving me burdened with doubts. Elíbom Prímom also feels distant, and I wonder why I remain subservient to his vision. Perhaps it is because without that I would be left utterly bare.

With war after war like tidal waves eroding the shape of the world, the Second Age comes. Sometimes I take note from afar, but mostly hear tell of the passing of mortality, such as the Elphadém diminishing further into twelve clans of Mankind, the Illiri. Allies of mine like Osré and Oshrémi keep me conscious of physical history, though I care little for it. The mortals no longer see me, even when I desire it. They have forgotten us Séorans. They have forgotten Elíbom Prímom. The split between our races is complete.

* * *

The storm abates the farther we fly from the center of the Upper Mountains. When we reach the southern border where the shadowed line of my hidden dell comes into view, the moon is bright, illuminating puffs of cloud that help light our way. It is then that I notice the Alöwean Sky Rider bent forward, her helmed head resting limply on the Erïeth's neck. Lüfet conveys that she is aware of this, undeterred, not only confident that the harness securing her rider to the saddle will hold, but that the manner of her flight will not allow her rider to fall.

Leading the way as a sparrow, I direct the Erïeth to land in the grassy clearing of the dell where I transform back into my Séoran form. There, Lüfet tells me how to unclasp the straps of the Alöwean's riding saddle; a gaze of raccoons help me with this, after which they lower the unconscious woman from the eagle's back and carefully rest her on a patch of soft grass.

Next, I translate instructions for the raccoons to remove the saddle from the Erïeth's back. When the task is done, the great eagle ruffles her feathers in liberation and looks at me with her fierce yellow eyes. "I thank you, honorable Séoran," she says.

"You are most welcome," I answer. "Call me Thian."

Lüfet studies the high ridges overlooking the dell, settling her attention on the ascending mountainside to the north.

"Are you hungry?" I ask.

"I am."

"Do not let me keep you." I indicate the mountain. "Spread wide your wings and enjoy the bounty of this region."

Calmly, Lüfet fixes her large eyes on me. "I will not leave Ashe."

Ashe. I study the unconscious Alöwean. "That is her name?"

"It is," the Erïeth says. "Ashe Pethus. I have come to understand most of her speech; for we have been together for thirty years, since I was taken as an eaglet from my mother's nest."

"Where were you born?"

"The Mountains of the Crescent Moon."

"That range is not far from here," I say, knowing the humans to call it Girgash. "You could return to your home."

"You misunderstand," Lüfet replies, lowering her head to meet my eye level. "My home is with Ashe. Our destinies are intertwined, directed by the Current of Life."

"What destiny do you foresee?"

The Erïeth straightens, towering feet above me as she returns her attention to the dark clouds still looming over the Upper Mountains. "The winds grow stronger, and the haze disorients. If we do not alter course . . ." Lüfet looks at me. "You may be able to help Ashe in a way that I cannot. Her spirit has long been molting without fresh growth. If nothing replaces that which has rotted and fallen away, she risks unbalance. Such a creature cannot fly. To persist in trying risks a devastating fall . . . for both of us."

I am not sure what of any lasting value I can offer an Alöwean, but remain intrigued by her ability to see me. "I will offer what I can," I say, "but would it not be better for you to speak to her? I could translate."

The Erïeth considers this for a moment, and then replies, "No." She prepares to say more, but then falters. "No."

Perhaps she is afraid of what such a change could mean for their relationship, perhaps complicating their general understanding. How much do they really know about each other to begin with, and how much is each limited by her distinct racial identity in terms of interpreting the other's actions?

Perceiving that Lüfet does not wish to be pressed on the subject, I reiterate, "I will offer what I can."

She nods, steps away, and then flaps her wings to take flight. I help channel some air up toward her, providing greater liftoff, but cannot offer more as fatigue from the day clings to my body.

"I will return," she calls, riding the current in ascending spirals out of the dell. "Take care of Ashe." She pipes a single, high-pitched note that echoes across the region. "Do not disappoint me, Séoran."

Watching the large bird navigate the air higher and higher, I marvel at such elegant, majestic strength. I do not understand Lüfet's loyalty to her Alöwean master, but admire its confidence.

The moon peeks above the western rim of the dell. Crouching down beside the still unconscious Alöwean, I have her helm removed by a raccoon and study her crimson face. Curious about her current mental state, I gently place my hand upon her brow. In her mind, Ashe stands before a small black pool surrounded by mist. A white swan materializes from the mist, gliding across the pool, a gentle ripple following in its wake. The swan looks at me. "Be wary."

My heart stops. "Phedra?"

I try to advance toward the pool, but the image vanishes. Returned to my dell, I quiver with confusion and hope. How could Phedra be present in the Alöwean's subconscious realm? I touch Ashe's head again, but her mind has quieted, resting in the silent depths of sleep.

I remember that her health is still threatened by the cold. Her core temperature needs to be increased, so I return my attention to the present.

I would warm her again myself, directing the air currents as I did in the mountains, but she needs something more pervasive and longer lasting, and my energy is too depleted from recent efforts.

With little more to offer, I have two does and the raccoons help me carry Ashe across the meadow to a thermal spring sheltered by trees. It is tricky for me to directly interact with physical matter, so they help remove her cold wet clothes—these mortals obscure themselves with so many layers—and then lower her into the pool, careful to rest her head upon a soft grassy portion of the bank.

Looking at Ashe, making sure she is settled safely, I am reminded that the Alöweans are our kindred, children of the Séorans and Elphadém. Her flesh resembles that of the Elphadém, as does her form, but there is something more that harkens to her Séoran heritage. I glance at my own hands and body, not so unlike hers, though less tangible and full of translucent light. Here could be an opportunity to reemphasize a fragment of the original harmony of creation: Alöwean and Séoran working together in common purpose. More importantly, there was the glimpse of the white swan. Could that be a call from Phedra at last?

I must learn more. Part of me is eager, but another trembles with doubt. After so many failures, so many rejections . . . Do I have the fortitude to explore the possibility one more time? Or do I delude myself in thinking that one white swan in one Alöwean's dream is actually connected to Phedra?

I must learn more.

I check on Ashe periodically through the night. While the sun rises in the east, I make a robe, the result of manipulating strips of raw wool between my fingers. My neighbors, a herd of silver-colored mountain goats, provide the material upon my request, grateful to shed the weight as the spring days grow warmer. Meanwhile, Osré and Oshrémi watch over Ashe while I forage what food is readily available in the area with the help of other small animals.

The day is waning when Oshrémi notifies me that Ashe is starting to stir. Quickly returning to the hot spring, I sit cross-legged and wait in the lengthening shadows until at last the Alöwean opens her brown eyes to the sky and slowly sits up in the water.

"How do you feel?" I ask.

"Warm," she replies, investigating her hands.

I give her time to orient to her new surroundings, and then tell her what has transpired since the mountain storm. When she is ready, I offer her the robe, which she accepts gladly from the doe carrying it, and introduce her to my home, providing what support I can with my arm as we walk and talk. Sharing the sunset together nourishes me with a feeling I had thought lost. Not since the early days with Phedra have I known such simple, joyful contentment. That Ashe was also born in the land of Chaléth in the Middle Kingdom reinforces my sense of connection. It is the first real good I have known for four centuries, since before the Elphadém Civil War. Our lives parallel in so many ways. I am confident that Elíbom Prímom has guided us to one other.

Lying next to each other on a hilltop outside the dell, Ashe and I watch the stars. She asks me, "Do you ever wonder what is out there beyond the myriad of lights and space?"

"Few have ventured beyond that which holds the tangible world in place," I answer. "My people call it the Canopy of Ethezimél." The sparkle of Rühílawé is up there, visible, a guiding light by which to one day return by way of Oceanus.

"I wish I could see the details more clearly," she comments.

"I can show you," I offer.

"Really?"

"A glimpse, anyway."

"All right."

I sit up, and indicate that she do the same. Moving behind her, crouched on my knees, I gently place my hands over her eyes like a visor. "Keep your eyes open."

She smiles as my hands manipulate the waves of light in such a way as to magnify what she can see: stars enlarged to reveal faint detail, color, and movement. Through our touch, I share her sight, feeling both glad that she is impressed while also saddened by the limitations of her Alöwean sight. "I am sorry I cannot offer you more."

"It is enough." With her hands on mine, she gingerly guides them around to take everything in.

I recall what I have heard about the Sentinels, those of the Fallen who ultimately denounced Üzmaveth. There was one Sentinel, in particular, who is said to have been the first to partner with a mortal here in Illirium. "Have you heard of Adáren and Nora?"

"The first name is familiar." Ashe continues to study the stars through my hands. "He was the first Guardian of Illirium."

"Yes," I say. "His success was influenced by the power of Nora, a Séoran."

"What kind of power?"

"An enhancement of his Alöwean abilities, for one," I answer, "such as stamina and sensory acuity."

"Why do you mention him?"

"I was just curious." Though hope too readily partners with haste, I begin to wonder if Ashe and I could enjoy a relationship similar to Adáren and Nora. The prospect fills my imagination with vague possibilities. Lachímel may be wary of the Sentinels, but I am not like them. Moreover, Phedra left Triönym for a new beginning, and I accompanied her with Alíndor's blessing. Is that not what a future with Ashe could provide—a new beginning for each of us? Or is it about some kind of return? Either way, perhaps I have been too focused on what has been lost. Now it is time to explore what has been found.

All the while, the white swan continues to appear in Ashe's dreams. Is it a call, a blessing, or a warning?

What have I found?

"Soon, I must go," Ashe announces late one morning as we sit beside the cascading waterfall that feeds the dell.

The statement stings my hope. I try to learn more, but she becomes elusive, talking about some errand in Rökad.

"I do not want you to go," I say. There is so much we might discover together.

She says something more, but in my grief I only hear the latter portion: "We will see each other again."

"When?" I ask.

"I do not know," she replies, taking my hand in hers—such a kind gesture.

I stare at her hands. "I could come with you."

She seems to consider this, but then says, "No."

"Why not?"

"It would not be good for you," she replies.

What do you know of my good? I look into her brown eyes, searching for some sign, some clarity about what I should do. Too many questions remain unresolved. The spirit of Phedra calls to me, I am sure of it; like approaching the coast and hearing the first boom of the waves, still distant but welcoming me to proceed. "Must I let you go?"

She looks taken aback by this question. I should have phrased it better. I have to maintain her trust, convincing her that I am an ally—at least until I can better decipher these preliminary clues.

"A friend would understand," she replies.

Yes, a friend. It has been so long since I have enjoyed the friendship of an equal. There, my window of connection remains open. Ashe does not need to know about Phedra; that will only complicate matters. Instead, I will focus on what I can offer, such as empowering her potential. "I am glad that we met," I offer. "You have opened my eyes to a broader world of possibilities. You give me hope that barriers can be overcome, and broken pathways mended." Speaking the truth is not synonymous with sharing everything.

"You saved my life," she says. "I will not forget you."

I watch her depart, but cannot accept it as final. I made the mistake of letting Phedra go, but not again. As the world is too dangerous, many of its dimensions unknown or forgotten by mortals, I will find a way to convince Ashe to keep me close—that it is in her best interest.

I just need more time.

10

The Door

Too late do I realize that the coming of the Alöweans to Illirium provided an opportunity to return to Rühílawé. Instead, as the Northern Wars rage between the Alöwean and Rök kingdoms, I continue to hide in my dell, helping it grow and thrive while the world outside grapples with itself. If only I had thought to hide myself on one of the Alöwean ships that sailed back across Oceanus after the Northern Wars concluded.

Lachímel finds me.

"How long will you remain idle, Thian Darhe?" he asks.

I consider whether he has always known where I am. Regardless, I show him the wealth of life I have nurtured in my dell—clear creeks, soft-barked trees, and swaying grass. "I fulfill my task," I say, though my tone lacks conviction. "Are not the happenings of Illirium yours to contend with? Did not Alíndor entrust the Elphadém to you, Captain of the Lower Kingdom? Where are the signs of your work?"

As I recline against a white birch tree, enjoying the eager embrace of tall cool grass, Lachímel stands stiffly, the whiteness of his eyes dimmed. "You still do not understand the nature of our struggle. Ever since the Corruption, that which Elíbom Prímom created has been under threat. So it will be until Üzmaveth and all his followers are destroyed."

"Üzmaveth could have been executed long ago," I counter, "but Alíndor believes in redemption." I used to admire that as strength, but lately I am not so sure.

"I do not understand it either," Lachímel replies. "Üzmaveth has been given too many chances; he is beyond salvation. Nevertheless, with the Divide now about to fade, nothing is safe." He glances at me. "Not even you."

"I have no quarrel with Üzmaveth." I would rather not think about his troublemaking.

Lachímel raises a brow. "He led Phedra astray."

"I did not say that I trust him."

"When the Divide falls," Lachímel continues, "my host may not be strong enough to stop whatever Üzmaveth has managed to prepare all these years."

"Assuming he intends to invade at all."

"He will come," Lachímel asserts, "and find a quarrelling Illirium ready to be devoured. The Illiri clans have forgotten us and remain in contention with each other. The Alöweans are no better."

"Is the Lower Kingdom lost then?" *Was it ever claimed?* The Fallen were condemned here in the Early Years. I still wonder what Elíbom Prímom intended in allowing us to come here.

"Not all is lost." Lachímel stares westward. The comment reminds me of his sister, Äelmich. "Yet, the original order of creation is nearly ended. A group of the Fallen calling themselves Sentinels work to establish their own kingdom, going so far as to partner with some of the mortals."

"Is that so threatening?" I ask, intrigued by the concept. Perhaps it provides a new way forward. "I am one for unity and peace, and care not for questions of dominion."

"You hide behind a façade of peace," Lachímel says, "but if the original boundaries set by Elíbom Prímom continue to crack, your influence will only diminish more, reducing you to a shadow under these trees."

"I will not take part in violence," I say, having long felt the decline of my power here. "There are other ways to achieve order."

"I wish that it were so." Lachímel's voice softens. "Sometimes we must fight to preserve that which is held most dear."

Phedra once said something similar. "What do you hold dear, captain?"

His gaze shifts north to the Upper Mountains. "I was originally charged by Alíndor to preserve the spirit of our race, but I also care about the legacy of the Elphadém. With Äelmich it can be so, even if we are only able to save a few."

I recall our conversation centuries earlier about the way back to Rühílawé. "I do not recall you trying to save Phedra."

"She rejected my counsel," Lachímel replies. "As I told you before, I do not know what happened to her."

"Could she have found a way back to Rühílawé without Äelmich?"

"Unlikely," he says, his back to me, still gazing at the mountains, "but Nïmwé could better answer your question."

Nïmwé, Warden of the Door of Rühílawé. I have only heard of the Door in relation to Lachímel's sister, Äelmich, who guides the spirits of the dead to its entryway. "Could I return through the Door?"

Lachímel looks at me. "No." His expression is stern. "It is not for the living, Thian Darhe. There are other doors for us."

Hope stirs anew within me. "What other doors?"

"The Alöweans have learned how to make lesser versions. There is even one here in eastern Illirium, in their capital of Anaríl."

"Have you passed through such a door?"

"It is not my purpose to return," he replies. "Not yet."

Alas, I am once again too slow to act. The Divide opens and Üzmaveth returns with fire, chaos, and death—what comes to be known as the Illirium War. His forces, surprisingly immense, move swiftly and concisely, leaving a smoldering ruin in their wake. Before I can reach it, the Door of Anaríl is overwhelmed and closed. When I learn that most of the Sentinels are also slain, I curse this place and its history.

Only one door remains open: the Door of Oblivion. It is here in Illirium, somewhere in that wasteland beyond the Kurshemnt Mountains that Phedra once showed me. I hear that the Door leads to Lïmbol, the region just west of the Middle Kingdom. That would be closer than any other way currently open, yet it is guarded by Üzmaveth's forces. As I cannot cross Oceanus by myself, the way being too vast, dare I go to the Door of Oblivion and request passage through in some stance of neutrality?

No. I do not trust anything connected to Üzmaveth. He is the source of too much grief and too many losses. Even Phedra, so aware and intelligent, was deceived by his ideology. I also recall my encounter with Rïven and the Ophidi, and imagine that the outcome at the Door of Oblivion would be no different. So, if not that way then where should I turn for hope?

Lachímel looked to the Upper Mountains. Though he said the Door of Rühílawé is closed to me, perhaps I will be permitted to pass if I explain my situation. It is worth a try.

One spring, after most of the snow has melted, I search the mountains, masking my passing by traveling in my sparrow form. I leave Osré and Oshrémi to watch over the dell.

There are so many crevices, valleys, and pinnacles; I find nothing. Once more, I perceive time defying my resolve. Whoever the warden Nïmwé is, whatever her status as a Séoran, she is masterful at keeping herself and the Door hidden.

But then I spot Äelmich walking under the mortal sun as a rugged grey ram with large curved horns. Though there are other mountain rams in this region, there is something about her presence that emanates the Unseen. It is my discovery of a lone Alöwean Sky Rider, in fact, that helps me spot the ram. The Sky Rider appears to also be following Äelmich, though far less successfully than me.

One night, under a clear sky of twinkling stars, I witness Äelmich in human form guiding a spirit of the dead up through a narrow valley. The visage of the spirit is like the faint glow of a candle, while Äelmich appears as a brown-skinned Illiri woman with thick black hair gathered up in a series of decorative knots. She bears a staff crowned with a pair of ram's horns. She does this, I assume, to look familiar in form to what must be the spirit of an Illiri departed.

Siege towers of cloud settle over the mountains. They do not concern me except that a blizzard will make it difficult to maintain my sparrow form while also keeping Äelmich in view. I must risk getting closer.

Hail begins to fall, and then snow. Undeterred, Äelmich ascends a steep rise to the face of a large cliff of solid stone, featureless save a natural walkway jutting alongside, starting from the rise at its right. Observing from across the canyon, with a curtain of snow blowing between us, I watch Äelmich direct the Illiri spirit to the center of the cliff. My heart leaps when an opening appears amidst the rock, bright like the midday sky.

I must get closer.

The wind is too fierce for my humble sparrow form, tossing me sideways, so I have to abandon it. Resuming my true Séoran form, I hover over the rock, swiftly continue down one side of the canyon and then climb up the other. In my primordial form, I am conscious of the chilling gusts passing over me, but they are now like a gentle caress. The howling also becomes quieter, and my vision sharpens.

When I arrive, the spirit of the deceased has passed through the Door to a valley rich with life: green grass dappled with flowers, tall swaying trees, happy clouds gliding across a blue sky. *Rühílawé*. The city of Rühílis, dwelling place of Alíndor, would not be far. Drawing closer, I begin to smell the salt water of the ocean, glimpse its glimmering blue surface beyond the fields to the left.

Closer.

I can almost feel the tips of sun-warmed grass tickling my palm.

A hand grabs my neck, driving me back into the cold, across the chasm, until my body slams against rock. I try to free myself from the Séoran's firm grasp, but she is too strong.

"Be still," she says, glaring at me with golden eyes. Her entire figure blazes white, and she holds a silver sword.

"I think he means you no disrespect, Nïmwé," a familiar voice says.

Looking past the one pinning me to the wall, I see Äelmich walking through the stormy air toward us, still appearing in her Illiri form wrapped in a grey cloak. A sword is strapped to her waist. "Why have you been spying on me, Thian Darhe?" she asks.

Meanwhile, Nïmwé, Warden of the Door of Rühílawé, continues to hold me against the wall. I raise my hands in submission. "I merely seek Phedra Darhe."

"Phedra rejected my guidance," Äelmich says. "She did not pass through the Door."

I glance at Nïmwé for affirmation. Her grip loosens, and she lowers me to stand on my feet. Still staring at me, her hand then leaves my neck as she withdraws across the chasm into the stone of the Door, the vision of Rühílawé vanishing with her.

"Can I not pass through?" I ask, unable to conceal the dejection in my voice.

"By Alíndor's decree, the Door of Rühílawé is not for the living," Äelmich replies, "nor those associated with treachery."

"I did not know what Phedra was doing," I protest.

"You did not care," Äelmich counters. "Too long have you ignored events around you. Too long have you wallowed in self-pity. It is time to rise from your slumber. You retain some power here. If you wish to honor Elíbom Prímom then rejoin your people. The allies of Üzmaveth are still inflicting harm throughout Illirium. In the Northland, Helëna, who incited the Second Unrest, is gathering new strength. We could use your help."

"I am a simple curator," I say. "What help can I provide?"

"You did much to ease the suffering of those hurt and dying in the Elphadém Civil War," Äelmich replies. "That was no small offering."

There had been something meaningful in that. "But my power means little without Phedra," I say. We were brought forth from the deep to serve together. "Are there no other Doors back to Rühílawé?"

"Your place is here, Thian Darhe. It is what you chose."

"It was Phedra who wanted to leave."

"You chose to follow," Äelmich says.

"Am I to be condemned like one of the Fallen then, a prisoner here in Illirium?"

Äelmich turns away. "I have much to do, Thian Darhe. No more excuses." She leaves me standing alone across the chasm from the Door of Rühílawé. Flakes of snow blow about my face. *What am I to do?*

The Door of Rühílawé is guarded and closed to me, and Phedra did not pass through. I have searched throughout Illirium for so long. I do not have the power to breach the boundaries of Üzmaveth's domain in the southwest, in the Desert of Oblivion and beyond. Even Lachímel and Gathírel, their forces united with the Alöweans across Illirium and Alöwe, were unable to repel Üzmaveth's invasion without significant loss. Üzmaveth has exposed everyone's frailty.

Only one has answers with any certainty. Yes, I must speak with the spirit of Elíbom Prímom, somehow gain admittance to the city of Rühílis where Alíndor dwells. If Alíndor can twice show mercy to Üzmaveth, despite the devastation he has caused, she has no reason to deny extending mercy to me or Phedra.

"Elíbom Prímom," I shout through the howling mountain storm, "Alíndor, if you can hear me, show me the way to you. Bless me with a sign." The wind exhales with agitation. "Show me. Please."

Lifting my head to the heavens, closing my eyes, I float up into the air, extend my arms, returning to my sparrow form, and let the storm send me where it wills. I imagine myself to be a dandelion pappus, and wish that I could spread myself in every direction like hundreds of filaments scouring the earth.

When I open my eyes, the shape of a rock outcrop materializes in the darkening storm. There is someone there, huddled against it for shelter. No, there are two: an Erïeth and an Alöwean woman. This must be the Sky Rider I spotted earlier.

After liberating myself from the air current, I approach the Alöwean and her mount, resuming my Séoran form. The Alöwean is wrapped in a blanket, shivering, while the Erïeth tries to shield her from the wind. The power of the Unseen emanates crimson from the woman. *Who are you?*

Looking at me, the Erïeth's expression eases in relief, her eyes pleading for help—less for her, and more for her companion. The eagle bows her brown-feathered head in reverence. Through the black pupils of her yellow eyes, I am welcomed into a deeper aspect of the eagle's communication. "Know me as Lüfet," she says. The words are not spoken, but rather shared through the interplay of her eyes, the tilt of her head, and the subtle movements of her body.

Gently, I touch her large beak to indicate my own respect and goodwill. She shifts to let me better see the Alöwean, and I am surprised to find the woman looking directly at me.

"Who are you?" the woman asks.

The question startles me. "You see me?"

"Yes," she replies, looking perplexed.

Can it be?

"I am glad," I say. I have not been seen by a mortal in at least an age. Possibilities rejuvenate my thoughts. Could this Alöwean be the sign I seek, a way forward through the vapors of my doubts? More questions arise, but I must put them aside for the moment, trusting that they will be answered in time. First, I must assure this woman by guiding her from this storm.

"Do not be afraid."

11

Rise

After all that I have been through, and with all that remains uncertain, I am still determined to speak with Alíndor. There are questions she can help resolve, especially about Phedra. There is wisdom I need, as well as power. Besides, I yearn to stand in the shelter of the Balmwéa Elïf once more and bask in the presence of Elíbom Prímom. I will return not as a simple curator, however, but something more—something new. I shall be a liberator, focused not on confronting the enemies of Rühílawé, but engaging those bound, wounded, or lost amidst the flailing conflicts of this life.

For now, here at the southern coast of Illirium, unable to cross Oceanus alone, I will use Raez to reach the shores of Rühílawé, the Upper Kingdom. I feed his imagination that Rühílawé is the Span, the land of the gods, and that it will provide him the sign that he seeks. That is not untrue. After all, I do believe in his quest and I want him to succeed; it is just not my priority. Raez thinks to use me. He thinks me powerless. I let him, knowing what I must do.

I also care for Ashe, but as she decides to stay back in Illirium, I accept that she has fulfilled her part. She is ready to take the next step in her own journey, and for that I am glad. One day, I intend to know the rest of her tale. Until then, I acknowledge my gratitude for how she guided me to Raez, and how our partnership, the three of us, brought us to this shore of opportunity. We were stronger together, but need not remain so to succeed. Each of us ventures forth, adding color to this mysterious, ever-changing world. There is hope in that, and there is possibility.

Awake, oh sleeper. Rise to the sun—
   to light,
   renewal,
   peace
   the span of Oceanus.

Acknowledgment

This novel would not exist without another man's specific vision. Our long-distance partnership began simply enough (though the setting of a worldwide pandemic was not so simple), yet quickly evolved into something more, something unique—something that probably could not be replicated. In short, his trust, support, patience, and creative ideas helped shape this novel. For that and all else, I am deeply grateful. Thank you, Angus.

About the Author

Passionate about art, outdoor adventure, and world travel, J.D. Grubb has lived chapters in the United States and Europe, and wants to explore every corner of the world. He currently lives in northern California. *Three Shades* is his second novel, building upon the world introduced in *There was Music*.

You can connect with him at:

- jdgrubb.com
- twitter.com/JD_Grubb
- facebook.com/JDGrubb
- instagram.com/jd_grubb
- youtube.com/@jdgrubb

Subscribe to his newsletter:

- mailchi.mp/4aa505527f08/jdgrubb-newsletter

Also by J.D. Grubb

There was Music

She defied them with survival.

Prisoner 43-1-12 contends with the voices of her past, present, and future in the war-altered world of Illirium. From a ranch outside a rural town, to a prison formed from city ruins, and a wilderness marked by supernatural encounters, *There was Music* explores the struggle between identity and the cost of survival, the power of music and the hope of healing.